The HEART REHAB EXPERIMENT

A hilarious and sexy
romantic comedy

STARLA DEKRUYF

This book is a work of fiction. Names, characters, places, and incidents either are products of the author's imagination or are used fictitiously. Any resemblance to actual events or, places, persons, living or dead, is entirely coincidental and not intended by the author.

THE HEART REHAB EXPERIMENT

STARLA DEKRUYF

Cover Design: Enni with Yummy Book Covers

Editing: Jeanine Harrell with Indie Edits With Jeanine

Proofing: Krista Dapkey with KD Proofreading

Print Edition ISBN: 9798985626902

Digital Edition ISBN: 9798985626919

For Paul Rudd. Thanks for inspiring the very best adorkable book boyfriend.

And for my husband, Jeremy. Thanks for having so much confidence you aren't intimidated by Paul Rudd.

Content/Trigger Warnings

This book is intended for readers who are 17+. Please note that there may be content in this book that may be triggering for some readers. This list is not exclusive, so please proceed with caution.

- One open door scene w/ mild details
- Mild explicit language/cursing
- Alcohol consumption
- Death (in the past/off page)
- Talk of cancer (in the past/off page)
- Grief

Chapter 1

Pete

Natalie would hate the weather today. It's too sunny, and the sky's too blue. *Where are the clouds? Just give me one freakin' cloud,* she'd often taunt the sky. And I'd generally reply, *Honey, if you don't like cloudless skies and sun, we probably shouldn't have left Seattle and planted our roots in Los Angeles.*

I glance up at the relentlessly clear sky, squeeze my eyes tight and curse the blinding sun. "Okay, you're right," I say aloud, my face still slanted upwards. "It's too sunny here. But I guess it's too late to plant our roots somewhere else—it's definitely too late for you." My throat goes dry. Propping my hands on my waist, I gaze out over the cemetery, cool sweat trickling down my spine. "And now, you're stuck here." I shake my head at the unfairness of it all before I face the sky again and yell, "Would it be too much to ask for a little rain? Huh? How about some clouds? Just give me one freakin' cloud!"

"I'm sorry, but do you mind?" a soft voice calls from a few yards away.

I suck in a breath and whip around, surprised when I discover a woman sprawled among the grass in the shade of a Catalina cherry tree. At first, I'm not positive she's talking to me. "Excuse me?" I glance over both shoulders before taking a few tentative steps toward her.

"This is the first real break I've gotten all week and I just need a moment to rest."

Now that I'm only within a few feet of the woman, I notice her eyes are closed. She's wearing a short black dress, revealing grass-stained knees. Her legs are crossed at the ankles and her fingers are clasped across her stomach. With her strawberry blonde hair fanning around her head like a halo, I'm not sure if I find the appearance mesmerizing or disturbing.

The woman opens one hazel eye while the other remains pinched shut. And it's in that moment I realize I've been staring at her for far too long.

"Sorry," I mumble, averting my eyes.

"I know what this must look like, with the stained knees and all," she laughs to herself. "But honestly, I'm not hiding or skipping out on a loved one's funeral." She glances at the pink, sparkly Apple Watch strapped to her wrist. "I have thirty minutes before my next client is scheduled to meet me here."

"Your client?" I rub at the back of my neck where my hairline is damp with sweat.

She sighs, propping up on an elbow and reaching out a hand. "Jules Sweeney, interventionist."

I shake her hand as if on autopilot—just as I've been doing all week—and introduce myself. "Pete Redd, unemployed."

I'm not sure why I say it, but she smiles. It's warm and fits her pale, lightly freckled face just right.

"Nice to meet you, Pete." She lies back down, resituating herself into the previous position, and shuts her eyes. "Now, if you don't mind, I really need a few minutes. You have no idea what kind of day I've had." After a brief pause, her eyes fly open, and I watch the remorse play out on her face.

But I start talking so I don't have to hear the apology. "Uh...yeah, sure...right." My words come out in a jumbled mess as I step backward. I try to process why this woman would be resting in a cemetery, never mind meeting a client here. And, just what in the hell is an interventionist?

"Dad." A gentle voice interrupts the awkward moment, and a calming hand squeezes my shoulder.

I drop my head.

"It's almost time," Tess says.

I turn and admire my daughter. Tess is a few years older than Natalie was when I met her our first year of college. She looks stunning today, in a long black dress with her dark-brown hair pulled away from her heart-shaped face. She looks like Natalie even more than usual with her hair this way. Both of our daughters, Tess and Cora, take after their mom in every way. Okay, maybe in appearance at least. But thankfully, they both inherited my sense of humor and taste in music. Despite being a beautiful pianist, Natalie had no clue what details and talent made a band awesome, and she sure couldn't carry a tune either.

The woman from the grass clears her throat. "In case you need it, I have several great therapists listed on my website. Google my name, you'll find me," she calls, eyes still closed. "I'm not sure what you're dealing with, but someone who yells at the sky like you did, has a lot of built-up emotions."

We both ignore her, but Tess gives me a pained smile as she slips her clammy hand into mine. Her touch forges an ache in my chest, but I attempt to hide it by not making eye contact with her. It's too arduous. Because when I look at Tess, all I see is a younger version of her mother staring back at me with those lively sienna-brown eyes.

"C'mon." Tess pulls me along with her and it feels as if my feet have been encased in concrete. They're heavy, and if it wasn't for her, I might just pop a squat right here on the well-manicured grass and never leave.

But I'm supposed to be the strong one. I'm the dad. The parent. And the only one my girls have left.

People are scattered around, chatting quietly. Rows of white chairs positioned around the casket are filled with people I don't even have the energy to attach names to. They mutter their condolences as Tess escorts me to the front row. Daniel Russo, my best friend since childhood, and ultimately the reason Natalie and I ended up in LA, stands when he sees me approach. He pulls me in for a hug, and it feels tangible and solid, and I want to sink into him.

Cora is there in the front row as well, standing next to Daniel. Tess's husband, Richie, holds out an open palm for her. She releases my hand and exchanges it for Richie's. Richie. What kind of a name is that, anyway? When Tess first brought him home to meet Natalie and me, she introduced him as Richie, not Rich and not Richard. Natalie and I shared a look. Because that's how it was between us. We could say all the words with a single look.

But, in this moment, I've never been so relieved to have Richie as a son-in-law. Tess needs a strong body to lean on. Because God knows, I'm hardly equipped to be that for her right now.

"Dad, finally." Cora wraps her arms around me, and I fall into her, breathing in her rosy scent.

I squeeze my eyes tight, and the tears break free at the corners. I cling to her, and I feel like I'm the child and she's the parent. This is how I've felt since Natalie got sick. It makes me angry. I'm angry the roles have been reversed for the past six months. I'm angry I haven't been stronger for them.

"We've been waiting on you," she says.

It feels like the intense, sweltering sun is baking me with this black suit jacket on. It also feels like it's frying my brain in the process. I lick my upper lip and taste the saltiness of the sweat there. The irritation and the indignation that my kids are having to take care of me burns in my chest. "Well, I'm sorry that I made everyone wait." I raise my voice.

"Dad," Tess says, a warning in both her tone and her sienna-brown eyes.

"I'm so sorry that my wife died"—I whip around and face my

family and friends—"and that I made everyone wait because...oh I don't know, I guess I'm not ready to bury her yet."

Sobs sound out, but I don't realize where they're coming from until it's too late. Cora is crying into her hands next to me, her shoulders trembling.

I mentally scold myself, and my throat constricts from the inconsolable ache there. Pinching my eyes shut, I shove my thumbs into them. I'm a jackass. "I'm sorry," I whisper, placing a hand on her shoulder and giving it a tender squeeze.

"You're not the only one who lost her, you know?" Cora spits out in between her fits of sobs.

"I know...I know." I run a hand down my unshaven face. What's the point of shaving anymore, especially on a day like today? What's the point in doing any of the mundane things ever again? "I'm sorry," I try again. Because these kids are the only thing I care about anymore. Cora and Tess are all I have left. And...Richie Rich.

Defeated, I slump into a chair, and now I'm burying my own face into my hands. "I'm failing at this miserably."

Tess gingerly sits next to me and rests her hand on my shoulder. "You're not failing at anything." Her voice is softer than I deserve.

"I'm failing at being a father."

"Dad." Cora sits on the other side of me, and I lift my head from my palms. She swipes at her wet cheeks. "Mom being gone doesn't change anything. You're still our dad. A great dad."

"The best," Tess says, her lips pulling into a genuine smile.

"Yeah, but now I'm going at it alone." I wipe the rough suit sleeve over my damp eyes. "I'm not sure I'll know what to do or how to take care of you without your mom."

"You'll be fine," Cora assures me. "We'll have to figure out a new rhythm. But Tess is married, and I'm starting college in a few weeks. You don't need to worry about us so much."

Cora is attempting to make me feel better by reminding me I don't have much of this parenting thing left on my own to do, but her words twist in my gut. She's heading to college soon, and Tess and

Richie are already their own family unit. Even though Cora's attending the University of California, Santa Barbara and it's only about a two-hour drive from LA, it suddenly hits me in this moment. The weight of the realization consumes me and forces me to remain planted in my chair. Once Cora is gone, I'll be alone. The word *alone* rings in my ears, sounding like a curse word on a child's lips, and the negativity of it wraps around my chest like a vice.

Since Natalie's diagnosis a little over six months ago, Tess has been at the house more often than not. And in the last week, she was there every day. What will I do in that big house all by myself?

"Unless," Cora mumbles, her attention fixated on her black heels as they dig purposefully into the prickly grass, "you'd rather I take a year off school?"

"No. No way. That's out of the question." I shake my head. Cora has been talking about her freshman year of college and rooming with her best friend, Jessica, since they were in grade school. Besides, Natalie and I have already paid the tuition. It's one of the things she made me promise, that I would make Cora go. I may be incapable of keeping some of the promises I made her, but I intend to keep that one.

"I will stay home, if you need me to."

"No, you're going, and that's final. Your mom made you and I both promise, remember?"

Cora's face tightens and she nods but says, "Well, it's not like she'll know."

"Cora," Tess scolds, "you're going. Dad's right, you both promised. This is not up for debate." Tess plays her older sister card, and I'm grateful.

"But I don't want Dad to go back home...alone."

"Hello?" I wave a hand in the space between my daughters who are still talking over me. "Dad's right here. And Dad will be fine."

"You're already not working. And not shaving. You're gonna go crazy in that big house all by yourself."

"I am not." I scratch at the scruff on my chin self-consciously.

"Cora," Tess interjects, "he was just yelling at the sky."

"Really?" Cora flashes me a look with worriment streaking in her amber-brown eyes. "Is that true?"

"No."

But at the same time, Tess says, "Yes."

The minister approaches, a gangly graying man, and he clears his throat. "Excuse me, but we should get started. I have a wedding to officiate in an hour."

While his tone may be sincere, his words are not. My blood boils beneath my skin and I find myself wishing it were him in that casket rather than my wife. She didn't deserve this. What she ever saw as promising in this guy as a minister I can't fathom in this moment. I guess I never got those good vibes from him the few times I accompanied Natalie to church.

I pull myself to standing. "Oh, I'm sorry you have a wedding to officiate. That's super important. Of course, way more important than a celebration-of-life service for my dead wife," I bite out.

Both Cora and Tess stand too. Daniel passes me a sympathetic look. He's about to step in. A best friend can tell when the other one is about to lose it.

The minister backs away, holding up his Bible as if he's summoning the demons out of me. *Go ahead and try*, is what I wanna say. Because, yeah, I guess I'm bitter about the fact that my wife is gone. That she had to be taken away from me. And away from our daughters.

He presses his thin lips together. "I'll give you a few more minutes." He slinks away.

I stab my hands through my earlier gelled and styled hair and exhale a string of curses under my breath.

"Dad." Tess elbows me, her wide eyes and chin motioning in unison toward the minister. "That's a Jesus-Man right there," she mumbles through clenched teeth.

And she's right. Not only is the minister witnessing my outburst of foul language, but all of my family and friends seated behind me, my parents and in-laws, my best friend and my two daughters as well. The very two daughters I'm so obviously failing.

I can't do this. I can't do this without Natalie. I should've been the one to go first. She was always better at this parenting gig than me.

It all feels like too much to bear. It feels unfair. Unfair that Natalie would leave this world first. And now, I find myself jealous of her. The guilt of being the one still alive tightens in my chest, unforgiving. I have this impulsive urge to climb inside that mahogany hardwood box and let them bury me six feet under instead.

"Dad," Tess says, her gentle voice reminding me of her mother's. "Do you really think Richie and I would let you go back to the house all alone? You're gonna come and stay with us. For however long you need."

My throat thickens as tears well up in my eyes again, causing my vision to blur and I'm instantly blubbering like an idiot. "No. I can't. I'm a grown man. I can't live with my daughter and her husband." I swipe the suit sleeve across my drenched eyes again.

"We're not taking no for an answer."

But I find myself considering her offer, the panic of being alone taut in my chest. "You sure I won't be a burden?"

"You're my dad, you could never be a burden."

I focus on her eyes, recognizing the sincerity in them. "Are you sure about this?"

Tess nods. "Absolutely."

"And you're okay with this?" I ask Richie.

"Most definitely. Whatever you need." He stands and puts his hand out to shake mine. I glance at it but instead of accepting, I pull his slender, lanky body into a hug.

"Thank you." I sob into his chest like I'm a toddler.

I realize in this moment that all of my family and friends are still waiting. And staring. Instantly, the annoyance of this kicks up in my veins. I turn to face them. "What are you looking at, Aunt Jan? You've never seen two grown, heterosexual men hug before?"

Tess and Cora simultaneously gasp while Aunt Jan harrumphs.

"Dad!" Tess scolds before leaning in and saying low into my ear, "Are you still taking the medication your doctor prescribed?"

I ignore her and mumble *sorry* to Aunt Jan before wrapping my arm around Cora's shoulder and folding Tess up underneath my other arm. I nod my chin at the impatient minister, signaling we're ready to begin—but I don't feel ready. How can I be ready to say goodbye to *my* person, my best friend and lover, the one I've shared my life with for the last twenty-five years?

As I slump into the chair and the minister begins reading Psalm 46:1-10, Natalie's favorite Bible passage from the first time she was sick, I force myself to zone out. It's the only way I can make it through this. That and having two of the strongest women I know at my side. Their support and plans to take care of me are probably more than I deserve.

An intensity burns in my core, that feeling of someone watching me, and I turn in the direction. I find the shadowed eyes of Uncle Bob, Aunt Jan's husband, fixated on me. Instead of pity resonating there, his eyes are accusatory. As if I'm to blame for their niece's death.

"What are you looking at?" I hiss.

Uncle Bob looks away, and Aunt Jan harrumphs again.

"Dad," Tess whispers, shoving a pointy elbow into my rib.

I focus my attention on the sky without feeling an ounce of remorse toward Uncle Bob or Aunt Jan. They were never close with Natalie, judging her for getting married too young and to me, a college dropout heading nowhere fast. But twenty years old hadn't felt young to us when we were so in love. And as for being a college dropout, I'd say my career as one of the top realtors at the best agency in LA makes up for that. But Natalie didn't need my career for us to live comfortably. She'd started designing her own online women's fashion line, *Natalie's,* eight years ago. In the last two years, she brought in nearly as much income as I did.

At the edge of the skyline, where it meets the tops of the eucalyptus trees, I spot one puffy, lonely, cumulus cloud. Gratitude manifests in my chest and spreads, reaching to my limbs. I can feel Natalie here, with me, giving me the comfort I need but can't get from anyone else.

I whisper, "Look, there's one freakin' cloud."

Cora squeezes my hand and Tess cradles her head on my shoulder.

If Natalie continues to give me small signs like this, especially when I need them most, maybe—just maybe—the three of us will make it. The three of us and Richie Rich, of course.

Chapter 2

Tess

Eight Months Later

I rush downstairs for breakfast and find Dad dressed in my pink robe with his brown hair disheveled and his face in desperate need of a shave. He's seated in the same spot he's always in when I come downstairs each morning.

My spot.

But it doesn't matter. It's been eight months, so it may as well be his spot now. I have resorted to the space next to Richie on the nook's built-in wooden bench.

But Richie isn't sitting this morning. Instead, he's scarfing down a bowl of oatmeal while hovering over the sink, the steam still rising. I hesitate at the kitchen island, glancing at them both, and feel uneasy about what I've walked in on this morning. It's not unusual for Richie and Dad to get into petty arguments. Some of my most recent favorites are about the weather, the traffic to Dodger Stadium, and how long the marriage will last between Justin Bieber and Hailey Baldwin.

I do my best to not only stay out of these frivolous arguments but to conserve the peace between them as well. But today, my stomach does somersaults. There's enough going on without having to stress over being the peacekeeper.

"Morning, Dad." I reach for a rosy grapefruit from the fruit bowl on the counter, bringing it to my nose for a sniff. The citrusy scent is intoxicating, stirring up idyllic childhood memories of eating these side by side with Mom on the sofa on Saturday mornings.

"Hey, Tess," Dad greets around a mouthful of cold cereal.

Today, his choice of poison is Cinnamon Toast Crunch. But suggesting a healthier option is hopeless. Dr. Lang—my therapist—says I need to give Dad time. Riding him about small things, such as his diet, could trigger reactions that indicate deeper emotions he may not be ready to deal with yet. So, I do my best to ignore him while he scarfs down a heaping bowl of children's cereal, and I slice my grapefruit in half.

Richie rinses his bowl and spoon and loads them into the dishwasher. He passes me a knowing smile I've grown accustomed to and gives me a quick kiss on the cheek. His smile means Dad is in his usual ornery mood.

"See you tonight. Eight o'clock. Mercury's." He picks up his briefcase from the floor by the back door.

"Right, dinner. I remember. Have a good day. Love you."

"Love you too." Richie gives Dad a nod, though I'm not sure he notices. "Bye, Pete."

"Oh, yeah, bye. Good luck today. Make lots of deals."

Dad doesn't understand Richie's job. And Richie has given up explaining it to him. He works as a senior project manager for Cavanaugh Industries, a commercial construction company his family has owned and operated for years. While he's excellent at his job and works hard, admittedly he did inherit some family money, not to mention a place of employment straight out of college at the family business. Hence the reason for Dad's nickname for Richie. Dad doesn't like handouts. Which is ironic, considering he's been living with me for so long.

After Richie slips out the door, I reluctantly sit down across from

Dad with my grapefruit. I wish he wouldn't give Richie a hard time. After all, we're the ones providing him with a place to live so he doesn't have to be in that big house all alone. If it wasn't for Richie reminding me of Dad's loss, I may have been tempted to send him back home months ago.

"Are you heading to the store this morning?" Dad stares into his bowl.

"Yep. We're down to only twelve more weeks before opening."

"That's good." He tries to sound upbeat but fails. "When will you be home?"

"Around the same time as usual. Seven o'clock." But when Dad gets in one of his moods, where he's practically inconsolable, I'm tempted to stay at the store later.

"And it sounds like you and Richie Rich have plans for dinner? Who are you going with?"

I purse my lips, ignoring his questions. "Dad, I really wish you wouldn't call him that."

He rolls his eyes dramatically. "Fine."

Honestly, he resembles a child sometimes. I had no idea how much he would regress after Mom died. Most of the time, I regret asking him to come stay with us for as long as he needs. But then we talk about Mom, get stuck in a memory, and the pity for him returns tenfold.

"What about this weekend? What do you guys have planned?"

"Richie and I have dinner plans with friends on Friday, then his company golf day on Saturday, and we have a friend's baby shower on Sunday."

"And men are supposed to go to that, a baby shower?"

I nod, before scooping a piece of grapefruit into my mouth, the citrus biting at my tongue.

"He could hang out with me instead on Sunday. We could go shoot some hoops."

"Sorry, Richie has already RSVP'd."

"To a baby shower? What kind of floopy, uppity-up party is this?"

"The kind you RSVP to," I say flatly.

Dad drops the subject and picks up his bowl. He slurps the sugary milk, and I press my lips together, fighting the urge to ask him to stop.

He stands, and the pink robe that was once mine, falls open. Thankfully, he's wearing a pair of plaid boxer shorts and a plain white tee underneath. Though the T-shirt has seen better days with the yellowish tint to it and orange Cheeto stains.

Dad claims that one day, while he was doing laundry dressed in only his boxer shorts, the UPS guy knocked on the door for a signed delivery. The robe was the closest garment to throw on. The problem is, he hasn't taken it off since that day. Only to wash it. Then it goes right back on.

"Hey, have you talked to Cora?" Dad asks.

I furrow my brow—the question coming from left field. "I got a text from her yesterday. Why?"

Cora and I are five years apart. While we get along fine, having that many years of an age gap is enough to not have much in common. Not only can I drink alcohol legally, but I married Richie when I was twenty and Cora was only fifteen, barely starting her period. I graduated college with a bachelor's degree in fashion design and technology at the age of twenty-two while Cora fretted over who to go to prom with. After Mom was diagnosed with breast cancer— the second time—and was teaching me all the ins and outs of her women's fashion line, Natalie's, Cora was partying her way through high school.

Dad shuffles into the kitchen in his worn slippers. "She's been distant lately. And last time I talked to her, she mentioned a summer internship at the University. I'm worried about her." He sets his bowl in the white porcelain farmhouse sink without bothering to rinse it, never mind loading it into the dishwasher.

"I'm sure she's fine. She's in college. She needs her space. Remember when I went to college? I barely called home the first year." I scoot out of the bench and take my bowl and saucer to the sink. But instead of setting my dishes inside, I toss the rind into the trash and rinse them, along with Dad's and load them all into the dishwasher.

"Yeah, I remember." He smiles before his face turns serious, and he leans against the counter. "But at least you called your mom."

My jaw clenches. And now, it's just me and Dad, frozen in that moment. Stuck in that memory of Mom. I want to rush into his arms and let him hold me like he used to when I was a little girl and woke up from a nightmare. But this nightmare is one I can't seem to wake up from.

"If you're worried about Cora, you should call her," I suggest.

"Yeah, okay."

Before he has a chance to escape into the living room, I go against Dr. Lang's suggestion not to push him and call, "Hey, Dad?" He glances at me over his shoulder, acting inconvenienced by my interruption. "Have you talked to Uncle Daniel lately?"

Daniel Russo is not only Dad's childhood friend and mine and Cora's godfather, but he's also Dad's colleague. The two often traded realtor listings. Daniel is usually a bit of a narcissist, but he has been wonderful since Mom passed. He goes over to the house once a week and takes care of the yard and the pool. Dad is too cheap to pay a yard service, so typically he takes care of it himself.

"Talked to him a few days ago. Why?"

"I wondered if he's found any good listings for you recently. Any *Pete Redd* listings."

His face pales and his jaw sets. "He hasn't mentioned any. Besides, kid, you know I'm not ready yet."

I tread lightly, hearing Dr. Lang's voice telling me it's not my place to manage his emotions. "I know, I just thought that maybe...if you dip your toes in. Maybe take on a joint listing with Daniel, then—"

"Tesssss." He drags out my name on a whine, interrupting me. "I said, I'm not ready." Pain etches on his unshaven face, his green eyes sunken in and heavy.

"But—"

"Soon. Hopefully. But not yet." He offers me a weak smile before turning and making his way into the living room. The sound of the TV coming to life soon follows, along with a potato chip bag crinkling.

It's not even 9:00 a.m.

I rub my temples and exhale. Every day it's the same thing. Why did I think today would be any different?

It's Friday night and we're at Mercury's, Richie's favorite restaurant, having dinner with our other couple friends. Carter and Dexter went to college with us and have been friends with Richie since they were children. Now, the three of them work together in the LA branch of Cavanaugh Industries. Carter met his wife, Alissa, on Match.com. She's a *Next Top Model* look-alike, with her glossy blonde hair, flawless skin, and measurements that should belong on Barbie rather than a human being.

Dexter met his vivacious redheaded girlfriend, Cheyenne, while he was positioned in the Austin, Texas branch of Cavanaugh Industries a few years ago. She's a few years older than the rest of us, is as sweet as honey, and has exquisite fashion sense, making her my go-to girl when I have questions about Mom's clothing line. She's been instrumental in getting the clothing boutique ready to open. Since she was spending so much time there, she finally agreed to allow me to put her on the payroll.

Alissa takes a sip of her chardonnay while Cheyenne gives me her opinion on my shoes, a pair of fuchsia slingbacks. I swivel my unsweetened iced tea in my glass and, every once in a while, glance up and make eye contact with the girls so they think I'm paying attention.

I'm not.

I can't stop thinking about Dad and how we're stuck in a rut I'm unsure we'll be able to climb out of.

Alissa clears her throat, and I'm suddenly back in the restaurant with the clinking of dishes and the camaraderie of the men. I glance at both women, my face hot under their quizzical stares.

"What?" I ask from my daze.

"I said, why aren't you drinking wine tonight?" Alissa's narrowed eyes take me in, considering.

I glance at the others seated around the table. Richie is carrying on a conversation about his golf game from last Saturday and how hole eighteen had been an epic shot, granting him a par. I lower my chin and voice as I say, "Richie and I are thinking it's about time we start trying."

"Ooooo, really?" Cheyenne claps her hands, bouncing in her seat. "This is so exciting."

"Are you sure about this?" Alissa sits back in her chair, crossing her arms over her ample chest. "You've barely been married three years. What's the hurry?"

"Oh, stop. Three years is plenty." Cheyenne flops a hand at Alissa, dismissing her, and I wish I could do the same, put Alissa in her place.

"I'm almost twenty-four," I say, incredulous. Why is it my job to convince Alissa I'm ready to start having kids? "Besides, if we want at least two kids, there's no telling how long it could take to get pregnant each time. There's a five-year difference between Cora and I."

"Yeah, but I thought that's because your mom was diagnosed with cancer after she had you?"

Her words sting, and I can't help but physically recoil as a result. Alissa isn't mean intentionally. She simply doesn't think before she opens her mouth and the word-vomit exits.

She must notice my reaction.

"Sorry, Tess. I didn't mean anything by it."

I force myself to swallow around the lump in my throat—the one that's present every time Mom is mentioned. And cancer.

"Well, we are tickled pink for you and Richie." Cheyenne recovers the moment and lifts her glass. "We should toast."

The men's conversation halts.

Richie leans into me, whispering in a low growl, "What are we toasting?"

I'm debating how to inform him, when Cheyenne blurts out, "That y'all are trying to get pregnant."

"You sneaky dog, you." Dexter slaps Richie on the back.

"Hot damn," Carter says. "Now that's what I'm talking about." He passes a knowing look in Alissa's direction.

She waves a finger in the air at him. "Nuh-uh, don't even think about it. You know I'm not letting all this"—she mimics an hour-glass shape with her hands—"go to waste in my twenties."

"Oh c'mon, you won't be thirty for like six more years. I can't wait to see little Carters running around."

"You know," Cheyenne interrupts, "reproductive rates drop and birth defects skyrocket the older you are."

Alissa flicks her blonde hair off her shoulder and shoots a death stare in Cheyenne's direction before saying, "I'll take my chances, thank you very much."

Cheyenne is still holding her glass awkwardly in the air. "Okay, y'all, maybe we should toast and keep our opinions to ourselves." Cheyenne pins Alissa with a side-eye while she continues with the toast. "To our good friends, Richie and Tess, may—"

"'May the odds be ever in your favor,'" Dexter interrupts, ripping off the famous line from *The Hunger Games*.

Carter chuckles along with him.

Cheyenne rolls her eyes so far back in her head I'm afraid they'll get stuck there.

To break the tension, we all take a drink. But when I glance at Richie, he's shifting in his seat uncomfortably and setting his glass down after gulping his domestic beer in one succession.

"Something wrong?" I ask quietly, aligning my silverware so they're in perfect order.

Richie, however, does not lower his voice when he says, "I mean, yeah, something's wrong." He rubs at the back of his neck. "I just don't think now is a good time."

My face heats about twenty degrees, embarrassment flooding my cheeks as all four sets of eyes stare at me, awaiting my reaction.

I blink. "But I thought...Richie, we've talked about this. I thought you wanted to have a baby now."

Richie reaches for my trembling hand and pulls it into his lap. "Oh, babe, I do. That hasn't changed."

"Then what's the problem?" My voice shakes.

He drops his chin and sighs, unable to look at me with those big blue eyes. "In one word? Your dad."

My mouth drops open before I somehow recover. "My dad? What does he have to do with this?"

"Buddy, that's two words," Dexter mumbles.

"Hush up," Cheyenne demands.

"Look, it's fine your dad is staying with us, really. But trying to get...intimate while he's in the next room is sort of...a problem."

"C'mon, Cavanaugh, you gotta push that to the back of your mind and charge through. Take one for the team. Get the job done." Dexter shakes a fist at him, his crooked nose that resembles Owen Wilson's sticks up in the air slightly.

"Dexter." Cheyenne smacks him in the gut.

"Gee. Thanks, Dexter, for putting it that way," I say. "Like making love to me is some kind of chore."

"You know I don't think that. I'd never think that. I love you and there's nothing I want more than to start a family with you. But—"

The *but* feels like a slap to the face.

"But maybe...we ought to wait. You know, until he's back home. *His* home. He's gotta move out eventually."

Yeah, right. Eventually. But when is eventually? Two weeks? Two months? What if it's two years? I'm equal parts saddened at the thought of him leaving and returning to his house alone and elated to finally have my spot at the kitchen nook and my robe back.

On second thought, he can keep the robe.

"So, listen." Alissa eases the tension, stretching across the table and spilling her boobs in the process. "I think I know what you need to do. There's this lady." She snaps her fingers together a couple times. "Jules Sweeney. She calls herself an interventionist and has an office in LA. My brother went and saw her after his wife left him when she had her opioid addiction. Anyway, he described the sessions with her as miraculous healings. You've heard me say it, he's a completely different person."

I shake the ice in my glass. "That's great, but I don't see what this has to do with the situation with my dad."

"I'm getting to that," she says, talking with her hands. "So, this miracle worker helps people with addictions that stem from traumas. She wrote a self-help book. It's a freaking *New York Times* best seller. The book has an entire section talking about a specific program for men who lost their spouses to death or divorce or whatever. The program she executes helps them get back out there. You know, dating again."

The word *dating* in association with Dad sounds foreign to my ears and tastes sour in my mouth. I straighten in my seat. "Oh, I don't think he's ready for dating." And to be honest, I'm not ready for that either.

"He doesn't necessarily have to start dating, but this lady can help snap him out of his depression and back into taking care of himself again. And convince him he's ready to move back home." She takes a breath and leans in closer. "Isn't that what you want?"

Is that what I want? I'm sure I don't want him depressed or being a slug in my home anymore. And I definitely don't want him living with me to be the reason I have to postpone having children.

"I think Alissa might be onto something. You're tired of seeing your dad mope around all day every day, aren't you?" Cheyenne asks.

I bite my lower lip and turn to look at Richie.

He shrugs a shoulder, his black hair flopping into his face. "It may not hurt to at least look into this. Ya know, reach out to this so-called miracle worker. Because after eight months of living with us, that may be what we need."

This entire conversation is making me uneasy, the nerves cause somersaults in my stomach. I shift in my seat, fidgeting with the silverware again. "What does this lady actually do? Does she fake date these men to make them feel better about themselves? Because that sounds terrible. And I don't want him in worse shape when it's over."

"Not exactly," Alissa says, taking a sip of her wine before continuing. "The men who agree to her program are aware of the details—that she's there to act strictly as a partner or a fill-in girlfriend, if you will. It's called her Challenge Program. She starts off trying to work through their trauma, then, she encourages them to make some positive changes. It's a six-week program that consists of six counseling sessions and six challenges."

"Challenges?" I question.

"Right. These usually involve getting them outside, doing something they once enjoyed. Like, a hobby, maybe seeing a Dodger game. Isn't your dad a Dodger fan?"

I nod.

"The biggest," Richie says, intrigued and now hanging on every word Alissa speaks.

"Then, like, for your dad...he's had a hard time going back to work, so she'd somehow plan for an opportunity to present itself where he'd have to—or want to—return to work."

"This all sounds a little too easy. Not to mention misleading," I say.

"Here's the thing, though. She gives the men back their confidence. Then, when she sets up a 'chance' meeting with a potential partner, he's more open to it, to a relationship, and *bam*"—Alissa claps her hands together and I jump—"her work is done. And your dad is out of your house and back home. Mr. Independent. Bye

bye, pink robe." She rests back into her seat, brushing her hands clean.

"I agree with Richie," Cheyenne says. "It wouldn't hurt anything to at least call the lady."

"But I know my dad. There's no way he would agree to her program."

"Not willingly." Alissa gives me a sly grin.

"What are you suggesting?"

"Tell your dad he's simply agreeing to go through the program, that's it. Strictly the counseling sessions and the challenges. Leave out the fill-in girlfriend part," Alissa says. When I don't respond right away, she says, "Listen, I have her book. I'll bring it by tomorrow, and you can read it yourself."

I'm beginning to warm up to the idea. I guess I could call this interventionist lady, no harm in that. And I could read her book and see what she's all about. I suppose if she's not actually trying to date Dad, it might be okay. And if it gets him back on his own two feet and in his house again, it would be worth it. Even better if she gets him out of the pink robe for good.

"A best-selling novel, nothing shabby about that," Carter chimes in.

"Okay," I say on an exhale. "I'll read her book. And...I'll call her." I glance at Richie, and there's something like optimism shining in his blue eyes. I can feel it too, blooming in the center of my core.

"It sounds to me like pimping out your father," Dexter jokes.

Richie punches a fist into his shoulder.

The hope I felt only moments before fizzles as fast as it sparked. Because Dexter is right—it sounds exactly like that. And how can I not feel like the worst daughter in the world for seriously considering this?

Chapter 3

Jules

Waiting in the never-ending Starbucks drive-thru is the last place I should be at 8:46 a.m. when I have a client showing up at my office at nine. I could skip my Friday triple grande flat white, but then I'd be stuck drinking the office Keurig coffee. And that's not a risk I'm willing to take on such an important day.

With eight cars already in line and wrapped around the building, I pull into a parking space and take my chances with the cafe. My ankles wobble in the too-tall heels. I'd bought the dumb shoes on a whim following a devastating breakup even though I knew they were uncomfortable. Unfortunately, I chose to wear them today—when I'm running late and expecting a new client.

Inside, I give a small fist pump upon finding only three people in line. Derrick, a tan and attractive barista in his late twenties spots me and smiles. Sometimes having clients all over the city has its benefits.

Maybe I won't be too late after all.

I reluctantly tap out a text to Angie Phillips, my assistant/roommate.

Me: *Running late.*

Angie: *Triple grande caramel macchiato.*

Me: *Done.*

I hold up two fingers to Derrick, who gives me a head nod from the other side of the bar. It's the least I can do since Angie will be stuck playing referee between my client, Jake Morris, a recovering alcoholic, and his mother. Jake has been my 9:00 a.m. every Friday for the last couple of months. Typically, I no longer see my clients once they complete the Challenge Program, but sometimes, I come across a one who requests additional sessions.

Jake Morris is that such client. He puts my ten years of experience as a licensed therapist to the test on a weekly basis. Last month, Jake's mother began joining in on our sessions. We've been making zero headway because Mrs. Morris is unable to forgive her son for everything he did to the family while he was deep in his alcoholism. I'd prefer to be stuck in the forever-long Starbucks line than be in Angie's shoes, even if hers are probably more comfortable.

Derrick gestures me over with a head nod and slides two cups across the counter. I hand him a twenty-dollar bill. "Thank you, Derrick. As always, you're a lifesaver." He tries to pass the money back to me, but I snatch the cups and back up.

"No, Jules, you're the true MVP." He places both hands over his heart and mock swoons.

Back inside my car, the scorching sun shines through my windshield. My Ray-Ban sunglasses are doing little to protect my eyes from the blinding light. When I pull into the parking garage of my office building twelve minutes later, the temperature drops a good twenty degrees.

With the two coffees in tow and my bag slung over one shoulder, I step onto the elevator in the fatal heels. A dreadful grinding noise rumbles in my ears, and I suck in a breath as gravity forces upward under my feet. The Temple of Doom—aka the elevator—stops abruptly when it reaches my floor and jolts me forward. I clutch the cups in my hands as I attempt to catch my balance but fail and stumble. The hot liquid sloshes out the spouts, and I swear, coffee is like a magnet to a white blouse. I curse under my breath. The Temple of Doom strikes again.

The elevator doors slide open, and I step out into a war zone. Jake Morris has his giant hands laced around the neck of his mother while she attempts to scream through the strangling. Poor Angie, with her spaghetti-noodle arms, is sandwiched in between, trying to pry the two apart.

"Jake!" I holler, rushing toward the huddle.

The sound of my voice, or maybe the mention of his name, is enough to snap Jake out of his rage. He releases his grip and steps back. His mother gasps, choking and bending over at the waist.

"My goodness, are you all right?" I set the coffee cups on Angie's desk and caress Mrs. Morris's back. "Ang, get her some water, will you?"

She does without hesitation, but not without taking an untrusting eye off Jake Morris.

"I'm sorry," Jake mutters, tears welling up in his eyes as he stabs his fingers through his disheveled hair. "I didn't mean to. Mom, you gotta believe me," he pleads.

Angie hands Mrs. Morris a paper cup, and she gulps the water.

"Jake, what were you thinking?" I massage tiny circles at my temples.

"I wasn't," he blurts. "She just makes me so mad sometimes, ya know? With her judgy eyes."

His mother sets the paper cup down, hikes the strap of her purse higher on her shoulder, and glares at Jake.

"See!" He points a waggling finger at his mother. "You see that? Judgy eyes."

He's not wrong. Mrs. Morris's glare toward her son is a mixture of fire and ice.

"That's because I *am* judging you," his mother finally snaps, finding her voice after near-strangulation. "Everyone is judging you. And me. And if you don't want help, you're gonna have to do this on your own." She spins around on her flat-heeled shoe, stabs the button for the elevator, and stomps on as it opens.

I sigh and turn to Jake.

"You see what I'm dealing with? You see how she is? She's impossible."

I snatch a pen off Angie's desk and scrawl on a Post-it Note before handing it to him. "Jake, I think it's best if you seek professional help. This is the name and number of a psychiatrist that specializes in alcoholism and their families."

He snatches it from my grip. "You're dumping me?"

"No. I'm trying to help you. And I believe I've done all I can. I'm not a psychiatrist. I'm not even a licensed therapist anymore."

At least, I'm not a practicing licensed therapist.

"This is her fault, ya know? Everything's her fault."

"I hear you, Mr. Morris." I rest a hand on his back and usher him toward the elevator. "Please, call the doctor I recommended."

"Yeah, okay," he mutters. The elevator doors open and he steps inside. "Hey, Jules, now that I'm not your client anymore...can I ask you out sometime?"

"I'm flattered. But I also don't date former clients either." I swallow around the lie. In the past, I did date a former client. Since the relationship ended in a complete and utter disaster, I figure it's not a bad rule to reinforce.

Finally, the doors close, and Angie and I are alone. We both slump into the chairs at her desk and pick up our coffee.

"Happy Friday to us." She smiles half-heartedly.

"Cheers to that." We knock our cups together before I take a large gulp of the bittersweet nectar.

"What happened there?" Angie gestures with her cup at my now-most-definitely stained blouse.

"The Temple of Doom happened." I glare at the old, untrustworthy elevator.

"Again? That's the second time this month." She tucks a strand of straight black hair behind her ear, kicks her feet up on the desk, and crosses her ankles. "You ought to invest in white blouses. Buy stock in them or something," she teases.

But I'm too focused on the cute wedged sandals strapped to Angie's feet. "Hey? Are those mine?" I raise a brow at her.

Her lips curve into a smile. "I didn't think you'd miss them. You've got, like a billion pairs of shoes."

"But not like those." I lean back in the chair and cross my leg, swinging my dangling foot. "And I don't have a *billion* pairs. It's not like I'm rich."

"I know," her voice goes up. "But it's not as if you're hard up either."

"That cash advance from my publisher is practically gone."

"Yeah, yeah, I know. You used it to pay the lease on this super reliable office space." Her eyes take in the room. The old renovated office space is less than fancy with the worn beige carpet and mauve-painted walls.

"It may not be glamorous, and the elevator might be questionable at best, but office space in a decent part of LA isn't cheap." I pull myself up to standing, my ankles wobbling before I straighten. I rummage around in the unlocked file cabinet next to Angie's desk, searching for the bleach Tide pen we keep on hand for the coffee spillage occasion.

"Okay, but when you're sent a large royalty check, can you at least look for new office space? On the bottom floor, preferably. You know I don't trust taking the Temple of Doom, and my feet are getting blisters from all those flights of stairs."

"Then maybe you should stop trying to cram your giant feet into my shoes."

She waves me off but laughs.

I finally locate the bleach pen, and my fingers tremble as I remove the cap and rub it on the front of my blouse. Anxiety burrows in my stomach like a tornado as thoughts of meeting with my new client run through my mind.

My phone conversation earlier in the week with Tess Cavanaugh was enough to intrigue me to at least agree to meet with her father. His story sounded similar to my other clients who have successfully completed my Challenge Program. Though, typically the trauma my clients face is the result of divorce. I've only taken a few through the program who were overcoming trauma caused by the death of a loved one.

Tess's situation tugged on my heart. My own father lived with me until a year ago when the dementia got too bad for either of us to handle. But my mom hadn't died, she'd simply left. By choice.

When Tess told me how much she loved my book, I was almost certain she'd only read the blurb on the back jacket because she quoted it nearly word for word. "I love the way you talk about coping with trauma and emotional turmoil without turning to addictive behavior. It's fascinating."

As she continued to ramble, I knew exactly where the conversation was headed. And I was one hundred percent uncomfortable with the direction. Tess asked me to take her dad through my six-week Challenge Program but not tell him how it usually works—that I set forth the challenges and accompany my clients on each one. I'm like a built-in friend that may or may not take the place of a significant other. I sort of fill that void until my client is ready to either move on or feels confident being alone again. For Pete, the end goal would be that he finally moves back home.

Even though I'd clearly made Tess's day by agreeing to take her father on as a new client, this will be a challenge for me as well. People who are interested in my six-week program come to see me willingly. They are fully aware of how it works and agree we are strictly friends during the course of the program. This will be the first time a client will have no idea of my typical role. I'm not sure how I feel about lying to a client. As a former licensed therapist, it feels unethical.

"You got this," Angie says, her ankles still propped on the desk.

"Don't let this new client or the circumstances of why he's here intimidate you."

"Yeah, yeah, I know." I toss the bleach pen back into the file cabinet, the stain proving to too big of a job for it. I flatten my black pencil skirt with my sweaty palms for the hundredth time this morning and pace the length of the office, my left foot already working on a blister.

"You're a professional. You can handle this."

"You're right." I stop pacing and look at her, squaring my shoulders. "I am a professional. I can do this."

Angie rolls her creamy-brown eyes, tapping a pen against her desk. "That's only what I've been telling you all week, but sure, listen to yourself and get amped up."

The elevator dings and the doors slide open, spitting out who I can only assume is my new client. He whips around, checking out the elevator like he's just been violated.

"Mr. Redd?" I say.

He spins back around to face me and smiles. It's a pleasant smile. One that's genuine and makes his green eyes sparkle. I'm not sure what his daughter was talking about, this man doesn't resemble a slug in the slightest. The three-to four-day-old stubble on his boyish face looks sexy on him. And somehow, slightly familiar.

I take a few steps in his direction. "Nice to meet you." I reach out my hand, just as Angie pulls out the bottom drawer of the filing cabinet, and it slides right out in front of me. It all happens so fast, but at the same time, as if in slow motion. The drawer cuts my path, my shins smack into it, and the collision sends me flying over it. My hands splay out, reaching for anything to hold onto to break my fall.

My attempt to break my fall results in me and my new, very attractive client nearly reaching third base.

"Ooooooh," Angie exhales. "Sorry!" But she's busting up laughing beneath a cupped hand.

"I am so sorry. Oh my goodness, terribly sorry." My face burns and feels like I've stuck it into a fire. He kneels down and holds me under the arm while I try to avoid looking into those glassy green eyes and scramble to my feet.

"Are you okay? That was quite a fall." While it's evident he's amused, he seems more uncomfortable than anything else.

My shins scream out in fiery pain, but I am a professional. I flatten my skirt and reach out again to shake his hand, ignoring the sting. "I'm fine." I force out a fake laugh, which comes out as anything but convincing. "Let's try this again. I'm Jules Sweeney."

"Wait. Jules Sweeney?" The same smile from earlier returns, and he shakes my hand. It's firm and warm and lasts much longer than it should. "I think we've met."

I'm lost in his beautiful eyes, transfixed. I shouldn't know what color my client's eyes are. But I'm having a difficult time looking away. "Um, what?" I finally mumble, my cheeks flaming.

"Oh shit," he says, tearing his hand from my grasp. "You're bleeding."

"Wh-what?" I glance down and discover he's right. Blood is trickling down both shins, threatening to spill into my shoes. This explains the burning pain. "It's nothing. I'm fine." I grab a couple of tissues off Angie's desk and dab at my bloody shins. The gashes don't look too bad. It seems as though I'll live, despite the fact I want to die from embarrassment.

"Would you like me to come back a different day? Because I can. My schedule is wide open." He has his hands pressed to his hips where his jeans sit low and at just the right place.

I swallow.

But his comment reminds me of why he's here. This guy needs my help, and I'm going to stop ogling him and do my job. Because I am a professional.

I toss the tissues in the trash. "No, no, that won't be necessary. I'm fine." I step aside, wincing, and gesture to the open door of my office. "Why don't we get started?"

His expression caves, his hope gone that he's not getting out of this. He stalks past me, taking on a childlike behavior. I've dealt with plenty of difficult clients, but most of them come to me of their own free will. It's clear he doesn't want to be here. Which will only make my job that much harder.

"Why don't you take a seat on the sofa, and we'll get started with the basics." I go to shut the door, but Angie catches my attention. She mouths, *He's hot*, along with gesturing a double butt grab. I wave her off, my face heating in the process, and I push the door closed. I take a seat on the white fabric chair kitty-corner to him.

Perched on the edge of the yellow leather sofa, he rests his elbows on his knees and clasps his hands in front of him. He's dressed in an LA Dodgers T-shirt and his short, dark-brown hair is sort of sticking up in a way that makes him more appealing, not less.

Why can't it be less? Ugh.

The mood in the room feels thick and hot. I pinch at my blouse, allowing a breeze of air to flow over me and cross my leg over my knee.

"Why don't you tell me why you agreed to meet with me."

I am well aware of his backstory; his wife died eight months ago, and he's depressed and unable to find joy without her. That's the reason *he thinks* he's here. But this is his first test. Will he be honest with me? Since he seems to be purposely looking everywhere except in my direction, I'm skeptical he'll be able to. His green eyes are busy checking out everything in my office until he has nowhere else to look than at me. When he does, he still doesn't make eye contact.

"My daughter Tess asked me to."

"So, there's no other reason?"

His eyes take another trip around the room again before they finally find mine. "What do you want me to say here, doc?"

"Oh, I'm not a doctor," I correct him. He arches one quizzical dark brow at me. It's sexy and sends an electric current tremoring through me. I clear my throat. "I'm an interventionist."

"What's the difference?"

"Less schooling." I laugh.

A smile actually breaks on his face. If we accomplish nothing else today, I consider that genuine smile a win. But it was a lie, of course. I completed all the necessary credentials and practiced as a licensed therapist for ten years. I had chosen to stop practicing.

He pushes back, leaning into the modern sofa. "And what do you think you can do for me?"

I swing my dangling foot, a blush crawling up my neck as I fiddle with the globe pendant necklace hanging from the gold chain. Possible inappropriate answers to his question spring to my mind. Focus. I need to focus here.

"What you get from me isn't really relevant here."

"You see, now you've got me even more confused. Because I think you inadvertently got my daughter's hopes up. I think she thinks you're gonna fix me." In his eye contact I see sadness reflected there.

My foot stops swinging. "Do you feel you need to be fixed?" I wince, regretting asking the delicate question so bluntly.

"What? No." He runs a hand down his face. "I came here for Tess. I promised her I'd at least give you a chance."

By the way he looks at me, with those shifty eyes, I'm not sure he will. The realization sends a pang in my heart and my own confidence wavers. "But you don't think I can help you?"

"Well, gee. Let me think about it. Can you bring my wife back?" His question takes me by surprise, but it's not an unusual one. I've helped clients with all different kinds of issues. Their first go-to thought is to request the impossible, the very thing they lost that can't be found, that can't be brought back. His eye contact is brief before it flitters away again. "That's what I thought," he mutters.

It's obvious this guy is a loose cannon and is prepared to bolt any second. But he is in desperate need of help, so I can't let him retreat. "How about you humor me and"—I pause to read over his info sitting in my lap on the iPad screen—"Tess. Try talking to me."

He rubs at his brows and sighs heavily. "Yeah? About what?"

"Let's start with something simple. Your daughters. I mean, they're the reason you're here, after all."

He glances at me. "Yeah, okay."

Okay. I exhale and prepare to take notes. But he's not talking long before I'm caught up in his words, consumed by his love for his daughters, and I forget to type a single word.

"They both look so much like Natalie. They have a lot of her personality traits too," he's still going on. "Sometimes I wonder if I played a part in creating them at all." He chuckles to himself. The sound vibrates in my chest and causes it to ache more than it should. "But then Tess, my oldest and who is usually so serious, will crack a joke at the right time, and I think, *Now there, that is my daughter.* And Cora, she'll turn on music and sing along, hitting every note. Natalie couldn't carry a tune if her life depended on it." His face distorts at the realization of his poor word choice.

It's my job to help him through these moments. But I'm caught up in his story, consumed by the heartbreak conveyed in his voice.

Suddenly, he scoots to the edge of the sofa. "I'm sorry, fake doc. But I don't think you can fix me."

I'm losing him again. I feel him slipping away. My brain scrambles with desperation as I attempt to reach for something tangible, words of encouragement, anything that will keep him here. Because I became an interventionist to help people. And for some reason, other than his adorkable charm and good looks, I want to help this man more than anyone else.

"It's not my job to fix you," I say, which is a lie. That's complete BS. It's exactly my job. "Because that would mean you're broken. And you're not."

"I'd have to say, fake doc, that I disagree." He pushes his splayed fingers through his hair, causing it to stick up in even more places, and it sets something simmering in my depths. "I haven't shaved in a week. I could probably use a haircut. And these are the first real clothes I've put on in a month."

"So I've heard." My brows pinch together as I double-check my notes. "It seems you've taken an interest in a certain item of clothing."

"Seriously? What *hasn't* Tess told you? And for the record, I don't know why she keeps making a big deal about that. She never even wore the thing."

I ignore his last statement. It's typical for clients who have experienced trauma to take ownership of something that brings them comfort. Apparently, for Mr. Redd, it's his daughter's pink robe. It could be worse. I once had a client who lost his sister and began wearing her favorite pair of red high-heeled shoes all over the house.

I focus on his first question. "Tess also said you haven't been back to work since before your wife passed."

He peers out the window. "Yeah, that's right."

"It's been eight months. That's quite a long time. Do you miss it?"

"I think you're asking the wrong question." He turns to face me. The look in his eyes is haunting and nearly steals my breath.

"What do you mean?"

"How can I miss anything when all I do is miss my wife? Nothing else feels relevant anymore."

"But you used to enjoy work?"

He nods. "I loved it. Matching the perfect home to the perfect person—man, it's like I was playing God or something. Like I was some sort of matchmaker." Underneath the unshaven face, and in the gleam of the sun from the window, he's suddenly beaming.

"What else did you used to enjoy?"

"Hiking. Not hard-core three-day-long crap-in-a-hole hiking. But like, trails and stuff. After Natalie and I moved to LA, we took the trail up to the Hollywood sign. It sort of became a tradition. We took the girls back to Griffith Park every year."

I can feel him slipping away, but this time, not physically, he's slipping into the past. And I can't allow him to stay there long. Even if he wants to. "What else?" I urge.

"The beach. When you live this close, who doesn't love the beach? Surfing, driving along the coastline, and Dodger games, of course." He pinches at the shirt he's wearing with the LA baseball team's logo printed on the front.

"So, let me ask you, have you done any of those things you just mentioned since your wife passed?"

He shakes his head, watching his own fingers as they fidget in his lap. "I don't really see the point."

"Do you think your wife would want you to give up all those things you once enjoyed?"

He shrugs. "Why not? It hardly seems fair to enjoy anything when she can't."

I turn off my iPad and lay it on the table in between us, clasping my hands together. I clearly need to come at this from a different angle. "But you enjoy being a dad, don't you?"

"Well, yeah, of course. They're the only reason I get out of bed every day."

A smile tugs at my lips. Bingo. But not only because his words and motives are sincere, but because I've found the sweet spot. The thing that will drive him to want to accomplish the challenges. The thing that will push him to heal and ultimately complete the program, thereby moving back home. His daughters. You don't have to have kids of your own to know that they can always be used as leverage. Good or bad.

"But they're grown now, right? Tess is married and—" I blank on his other daughter's name.

"Cora," he provides for me.

"Right, thank you. And Cora is away at college?"

His expression falls, his lips drooping at the corners. He nods.

I won't allow him to wallow, I keep the session moving. "I have your first challenge. Before we meet next Friday, I want you to do one thing you used to enjoy." I pause, hoping he'll understand so I don't have to elaborate. But his face is void of any expression. "Something you enjoyed before your wife passed." I expect his expression to change, but it doesn't. "Do you think this is something you can handle?"

He shifts uncomfortably. "Probably not." He pauses. "Maybe."

He drops his head. "I'll try. I'd do anything for my daughters," he mumbles.

He stands abruptly so I follow suit, my shins throbbing, and I check the time on my Apple Watch. "We still have a few minutes."

"I think I'll leave on that note. With instructions to follow." He takes his time shuffling to the door.

I follow him. "It's not really instructions, but more a challenge."

I open the door, but before he steps through, he says, "Nah, I'd rather think of it as instructions. It gives me a purpose, ya know?"

And I do know.

Chapter 4

Pete

I finally make it out of the city, and the open road stretches before me. With a few routes to UCSB, I decide to take Highway 1 along the coastline. This route will add thirty minutes to my drive, but I haven't seen the coast since before we lost Natalie. And while I'm well aware of the possibility of my emotions getting out of control, I take the risk.

The app on my phone showed questionable weather for today, so I left the top on the Jeep. But the humidity and lack of rain cause me to now regret that decision. I push on the buttons, and all four windows slide down simultaneously, allowing the scent of the salty sea air to infiltrate the inside of the Jeep.

In an instant, memories fill my mind, taking me back to all the times Natalie and I made this same drive to Monterey. After we moved to LA from Seattle—when the girls were small and we needed a break—we'd go on weekend getaways to a resort right on the cliff overlooking the ocean. We'd order room service and sleep late. It was really the only time I'd see a glimpse of the Natalie I knew pre-kids. The Natalie who relaxed and drank a little too much wine, and who worked her sex appeal to the max.

It's noon when I pull into the visitor parking lot at the Santa Barbara campus of the University of California. Lots sixteen and eighteen are full, so I make my way to lot twenty-two and pull the Jeep into the first empty spot I find. I flip the visor down and check my reflection in the mirror. Dark, puffy circles shadow my eyes. It will be enough to cause Cora to worry—that I'm not getting enough sleep, not getting enough to eat, not getting outdoors enough.

But at least I shaved this morning. The last time Cora and I talked over FaceTime, she commented on the scruff on my face and asked if I'd lost my razor or something. I'm wondering now if the facial stubble may have helped me to fit in better on campus.

I climb out of the Jeep and inhale the clean air into my lungs. There's less smog here than in LA and more cloud coverage as well. For the first time in a long time, something familiar bubbles in my chest; it's oddly comforting.

I pay for a parking permit at the kiosk and place it on the dashboard. My phone pings with an incoming text. I slide it out of my pocket and find a text from Jules Sweeney displayed on the screen. Nerves flutter in my chest.

Jules: *Good luck on your first challenge!*

I shake my head. Challenge? I thought we agreed on calling them instructions.

Jules: *Remember, do something you used to enjoy.*

I consider where I'm at, who I'm here to see. While this isn't necessarily something I used to enjoy doing because I've never visited Cora on campus before, Cora *is* someone I enjoy spending time with.

Me: *I'm on it.*

Jules: *Great! Can't wait to hear all about it at your session next Friday.*

I don't bother responding, instead I pull up Cora's address in my

Notes app and spin around in each direction. Cora is in building C, floor four, room 401. I spot building C kitty-corner and across the parking lot. I take off toward it, my black Chuck Taylors moving swiftly over the asphalt.

There are college students dispersed all around the campus, sitting in the long grass or leaning against oak trees with headphones on. They all look so comfortable and in their element. Maybe if college had been like that for me, I wouldn't have dropped out. Nah, who am I kidding? All I did that first year was party and play music.

Until I met Natalie.

Two young guys push out the doors of building C. I grab ahold of the door before it can lock behind them and slip inside, glancing over my shoulder to get a better look. The guys are dressed in wrinkled clothing, barefoot with shoes tucked in their arms, and their hair is disheveled. An uneasy feeling snakes through my gut. I remind myself Cora is nothing like me. She's a good kid, always has been. So is Tess. And for about the millionth time, I feel lucky both girls take after Natalie.

I receive a few *stranger danger* looks from a group of girls as I make my way through the lobby, passing mismatched sofas and a Ping-Pong table. My attempt at trying to fit in with the shaved face and Chuck Taylors has failed. Most kids either look like California surfers, future *Desperate Housewives*, or the worst yet, Portland hipsters.

I enter a hall where I find stairs that will lead me up to the fourth floor, and I stop off to the side. I tug my socks all the way up, cuff the bottoms of my jeans three times, and slip the hood of my Dodgers sweatshirt over my head. I take my sunglasses out of my back pocket and push them on before shoving my hands inside the front pouch of my sweatshirt and shuffle toward the stairs.

On my way to the fourth floor, I pass a group of guys who make it obvious they don't approve of my look.

"What's up?" I say as I pass, my words coming out in a growl.

They chuckle as I take the stairs more confidently than I should.

By the time I reach room 401, I don't even care that I look like an idiot, I'm giddy with excitement. I'm like a kid on Christmas morning who's hoping for a puppy.

I rap on the door, quietly at first.

When no one answers, I try my chances with the knob, wiggling it. No luck. And it's a proud father moment, knowing my daughter listened to my instructions and warnings and is keeping her door locked. I slip my phone from the front pocket of my jeans, debating if I should text her. It's after twelve o'clock now, she can't possibly still be sleeping.

I try the door again. But this time, I rest against it and sort of tap and scratch on it, along with whispering Cora's name. "Cora? Cora, Cora, Cora? C'mon...open up. I'll wait out here all day if I have to." I jiggle the knob again.

Seconds later, the door finally unlocks. But it only opens a crack. I stick my face through it, grinning wide. But it's not the sweet face of my daughter on the other side. Instead, it's Jessica, Cora's childhood best friend and college roommate. Her dark eyes are gigantic, and there's an obvious terror shining in them.

Before I have time to greet her, she screams. Like, full-on shrieks. The door opens wider, and she points a tube of lipstick at me while she continues to scream. Only, it's not lipstick, it's a stun gun disguised as lipstick. I recognize it as the same one I gave to Cora the day I dropped her off at college.

The recognition comes too late.

She presses the end of the tube to my chest and it sends burning electrical shocks coursing through my body. The device only comes in contact with my chest for maybe three seconds, but each second feels like an eternity as new piercing currents hit me repeatedly. My muscles lock up, and the overwhelming sensation along with the excruciating pain, sends me collapsing to my knees. I clutch at my chest and curse obscenities that sound more like gibberish.

I pinch my eyes shut against the sting and sense a commotion around me in the hall. Finally, Cora is kneeling at my side.

"Jessica!" Cora yells. "It's okay. It's my dad."

Jessica finally stops screeching though she's panting hard and fast. And so am I.

"Dad, are you okay?"

My nervous system is slowly sending notifications to my muscles, and I allow Cora to help me up from the floor. "What the hell was that for?" I spit out.

"I'm sorry, I'm so sorry," Jessica mutters through the cupped hand over her mouth. "I thought you were an intruder or rapist or something."

"If I were an intruder, why would I knock?" I tear off my sunglasses.

"I don't know," she answers, the lipstick stun gun trembling in her hand.

"Hey?" a guy interrupts. "Is everything okay here?"

"It's fine, it's just my dad," Cora says. "Dad, this is my RA, Alden."

He shakes his head and puffs air out of his cheeks. "All right, people. Everything is fine. There's no threat, only another neurotic parent." Alden presses his hands to his hips and proceeds to reassure all the concerned college residents they have nothing to fear.

"Dad, what are you doing here?" Cora hisses. "And why are you dressed like that?"

I glance down at myself, forgetting my change in usual appearance—my failed attempt to fit in. "I wanted to surprise you." I lift my hands in a sort of jazz-hands gesture. "Surprise."

Cora does not look impressed. But she tries to fake her enthusiasm and forces a smile. Though she forgets—I raised her. I know and can decipher each of her smiles. And this one? It's not a pleasantly surprised smile.

"It's good to see you, Dad." She closes the awkward gap between us and hugs me. It's genuine, but I can't help but feel the sting from her reluctance.

"It's really good to see you too, kid."

Cora pulls away and tentatively takes the stun gun from Jessica's hand. "You okay?"

"I'm fine. But really sorry, Mr. Redd." She presses her lips together. "Next time you wanna visit Cora, maybe wait until we open the door before trying to open it yourself and jiggling the knob. And maybe"—her eyes drift up and down the length of me—"don't look so creepy."

I forgot about the hood still over my head and flip it off, pushing my fingers through my hair. "Right. Sorry about that. I didn't mean to scare you."

"And I'm sorry I thought you were a rapist and zapped you."

"I suppose then, we're even." I grin but clutch at my chest subconsciously.

She gives me a faint smile before backing away and crawling into her bed, pulling the covers over her head.

"Were you still sleeping?" I slide my phone out of my pocket and check the time. "At 12:08?"

Cora crosses her arms, leans into the doorjamb, and ignores my question. "So what's going on? What are you doing here?"

"What? I came to spend the weekend with you." I raise my arms at my sides, like I've presented her with the best gift of all time—me.

She blinks. "The weekend?"

"Well, today and tomorrow. I'll head back Monday morning."

"Monday morning?"

"Yeah. I don't want to interfere with your classes."

"But where will you stay?" She glances at the tiny room where even a sleeping bag in between the two beds would be a tight fit.

I raise my arms again. "Duh. With you, of course, roomie." I grin, wide and cheesy.

Her face pales, and she's speechless. I'm pretty sure I've interrupted her weekend plans. But I don't allow her less-than-thrilled reaction to my news deter my plan. Cora and I always have fun together. This time it will be no different.

A groan escapes from underneath her roommate's blankets.

"We are gonna have the most epic college weekend. You wait, I'll show you how to party." I make my fingers into devil horns on each hand and let out a, "Woo-hoo!"

"Dad, you only went to college for a year," she grumbles and shuffles back to her bed, climbing inside and underneath the covers.

No way did I come all this way to surprise Cora at college and not at least do something with her. And no way am I about to fail at my first challenge. I can't help but wonder if this is the kind of challenge Jules had in mind.

Dropping onto the foot of the bed, I pull back the covers and brush the dark-brown hair away from Cora's face. She pries open her eyes and looks at me, a pout forming on her lips. "C'mon, kid. I came all this way. At least throw me a bone or something. Let's eat. Or go check out some local music. Anything."

"Yeah, okay," she says while exhaling a breath, "but you're buying."

I chuckle. "Of course."

Cora climbs out of the bed.

My vision travels across the room to where Jessica's body is hiding underneath a heap of blankets on her bed. "What about her?" I nod toward her with my chin.

Jessica grunts. "Don't even think about talking to me for at least two more hours," she mumbles.

"Cool," I respond.

She grunts again.

I turn to Cora and raise my brows and whisper, "We'll bring her back something. Her parents wouldn't forgive me if they found out I was here and didn't at least feed their daughter. On second thought, maybe they owe *me* lunch. Considering she did try to kill me."

Cora stifles a laugh.

"I said I...was...sorry." Jessica mutters each word slowly.

Cora rummages around in the cramped closet, picking out some clothes to change into and slipping out of the room to use the bathroom. I wait, perched on the foot of the bed, and slide my phone out of the front pocket of my jeans. The text from Jules sits there, a bubble underneath with the curser flashing in it but no words from me typed yet. I think about listening to some live music with Cora, maybe hitting up a college party, if she'll let me tag along.

I finally compose a response.

Me: *I'm about to do something I used to enjoy.*

Jules: *Great!*

Me: *And with someone I enjoy.*

Chapter 5

Tess

This is only the second night Richie and I will have to ourselves in eight months. As much as I thought Dad's surprise was an erroneous idea, I couldn't bring myself to discourage him. He was so enthusiastic when he told me about his plan for his first challenge. Going to see Cora wasn't a terrible idea. But surprising her was.

I feel like an awful sister for not at least giving Cora a heads-up. But not awful enough to deter Dad from going, despite the several rage texts I've already received from her. I need this weekend. Richie and I need this weekend. I hadn't imagined how problematic it would be to have Dad live with us. The strain his presence has put on our marriage, and now our future plans, is evident.

Now, his extended stay with us is like the elephant in the room. The one we don't speak of. The elephant used to be cancer. After Mom was diagnosed the second time, with terms like *inoperable* and *terminal*, none of us could bring ourselves to even say the C-word. Now Richie and I don't talk about how long Dad has been living with us, the stress he's put on our love life, and how long he'll be here.

I'm fitfully attempting to get my to-do list done at the store by a decent time tonight. But there are boxes of clothes to inventory and shelves for displays to build. Cheyenne has promised to come in today to help me.

Richie is golfing with Dexter and Carter. He and his buddies sometimes get carried away and lose track of time—turning it into a full day and night of golf, followed by food and drinks. I send him a text to remind him of our evening plans and ease my anxious mind that he's going to forget.

Me: *Looking forward to our evening together.*

I wait for what feels like forever and open a box filled with individual wrapped fall floral printed dresses. My phone pings.

Richie: *Me too. Imagine—an entire night to ourselves.*

Me: *You are gonna get so lucky.*

I add a kissing and flame emoji, my cheeks burning as I hit send.

Richie: *Oh yeah? Can't wait.*

The smile starts in my chest and fans out nearly ear to ear while the anticipation of being entangled with Richie thrums in my depths.

Me: *Love you.*

Richie: *Love you too.*

Knocking on the glass doors jolts me back to reality. Cheyenne stands outside on the sidewalk, two coffee cups in a drink carrier in one hand as her other hand raps on the door.

"Hey," I greet her after unlocking the door and holding it open so she can slip inside.

"I bring gifts," she sings, her red hair flowing behind her as she nearly skips toward the register kiosk in the middle of the store.

"The best kind of gifts," I say, locking the door behind her.

"Right?" She holds my coffee out to me and tosses the drink carrier into the recycle bin tucked underneath the counter.

"You are a godsend." I take a sip, the bitter deliciousness warming my tongue.

"Save your charmin' till later, after we've finished your lengthy to-do list." She winks.

Simply having her positive presence inside the store alters the aura in my ongoing cluttered mind.

"Okay," I say on an exhale, pulling the pencil from behind my ear and going over the inventory list attached to my clipboard. "We received sixty boxes from the warehouse this morning. All of which has to be checked and rechecked and confirmed in Excel. Then, the display walls need to be built so they're ready for inventory. And the walls in the window displays need to be painted."

Cheyenne sits on a round, high stool behind the counter in the kiosk, clicking on the laptop. "I've got the Excel spreadsheet right here." She spins around to face me. "I'll take care of the inventory. You get the shelves on the walls built. I know that's most important to you. Then I'll help with the painting."

I prop my hands behind me on the counter and pull myself up, sitting cross-legged and sighing. "It's all important."

"Right, I know. But something tells me you'll want to get the display just right. These designs are your babies." Her Southern accent comes out more on the word *babies*. It's hard for me to imagine she didn't over enunciate the word on purpose, though.

But I choose to ignore it. My body is feeling enough pressure knowing I'm putting the baby issue back on the table. "No, you're right. Thanks." I give her a tight smile and push my fingertips upwards against my scalp, where my hair is pulled into a topknot.

"Okay." She tilts her head at me, narrowing her eyes. "What's really going on, hon?"

I take a sip of the glorious brew and weigh my words. I'm not sure how much information I want to give away and how much I want to keep to myself. "I haven't told Richie I stopped taking birth control." The words tumble out unintentionally, and I drop my chin, pinching my eyes shut. But now that my secret is out, the tightness in my chest releases slightly. It feels good to tell someone, to get it out in the open.

Cheyenne is quiet for a beat. "Wow."

"Yeah," I say, glancing up at her.

"Okay." She takes a drink of her own coffee, something really sweet, like, I'm-concerned-her-teeth-are-gonna-fall-out-in-a-matter-of-only-a-few-years sweet. "Even after he expressed his desire to wait until your dad moves out before you start trying to get pregnant?"

I nod, the tightness in my chest returning. Just whose side is she on here?

"Well, Richie is a reasonable man. And he loves you. I'm sure if you talk to him about it, he'll be on board."

"He is. And he does. But I'm not so sure."

Cheyenne narrows her eyes at me from above the brim of her coffee cup. "Tess Gabriella Cavanaugh, are you telling me your plan is to not only seduce your husband but also trick him into getting you pregnant?"

Being called out by my best friend feels like I've just taken a punch to the jaw by a professional MMA fighter. It feels even worse because she's right. "I'm not gonna get pregnant that fast. I only stopped taking the pill a few days ago. I plan to talk to him. But I shouldn't have to seduce my husband." I press my palms to my face. "It shouldn't be this hard," I mumble into my hands.

"No, you're right. But every relationship has its ups and downs. And y'all are perfect together. Y'all will get through this."

"Yeah, I know." Because deep down I do know.

"But I still think you should tell him."

"Yeah, I know that too." I sigh and hop off the counter. There's too much work to do to sit around. And working keeps my mind off Dad and Richie and having a baby. Or not having a baby. "C'mon, let's get back to work. Those clothes aren't gonna inventory themselves."

"True that." Cheyenne holds up her coffee cup. "And hey, it's only a matter of time before you and Richie have your house back to yourselves. I'm sure this therapist lady knows exactly what she's doing."

"I sure hope so," I mutter.

Chapter 6

Jules

Beads of sweat trickle down my temples as I push the mattress up with as much strength as I can muster. "Pivot, pivot," I grunt, with a chuckle.

Angie has a hold of the other side of my mattress, trying to stabilize it so it doesn't end up swiping everything off the top of my dresser, along with us in the process.

"I'm pivoting!" she hollers.

"Okay, I'm bringing it down on your end. You ready for the added weight?"

"Yeah, yeah, I've got it. Let go of it already."

I give one last push of the mattress, but when I do, my clammy bare feet slip against the soft carpet and I lose my balance. I topple on top of the mattress, spread eagle and Angie yowls. Kobe, my Frenchie, lets out a string of barks and bounds on top of the mattress next to me, assuming we're playing some type of game or something.

"Kobe, down!" I give him a shove and scramble off, rushing to Angie's aid. She's pinned against the wall, the mattress pressing into her.

"Oops, sorry."

"Get this thing off me," she says, groaning.

Kobe continues to bark. I squeeze in between the wall and the mattress, and together, we push it and slide it into place on top of the bed frame. We both crumple to the ground in a sweaty, breathless, giggling heap. Kobe finally stops barking and jumps in my lap.

"I'm so sorry, Ang," I say between my laughter.

"Next time you need help flipping your mattress, I'm out."

"But you're so good at it," I tease.

"Oh, I know I am. It's your clumsy ass who isn't."

We laugh again as she stands and pulls me to my feet. Kobe weaves in and out of my legs before getting distracted by a stuffed squeaky toy.

"Well, thank you." I pull the stack of folded clean sheets off my dresser. "Hey, you wanna do me another favor?"

Her brows shoot up into her hairline, and she shakes her finger in my face. "Nuh-uh. I'm not helping you make your bed too. You're not six."

I exhale a laugh. "That's not what I was gonna ask you."

Her eyebrows remain arched as she awaits my request.

"You wanna go with me to visit my dad? You know how I hate going alone." My voice sounds pitiful, I know it, and I don't care.

Her expression changes, her features softening. "Sorry. I can't today. I promised my brother I'd go watch my nephew's karate tournament."

My shoulders slump, and disappointment flows through my veins. But this is not Angie's burden to carry. Sometimes I'm jealous of her and the fact that she has siblings and two parents who are healthy and still married. At least if my parents had had more kids, I wouldn't be in this alone. "No worries. Thanks anyway."

She lightly pushes a fist into my shoulder and smiles. "I'll catch ya next time. Tell Jimmy I say hey."

"Yeah, okay, I will."

She turns and walks away. Kobe has made his way to his dog bed in the corner on the floor with his toy. I unfold the fitted sheet and shake it out over the bed. From the corner of my eye, I see Angie taking hold of one end of the sheet.

She sighs. "Have you heard from your newest client? The adorkable dad?"

I guffaw. "Don't call him that."

"Why? We always nickname your clients."

"I know." My cheeks burn. "But—"

"But you don't think he's dorky?" she teases. "You know he totally is. But he's completely adorable. Nice butt too."

I can't deny it. None of it. Even the butt comment. The guilt races through me for even thinking about my client in this way.

"Do you know what he's chosen for his first challenge?" Angie tucks the corner of the sheet under the mattress.

"No. But I'm anxious to find out." I tuck the final corner and take the flat sheet off my dresser, unfolding it.

Angie takes a hold of one end, and we fluff it out together. "Me too. The first challenge is always a crapshoot." She grins. "Remember that one client who misinterpreted the first challenge as, 'try something you know you'd *never* enjoy' and went bungee jumping?"

We both laugh, and as terrible as that ended up, I can't help it. How that client got the first challenge so wrong is beyond me. Needless to say, he canceled the program, and I never saw him again.

The thought of that causes a pang of worry to course through me. What if Pete misinterpreted my challenge and does something stupid like my bungee-jumping client? I have an inexplicable desire to help him; I'd hate to have it end already. And yeah, Angie is right. He definitely has that adorkable quality I never realized I found attractive.

PULLING INTO THE LARGE, NEARLY EMPTY PARKING LOT AT THE Norwalk Memory Care facility, I suck in a deep breath of warm afternoon air before stepping out of the car. Anxiety thrums through me as I take the path to the front door and enter the building. Not being aware of Dad's state before arriving is always nerve-racking.

I greet Charlene, who's seated behind the desk. We make small talk, but mostly it's her telling me how she recommended my book to another friend for their child who's suffering from some kind of trauma. I probably have Char to thank for half of my book sales, so even though she's a little nosy, she has the kindest heart.

When the doors finally unlock with a buzz, allowing me to slip away, I push through them and head down the hall to Dad's room. I'm surprised when I find his door propped open, and my pulse kicks up. But after I enter and find everything in place, including him dressed in a bright Hawaiian shirt and seated in his recliner, my heart slows back down to its usual pace.

Dad doesn't even glance in my direction. He's staring out the window, no book in hand. I peer out the window, trying to see if he's looking at something specific. But besides a bird perched on a branch in a nearby Catalina tree, there's nothing.

His room is small. There's a bed, his recliner, a wooden end table next to it, an uncomfortable oddball chair with a high back, and a mini refrigerator I keep stocked with Yoo-hoo. His old guitar from his touring days with the rock band The Hughes sits in a holder on the wall. A photo of the entire band inside a frame rests on the windowsill. The sight of the guitar along with the photo causes a pinch in my gut—a reminder of better days before the illness altered things.

I take a seat in the high-back chair. "Hey, Dad."

He doesn't turn to look at me, doesn't even blink. If this were anyone else ignoring me, I'd take offense. But this is Dad, and I get the impression now he's having a rough day. My quick heartbeat returns, and I fiddle with my hands in my lap. There's no telling how this visit will go.

"I brought you a couple more books from the library." I pull the stack out of the bag, hoping this will catch his attention. Reading is about the only thing that keeps his sanity these days.

He finally glances in my direction, his eyes glossing over me to zone in on the books. I stand and set the stack on the small table next to his chair. He picks one up, and his vision moves over the cover and title. Patting his shoulder, I refrain from kissing him on the forehead and force myself to back away.

"Thank you for the books." He smiles. It's warm and genuine, and the familiarity of it nearly cracks my heart straight down the middle. Because I can see it in his shifty eyes, hear it in his unsure tone, he doesn't know who he's thanking.

"You're welcome." I step backward until my legs hit the chair, and I drop myself into it. "I think you'll really like that one." I nod in the direction of the book he's still mulling over.

"Yes, I think I will." He glances up at me. "Something tells me you've been here before."

No matter how many times this happens, his words still pinch painfully in my chest. "Yes, I've been here. Several times, actually."

"You're the one who brings me the books?"

"Yes, that's right."

He pats at his graying hair. "I do hope you'll forgive me for not remembering you."

You have no idea. "Of course," I choke out the words.

"And I hope you'll continue to bring me books."

The sorrow sticks in my throat, the words unable to form. I nod and force a pained smile.

Sometimes when Dad is like this, I'm tempted to tell him about the book I wrote. The one that's a New York Times best seller. Sometimes I'm tempted to tell him when he actually knows who I am, too. But I never do. There's no point to it. Either way, he won't remember. The irony of it all is too much to bear at times—the only thing keeping Dad going right now is books and I can't even tell him about the one I wrote.

Chapter 7

Pete

Cora convinces me to uncuff the pant legs of my jeans and put on a baseball hat. She changes out of her pajamas because apparently she *was* still sleeping at noon and puts on a pair of leggings and the Dodgers sweatshirt I bought her last spring. She's agreed to be seen with me only because I'm buying her lunch.

Cora wants to take me to a sandwich shop that's within walking distance of campus. She tells me it's her favorite place so I'm glad she's decided I'm worthy to be brought there. Especially after she voiced how upset she was with me for not calling first. My guess—she's more upset with Tess for not warning her.

Our entire walk to the sandwich shop, Cora texts Tess, but tries to tell me she's texting a boy. My kids must really think I'm an idiot and don't know them at all.

Inside the sandwich shop, it's filled with mostly college students. Even though I'm only forty-five and look young for my age, I still stick out easily. I pay and follow Cora to a booth with red vinyl seats. She climbs in and sits on a propped-up leg, and I slide in across from her.

I stare at her as she taps away at the screen with her thumb, and her other hand works the straw out of its wrapper. Her dark-brown hair is pulled up high on top of her head in one of those twisty knots that looks like if anyone bumps into her, she'll tip right over.

She's ignoring me, but I can't help smiling at her. She's beautiful and has too many traits of her mother's to mention. Though hers are different from Tess's. Where Cora's hair is the same shade of chestnut brown Natalie had, Tess's eyes are the darker brown like Natalie's and Cora's are a lighter golden brown. Tess's facial features are more defined where Cora's are softer and still have that babyish look to them.

My eyes burn as the tears form without intention.

Cora chooses now to pull her attention away from the screen. "Dad, you okay?" She sets the phone upside down on the tabletop, eyeing me skeptically.

I clear my throat against the thickness and pick up my sandwich, pulling back the paper wrapper. "I'm fine."

"Tess said you've been a little down."

"What? No, I'm not down."

"Dad. She said you've been practically living in her pink robe."

"What?" A blush creeps up my neck. I don't get embarrassed easily, but something about my kids not thinking I'm okay makes me feel inadequate somehow. "No. She said that?"

Cora nods, her lips curve around her straw and her dark brows lift in question. She doesn't believe me.

"Well, I can't help it if it looks better on me than her." I grin. "Somebody ought to be showing off their legs in that house. We're Redds. We can't help it if we have sexy legs that must be put on display." I swing my leg up and drop it on the tabletop with a thud. "I can roll up my pant legs again and show these bad boys off if ya want me to?" I give my leg a slap.

"No, no," she repeats, her hands outstretched at me. She giggles, despite the redness in her cheeks, and crawling down her neck.

We eat and chat, and it's almost like old times again. Except it's not. Because now that Natalie is gone, it will never be like old times.

"What's the deal with this summer internship you mentioned a few weeks ago?"

She stares at her sandwich. "It's for the Santa Barbara Independent."

"Where would you stay?"

"Jessica's aunt has a spare room she said I could crash in."

"How long is the internship?" I try not to sound as if I'm prying, but she knows me well.

"Twelve weeks," she says, wincing. "But I haven't even decided yet if I'm gonna apply." She fiddles with her straw.

The idea of her not coming home all summer has my throat feeling thick. I momentarily consider if this is something I should reach out to Jules about. I'm in desperate need of a subject change and force myself to suck in a deep breath. "So, what are we doing tonight? What party are we crashing? What rave are we hitting up?"

Her eyebrows snap together. "Dad, no one goes to raves anymore. This isn't the 90's. But"—she chews on her bottom lip—"there is this one party I was thinking about checking out. At least, before you showed up at my door unannounced."

"Okay." I clap my hands together. "Let's do it." I enunciate each word and Cora hates it when I do it.

"You know I cannot take you to that party."

"C'mon, why not?"

"You're my dad."

"But I'm a cool dad."

She eyes me skeptically. "Even still."

"C'mon," I try again. "I'll be good. I promise to be quiet and not embarrass you. Please, please, please."

Her face relaxes and she caves. "Fiiiiine," she drags out the word. "But"—she stabs a finger at me—"you better be cool. And you better not embarrass me."

I give her the Scout's honor sign, except I have no idea if I'm doing it correctly. I wasn't in the Scouts. Because obviously, I had much cooler things to do.

She rubs her temples. "Please don't let this be a huge mistake. Oh, and you better not have packed the pink robe."

"I did not, promise." We scoot out of the benches and throw our trash away. "Did Tess tell you it's really that bad?"

Cora rolls her eyes, and I shrug. Nah. It can't be *that* bad.

THE PARTY IS WITHIN WALKING DISTANCE OF CAMPUS AT A TWO-story house set back off the street, tucked between the homes on either side. It's the perfect party house with its balcony stretching across the second floor. Kids are hanging out on the front lawn smoking and the door is wide open.

An uneasy feeling snakes through me at the realization that I'm not sure what will happen if the cops show up and I'm the only adult here. But again, I promised Cora no judgments.

A boy dressed like a hipster in too-tight jeans and laced boots stands at the doorway, his arm outstretched and blocking the entrance to the house.

Cora leans into me and whispers, "Be cool. You promised."

I nod. Though if this douchebag continues to check out my daughter, I will definitely have to break my promise.

"Hey, who's the old dude?" he asks around a chuckle, his eyes full of amusement.

"Just a friend." Cora ignores his intense ogling and peers past him into the house.

"You into older guys? Because I'm a senior. And you have freshman written all over your..." He pauses, his eyes scanning Cora's body again, and my own body ignites like there's a fire in me ready to unleash. "Face," he finishes, a cocky grin on his lips.

It takes everything in me to not punch that smile right off *his* face. "She's with me," I say through gritted teeth.

"All right, all right." He sticks his hands up in surrender. "No need to flare up your hemorrhoids, gramps."

"Dad," Cora hisses after we shuffle past. "What was that?"

"What was what?"

"You promised you'd be cool." She waves to a couple people as we sidestep our way through the house.

"Hey, that *was* me being cool, kid. I could've beat his ass for the way he was looking at you."

We step into what looks like the center of the party. There's a makeshift stage in the corner by an old brick fireplace. A couple of guys set up equipment, a girl tunes a guitar, and another girl unravels a mic cord. Live music either means this party just got a hundred percent better or a hundred percent worse. You never can tell until the band starts playing.

"Dad." Cora tugs on the sleeve of my sweatshirt. "You can't beat up every guy who looks at me."

"Well, why'd you have to go and grow up on me?" I set my open hand on her face and palm it like a football. She shrieks and shoves me.

"Dad!" It comes out louder than she planned, and she bites at her lower lip, glancing over her shoulders to check if anyone noticed.

I can't help it, I laugh. I pet her head like she's a puppy. This time she steps backward, out of my reach.

"Okay, stop." But she laughs. "I'm gonna go find us a drink. You stay here." She backs up before turning around, and I lose her in the crowd.

I listen to Cora and stay put, feeling slightly awkward after being referred to as an "old dude" and "gramps," but what had I expected? I'm probably the age of most of these kids' parents, maybe younger than some. Natalie and I were always the young parents at all the school functions. I can picture her here with me now. She would've loved to be here. No doubt she would've fit right in. She fit in everywhere we went.

I pull my hood back over my head and shove my hands into my

jeans pockets while I watch the band warm up. I'm slightly less noticed underneath the hoodie. I know this because kids shove into me without hesitation.

The members of the band argue, some of them check their phones, another one picks up a red plastic cup and chugs the entire thing before crushing it and chucking it across the room. By the looks of the bass sitting in its stand, untouched, the band is short a member.

I bounce on my toes, glancing around, and scanning the crowd, no sign of Cora. I look back to the band and blow air out of my cheeks before stepping closer to them. "Hey, you guys need a bass player?"

They're skeptical, I can read it in their eyes. One drinking out of a plastic cup even chokes.

"You know how to play real music?" The girl with the guitar strapped to her chest asks. She's got long straight blonde hair and is dressed in a faded black Led Zeppelin T-shirt.

I nod.

She looks me up and down. "All right, let's see what you can do."

"Oh? Seriously?" I stifle a laugh. I'm as surprised as the rest of the band. "I mean, cool." I pick up the instrument. It's on the cheaper side, but no matter. Back in high school and college, I could make any instrument sound good.

I'm a bit rusty at first. But after a couple of runs, it comes back to me. And it feels good. I'd forgotten what it's like to hold this familiar instrument in my hands, to dictate the music that comes from it.

"Not bad." The girl with the mic pushes her fingers through her blue hair before resting an iPad on a music stand in front of me. "This is our opener." She taps at the screen. "Think you can handle it?"

I scan the notes, not really paying attention to the lyrics, and discover they're easy. I don't want to come across as cocky—oh wait, yes I do. "Yeah. I think I can handle it." I smirk.

Zeppelin girl strums a few chords, and the crowd turns their attention to the stage. Most focus their attention directly on me. Their eyes are quizzical, and some go slack-jawed. There's even some booing and laughing.

The blue haired girl with the mic introduces the band, having to yell over the crowd's criticism. "We're Feminist Foxes."

Of course they are. I refrain from rolling my eyes even though I really want to. At about the same time, Cora weaves through the crowd, holding a plastic cup in each hand. When she spots me, she freezes, and to say she looks horrified would be an understatement. She mouths, *What are you doing?* and I swear I can hear the hiss in her voice. But the song is starting, so all I can do is shrug both shoulders and begin playing.

I find it surprising how easily I keep up with the rest of the band since I haven't played bass for about a hundred years. While the guy on drums knocks out the beat, the blue-haired girl with the mic hollers about broken promises, and I wonder who did this girl so wrong? But I continue playing. It doesn't take long before the crowd is joining in with the lyrics and dancing. I even catch Cora swaying her hips, and she allows a smile to slip in my direction.

The song finishes and the crowd cheers. One guy standing on top of a table shouts, "Go old dude!" And everyone in the house screams. Then they all start chanting, "Old dude, old dude, old dude."

Would I prefer a better nickname if I were part of an actual band? Sure. But this still feels pretty cool.

Cora hands me one of the cups from her hands. "You look thirsty," she says above the noise.

"Thanks." I take a swig and then choke. It's pure vodka. Dad mode kicks in. I give her a stern look. "Cora?"

"Don't worry, I'm drinking sparkling water. One of us needs to stay sober. I have a feeling this isn't going to end well, despite your promise." She gives me a tight smile.

How could this not end well? I'm totally killing it. I'm the coolest guy in the room. "I think it's unanimous, they love me."

The blonde with the guitar and the Zeppelin T-shirt nudges my arm. "You up for another?"

I raise my brows at Cora. Not so much asking for permission but more to say, *See, they love me.*

"Yeah, yeah, go. But remember, don't embarrass me."

I chug the rest of the vodka, the clear liquid burning as it slides down my throat. The warmth spreads in my stomach. This is the first time since Natalie died that I have felt even a smidge of being alive. And I revel in the moment.

We play another angry chick song followed by a pretty bad rendition of The Cranberries "Linger." We're starting to lose the crowd, so I lean over to the girl with the mic. "Hey, you know Tom Petty's 'Free Fallin'?"

She blinks at me. "Who's Tom Petty?"

"You're kidding, right?"

She shakes her head, the blue hair swishing back and forth.

The guy on the drums says, "Hey, man. I know Tom Petty."

"You do?" I'm excited. It's thrumming through me. Or maybe it's the alcohol. But it doesn't matter. Because I am alive.

Based on the amount of pot smoke wafting through the house, I'm honestly shocked these kids aren't familiar with Tom Petty. Regardless, I'm stoked to educate them on good music. "These kids are gonna get schooled tonight."

"What?" the girl asks.

"Never mind." I turn to the guitarist and ask her to play a D chord. "Here." I hand the iPad to the Zeppelin T-shirt girl. "Google the music for Tom Petty's 'Free Fallin'."

She looks at me, her lips quirking up at one side.

"Yeah, I'm old. But I'm not an idiot. I do know how to use the internet."

She finally cracks a full smile in my direction before speaking into the mic. "So, old dude has a special treat for us tonight."

The same guy on the table shouts again, "Go, old dude!"

The students in the crowd cheer, and I lead while the other band members follow. The crowd is skeptical. Maybe they're too stoned for Tom Petty? If that's even possible. Cora has her face buried in her hand, and she's moved to the back of the room, closer to the front door. She's sure I'm going to embarrass her and she's preparing to bolt.

But as I lead us into the chorus, a few kids sing along. It amps me up. The combination of the alcohol and the adrenaline pumps through my veins as if charging my body with electricity. I reach the last chorus of the song and drop to my knees. I squeeze my eyes shut and slap the bass, singing at the top of my lungs till they burn. It's doubtful anyone can even hear me over the instruments and the rest of the crowd singing. I open my eyes, ready to relish in the moment as goosebumps shoot down my arms. And it's then I see Cora. The hipster douchebag from the doorway when we first arrived at the party is standing next to her. He's close, too close.

I continue to play and sing, but I'm distracted. From the corner of my eye, I watch as the guy pushes her against the wall, runs his hands all over her body, and smashes his disgusting, douchey lips against hers.

Cora sets a hand on his chest and shoves him, but he forces himself on her again. My skin goes from electric goosebumps to tingling in anger in an instant. I don't think. I rip the mic from the blonde's hand and yell into it, "Hey, douchebag? Get your hands off my daughter."

The band's instruments halt, and the crowd goes silent as if someone has scratched a record.

The guy still standing on the table shouts, "Whoa, old dude is Cora's dad?" He chuckles into his fist while others join in, laughing quietly.

"Who's gonna make me? You?" the douchey hipster taunts.

"You're dead," I say, clear as day. I slip the bass over my head and hand both the guitar and the mic to the blonde. "Thanks, ladies, it's been real," I mutter before I rush toward the front door. Cora's gone, and so is the hipster douchebag. I run outside, checking in every direction once I'm on the porch. Beneath the glow of the streetlamp, I catch a glimpse of the back of Cora, her pink tank top shimmering.

"Cora!" I jog to catch up to her.

She walks fast, her arms crossed tightly and hugging her body.

"Hey, are you okay?"

"No, I'm not okay, Dad," she bites out.

"I could kill that guy." I smack my fist into my palm. It stings, and I shake my hand out. I'm not the fighting type, and I'm not intimidating, but it doesn't go unnoticed that the guy is nowhere to be found.

"He's not who I'm upset with," she spits.

"What? You're mad at me?"

She stops, her breathing accelerated. "I asked you to do one thing. One thing." She holds up a finger at me. "To not embarrass me. And you couldn't even do that."

The guilt presses down hard, like an unforgiving weight on my shoulders, reminding me of the failure I am. "You're right. I'm sorry. I didn't mean to."

"Why'd you come here, Dad?"

"What?" Her question is like a slap to the face. "To spend time with you. I've missed you like crazy."

"No." Her face is stony.

I rub my forehead.

"You came here for you. To make yourself feel better. Because you miss her. You didn't come here for me."

"Hey, kid, c'mon. That's not fair."

"You're right. It's not fair." She crosses her arms again, and I resist the urge to pull her into me like I used to, to protect her and make all the pain disappear.

"Look, I know you're having a hard time. We all lost her. We all miss her. But the rest of us are trying to make the best of things. I suggest you get your crap together. Or you're gonna be grieving all alone."

She stomps off, leaving me standing by myself, the reality of her words haunting my ears.

Chapter 8

Tess

I spill the wine all over the kitchen island because my hands are shaking from my nerves being completely shot. I should not be this nervous. Why am I so nervous? This is my husband. This is Richie. He's not some stranger I hardly know.

It's not like he's gonna get that bent out of shape about it. So what, so I went off the pill. Who cares? Women who want to have a baby go off the pill every day. What's the worst that can happen? He'll get pissed and tell me he's still not ready?

Before Mom died and Dad moved in, Richie wanted a baby. I have to cling to the hope that his desire for starting a family hasn't changed.

Using a huge wad of paper towels, I soak up the wine and wipe it clean with a Lysol wipe.

"Everything okay in there?" Richie calls from the living room.

"Yep," I holler back, "it's all good. Spilled a little wine."

"Need some help?"

"No, I got it."

"Want me to start the movie?"

"Yes please."

I refill the wine glasses and carefully maneuver both of them into the fingers of one hand and carry the cracker and cheese tray in the other. Propped on the edge of the sofa, Richie takes the tray from me and slides it onto the coffee table. I hand Richie his glass and bend, pressing a soft kiss to his lips.

While he's dressed in a T-shirt and a pair of gray jogger sweats, I'm not only wearing a maxi dress and a sweater, but I even left my lipstick on. I tuck my bare feet underneath me, situating the dress over my legs. Part of me wishes I would've put on more comfortable clothes too. But how does one seduce her husband dressed in jogger sweats?

Richie doesn't seem to notice either way. He presses play on *I Love You, Man*, one of our favorite go-to movies starring the hilariously charming Paul Rudd and the stunning and talented Rashida Jones. Richie shovels cheese and crackers, one after the other into his mouth. It's questionable if he's even chewing them, but rather he's more inhaling them. Sometimes you'd never know how proper of an upbringing Richie had. Like now, for instance.

"Wanna save some for me?" I tease. With all the anxiety I'd felt today, I hardly had more to eat than a protein bar the smoothie Cheyenne brought me at three o'clock.

"Sorry, babe." He holds the tray out to me, and I take two crackers and two slices of cheese.

"Thanks."

I nibble a cracker. Richie takes a sip of his wine and places a hand on my knee. It's the first real attention he's given me all day and I hate to admit it, but my body reacts to his simple touch. An instant heat travels across my skin and a craving begins in my depths. As nervous as I am about telling him, I also want him. With Dad out of the house, Richie and I have the freedom to be intimate anytime we want. Anywhere we want.

After I finish my cheese and crackers, my appetite for food is gone, and I only have an appetite for my husband. I pick up my glass and gulp down what's left of the wine, my throat puckering as I swallow. The alcohol creates a blanket over my nerves. It's now or never.

I caress the nape of Richie's neck while his hand that rests on my leg gives it a squeeze in response. But his attention is still on the movie. My fingers twirl, circling at his hairline before slowly working their way up farther into his hair. After a few years of marriage, I'm quite familiar with my husband's most pleasurable spots. He tilts his head into my hand but doesn't look my way.

Has it been that long since I've had to initiate things that he doesn't recognize it? I mean, sure, Richie is usually the one who does it since I'm always exhausted after spending hours going over clothing designs, talking with the merchandisers and the manager at the warehouse, and trying to prepare for the boutique's opening. Lately, if I want to show him I'm in the mood, all I have to do is start stripping off my clothes.

But tonight, I want it to be different. I want to take our time. I want to focus on all the pleasure spots—his and mine.

I dance my fingertips over the back of his ear, sliding downward where I give his earlobe a slight tug. His hand glides up my leg and he turns to face me. Ah, it's about time.

"Well, hey, there." He gives me a smoldering look.

"Hey, yourself," I murmur, still running my finger along his ear.

"I suppose we should be taking advantage of the time we have alone."

I smile, placing my hand on the back of his neck again and direct his head closer to mine. But he doesn't need much direction. He remembers how to kiss me like he wants to steal the breath from my lungs. It's drawn out and intense and my head goes dizzy.

Richie slips the cardigan off my shoulders and presses gentle kisses to my skin he's just exposed. I shove my splayed fingers through his hair as he pushes down the strap of my dress. He devours my lips, shoving his tongue in my mouth and tangling with my own. I work his earlobe again, tugging it, and he lets out a moan.

When he cups a hand to my breast and pushes more forcefully

with his tongue while easing me onto the sofa, I gasp. He reaches a hand up my dress and it's then I remember that I wanted us to take our time. To take advantage of our entire evening. To refamiliarize ourselves with one another's bodies. And maybe to also let him know about my decision to go off birth control.

I grab onto the fabric of his shirt, and as much as I want to pull him closer, I push him back.

"What's wrong?" he pants.

"Nothing," I breathe out. "I just want to take our time. Ya know, we don't have to rush it, we have the entire night."

He grins. "Yeah, okay." He dips his head and kisses my neck and my shoulders and the top of my breasts, and my skin sizzles under his burning lips.

My phone pings, signaling a new text. "Ignore it," I whisper breathlessly.

But it pings again and then, almost instantly, another ping follows.

He sits up on his knees. "Could be important."

"Ugh," I groan. "It probably isn't." But as I sit up and reach for my phone resting on the coffee table, a sick sense of dread falls to the pit of my stomach. I read the screen, it's a text from Cora. They're all texts from Cora.

Cora: *Dad has officially lost it!*

Cora: *He's ruined everything!*

Cora: *I left him at the party.*

After I scroll through her texts and tap a reply, another one comes in.

Cora: *Call me—911*

Richie reads the texts from over my shoulder, giving me a few soft kisses on my neck. "Better call her."

My insides are torn. Cora doesn't send 911 texts often, so I know this is serious. But who knows when I could get a night alone with Richie again? Part of me knows I only have myself to blame. I could've warned her that Dad was coming. But I'm not sure why she thought it was a good idea to take Dad to a party. Especially when he's been so depressed.

"It's fine. We have all night, remember?" Richie says reassuringly, kissing me on the top of my head before resituating himself on the sofa to focus back on the movie.

The desire I felt only moments before fades and transforms itself into fervent anger that courses through my veins. I've put up with Dad for the last eight months. Cora couldn't even handle him for one night. I sigh, scrolling through my contacts until I land on Cora's. And for the first time in a long time, I wish I didn't have a little sister. Or maybe, I wish I didn't have a Dad who couldn't seem to pick up the pieces of his life and be a parent.

On Monday morning, I dress in a pair of old jeans and an LA Dodgers T-shirt, then pull my hair into a messy topknot and head to the store earlier than usual. Being at the store is the only place I can find some kind of normalcy in my life. And even though it's early, there's enough on my to-do list to make my excuse believable. I can't see Dad sitting in my spot, wearing my robe, and slurping up the milk from his cereal bowl. Not today.

When Dad came back yesterday from his visit with Cora, he looked in worse shape than before he left. I'm not sure what he thought he'd accomplish by going there, surprising her, trying to have the college experience. All it seemed to do was push Cora into the decision to apply for a summer internship at the Santa Barbara paper. I clench my jaw thinking about it as I prep the display wall for painting.

Natalie's Clothing Boutique will open in August with a fall line, so while the entire store will be white, I'm painting the wall in the window displays in cool autumn tones of burgundy, gold, and green to contrast the colors of the clothing. It's the last line Mom designed. But I try not to think about that. If I do, my emotions will run wild, and I won't get anything done.

Carrying a gallon of paint in each hand, there's a knock on the glass doors. I turn and find not only Cheyenne but Alissa as well. I was prepared to fill Cheyenne in on my disastrous weekend and tell her things didn't go according to plan on Saturday night with Richie. But having Alissa here makes me second-guess spilling the details of my love life. Or lack thereof.

After I unlock the doors, Cheyenne pushes through, carrying a tray of green smoothies with Alissa on her heels.

"Good morning," I say, keeping my voice light.

"I brought reinforcements," Cheyenne says.

"I see that." I smile at Alissa.

"No, no, not Alissa." Cheyenne heads straight for the kiosk in the middle of the store, which has somehow turned into our little oasis in this mess over the last few weeks. "Power smoothies," she sings.

"Well, whatever you brought, I'll take it. I can use all the help I can get."

Alissa glances around the store, taking in the space. It's been about a month since she's been here. The walls weren't even covered in drywall then.

"It's looking really great."

"Thanks."

"I mean, I thought they'd be done with the floor by now. But at least you've got working plumbing, right?"

"Not exactly."

She whips around to face me. "The bathroom still isn't done?"

"There was an issue with the tile. Some sort of back order or problem with shipping, I'm not really sure."

Alissa makes a tsk-tsk noise, shaking her head. "Tess, this is what I told you happens when you try to cut corners."

"I didn't try to cut corners."

"No?" Her blonde brows shoot up. "Didn't you say you didn't want to use my tile guy because he was too expensive?"

"I did say that, yes. But why would I choose to pay twice as much for the same job? Especially when they both had the same referrals and five-star ratings?"

"Fine." She holds up her hands in surrender. "All I'm saying is my guy would've had it done weeks ago."

I don't mention that a few weeks ago, the floors weren't even ready for tile. "It's fine. We're not in that big of a hurry."

"Tell that to yourself," Cheyenne says. "You're the one who's been spending countless hours here, putting in work you could pay someone to do, or work that could be spread out. Your grand opening is how many months away? Three?"

I nod, chewing on my bottom lip, and hesitating to answer, "But I want everything to be perfect."

"It will be." Cheyenne pats my hand with hers. "Or at least darn near perfect. Especially because you've got us."

"Here," Alissa hands me a smoothie. "Drink up and then fill us in on your sexy time the other night." She waggles her thick blonde brows at me.

I shoot Cheyenne a look and all she gives me in response is a shrug and a wince. Regardless that the three of us are close friends, there are some things I purposely choose not to tell Alissa. This is one of those things. So all I can do is stare down at the green sludge in the clear plastic cup, mulling over how exactly I'm going to summarize Saturday evening.

"Well?" Alissa takes a sip of the smoothie, the thick liquid taking its sweet time moving up the straw.

I glance back and forth between Alissa and Cheyenne before saying on an exhale, "Nothing happened."

"Oh no," Cheyenne says, disappointment conveyed in her tone. "You told him and he was upset?"

"No, not exactly."

"Tess, you didn't tell him?"

The answer to her question feels more complicated than it should. Because it should be easy. No, I hadn't told Richie I stopped taking the pill. But it's not because I hadn't planned on telling him. It's because I hadn't had the opportunity. When I called Cora, it'd changed the course of our entire evening.

"Our evening alone got interrupted. Cora texted me a million times." *Okay, so it was only a handful of times.* "So Richie insisted I call her after she sent a 911 text."

"I can see where this is going," Alissa groans.

"Cora and I talked for over an hour. By the time I got off the phone, Richie was asleep."

"So why didn't you wake him up?"

"Once a guy is sleeping, there's no waking him up."

"Not true," Cheyenne says. "All it takes for Dexter to wake up is me taking my clothes off." She giggles. "A man cannot turn down a naked woman."

"Naked? All I have to do is breathe, and Carter is in the mood." Alissa laughs.

I can't help it, I laugh too. I'd been apprehensive about having this conversation with Cheyenne all weekend. And I never planned on telling Alissa at all. But now that it's out in the open, it feels good. This is the first time I've laughed since Saturday.

"So, what happened?"

"My dad happened, what else?" I pace the floor, pushing my fingertips into my scalp.

"What, he came home early or something?" Alissa asks.

"Oh, he did come home early. But not that first night. The first night he'd gone and pissed Cora off so bad she ditched him at a party. I had to talk her down from the ledge."

"Literally?" Cheyenne asks, slack-jawed.

"No," I say. "Not literally. But she was pretty embarrassed. She was ready to not even let him back into her dorm room that night, if he even made it back at all."

"So, he found his way back?"

"He's old, he's not a moron. He had his phone. He used his map or Siri or something. But not until Cora had called me and we talked for over an hour. By the time we got off the phone, my dad had found his way back to her room and she'd calmed way down. We both know Dad can be intense. But he's way worse now that my mom is gone." My throat constricts, tightening around my words.

"Hopefully this Jules lady can help him like she helped my brother." Alissa takes a seat on one of the round stools inside the kiosk.

"I hope so. But it's not looking too promising." I try the smoothie, taking more effort than should be necessary to suck on a straw. "I mean, what kind of instructions could she have given him that would make him think surprising Cora at college, attending a party with her, and playing bass while singing with a band at a house party would be a good idea?"

Cheyenne gasps. "He didn't?"

"Oh, but he did," I deadpan.

Alissa looks almost too afraid to ask, but she does anyway. "What did he sing?"

I answer on a sigh, "'Free Fallin' by Tom Petty."

Alissa shakes her head and blows air out of her cheeks. "That's bad."

"Oh, c'mon, it could've been worse, y'all," Cheyenne says.

"What's worse than Tom Petty?" Alissa asks.

"What I wouldn't give for a video of his performance." Cheyenne tips her smoothie toward me. "I'd even settle for a picture."

Alissa giggles. "Let's check YouTube."

"Oh, good idea."

I bury my face in my palm while they hover over Alissa's phone and I wonder how on earth I will ever get my old Dad back. Or if he's even still in there.

Chapter 9

Jules

Kobe, my fawn-colored Frenchie, has come into the office with me today. My usual dog sitter headed to Santa Barbara for the weekend and decided to leave early. He's a good dog but to say he and Angie don't get along would be an understatement.

I step out of the elevator, a drink carrier balanced in my hand, and Kobe tucked underneath my arm. I decided bringing a peace offering to Angie in the form of her favorite coffee was better than warning her Kobe was coming in with me.

"Triple grande caramel macchiato," I sing.

Angie props a hand to her jutted hip and narrows her creamy-brown eyes. "What is *he* doing here?"

"I'm sorry, okay. I had no other option. But don't worry, you won't even know he's here." I set the coffee on Angie's desk and place Kobe on the floor. Without hesitation, he prances right over to Angie's handbag—not only her favorite but her *only* Coach bag—lifts his hind leg, and pees.

"Oh, c'mon!" She throws up her hands. "Are you kidding me?"

"No, no, Kobe! That's a bad dog." I pick him up and shoo him into my office where he has a bed in one corner for the occasional Bring Your Child to Work day."

Angie grumbles and curses while she holds up the bag, and pee drips out from underneath it.

"I'm so sorry, Ang. I'll pay for the cleaning." She narrows her eyes at me but doesn't say a word. Her silence is the harbinger of rage. She won't even yell at me. "I'll replace the bag. Whatever brand you want."

"Any brand?" Her brows raise.

"Fine, yes, anything. And look, I brought coffee," I say by way of a distraction.

"I know you're only trying to bribe me."

I bite my lower lip.

"Luckily for you, bribing works on me." She removes both coffee cups from the carrier and hands mine to me after reading the description on the side. "Who's Jeremy?"

I snatch the cup from her. "What?" There's no playing dumb here, my face blushes too easily and is always a dead giveaway—my tell if you will. "He's a new barista. Apparently I am"—I use air quotes with my free hand—"a breath of fresh air."

She smirks. "So are you gonna call him?"

"No. Definitely not."

"Oh, c'mon, this Jeremy guy could be the breath of fresh air you need," she says the last words in an airy tone.

"Doubtful."

"Or maybe he can dust off those old lady parts of yours so you stop fantasizing about a certain client." She waggles her brows.

As if on cue, the elevator dings and Mr. Redd shoots out the doors, stumbling to catch his footing. He smooths his John Mellencamp T-shirt and appears a bit flustered at first. But the Temple of Doom would do that to anyone. When he looks at me, his green eyes soften, and he grins. My chest gives this sort of heave, and I set my hand there to push my heart back in place.

There's something different about him today, besides his clean-shaven face. While he still looks attractive this way, I think I prefer the three-day stubble. I clear my throat of the desire lodged there. "Mr. Redd, you're a few minutes early."

His expression falls. "I know. I thought doctors liked it when patients were early. I can leave and go wait in the car, then come back if you want?" He hikes a thumb over his shoulder.

"No, no," I wave him off. When I do, the coffee slurps out the spout and dribbles down my blouse. Of course. I sigh.

"That won't be necessary. C'mon, let's go into my office."

"Do you wanna clean that up first?"

I glance at the caramel-colored liquid on my pale-blue blouse and shrug as I return my gaze to him. "Would you be surprised if I told you this happens all the time?"

He looks from me to Angie as if waiting for confirmation. Ang nods at him and takes a sip of her own coffee.

"Why don't you keep backup shirts in your office if this happens so often?"

Now that was a good question. Why hadn't I thought of it? "That's not a bad idea. I'm gonna try to remember that. For now, why don't we get started?" I gesture to my office with my coffee cup.

Before Pete passes Angie, he gives her a perfunctory nod. "I don't think we've officially met. Pete Redd." He holds out his hand.

She accepts like she's been gifted with a medal of some kind. "Angie Phillips. And the pleasure is mine." She smirks, making it obvious she's checking out his backside as he passes. She fans herself dramatically, and I clench my jaw while my face flushes.

I open the door for Pete to enter first, mostly so I can remind Angie of proper professional behavior. But when I do, Kobe hops over to greet him and jumps on his legs. "Sorry. I forgot to warn you about him." I nudge Kobe and whisper in a hiss, "Down." But he's insistent and jumps up again.

"Whoa, who's this adorable fella with the sharp nails?" Pete indulges Kobe by reaching down and giving him a good amount of attention.

"This is Kobe. And yes, I've missed his last two grooming appointments so they're a bit overgrown." I pick him up, and although he's small, he's heavy and feels like dead weight in my arms. "Again, I'm so sorry." Kobe sneaks a lick to my cheek. I'm not sure if Pete is a dog guy, but if he's not, I can bet I've completely grossed him out. I place Kobe on his bed in the corner with his favorite toy and hope he stays put.

"Kobe? That's an interesting name for a dog."

"He's named after Kobe Bryant."

Pete's dark brows raise. "As in, LA Laker Kobe Bryant?"

I feel my cheeks blush while a pang of sadness hits regarding the loss of such an invaluable person. "That's the one." I move toward my chair and the sofa. "Kobe was mine and my dad's favorite basketball player back when the two of us used to go to the games together." The words exit my mouth naturally, which takes me by surprise. I don't talk about Dad often, especially not with clients. But with Pete, it feels easy.

"You *used* to go to games together?" he questions.

"We haven't been to one in a while." That's all I can give him. I clear my throat. "Okay, let's take a seat and get started."

We both sit at the same time. Pete is extra fidgety today, appearing more nervous than the first time we met. Typically, by the second meeting, my clients relax a bit, they know more of what to expect. But I have a feeling I know why he's anxious.

I set my iPad on my lap with his file tab open so I can check my notes easily. But I don't need them. Pete's story has made a lasting impression. Also, Tess called me on Monday and gave me the rundown on how Pete's first challenge went. I'm grateful she did because after Pete sent me the text on Saturday informing me he was spending time with someone he enjoyed, a bit of unwelcomed jealousy had pinched in my gut.

"Let's get right to it, shall we?" I smile. He doesn't respond, only fidgets his fingers in his lap. "How did your challenge go?"

"Eh, okay."

"Did you complete my instructions?"

"I did." He pauses before continuing, glancing toward the window. "But I'm not sure it did much good."

"No? Why's that?"

"It made things worse."

"In what way?"

He stands, and I sit upright, my back stiffening. As he begins to pace in front of the window, I check over my shoulder, and Kobe is sitting at attention. "Kobe, leave it," I command. He lies back down, chewing his toy again. "Pete," I say. "Did you really go to your daughter's college last weekend and embarrass her in front of her friends?"

He whips around from the window to face me, his face full of confusion.

"Tess told me."

He rolls his eyes and throws his hands up. "Of course she did."

"She thought I should be prepared."

"Yeah? Whatever happened to doctor-patient confidentiality?"

"Pete, again, I'm not a doctor. And you're not my patient. We never signed anything."

"Maybe we should have," he says gruffly.

"Are there things you don't want your daughters to know?"

He groans. "No, of course not. I'd tell my girls anything."

"Or me?"

He simply grunts.

"Why don't you sit back down and tell me what happened."

"Why? You already know." But he does sit, slumping into the sofa, his defenses gone.

"Tell me your version."

"I wanted to see my daughter. Is that a crime? You said I should do something I used to enjoy. I missed Cora so I thought I'd go surprise her."

"That's nice," I insist.

"But I messed everything up." He rubs a hand over his face.

"In what way?"

"Oh, I embarrassed her, I guess. But you didn't see that slime ball with his hands all over her. She needed my help. I'm her dad." His voice cracks with the last words, emotion consuming them.

"But I don't think that was the underlying issue."

"What do you mean?"

"Why did you go to see Cora?"

"What? I just told you why." He slides to the edge of the sofa, his defenses up once again.

"Listen, hear me out. I think you thought Cora missed you too and by surprising her, you'd both be happy being together again. There's nothing wrong with that. But I think subconsciously, you wanted to be with Cora because she makes you feel more whole and fills a void you're now missing with your wife gone."

"Yeah, that's exactly what Cora accused me of." His face is stony. "She said I only went there to see her because I missed Natalie."

"And what do you think?"

"I think..." He presses his lips together in a firm line before looking me directly in the eyes. "You're both probably right."

I recognize this is a pivotal moment for Pete. As his interventionist, empathy is okay, expected even. But attraction is not. I should not be feeling anything beyond empathy for this man. I can't go down that road. Not again. It not only caused me to shift careers, it nearly broke me the last time. Regardless of the successful book sales.

"Okay, let's focus on the future." I bend and clasp my hands together. "Let's talk about what happens next in case she gets accepted for the internship at the newspaper." His jaw drops, but I push through. "Now, I don't want to tell you how to parent, but might I suggest you talk to Cora?"

"Do you have kids, doc?"

"You can call me Jules. I'd actually prefer it."

"Noted."

"And no, I don't have kids." I keep my eyes focused on the iPad screen.

"No kids?"

The shock in his voice is not missed. I've heard it a bazillion times. From family, friends, even strangers when they find out I'm nearing forty and don't have kids. He's not the first. But for some reason, it still stings coming from him.

"I noticed no wedding ring either. You're not married?"

"Nope, not married. But Jeremy"—I pick up my coffee cup and point to the writing scrawled on the side—"could be a potential suitor."

Pete chuckles and the sound pulses throughout my body. I smile.

"Anyway, we're here to talk about you not me."

"Too bad," he mumbles.

"Excuse me?" At first, I think I imagined him speaking at all.

He fidgets his hands again. "Nothing. I just meant, it's too bad you're not married. Marriage can be a pretty awesome thing. And you're, you know..." His face reddens. "An attractive woman."

Now I'm certain I'm blushing. Heat travels all the way to the tips of my ears.

"Sorry, that was probably way out of line, I'm your patient. I was only stating a fact. You know...paying you a compliment," he rambles.

"Pete," I interrupt, "it's okay. It's very sweet." I clear my throat. "Anyway, I have another challenge for you." I stand, nerves zinging through my legs as I walk to my desk and pick up the envelope lying on top.

"I hope this time you give me more directions." He exhales a light chuckle.

There are definitely more directions to this challenge. But after his compliment, I'm hesitant to follow through with this one. I pull off the sticky note attached to the envelope with my name scrawled across it.

"Here." I hand the envelope to him and sit down.

He eyes me skeptically while he removes two Dodgers tickets for tomorrow's game. "I'm confused. Totally stoked but confused."

"I agree you need more directions with this next challenge. And a chaperone." I smile.

He points the tickets in my direction, arching a brow. "You?"

I nod. "Attending games is something you used to enjoy. So, you up for the challenge?"

When he grins at me, that same one from the first day I met him, my chest heaves again. I really need to get a handle on the effect his grin has on my body. I am a professional, darn it.

"Yeah, most definitely. Challenge accepted."

Chapter 10

Pete

The pink robe is in the washing machine, my face is shaved, and I'm even dressed in clean clothes. Including one of my favorite Dodgers T-shirts. Cora bought it for me at the last game we attended together.

I pick up my team cap from the dresser and shove it on my head before jogging down the stairs. As I cram my wallet, phone, and keys into the pockets of my jeans, I catch sight of Tess in her office. I tiptoe toward the door that's open a crack and peek my head in. She glances up, hovering over a large sheet of clothing designs, pencil in her hand. Her hair is pulled back and messy, with several pieces framing her face.

"Hey, Dad." Tess smiles.

"How's the latest line coming along?"

"It's good. But this will be the first line without Mom's direction."

She's worried. I see it etched on her face.

My first instinct is to freak out with her. To say she can't do it without Natalie. Because her mom had a keen eye for fashion and always knew what would be in next. Like she had a sixth sense or something. But Tess needs me to be optimistic and supportive. So I reach deep down for all I can muster.

"You'll be great. Mom would be so proud of you." It's not enough. But for now, it's all I got.

She smiles, tucks the dark, loose hair behind her ear, and a shiver of familiarity runs through me. An image of Natalie from those first few years, staying up late, hovering over clothing designs on butcher paper stretched across our coffee table. I'd have to convince her to come to bed, enticing her with a glass of wine and me singing an Eagles song in her ear, threatening to do a striptease right there in our living room if she didn't put down the pencil.

"Thanks, Dad." Tess smiles and shakes me from my memory.

"Okay." I push away from the doorframe. "I gotta go."

"Where are you headed?"

"As if you don't know." I grin. "Bye. See ya later tonight."

"Have fun," she hollers right before I slip out the front door.

My phone pings with a text just as I slide behind the steering wheel of my Jeep.

Daniel: *What are you up to today?*

At first, I consider lying and am quickly confused by that reaction because Daniel and I don't lie to one another. But there's something about this whole seeing-an-interventionist thing that makes me feel embarrassed. Or maybe defensive for some reason. But he's already aware of most of the details anyway.

Me: *I'm heading out on my next challenge. A Dodger game with the doc.*

Daniel: *A Dodger game? That doesn't sound like much of a challenge.*

Me: *Maybe she's going easy on me to start with.*

Daniel: *Or maybe the doc has a thing for you.*

That's ludicrous, she's like my therapist. I sigh heavily and click my seatbelt in place. Maybe this was another reason I didn't want to tell Daniel.

Me: *It's not like that.*

Daniel: *Is she hot?*

Me: *I gotta go. Gonna be late.*

I'm about to toss the phone into the glove compartment, the whole out of sight, out of mind thing, when my phone pings again.

Daniel: *Ok, fine. Just be sure to check your email. I sent a couple listings your way.*

Now I really wish I had thrown my phone into the glove compartment before seeing that last text. I groan, run a hand down my face, and send a quick reply.

Me: *Thanks.*

Jules and I agreed to meet at the stadium. She said it would be less formal this way rather than me picking her up. She also said if I couldn't go through with it, there would be less pressure since I had both tickets in my possession.

But I'm here. I made it. And as I watch the excited fans enter the stadium in a blue blur, I feel something like hope in my chest. Something I haven't felt in a while. Almost like the feeling I had while playing bass with the band last weekend. Maybe Jules actually knows what she's doing. Fake doctor or not.

I spot her weaving through the crowd of fans. She's not hard to miss—she's the only one not dressed in blue Dodger apparel. The sun bounces off her strawberry blonde hair, causing it to look more golden than red. And she's got an olive-green T-shirt on, making her hazel eyes pop.

I pull down the brim of my hat, attempting to avert my gaze. I'm not supposed to notice her eyes. Or find it cute how she fields the ticket brokers as she makes her way toward me. She sort of trips over her own feet or maybe a crack in the concrete, but she catches herself, and I place a hand on my chest, exhaling a sigh of relief.

When she's finally in front of me, I clear my throat and try to hide my amusement. "Hey."

"Hey, Pete." She smiles this scintillating, warm smile that reminds me of the sun.

Why am I comparing this woman's smile to the sun?

I shake her hand but break it off quickly. Her hand is clammy, and it feels too nice in mine. More than nice. It sends a lusty current zinging through me. Feelings I shoved down months ago. *What are you doing?*

"Should we go in?" I ask, feeling flustered so I stuff my hands into my pockets.

"Sure."

We enter the stadium side by side. The silence between us is awkward, and I realize we don't know one another that well. I suppose she knows me more than I know her. I've learned she's not married, doesn't have kids, has a dog named Kobe with freakishly sharp nails, and she's a little clumsy.

We walk through the tunnel, and she glances in my direction, smiling, right before she slams directly into the chest of a burly man. She bounces off him like a basketball on a backboard, landing on her butt.

"Whoa, are you okay?" I crouch next to her. Okay, maybe she's *a lot* clumsy. I help her to her feet.

She rubs her backside. "I'm fine."

The burly chested man continues walking. I holler after him. "She's fine by the way, in case you wanted to know, you big buffoon."

Jules elbows me. "Pete," she hisses under her breath. "That guy is huge."

The man stops abruptly and turns around. It's then I notice how taut the sleeves of his Dodgers shirt is over his biceps. My breath catches as he takes a few steps toward us.

Jules grabs ahold of my hand and pulls me back before raising our joined hands in the air and shouting, "Woo-hoo! Go Dodgers!" She lowers our hands and whispers, "Run." She drags me along with her, and we're almost sprinting before I glance over my shoulder and realize the buff man isn't even following us.

I tug on her hand to slow us down. "I think we lost him," I say through laughter.

She stops, releases my hand and rubs her backside again. "Oh, good." She smiles, biting her lower lip.

We head into the stadium and find our seats. The scent of hot dogs, buttery popcorn, and even sweat causes nostalgia to build in my chest. It feels strange being back in these bleachers.

The last game I attended, I brought Cora. But the time before that, it had been only Natalie and me. She loved the Dodgers. Sometimes I wonder if she loved them more than I did. It became sort of an addiction for her. Besides being a baseball fanatic in general, I think she needed something to connect her to the city. Sort of like confirmation we'd made the right decision to move to LA and plant our roots here. Although, every once in a while, I caught her trying to be discreet about rooting for the Seattle Mariners.

Glancing over at Jules, I'm suddenly aware of how awkward she looks. She's sitting with her hands wrapped around the edge of the bleacher. She has zero Dodger apparel on and isn't even sporting their colors. It's almost as if she did it on purpose.

I lean over and say, "So, you're a big fan of the Dodgers?"

She whips her head to face me, taking in my expression. "Oh, yeah." She grins, nodding convincingly.

My lips quirk into a smile. "You've never been to a game, have you?"

"Never," she admits. Her honesty is endearing. "That obvious, huh?"

"A little," I lie.

"I've always meant to, just never got around to it, I guess."

I scratch my chin and glance around at the hard-core fans dressed head to toe in team apparel. I'm sure they're wondering what this lady dressed in nothing Dodger blue is doing at a Dodgers game. The last thing I want is these fans becoming unhinged and thinking Jules is rooting for the opposing team—the Oakland A's—dressed in that green shirt.

I nudge her with my elbow. "Let's go get you a shirt or hat or something. When you sit here, you gotta represent your team. You gotta show your respect."

"And I'm guessing you don't want to be seen with me like this?" she asks, a challenging smile on her lips.

I shrug and raise my brows as if to say, *Guilty*.

"Okay," she agrees, standing. "But you're buying."

"Gladly."

When we return to our seats, we have popcorn in a Dodgers fan container, bottled water, and Jules is decked out in team apparel. While it cost me a small fortune, I'm satisfied. And I think she is too. She's wearing a Dodgers T-shirt and hat and sports a foam finger. She perches on the edge of the blench, excitement bubbling out of her.

I lean into her. "Happy now?"

She grins a cheesy smile. "Very."

And I am too. It feels good to be responsible for making someone else happy. It's an achy—but a welcomed achy—feeling in my chest.

"So, why the Dodgers?" She shoves a handful of popcorn in her mouth.

I blink at her. "That question doesn't make sense. Why *not* the Dodgers?"

She shakes her head, and talks around the popcorn. "I meant, why not the Angels instead?"

I cover her mouth lightly and glance over both shoulders. "Shh, we never speak that word. Especially not here."

She laughs underneath my hand and I release her mouth, chuckling.

"Okay, for real? After Natalie and I moved here, we knew we needed to embrace all we could to make LA feel like home. Our first night in our new home, Natalie spread out a sheet on the living room floor, and the four of us sat and ate Chinese takeout. We literally flipped a coin. Heads, Dodgers; tails," I lower my voice and mumble, "Angels."

Her face is amused. "Seriously? You based your entire fandom on the flip of a coin?"

"I thought you'd find the story sweet." I shrug.

"No, no, it is." She touches my arm. "I'm just surprised is all."

The game begins, and the first pitch to the Dodgers' leadoff batter results in a double. They're off to a good start. When I glance at Jules, her eyes are big and wide, and it's as if she's taking it all in. I wonder why she's never made time to attend a game. What has kept her so busy? Besides trying to help loser schmucks like me.

I settle against my seat back—baseball games are long. But that's what I love about them. Hours of no one expecting anything from me.

Jules asks a few questions, and it doesn't take me long to realize she doesn't know much about baseball.

"I've always been more of a basketball fan. The Lakers," she admits. "My dad was a huge fan, so I figured I'd better get interested or I wouldn't have much in common with him."

"Was? He's since passed?"

She's propped on the edge of her seat and glances over her shoulder at me. "No." She adjusts the hat on her head. "He's got dementia. Most days he doesn't even remember who I am, never mind that he loved basketball."

She says it so matter-of-factly that I'm not sure I should say anything in response. But I do. "I'm sorry."

"Thanks. It's been a few years, so I'm getting used to it."

But she doesn't look used to it. It clearly affects her. I can't imagine not remembering Tess and Cora. "And your mom?"

She sets her hand on the globe pendant hanging around her neck. "Ahh, now that's a story for another day. Besides, you're my client. Not the other way around, remember?"

I do remember. But sharing this game with her feels intimate, like we've connected on a new, deeper level. "Right," I say.

We stare at one another, and neither of us seems able to look away. Her eyes convey words that I want to command to come out. I want her to feel comfortable sharing with me verbally what her eyes are saying silently.

We hear a loud *crack*—the wooden bat coming into contact with the ball—and just like that, our connection is broken. We turn our attention to the field. The entire stadium is on their feet, including us, as we watch in anticipation while the ball flies through the air as if in slow motion. The ball zips toward the crowd about four rows below us and the stadium cheers in a thunderous roar. The announcer hollers through the stadium speakers, "Home run!" And the words flash on all the large screens in bright colorful lights.

Jules and I turn to each other, cheering, whistling, and jumping, and before I know what's happening, she launches herself into my arms. I squeeze her tight and swing her around. It feels natural and right, like the world has corrected itself. I inhale the intoxicating fruity, floral scent of her hair without thinking, and when I realize what I'm doing, I set her back down on her feet abruptly.

"Sorry," she mumbles, adjusting her T-shirt.

But I'm not sure she's the one who should be apologizing. I just sniffed her hair like a weirdo. "No, I'm sorry."

"Pete, you don't need to be sorry. I got caught up in the moment... in the excitement."

"Right. Same." I pull down the brim of my hat. "Besides, you're my—" I pause, because I'm still not sure what to call her. "And I'm your client."

"Right," she agrees. "You are. But that doesn't mean we can't be friends."

"Friends?" The term feels less than. A write off of the attraction I've been feeling along with the vibe I've been getting from Jules. But it also erases a smidge of my guilt.

She nods.

"Okay, friend." I grin at her and if I'm not mistaken, I notice a blush crawling up her neck and pooling into her cheeks. I'm sure I'm mistaken. It's probably a sunburn. Today, the sun is bright and shines relentlessly down on us.

Yeah, that must be it—a sunburn.

Chapter 11

Jules

If Pete continues to grin at me, and the scorching sun doesn't let up even the slightest, I may strip off this Dodgers T-shirt right here, right now. But that would surely put a stop to our day. And I haven't had this much fun since Angie and I snuck into that expensive workout on the beach and got caught. The instructor chased us almost a mile down the beach before finally giving up. Ang and I were so out of breath we collapsed onto the sand and laughed so hard my stomach hurt for two days after. So, in a way, we still ended up getting a free workout.

I'm familiar with basketball and how fans support the team, but baseball is like a completely different universe. Besides the blaring sun, I find I veritably enjoy the way the sport leisurely maneuvers from step to step. There's time to sit back and relax, time to take it all in and appreciate it. But when there's a good hit or a home run, the fans represent. Experiencing this for the first time with Pete isn't awful either. My body is still thrumming after I catapulted into his arms. I felt an electric shock surge through me when our bodies made contact, and I'm fairly certain he felt it too. But we can't do anything about it. I'm supposed to be helping Pete heal. And I won't go there again with a client.

"Bases are loaded." Pete scoots to the edge of the bench.

I do the same, my heart beating fast in my chest.

The batter takes a couple practice swings before stepping up to the plate and getting his feet into position. When his stance is perfect, the catcher flashes signals with his fingers to the pitcher. I have no idea what they mean, but I suck in a breath and wait in anticipation. The pitcher winds up and releases the ball. I don't even blink. *Crack!* The bat connects with the ball, and the player takes off in the direction of first base. The ball flies toward us. It's a home run for sure, and every single fan is up on their feet, shouting and cheering. This time, I refrain from throwing myself into Pete's arms.

But suddenly, the ball is coming in fast and close.

Pete shakes my arm. "It's coming for you. Catch it in your hat."

I don't even have time to think. I tear off my hat and hold it out. I feel a bit silly, but then I realize Pete is right. The ball is headed straight for me. I line up my hat, but before the ball sinks into it, the guy next to me shoves me, stretching his gloved hand right in front of my face. The sound of the ball smacking into his glove happens the same time my head comes in contact with the seat backs in front of me, sending a shooting pain radiating on my forehead.

"Hey!" Pete hollers. "That was a dick move. You know she had that."

"Then I guess she should've caught it."

"It's fine." I wave him off.

"No, it's not fine."

Pete is too distracted to help me up this time, so I use the back of the seat to pull myself to my feet.

"What are you gonna do about it?" the guy asks.

"Man, just give her the ball."

I press my hands to Pete's chest. "I don't need the ball. He can keep it." Pete tears his hat off and rubs his head. "I don't need it. I have this." I hold up my Dodger's number one fan foam finger. "And it's way better." I plaster on a persistent smile.

Pete finally focuses his attention on me. His expression changes from pinched and frustrated to open and worried. "You're bleeding."

"What?" My hand shoots up to the spot on my forehead where his eyes zero in. Sure enough, there's dark-red blood oozing from my head. "I think I hit it on the seat."

"Are you okay?" He crouches to get a better look.

"I'm fine."

"We should go and get you checked out. What if you have a concussion or something?"

"Don't be silly. It doesn't even hurt." I stick the foam finger to my head to stop the bleeding. "See, it's totally fine. Besides, the game's not over yet."

"C'mon, let's go. We've got them. There's no coming back after that last three-run homer."

When I realize it will be impossible to change his mind, I pick up my hat, keeping the foam finger pressed to my head, and follow him out of our row. Back out in the tunnel, Pete leads me to a hot dog vendor and asks the older cashier if we can get a Band-Aid from their first aid kit hanging on the wall. He's hesitant at first, but when I lower the foam finger, he fetches the kit. He gives Pete one large Band-Aid and an antiseptic wipe. We both nod our thanks, and Pete takes me by the shoulders, steering me to the end of the counter.

"Hop up there, and I'll clean you up."

I jump on the counter as Pete rips open the package for the antiseptic wipe.

"Okay, ready? I'm not gonna lie to you, this will sting."

He looks into my eyes, and a calmness washes over me. Something tells me he's a good dad. An honest dad. Much like my own. Dad wasn't perfect, but I've learned over the years, no one is. As long as they do their best, that's what matters.

I nod, folding my lips in between my teeth.

He swipes the wipe across my forehead, and he wasn't wrong, it stings like hell. I inhale a breath and hold it, biting back my desire to release a string of curses. But as I exhale, he leans in close to me and blows over the cut. It sends a cool, welcoming sensation that not only relieves the sting but also sends goosebumps racing down my neck and arms, as well as a humming in my depths. My exhale turns into more of a moan, and I suck in my lower lip. He either doesn't notice or has a good poker face.

"Um, what are you doing?" I whisper.

"Making sure it's dry before I put on the Band-Aid."

Duh, of course.

Pete unwraps the bandage and covers the cut on my forehead, smoothing it out gently with his fingertips. "Better?"

I run my own fingers over the bandage, the cut underneath throbbing. "Much. Thank you." I hop down from the counter on wobbly legs.

"C'mon, I'll walk you to your car."

I don't argue. Because even though this isn't a date, I'm not ready to say goodbye.

Conversation is easy but the secret I know that he doesn't is hanging over my head. I was hired to break him free from his depression so he'll move out of his daughter's home and get back to enjoying his life again. But I think I'm getting the better end of the deal. Pete is funny and not bad on the eyes either. Spending time with him doesn't feel like work.

"This is me," I say, when we reach my car.

He shoves his hands into his pockets and bounces on his toes. "Thanks for the tickets. And for coming with me. I had fun."

"So did I."

"Also, I think you're a lot smarter than what you give yourself credit for."

Blush creeps up my neck and heat spreads to my cheeks as I unlock my car. "I never said I wasn't smart."

"No, you didn't. But do you know how many times you've reminded me you're not a doctor?"

"Because I'm not." I resist telling him that not too long ago, I was a licensed therapist. And that I'm no longer practicing by choice.

He puts up a hand. "Okay, enough. To me, you might as well be."

I open the door and rest my hand on the frame, intrigued. "Why's that?"

"Because you just did more for me in one afternoon than my regular doctor and therapist have done in eight months."

The compliment hits me out of nowhere. His words balloon in my chest, and I struggle over what to say. My throat thickens, so I say nothing.

"Yeah, well...anyway." He rubs the back of his neck. "I should let you go. You've already wasted almost your entire Saturday on me."

"I'd hardly call it wasted." I raise my brows and pinch at my shirt. "I got new clothes out of the deal."

He grins. And it turns my wobbly legs into cooked spaghetti noodles, making it difficult to move. "Bye, Pete. I'll see you next Friday."

"Right, next Friday. See you then." He turns to leave, and I slide into my seat.

It feels like I should say something else, do something else. If this had been a date, I'm sure we'd follow up the game with dinner or drinks. Possibly a kiss goodnight—or more.

But this is not a date. I reluctantly pull my door closed and fasten my seatbelt. It's best this way. Besides, I've got another man expecting me today.

THE MEMORY CARE FACILITY IS CLEAN, AND THE PROPERTY IS spacious, surrounded by the shade of eucalyptus and palm trees. It's a bit of a drive to Norwalk, but since this is the neighborhood where Dad grew up, I knew he'd be more comfortable here than in LA.

Under the circumstances, he seems happy here, and the staff of mostly women treats him well. It might have something to do with the fact that he's one of the youngest and most attractive guys in the facility. Sometimes I wish a woman would see his potential and kind face, get a glimpse of the man he once was, and snatch him up. To promise to take care of him for the rest of his life. But that's not likely. I couldn't even do it. I tried. After Mom left, he moved in with me, and we lasted four years. I'm surprised now it was that long.

I park my car and walk to the front entrance of Norwalk Memory Care Facility. Charlene sits behind the front counter, her short, graying hair is tucked behind her ears, and she's busy painting her nails.

"Hi, Charlene."

Her blue eyes sweep up to meet mine before her penciled brows arch. "Hey, Jules. My, don't we look festive today."

I'd forgotten about the Dodgers hat and shirt. "Right. I just came from the game."

"That's nice, dear." She continues to swipe the brush across her nails, painting on a candy apple red shade to match her lipstick.

"Can you buzz me in, please?"

"One second," she says, taking her time to dip the brush into the bottle and paint another nail.

"How is he today?" Asking this question always makes me nervous, but I ask it anyway.

She pauses with the brush pinched between her fingers and gives me a confident smile. "It's a good day. Jimmy is in high spirits."

Relief floods in my chest and I even make an audible exhale.

"You have a nice visit." The hall doors unlock with a *click*.

"Thanks," I call over my shoulder before pushing through the door.

What Dad hates most about this place is the fact that he's locked in. Most of the time, he forgets. That's a good day. On the days he remembers, let's say the staff earns their pay. But the worst thing is I never know what kind of day it's going to be until I see him. Charlene can prepare me only slightly since his mood can shift in a matter of seconds.

The door to his room is open, my chest gives another small heave and I sigh. It's a sign he's still having a good day. I peek my head in. "Hey, Dad."

He's sitting on his leather recliner, a hardback book propped on his lap. We'd brought the recliner here from my house when he moved in because he loves it, never mind that it matches my leather sofa. But I would've brought all of my furniture here if it meant he would've had an easier transition.

Dad peers over the worn pages, his reading glasses perched on the end of his straight nose. It takes a few beats, but a warm smile stretches across his face. "Jules."

Ah, it's definitely a good day. When Dad remembers me, it's always a good day. They seem few and far between lately. I stride over to him, wrap my arm around his neck, and kiss him on the top of his downy, graying-brunette head.

He closes his book and slides it onto the side table, where a stack of historical novels sits. I pick up four to six books from the library for him each week.

"How many more books do you have left?"

"This is my last one." He pats the cover.

"Wow, you really plowed through this stack." I open the empty bag hanging on my shoulder and load the books into it. "I'll return these and bring you a new stack tomorrow."

"Good. Just make sure they're more historical and less erotica." His thick brow quirks up.

I bite back a laugh. A few of the books may have had a romance subplot, but I'd hardly call them erotica. "I'll keep that in mind." I check Dad over. He looks good today. He combed his hair and is dressed in clean clothes. A pair of khaki cargo shorts and a Hawaiian style short-sleeved button-down is his go-to outfit these days. "Do you feel up for taking a walk outside?"

"You mean a chance to break free from this place? Absolutely."

He pushes the recliner down and stands. Dad's brain may be malfunctioning, but his body works admirably. He's seventy and in excellent shape.

I bend my elbow and offer it to him, but he doesn't accept. "I'm not a decrepit," he spits.

"I know that, Dad." The last thing I want to do is upset him. Sometimes the chemical reaction in his brain triggers from anger and moves to confusion. "I wanted the honor of escorting my dad."

He waves me off but does manage a smile.

Outside, we follow a concrete pathway that weaves around the facility. There are benches along the way and a gazebo surrounded by colorful flowers.

"Since when are you a Dodger fan?"

We've made our first turn in the concrete path when he finally notices or decides to ask.

"Since today, I guess." Because it's the truth. And I can't lie to my dad.

"The hat looks good on you."

"Thanks." I self-consciously pull the brim down, attempting to hide the Band-Aid on my forehead.

"Hey, whatever happened to the Lakers hat I bought you?" he asks after we stop at a bench and sit.

He's referring to a hat he'd bought me at a game he took me to on my sixteenth birthday. That he remembers, but most days, he can't even remember I'm his daughter.

"I lost it at the beach. The wind lifted it right off my head and took it out to the water. I tried to get it but the waves took it too far out."

"You never could keep anything nice," he huffs. There's an undercurrent of anger in his tone.

"I still have the signed jersey you gave me on my eighteenth birthday."

"What jersey?"

"The Lakers one. The one autographed by Kobe Bryant. You had it put in a display case."

His hands fidget in his lap and his eyes are unable to focus. It's his tell—a sign an episode is coming. After nearly six years, I've picked up on the signs.

"I'd never spend that kind of money on something for you that you'd just wind up breaking. Or losing," he sneers.

Tension knots across my shoulders. I lower my voice. "Did you take your meds today?"

He whips his head to face me. "What? Why wouldn't I take my meds?" His voice rises. "Do you think any of these people would let me forget to take my meds? They're stricter than my captain in the army."

"Dad," I say quietly. "You weren't in the army."

"Of course I was. I was a major general. Oh, what would you know?" He waves me off, glancing around with wild eyes.

"Okay, Dad. I think you've had enough sun. Why don't we get you back to your room so you can rest?" I stand and reach under his arm to lift him.

He flinches at my touch, retracting his arm. "I'm not going anywhere with you."

"Dad." Panic heaves in my chest.

"And quit calling me that. I don't even know you. I don't have any kids. I never wanted kids. I told Susana that."

His words sting. It's not the first time he's said them, though he only ever speaks them while he's having an episode. He may have a difficult time remembering me, but he always remembers my mother.

Two nurses approach and help Dad up. He struggles in their grip but there's no thrashing this time, thank goodness.

"Easy now, Jimmy. We're gonna help you back to your room," one of the nurses says, his tone calming.

I stand there, feeling helpless—as always. "Bye, Dad," I mumble. "I'll be back tomorrow with the books. And more Yoo-hoo."

But Dad isn't coherent, and he doesn't comprehend what I say. Besides, he's too busy cursing at the nurses who are dragging him back inside.

Chapter 12

Tess

At a Starbucks downtown, the barista calls out my name. I shuffle past a cluster of elderly women dressed in matching neon-pink tracksuits to pick up my drink from the bar. I nod my thanks and squeeze into the corner where the only open table remains.

I scroll through emails on my phone, along with three texts from Cheyenne, who's already at the store. Apparently, there was a mix-up with our order for the keyhole-neck blouses. I send a quick reply, letting her know I'll be there soon.

"Hey, sorry I'm late," Jules says, sounding nearly out of breath. She waggles her fingers in a wave to a young guy working behind the espresso bar before sliding into the empty seat across from me.

"No worries." I shake my phone at her. "Still getting work done."

She laughs. "Sounds familiar."

"That a friend of yours?" My chin tilts in the direction of the young, attractive barista.

She glances over her shoulder at him before returning her focus to me. "That's Derek. A past client." She takes a sip of her coffee. "So, what did you want to discuss?"

I finally get a good look at her, there's a fairly recent cut on her forehead. "What happened there?" I gesture toward her face.

Her fingers brush over the wound mindlessly. "Your dad didn't tell you?"

"No." I shake my head.

"Baseball game."

"A baseball hit you?" I nearly choke on my coffee, leaning forward.

"No, no." She laughs. "I got knocked over trying to catch a home-run ball. Hit my head on the back of the bleacher."

"Whoa. I'm sorry."

"Occupational hazard." She tilts her head and shrugs one shoulder.

"Okay. Well, besides the injury, you had a good time at the game?"

"I think the correct question is, did your dad have a good time?" She looks pointedly at me.

"Right. I think he did. He didn't sleep all day Sunday which is a good sign. And he called my husband Richie. That's it. No nickname. No Richie Rich."

She looks at me, clearly confused.

"Never mind." I wave her off. "So what do you have planned for this week's challenge?"

"I have a few ideas." She pauses and I sense her hesitation but I'm not certain why. "Look, don't get me wrong, I want to know anything about your dad or the situation that could be helpful. But maybe, I don't have to tell you everything."

Ouch. I had thought by her agreeing to meet with me, it meant she wanted my help.

"No offense or anything."

"Gotta admit," I say, "a little offended."

"It's just that, for this to work, it should be raw, more organic, ya know? If you and I are telling each other everything, you're gonna have a harder time noticing any progress we're making."

It makes sense. But it doesn't mean I like it. I lean back in my seat and sigh. "Fine, fine, I get it."

"Good." She gives a perfunctory nod. "But please, definitely reach out if you need anything. Or if something should come up."

"Like what?"

"I don't know. Anything unusual. Like unusual behavior or if you notice backsliding. Anything that could push back the program."

"You still think you can do it in six weeks?"

"Yes, I think so."

"It's already been two," I remind her.

"And we're right on track." She winks before taking a sip of her coffee.

Jules's confidence makes it easier for me to relax. She's supposed to be the best, and I need to trust her. But part of me still feels guilty about doing this at all. She's not supposed to be playing with my dad's heart. But I know Dad. He doesn't do anything without getting his heart involved.

I push my chair out and stand. "I gotta get to work."

"Right, same." Jules nearly pushes her seat into the middle-aged woman sitting behind her. "I'm so sorry." She gently pats the woman's shoulder.

The two of us walk out side by side. I gulp in the thick, hot air and it clogs my lungs.

"Remember," Jules says before we part ways in the parking lot. "Text or call me if you notice anything unusual."

I nod. "Hey? What about the robe?" I say, the question coming out as the thought enters my mind.

"What about it?"

"He actually took it off. And washed it."

Jules pumps a fist slightly into the air and there's a satisfied grin on her face. "Like I said, right on track." She turns around and heads for her car, leaving me standing there, wondering how that is progress.

Sure, he'd taken the robe off and washed it. He'd also washed his

Jeep—something Richie has taken over handling since Dad moved in. But after he returned inside the house, he put the robe back on.

I sigh against the warmth from the sun. Maybe Jules is right. Maybe things are moving right on track. And maybe, just maybe, Richie and I and our future plans will be back on track soon as well. We've made it eight and a half months already, what's one more?

IT'S LATER THAN I TYPICALLY ARRIVE AT THE STORE. THE parking garage downtown is fuller than usual, and I have to park my car two levels higher. The store is unlocked, and I find my contractor, Barney, standing in what should be a finished bathroom. A yellow hard hat rests on his salt-and-pepper head of hair, and his calloused hands press to his hips. He's talking with two other men I recognize as the plumbers he's hired. Their conversation looks intense, and I'm in no mood to hear bad news today, so I make a beeline to the center of the store where I see Cheyenne pulling stacks of blouses from a large box.

I'm instantly aware that the blouses are one of the last pieces Mom ever designed. I glance around, taking in the sight of all the boxes stacked around the kiosk. The existence of Mom's entire last line—each of the last designs she ever created—sits in those boxes. My heart squeezes, and my throat goes dry at the thought. Doing this without Mom's help feels crippling. But she'd never planned on opening an actual clothing boutique. She'd planned to keep Natalie's as strictly an online business. While she was sick, we talked about it. She said it was up to me. I wished she would've given me her blessing, at least.

But here I am. Hoping I'm doing the right thing. Hoping I'm making her proud—of both the clothing brand and me. There's a lot of hoping happening here, and hope isn't my usual cup of tea. There's no certainty to it, no promise.

"Tess," Cheyenne says. "Thank God you're here. Look at this." She holds up a stack of white, keyhole-neck blouses, each wrapped in clear plastic. "They're all white."

"Okay." I stretch out the word, my brain trying to process what she means. "What's the problem?"

She looks at me, mouth agape, before tearing into a new box and pulling out another stack of blouses. "They're *all* white. *All* of the blouses are white."

Cheyenne's right. I kneel in front of another box and push the flap back.

"White," she states, before I have the chance to.

"Right."

"All six boxes," she reiterates, presenting them with her hand.

I push back to standing and press my hands to my hips. How did we end up with six boxes of the exact same white blouse? The store can't afford mistakes. Especially not this early in the game.

"I'll check the Excel sheet," I say as I move around to the inside of the kiosk and sit in front of the laptop resting on the counter. "Was the packing slip in the box?"

"Right here." She sets it in my hand.

I scan the page while the computer powers on. "It shows 360 white, keyhole-neck blouses." I glance over at the computer in time to catch Cheyenne cringe.

"Think we'll be able to return them?"

"Depends. If this was my mistake, then no."

Cheyenne looks at the boxes, her forehead scrunched into a frown. "What will we do with 360 white blouses?"

"Um." I press my lips together, considering. "We price them to sell and convince everyone white blouses are the in thing this summer?" I shrug my shoulders.

"Hello?" Her jaw hangs open at the end of the word, and she

arches her brows at me. "The shop isn't opening until late August with a fall line. No white after Labor Day, remember?"

I groan. "I guess we'll have to do some serious convincing."

She juts out a hip and props her hand on it. "More like, you're gonna have to wish upon a magical unicorn's behind to pull that one off."

Her choice of words along with her Southern drawl lightens the mood, and I smile. "Then that's exactly what we'll do."

Barney approaches the kiosk and clears his throat. I glance away from the laptop's Excel spreadsheet, and he removes the hard hat from his head and swipes the back of his hand across his sweaty brow. "I'm gonna need you to talk to the plumbers with me. Maybe you can convince them that getting your bathroom done is more important than heading over for their next job at Hooters."

"I thought that's what I'm paying you for," I say, annoyed.

"I just thought...if you talked to them—"

"Oh, don't you worry," Cheyenne interrupts, touching his arm like they're old friends. "This one has serious mad convincing skills. She's got a magical unicorn and everything," she says sarcastically but follows it with a wide bright smile.

Barney frowns at her.

I exhale and stand, ready to push my laptop closed when something on the spreadsheet catches my attention. "I'll be there in a minute, Barney. Don't let the plumbers leave. Promise them lunch. On me."

I quickly scan the info on the spreadsheet and sure enough, I spot it. I gasp aloud. Six boxes of keyhole-neck blouses. All six white. Signed by...Cora? But when? How?

"What is it?" Cheyenne moves around the kiosk, peering over my shoulder to study the computer screen. "What are we looking at?"

But I can't speak, I can only stare at Cora's name written there in the *Approved by* tab.

"Cora?" Cheyenne's voice goes up an octave. "But...when?"

I shake my head.

"You gave her authority to approve orders and not me? Your best friend and what may as well be your partner?"

"Cheyenne," I say softly.

"I know, I know, she's your sister." She waves me off and straightens. "Well," she sighs, "I guess you should start practicing those wishing skills. You got that unicorn handy? Better tell him to bend over."

Chapter 13

Pete

The sun is roasting, and the air is dense with humidity today, but I don't even mind. It's Friday which means I have my appointment with Jules. I'm anxious to hear what my next challenge will be. The last two were difficult but manageable. If her plan is to challenge me to do the things I once enjoyed, maybe it won't be so bad after all. Especially if Jules continues to accompany me.

Before I climb into my Jeep, I spot Richie on the edge of the driveway, strapping on his bike helmet.

"It's pretty hot out today," I call to him.

He turns to face me. "Yeah." He fiddles with the strap under his chin.

"Do you want a ride to the office?"

"Nah, I'm good. I could use the exercise." He swings his leg over and adjusts himself on top of the bike.

Richie is tall and lean and probably has zero percent body fat. The last thing he needs is more exercise. I try not to feel offended that my son-in-law would rather bike to work and risk heat stroke than be in a car with me for thirty minutes.

I slide behind the wheel and start the Jeep, messing with the radio. Rush's "Tom Sawyer" plays, and the distraction of one of my favorite songs helps keep my mind from going to places I don't want it to go. Like why I'm living with Richie Rich and Tess in the first place. And worse, the anxiety over the loneliness I'll feel once I do return home.

THIS TIME, WHEN THE ELEVATOR SPITS ME OUT INTO JULES'S office, I'm ready for it. I brace myself, landing the dismount with both feet together. I bow, and I shouldn't be surprised when Angie claps, but I am.

"It's only your third visit, and you've already mastered the Temple of Doom. Nice work," she says.

"Why, thank you." I salute her with a tip of my imaginary hat before glancing around the office. There's no sign of Jules. But Angie is drinking from a Starbucks cup, so I assume she's here.

"You can go ahead into her office. Jules is in the bathroom changing her shirt." She props her feet up on the desk, crossing them at the ankle.

"She took my advice?" I sound more excited about this than I should. I don't wait for a response, and instead open the door of Jules's office.

"Watch out for Cujo in there."

Cujo? I step into the office, and Kobe barks as he scurries toward me. I crouch beside him before he can jump on me and scratch me with his dagger nails.

"Hey, buddy." I pet him on the top of his head. Jules enters the office in a flourish. She's dressed in a fitted black skirt, showing off her killer legs and a peach-colored blouse. I can't help but notice the buttons aren't aligned.

"Hi, Pete." Jules smiles, and it lights up her entire face like a sunbeam after a thunderstorm. My body heats about a thousand degrees. She reaches out to shake my hand, and something like disappointment hits me square in the chest. The gesture feels too professional. I suppose I expected a different greeting after how much fun we had at the baseball game. Maybe a hug? But nah, that's weird. Why would she hug her client?

"Hey, Jules. How was your week?" I take a seat at my usual spot, the end of the sofa closest to the window.

"That's supposed to be my line." She holds out a dog toy and entices Kobe back to his bed with it.

"Okay, fine. My week was...uneventful," I say. "And yours?"

She sits on the yellow chair, frowning. "Uneventful, huh?"

"Oh." I point at her. "I washed my Jeep. First time in nearly nine months."

She bobs her head, as if considering if this is newsworthy. Or, progress-worthy is probably more likely. She's got her iPad on her lap and taps at the screen.

"Richie has been washing it for me. I'm not really sure why. Because up until the last few weeks, I haven't even been driving anywhere."

"Interesting."

"Why? Why is that interesting?"

"Did you ever think that maybe he's been keeping up on washing your Jeep to encourage you to go somewhere? To go do something?"

I shrug. I hadn't actually. "You think he was trying to get rid of me?"

"I didn't say that." She pauses, her hazel eyes focused on me with purpose, like she's trying to peer into my soul. "Do you think he is?"

I consider the question. Do I? Richie said I could stay for however long I needed, and I believed him.

"Nah. Richie loves me. We get along great. The three of us stay in most weekends and watch Netflix. Unless they have plans with their friends. It's nice. It's sort of like old times. Only Richie is there instead of Cora." I don't mention the gaping absence I feel every night without Natalie.

Natalie, who would watch TV sitting with her back pressed into the arm of the sofa and her bare feet tucked underneath my thigh. It didn't matter if it was one hundred degrees outside and the AC was set to seventy-eight, she perpetually had cold feet.

Jules taps away at her screen while I talk. Her expression is tight, closed off, and I feel like I've said something wrong.

She finally glances up. "Anything else?"

I refrain from saying that I feel like the baseball game was a huge step toward me being okay—not great, but okay. A step toward me learning how to live without Natalie. But I'm not convinced it's true. Some days, I still miss her like she's air, and I can't catch my breath.

So I simply shake my head.

Jules remains quiet, reading over what she's added to my file. Part of me wants to take a peek, but a bigger part of me doesn't. I think I'd rather not know how truly broken I am and how far I still need to go before I'm somehow Frankensteined back together.

"What do you have for me next, doc?"

Jules frowns.

She's probably thinking we'd moved past the *doc* title, but I thought we'd moved past the cordial handshake. Clearly, we're not on the same page.

Rather than commenting on the nickname, she ignores it and stands, picking up a notecard from her desk. She hands it to me, and I read it out loud.

Dave Bentley
346 Oceanview Ct.
Pismo Beach, CA 93449

"I don't understand." I glance up at her. "What is this?"

"Dave is a friend of mine. He's moving to Singapore and he needs to sell his home."

Everything falls into place at once. The details on the card, her words, my next challenge; they all click into place like pieces to a puzzle. I toss the note card onto the table and lean back into the sofa, agitation expanding in my chest.

"I'm not ready to return to work."

"If not now, then when?"

"I don't know," I say in between gritted teeth.

"Why not start with this one." Her eyes gesture to the note card. "It's a big house in a fantastic location. No doubt it will sell fast, and you'll make quite the commission on the deal."

"I don't need the money," I say, my words coming out harsh. I don't want to be angry, but I am. What gives her the right to dictate when I'm ready to return to work?

"Okay. That may be true. I apologize for approaching your next challenge with the incorrect angle. Money is definitely not the driving force of your challenges. Enjoyment is. And you used to enjoy your job." She reads from her iPad, "'Matching the perfect home to the perfect person is like playing God or something. Like I'm some sort of a matchmaker.'" She glances up at me.

She throws my own words in my face, something my therapist used to do. It's one of the reasons I stopped seeing him. Jules may not be a therapist, but she's sure acting like one now. What kind of credentials does it take to become an interventionist anyway? It's something I should've thought about and researched before agreeing to this in the first place.

"Will you please at least consider it? I think it would make a huge improvement in your progress."

"Do you honestly think I've made progress? Because I'm not entirely sold here. So I took the robe off for a few hours, I washed my Jeep, I went to a baseball game. So what?" I spit out. "I think we're grasping at straws here." I stand and stalk to the window, gazing out below at the busyness on the street. Cars zoom by, some pull into the parking garage below, people jog on the sidewalk dressed in exercise clothing.

"Despite what you think, your hurt and anger are hindering you from noticing the progress you have made. You and I both know going to that game was bigger than the game itself. It was a huge step in your progress," she says, her voice soft.

I rest on the windowsill and bow my head, exhaling a sigh from deep within my gut. She's right. As much as I don't want to admit it. Going to the Dodger game without Natalie was a huge step. And not only that. Jules and her quirks and infectious personality were enough of a distraction that I hardly even thought about Natalie. If I want to get even a smidge of my old life back, I have to at least try. I owe my girls that much.

I turn around and lean against the window frame. "Pismo Beach, huh?"

Jules nods.

"Gonna have to take Pacific Coast Highway."

"We can take it part of the way, but we don't have to."

I love that strip of the highway. Or, at least I used to. That specific strip of PCH bordering the coastline is beautiful, but it also carries heaps of memories. Some too painful now that Natalie is gone. And some too painful to drive it alone.

"Will you come with me?"

She smiles. "I'd love to."

Chapter 14

Jules

Having Pete ask me to join him in his next challenge had been part of my plan, but I'm relieved he actually wants me to be there. The last thing I wanted to do was invite myself. It's another sign he's making progress.

Pete's typical promptness doesn't disappoint, he knocks on my front door before 9:00 a.m. When I open it, his back is to me. He turns around, and I'm blinded by that big goofy smile of his. Warmth radiates throughout my entire body.

"Good morning," he greets. "Sorry, I'm a few minutes early."

"It's fine." I step aside. "Come on in."

He enters hesitantly, glancing around. "Where's Kobe?"

"He's with the dog sitter. I figured I'd better make arrangements for him since we'll probably be gone most of the day."

"And Angie won't watch him for you?"

I stifle a laugh as I step through the arched doorway and into the kitchen. "I love Kobe too much to do that to him. Angie and Kobe are like bickering siblings who are out for revenge on one another."

Pete chuckles, taking in the space around him. He runs his hand along the wood beam in the entryway while I fill my travel mug with coffee. First rule of surviving a road trip, always bring coffee. I shove a sweater into a bag along with my iPad and a book. Second and third rules, always bring a sweater and something to read.

"You might wanna grab a hat. The top is off the Jeep."

"Right." I hurry down the hall to my bedroom and grab a hair tie and my Dodgers hat off my dresser.

When I rush back out to the front of the house, Pete says, "I've always loved Spanish bungalows. What year was it built?"

"Me too. I think 1940." I hike my bag over my shoulder and grab my coffee. "Hey, did you want coffee?"

"Nah, I already had two cups this morning. Thanks, though." He eyes the bag on my shoulder and arches a dark brown brow. "Whatcha got there?"

"Just some reading material."

"You think my company is gonna be so boring that you need to bring reading material?"

"No, not at all. But you never know when you might find yourself needing something to read."

Angie shuffles into the room, her slippers sliding against the wood floor. Her face muddied with sleepiness, I await the blow; her unhappiness for being woken up early on a Sunday. But her expression changes from tight to amused when she notices Pete.

"What did I do to deserve this treat of seeing you on a weekend, Pete?"

He shoves his hands into the front pockets of his jeans and blushes like a preteen.

"Thanks to Jules, I'm going back to work today," he says with confidence, but then glances at me. "Maybe, I mean. As long as the house and the seller are manageable. As long as it feels like this is something I can do."

It's expected that he would still have doubts about returning to work, but I'm hopeful he'll feel more comfortable once he sees the house.

"If anyone can help you get over first-day jitters, it's Jules." Angie winks at Pete, but it's so exaggerated, anyone within five hundred miles wouldn't miss it. "And I'm not just saying that because she signs my paychecks."

"Okay," I say, opening the front door and shoving Pete out onto the porch. "We should get going." I whip around to Ang and whisper, "What was that?"

She plops a hand to her hip and peeks around me, checking Pete out from head to toe and back up again. "Damn, if you honestly aren't interested, I may have to jump on that." She licks her lips.

"Angie!" I gasp and smack her on the arm. "Stop that. And remember"—I stab a finger in her face—"he's our client so he is off-limits. For both of us."

"Okay, all right, chill." She throws a hand up. "You don't gotta worry about me, but ya might wanna give that same speech to those old-hot-and-bothered lady parts." She points down, and I swear I turn three shades of red in an instant.

I cover my face with my palm. "We're leaving now." I hike my bag over my shoulder but whip back around and whisper, "And my lady parts are not old." I stomp to the passenger side of the Jeep where Pete is holding the door open for me. Angie's laughter doesn't die out until Pete finally shuts the door. If he heard any of that conversation, I'll be humiliated.

I mean, sure, it's been a while since I've put my lady parts to good use, but that doesn't mean they're old. I won't even be forty for a few more months. As I adjust myself in the leather seat of Pete's Jeep, yanking down the hem of my summer dress, I shudder thinking how long it's been since I've been intimate with a man. Maybe Angie is right. Maybe my lady parts are old.

"Everything all right?" Pete glances over at me.

"What? Yes. Everything is great," I say, flustered. "I'm hot," I blurt. "It's hot, I mean. Outside."

Ugh. Angie and her big mouth.

"Do you think it's too hot? Ya know, to have the top off? Because I can run home and—"

"No, it's fine," I interrupt. "It'll be nice." I smile wide.

"Okay. Good. That's exactly what I was thinking." He grins and it sends a humming all the way to my depths. And if that's not a clear sign my lady parts are young and alive, I don't know what is.

When we finally reach the stretch of the highway where it meets the coastline, our conversation becomes easier as the speed limit slows and there's less wind. The sky is as clear as glass today and so majestically blue. The earlier fog has lifted, and we have a distinct view of the coast below. I pinch my eyes shut and inhale a breath of the sea air. It's cool and welcoming. When my eyes flutter open and I glance over at Pete, I catch him watching me. I'm instantly self-conscious and pull at the hem of my dress.

"What?"

"Nothing." He faces the windshield. "You look really relaxed."

"I feel relaxed." Or at least, I did before I caught him staring at me.

"I don't think I've seen you this relaxed. You're usually moving so fast and running into things and spilling coffee." He chuckles.

"I admit, I tend to have a lot going on in my mind. Sometimes my brain moves faster than my body does." I laugh at myself. He's not wrong. I've been called clumsy more than once in my life.

"It's nice," he says. "Ya know, seeing you like this."

His comment, along with his inviting grin, causes my body to buzz. *Easy, girl. It really hasn't been that long.*

Chapter 15

Pete

Music, light conversation, and ocean breeze causes the drive to fly by. Not only has the view been spectacular today since the weather decided to cooperate, but the company hasn't been bad either. The barista who hit on Jules last week was right, she *is* a breath of fresh air. Her personality is infectious. And showing off her killer legs in that dress isn't terrible either.

I'm not sure she's aware of what she's doing to me, but the way she gifts me a flirty smile here and there, I think she does. And I'm not sure where the line is. She's technically not my therapist, and I'm not her patient. And yet, I am her client, and Tess *is* paying her to help me.

Tess.

And there it is. My reminder of how stupid I was to have even allowed my mind to go there. To think there was a chance for something to happen between Jules and me. And besides, it's only been about nine months since I lost Natalie. There's no way I'm ready to move on, am I?

Regardless, here I am, spending the day with this incredible woman who challenges me. Literally. Not only do her challenges make me feel alive and give me joy in the things I once did but being around her also causes me to notice the beating of my heart and to be aware of the breath from my lungs. Things that were too painful only a few weeks ago.

I pull off the highway and turn down Oceanview Court, which leads me to a dead-end.

"This is the place," Jules says.

I park the Jeep in the driveway of the last house, a Spanish Mission-style home.

We climb out, and I inhale, filling my lungs with a savory scent of ocean air while glancing up at the house. It's not as gigantic as some of the homes I've sold in and around LA, but it has character, I can already tell. The decorative railings and red tile roof, along with the details of the carved stonework, set this one apart from the rest. It also features the big selling point unique to Mission-style architecture—the second-floor balcony that spans the front of the house.

We take the stone walk, which is true to the design and matches the driveway. The double front door is arched and reflects the fine craftsmanship of the era with pillars surrounding it. Jules looks in my direction before knocking, and I give her a nod.

I have a good feeling about this one.

Nine months ago, when I pictured returning to work, I'd begun sweating, my breathing had quickened, and my fingers would get fidgety. But as I stand here, staring up at the impressive woodwork of this door, Jules at my side, I feel okay.

The front door swings open, and a man who appears to be in his early forties greets us with smiles and handshakes. Well, I get a handshake, Jules gets a full-on front-body hug. There's even a slight lift to the hug. The kind where the feet are lifted off the ground a little. I find myself offended. How does this guy know Jules and I aren't together?

I clear my throat. The guy releases Jules and pushes his longish dark-blond hair away from his face in one of those one-handed douchey gestures.

While Jules readjusts her dress, pink staining her cheeks, she finally says, "Pete Redd, this is Dave Bentley. Dave, Pete."

I give Dave the courteous chin nod followed by, "Nice to meet you." I throw in a "Your house is magnificent," for good measure, as well as to remind us all why we're here to begin with.

Dave rests both hands on his trim hips, causing his navy-blue sport jacket to flap backward as if on command. This guy must be an actor because he's got that move down. I've sold houses for actors before, and they weren't all terrible to work with. Most were cooler than you'd imagine. Jules never mentioned what Dave does for a living, but all signs point to actor.

"Thanks, man, it's a real shame I gotta sell. But my girlfriend accepted a job offer in Singapore, and I can't imagine being that far apart from her. Sorry, where are my manners? C'mon in." He waves us inside, and I gesture for Jules to go first. I shut the heavy giganta-souraus door behind us. "I'll show you around the house and then Jules here tells me you need to feel a good vibe or good omen or something before you'll take it on. And hey—" He holds out his palms. "I get that, totally feel you, bro."

Bro? But out loud I say, "Sounds good, thanks."

Jules smiles. She appears less nervous than when we first arrived, but she's still fidgeting with the globe pendant hanging on the chain around her neck.

"You two want something to drink? Sparkling water, wine, beer?"

I try to hold in my eye roll at his offer of sparkling water. "Plain water is fine, thanks."

We follow him through the open entryway, and down a hall until we reach a large kitchen. He already has his head shoved inside the fancy commercial stainless steel refrigerator and calls out a muffled, "Bottled water?"

"Yeah, sure, that'd be great."

He pops his head out and hands me a bottle. "Jules?" His light eyebrows raise in question.

"I'm good with water, too."

"I think I've got a bottle of that wine you like." He smirks before his head dives back inside the fridge. So he doesn't notice the pink staining Jules's cheeks again and the dip to her chin toward her chest.

"No, no, don't be silly. That would be a waste for just me."

"Oh, c'mon, you know I wouldn't mind. Besides, I bet you can polish off this entire bottle yourself. In fact, I think I've seen that first-hand." There's teasing in his voice, and it seems to affect her, as evidenced by her body language.

"Dave, we're working here."

He finally emerges from the fridge and twists the cap off a bottle of sparkling water before handing it to her, along with a wink.

"Thanks." She accepts the bottle grinning from ear to ear.

I twist the cap off my water and take a long swig, allowing the cool—sans bubbly—liquid to relieve my hot throat. "Remind me again how you two know each other." I gesture at the two of them with my bottle.

They share eye contact while they both drink.

Jules swallows before saying, "Dave was my client. Years ago. I'm pretty sure I told you that."

"No, I don't think you did."

"Jules was the best teacher," Dave says, winking at her yet again, with eyes the color of mud.

Does this guy have something in his eye? Every time I look at him, he's winking at her. Or do they share that much history? My stomach muscles clench, and I use the water bottle to cool my hands that have suddenly begun to overheat. I recognize these emotions. It's just that I haven't felt jealousy in a long time.

"Teacher?" I hear myself say out loud before I can stop. "Is that what we're supposed to call her?"

"No, don't be silly." Jules waves a hand at me.

Dave shrugs. "That's what I liked to call her. She taught me a thing or two." A wink again. "But I also called her my friend. And let me tell you, I'm damn lucky to call her that."

"See," Jules says, "a friend. That's what I told you to call me."

"And what did Jules teach you? Or do for you? What kind of trauma were you trying to overcome? If you don't mind me asking?"

"I don't, not at all. When I first met Jules, I was a wreck. My wife wanted a divorce and left me for someone else. I was devastated. After ten years of marriage, we had built a life together. I knew how she took her coffee. We owned three homes together. We put up with each other's in-laws, ya know?"

I do know. Though, I had him beat by over a decade. I can't imagine if Natalie had wanted a divorce. Maybe separation by death is easier. Because at least then, neither of you made the choice to leave the other. But the ache I feel as a result of the gaping hole in my heart tells me otherwise. Separation by death isn't easier.

"Anyway, Jules helped my sister's friend who was going through a similar thing and she thought Jules could help me too. And she did." He smiles at Jules. There's no wink this time, thank goodness. "At first, I sort of felt like a wuss. But Jules helped me realize I didn't need to feel bad for loving my wife so much that I mourned her. I mourned the loss of our marriage and my failures. And she made me realize my worth. That it wasn't entirely my fault my wife left me."

"And good thing," Jules says, spinning slowly in a circle. "Otherwise you wouldn't have been brave enough to move on, to sell this house, and move to Singapore."

"Or help you with your client's challenge."

Jules and I both look at Dave.

"C'mon, Jules. It wasn't that hard to figure out. I haven't heard from you for over a year. When you called and asked for a favor for one of your clients, how could I say no. Especially after the way I treated you."

At his words, I didn't mistake the earlier tension. Maybe what I assumed was sexual tension was the opposite. I give Jules a sideways glance, and she's fidgeting with her necklace again.

"And I'm glad to help. Getting through therapy isn't easy."

"Thank you, Dave. We appreciate that," Jules interjects.

"Besides, I heard you're some kind of a miracle worker," Dave says to me.

"Matchmaker for houses and buyers," Jules corrects.

I rub at the back of my neck. "Oh, I don't know about that."

"So, what do you say? Feel like working your matchmaking skills with my home?"

I take in the space around me. From this spot in the kitchen, there's a full view of the arched opening into the dining nook, about half of the living room with more archways, and a glimpse into the backyard which reveals a wood deck, a pool, and a hot tub. These Spanish Mission-style homes are hard to come by these days. It's something I can sell fast.

Dave's phone rings, and he yanks it from the front pocket of his sport jacket. "I gotta take this."

"Let me check out the rest of the house, but I'm thinking this is something I'd be interested in taking on."

"Well, all right." He grins. "Be my guest." He waves me on as he speaks into his phone, "Go for Dave."

Jules and I give ourselves a tour of the home, awkward silence stretching between us. Each room is as great as the kitchen—rounded archway after rounded archway, each one complementing the other. If this had been a year ago, I would've taken it on in a heartbeat. But I'm feeling rusty. I haven't gone this long without selling a house since my early years when I first started.

I really only got into real estate because of Daniel. He told me the market was insane, and I'd make a killing. Daniel and I met growing up in Seattle. He moved to LA right after Natalie and I got married and relentlessly tried to get us to follow him. He said the market moved much faster in LA, and with only one sale every few months, you could be set financially for a year.

But Natalie wasn't keen on the idea of moving to LA. Our families were still in Seattle and we had a small child. Natalie was still going through chemo after her first diagnosis of breast cancer. She was too sick to work, and as a college dropout myself installing cable, the medical bills were killing us.

After she went into remission, my promise of sunny skies to lift her mood, and with me acquiring a real estate license, Natalie agreed to the move. Who would've guessed the sunny skies were the worst thing for her mood? She hated that every day was sunny. She missed the gloomy, misty days of Seattle. But I took to my job quickly and found not only was Daniel right regarding the market, I also really enjoyed it. And I was good at it too.

Dave is still on his call when we finish the tour, so Jules and I take the bottle of wine he previously offered, along with two glasses, and head outside. Jules walks to the edge of the yard and leans over the black wrought iron railing that overlooks the bay.

I open the bottle of wine and fill the two glasses, glancing up every few seconds to watch Jules. The sun is beginning to set. It's at that perfect place where it rests above the shimmering water and hangs barely below the clouds, teasing and creating a marigold sky. The air is still warm on the skin, but there's a cool breeze blowing through Jules's hair, lifting her floral dress at its hem. It's a stunning sight, and I take my time reaching her with the wine.

"Technically, we're still working," I say, nudging her arm with the glass. She accepts with a smile and tucks her wild strawberry blonde hair behind her ear.

"So you've decided to take it on?"

"Sure, why not? Gotta start somewhere, right?" I shrug.

"I'm so glad to hear that, Pete."

I glance over my shoulder. "If Dave would come out here, we could toast or something."

"Or we could toast without him." She holds her glass out to me, her face shining with possibilities.

She's giving me all the signs, but I've been out of the game so long I'm not sure I'm reading them correctly. I grin and clink my glass to hers.

We both take a sip of the wine. It tastes expensive. Most likely, it is. I'd prefer a beer, but I can't help but feel a little satisfaction at drinking Dave's high-priced wine.

Jules's big hazel eyes peer over the brim of the glass, staring directly at me. I'm not sure if she's meaning to give me the look she's giving me, but it causes my hormones to stand at attention. Suddenly, they're not only awake, but hyperaware. They're fighting with my brain, which is tries to slam the brakes on these feelings—feelings I shouldn't be having.

Jules clears her throat, pulling me away from my trance. "This is some view, huh?"

I tear my gaze away from her before I do something we'll probably both regret. "It is. Dave is a lucky guy."

She elbows me playfully. "No, you're the lucky guy. You get to sell this place. Which means you'll get to highlight all the good points. And now that you've been here, you know firsthand."

"That's true." I don't tell her the best aspect of this house is her. Instead, I choose to tell her something I've never told anyone. Not my girls and not even Daniel. "It's similar to the style of home I've always wanted to buy."

She turns to face me. "Really? But don't you live in a ranch-style home?"

"I do. I loved the home because Natalie loved it." It feels natural to talk about Natalie with Jules, even here, outside the office. "But it wasn't my first choice. My friend, Daniel, showed us some Spanish-style homes that I loved but Natalie didn't and several ranch-style homes that she, of course, loved." I shrug. "We compromised. Happy wife, happy life and all that jazz."

"That doesn't sound like a compromise."

"My wife was so sick and weak after her chemo treatments she couldn't even carry or pick up Tess. I guess when you see someone you love at their weakest, and then they're given a second chance at life, you'll do anything for them."

"Even if it means sacrificing what you want?"

I nod. "Even then."

We're quiet for a while. I worry the mention of my wife, the cancer, and my obvious love for her has ruined what was a nice moment.

But then she says, "It's inspiring to see you accepting this challenge with open arms. I'm really proud of you."

"Well, I don't know about 'with open arms.' I definitely had my reservations. I still do. But I feel ready. It's time to get back to work. And I have you to thank." I tip my glass in her direction.

"You were ready, you just needed a little push."

"Maybe."

We watch silently as the sun slips into the water and the sky changes from a warm glowing orange to violet and then indigo. Nearly instantly, the air cools, and I catch Jules shiver next to me. I shrug out of my sport jacket and cover her lightly freckled shoulders with it. She tugs it on further and smiles.

"Thanks."

It looks better on her anyway. I didn't realize how douchey I looked in it until I saw Dave in his.

"So, Dave?" I say it as a question because that's exactly how I intend it. And from the head-to-shoulder tilt along with a smirk, she reads the intention.

"Yeah," she mutters, "what do you wanna know?"

"You two were a thing?"

She nods, her attention back on the water now. "For a short time. We ended things about two years ago."

It's more obvious to me now why she reacted the way she did to his words, his winks. She may be over him, but clearly, he did a number on her.

"I gotta admit. I'm a little surprised."

She turns to face me, an elbow leaning on top of the iron fence, her wine glass balancing on her hand. "Why's that?"

I shrug, hunching both shoulders nearly to my ears while I think of how to answer that. "It's that, you're so..." My words fall off. *Attractive, sweet, endearing.* "And he's so—"

"Cocky? Self-absorbed? Conceited?"

"I was gonna say douchey. But those work too."

She giggles. The sound vibrates in my chest and works itself all the way down to my toes.

"He's not, entirely. He just doesn't make a very good first impression is all."

"If you say so."

"Okay, maybe he's a tiny bit douchey." She laughs again.

"So, what happened?"

"Let's say, we wanted different things."

"Different how? Different priorities? Different futures?" I'm prying. But anyone who would willingly hurt this woman has to have a valid reason. And I don't see what his could have been.

"Both," she says matter-of-factly.

"Okay, then let me ask, what do you want?" She's looking at me with those big shimmering hazel eyes. I clear my throat. "In your future, I mean?"

"I don't know exactly."

"I call bull."

Her light brows raise. "Excuse me?" There's pain reflected in her voice.

"You're almost forty, don't tell me you don't know what you want."

She narrows her eyes at me and then exhales dramatically. "Okay, fine. I want to keep helping people. I want to expand my interventionist business. I'd like it if my mom would make an effort to maintain a relationship with me. I'd really love to attend another Laker game with my dad. I want Angie and Kobe to get along." She lets out a mock laugh. "I'd like to, one day, settle down with someone who loves me for me. All quirks included. Someone who isn't gonna leave me as soon as things get tough. A partner who will stick it out and figure things out with me, not run the second it gets too hard. Like my mom did when my dad was diagnosed with dementia." She stops talking, sucks in a breath and gives me a sheepish smile. "I guess you were right. I have had time to think about this."

"Told ya." I smirk.

She blushes and tucks her hair behind her ear.

"You wanna talk about it? Your mom? Your dad?"

"Not really. Not yet."

I nod.

"I'm probably hoping for too much. You know, out of life."

"I don't think so." She stares into my eyes again, her body moving closer to mine, and I can't help but be drawn toward her like she's a magnet. "There's nothing wrong with knowing what you want and fighting for it. It's a rare quality these days." Not to mention sexy as hell.

"But I don't want to get my hopes up."

"Why not?"

"Because I hate to be disappointed."

Without thinking, I reach out and tuck the same unruly strand of hair behind her ear, and she bites her lower lip. It causes the air to thicken around me and my body to ignite. "How do you know you'll be disappointed?" My voice sounds haughty.

"Life experience, I guess."

The magnetic pull draws me closer, and I lean in. She's closing in toward me too. My heartbeat quickens, and my palms sweat. I'm like a schoolboy again, everything feels exciting and new. I squeeze my eyes shut and take my chances. My lips brush against hers in a whisper, and tiny white spots burst behind my eyelids as my craving for her surges. I have an intense urge to push her against the fence and see where this single kiss will take us.

Dave's voice sounds out in the distance, interrupting any further intimacy. "I see you two are already celebrating without me."

We pull apart as if lightning struck between us. Jules even pushes me in the chest slightly with her palm. And I'm not gonna lie, it stings.

Dave approaches, crossing the grass, and I notice he has three wine glasses in one hand and a bottle of wine in the other.

"What? No, of course not," she stutters and tosses her glass of wine up and over her shoulder.

The sound of the glass shattering on the rocks behind the fence causes me to jump, even though I'm expecting it.

"I could go for some wine to celebrate," Jules says, then looks pointedly at me.

"Oh, yeah, me too." I hide the glass behind my back.

But poor Dave has arrived and stands there trying to figure out what he's missed. And honestly, so am I. Did I really kiss Jules? And did she toss her glass over the fence to act like we hadn't started celebrating without him?

Chapter 16

Tess

It's been nearly a week since I sent Cora a text asking her to call me back. It's a longshot to get her on the phone for a real conversation since she prefers texting. So when my phone rings as I'm applying makeup in preparation for a date night with Richie, it takes me by surprise.

"Okay, okay, what's so important that you couldn't tell me by text?" Cora complains.

"I asked you to call me five days ago. I told you it was urgent. When you text me 911, I call you back within seconds." I brush a smoky gray eyeshadow across my eyelids.

"Well, I guess you should've texted 911 then."

I can hear the snark in her tone. "Are you drunk?"

"What? No. Lay off, Tess. You're not my mother."

Her words sting, and it takes me a few seconds to recover, the makeup brush frozen midair in my hand. "So listen, the urgency is about the store. Remember how I gave you permission to sign off on orders?"

"Yeah?" she drags out the word.

"Well, the shipment that arrived is wrong. We received six boxes of white keyhole blouses rather than one box of each color."

"Oh man, seriously? That sucks."

"Right. It does suck. Because what am I gonna do with six boxes of white blouses? In the fall, mind you? You know the saying, no white after Labor Day?"

"That's an old rule, silly. No one actually follows it," Cora teases.

I push away from the bathroom counter, unable to look at myself in the mirror any longer as my cheeks grow hotter with frustration. "Well, you'd better hope that's true. Because do you know whose signature is in the approval box? It's yours, Cora. How did you approve six boxes of the same color blouse? What were you thinking?"

There's silence on the other end of the phone at first. Followed by an elongated sigh. "I'm sorry."

"What happened?"

"I don't know. I remember being at the shop, and you asked me to review the order. You were busy arguing with the contractor about something. I got a text from this guy I've been talking to. I don't know, I guess I got distracted."

"You got distracted? Cora, Mom wanted you included in the business and that comes with a responsibility. I trusted you."

"Yeah? Well, maybe you shouldn't have. And maybe I shouldn't be included in the business."

"Don't say that."

"The clothing stuff, the designs, the shop, that was never my thing. That was yours and Mom's. Listen, I'll try to help out with the mix-up. Whatever you need me to do, but then that's it. I'm done."

Tears prick my eyes, and I stop them from fully forming. "You don't mean that." My words choke out. "You're just upset, and I'm sorry. We're both upset."

"No, I do mean it. And I'm not upset. I actually feel good about this decision."

"Why don't we talk about this when you come home?"

"Home?" There's a muffled bitter laugh on the phone. "Fine. We can talk about it next time I'm *home*. But it will be a while. I got accepted for the newsroom internship position."

I'm speechless. My emotions jump hurdles in my mind over any intelligent word choices.

"I gotta go."

She disconnects the call, and I press my back against the bathroom wall, sliding down to the floor. Bringing my knees to my chest, I drop my head and allow the tears to come. They flow easily and vibrate in my chest. My body convulses with each new wave of a sob. I cry for Dad and his loneliness. I cry for myself and all I've lost. I cry for Cora and all she's lost. But mostly, I cry for the unfairness of it all. That two young women have to navigate the rest of their lives without the direction and nurture of a mother.

Will the same horrendous disease that took our mother take us as well?

Somehow, I manage to pick myself up off the floor and make myself presentable for my date night with Richie. I step into a bandage fringe dress in a steely gray color. It's one of my original designs that Mom never approved of. She thought it was too different from the bohemian-chic style of Natalie's. This particular dress will be on sale with the late fall line—the first one to not include any of Mom's designs. The dress features wide straps, a V-neckline, and hugs my curves. It has a good foot of fringe at the hem. It's fun and flirty. The exact mood I'm going for tonight.

Richie and I haven't had a romantic dinner out with only the two of us in so long. I can't even remember when the last time was. Either Dad tags along as the third wheel, or Richie invites Dexter and Carter. I don't typically mind. I love Cheyenne and Alissa. But I'm grateful it's only the two of us tonight.

We go to Mercury's off Sunset Blvd. Richie claims they have the best steak. They could have the worst steak and I wouldn't care. My only goal for tonight is that he's in a good mood. When I break the news to him that I've gone off birth control, I need him to be putty in my hands.

Richie orders a steak with a side of steamed seasonal vegetables because he's decided to go off carbs. I'm not that disciplined so I order a baked potato and bread with my steak. My nerves bounce around, and I attempt to listen while Richie explains how his business trip to the Texas office went last weekend. His dad opened the branch over ten years ago when Richie's parents decided to retire there. It's where Richie's grandparents live so it made sense. But having him travel back and forth does get old. I'm only now considering how this could affect us once we have a baby.

But regardless, I've decided, no more waiting. We can't continue making excuses and putting our lives on hold while Dad heals and gets back some of his own life. Although, since he's been seeing Jules weekly and performing the challenges, he's made huge improvements. Okay, maybe not huge, but improvements at least.

"More wine?" I ask Richie, holding up the bottle.

Richie raises one thick, black brow at me, a smoldering expression across his face. "If I didn't know better, I'd think you were trying to get me drunk."

My face flushes, feeling both caught and guilty. "Don't be silly. But we are taking an Uber home...so if you want to?" I say, hoping my tone doesn't sound desperate.

He smiles and tilts his glass, allowing me to fill it. "You know I don't usually drink much. I could've driven us."

"I know, but I wanted you to relax. I wanted both of us to relax. And not having to worry about who's gonna drive helps."

"You're right. This is nice." He swirls his wine before taking a sip. "And you look amazing. Did I forget to tell you that?"

"Thank you. This is a dress from the late-fall line. One of my own designs."

"It's like you designed it solely for that rocking body of yours." His blue eyes darken, and my body scorches like fire under his pressing gaze.

I set my hand on his leg and run it up his thigh, teasing. He leans in close and his finger grazes my cheek before he kisses me. His lips press gently, but I recognize the want. He pulls away and kisses me on the forehead.

"Ready for the check?" I whisper.

"I've been ready." He makes eye contact with our waitress across the room and holds up a finger. "After the first glimpse of you in that dress, I wanted to skip dinner and head straight to dessert."

I feel my cheeks blush. After three years of marriage, we're still like newlyweds, and his compliments turn me into a gooey, hot mess. I continue to tease him with my hand on his thigh, caressing it just close enough to inappropriate public touching. He's usually very anti-PDA so I assume the alcohol is already working its magic.

This feels like a good time to discuss my wanting to start a family, but I need to ease into that conversation gingerly. Maybe I'll have to wait until we're back home, and I've got him hanging on the edge of pleasure.

"You're gonna have to stop doing that if you ever wanna get out of here."

"What?" I blink, confusion swimming in my mind.

His eyes gesture under the table at my hand on his leg. "I have to be able to walk out of this place." He chuckles.

I retract my hand and giggle. Richie pays the bill, and we both down what's left in our wine glasses. He covers my bare shoulders with his sport jacket, and we rush out of the restaurant like horny high school kids, our desire for one another consuming us.

We step onto the sidewalk into the inky night and wait on the curb for our Uber, unable to keep our hands off each other. Apparently, something about being outside in the darkened night is enough for Richie to no longer feel like he's in public. Despite the people who brush behind us on the sidewalk and the other couples waiting alongside us for the valet to deliver their cars, he doesn't let up on his grip around me.

Richie spreads hot wet kisses down my neck that cause me to

giggle. He runs a hand up my side before palming my breast, and I inhale a sharp breath.

Our Uber arrives just in time. Otherwise, we may have given our audience an R-rated show right here on the curb free of charge. Inside the car, Richie is determined to keep our make-out session going. He kisses me with so much desire his tongue feels like it's at war with my own, and I'm not sure who is winning.

My mind is distracted by the pressing conversation I need to have with him, the worry of Dad already home waiting for us, and the concern Richie may try to finish us both off in this Uber before we even make it home. His hand slides under my dress and tugs on my underwear. I gasp and force my brain to focus. I give him a slight push in the chest and move his hand.

He pulls back, and his blue eyes search mine while we both pant, and the quick beating of my heart pounds in my ears.

"What's wrong?" he says, breathily.

"Nothing." I give him a gentle, reassuring kiss on his lips. "But I'd rather wait until we're home."

He sighs and sits back, retracting his hands from me. "Yeah, I know."

There's an instant wedge separating us, and I shudder at the ice-cold breeze that flows between us after he breaks away from me. I'm suddenly aware of the stranger driving us, and my cheeks flush with embarrassment.

"We can open a bottle of wine, put on some music," I hedge.

He looks at me passively and pats my knee. "It's a nice thought."

"What's that supposed to mean?"

"You and I both know *he'll* be there when we get home. He'll be bored, expect company. You'll feel bad, end up giving in, and we'll watch a movie with him. You'll fall asleep on the couch, and when I wake you up to go to bed, you'll have a headache from the wine, and we'll cuddle until we're both asleep again."

I can't help but stare at him, incredulous. And yet, he's not wrong. That's exactly what will happen. Because it's a pattern we've been repeating for several months.

"Don't get me wrong," he says, less irritation in his voice now. "I love falling asleep with you in my arms. But sometimes, it would be nice if we could return to an empty house after a date." He leans into me and lowers his voice. "I don't wanna be restricted to our bedroom when we have an entire house. I miss our kitchen sex, and a movie ending with sex on the sofa, and making love on your desk in the office."

It's been a while since he's voiced this to me. And I've missed it all too. "Me too," I whisper.

He runs his hand through his black hair. "I know his sessions with the interventionist have helped. Believe me, I've noticed. But he's still home. A lot. And I feel bad complaining, I mean, he's your dad."

The Uber driver decides now is a good time to let us know he's been paying close attention. "Bummer, dude. This one has daddy issues, huh?" He hikes a thumb over his shoulder in my direction.

"Excuse me?" I say.

Richie pats my knee. "No offense, buddy, but this really isn't any of your business."

"I beg to differ. You can't go home and get freaky because daddy's home. So you wanted to do it in my car."

Richie stiffens next to me and clears his throat. "I can assure you, nothing was going to happen, sir."

"Sir?" The driver waves a dismissive hand. He points to his name on the dash. "Call me Jeff. And the trick is you gotta get her dad out of the house. Have his buddies take him out."

At first, I'm embarrassed and offended. But the more "advice" this guy gives, the more it gets my wheels turning.

"Richie, we could go to Dad's house."

"What?"

"Dad's house. It's empty. And I have the code to the lockbox for the key." I allow a sexy smile to play on my lips as I return my hand to his lap once again, not even caring the Uber driver is getting a free show.

Richie shifts in his seat. "Hey, Jeff. Change of plans. I've got a new address for drop-off."

When we arrive, we race out of the backseat and hurry up the front steps of Dad's ranch-style home. The house is lit up, signaling it's after 10:00 p.m. because the lights are on an automatic timer. Richie stands behind me, pressing a trail of kisses down the back of my neck as his confident hands run over my hips while I punch in the code on the lockbox.

"We're in business." I hold the key in the air triumphantly.

Inside, everything looks the same as usual. I was here last week watering Mom's indoor plants. It was harder to come the first few weeks after Mom passed away. Sometimes, I'd wait until Cora was visiting for a weekend so I wouldn't have to come alone. But now, when I return, I feel a sense of peace. I wish Dad would feel the same kind of peace. I also wish I would have thought about sneaking in here with Richie before now.

I toss my purse onto a chair in the living room. Everything looks untouched. I don't allow my eyes to linger on all the familiarities—namely, the family photos. I don't allow the memories to take hold of me.

"Isn't this perfect?" I ask.

He presses a finger to his lips. "Shh. Do you hear that?"

My throat constricts and my body stills. I shake my head.

"Yeah, me neither. Ahh...it's quiet. And best of all, we're alone." He wraps me up in his strong arms, lifting me off the ground, and giving me a little spin while kissing me.

"I told you it's perfect."

He returns me to my feet and shoves his jacket off my shoulders, pressing his lips to each one before taking the jacket all the way off.

"I'm gonna open a bottle of wine," I say.

"Perfection." He tosses his jacket onto the floor.

Richie steps out of his shoes. "I'm gonna put on some music."

"Music, yes." I remove two glasses from the wine rack where they hang. "Oh, I have an idea."

He turns to face me, eyebrows playful.

"Hot tub."

"Hot tub?"

I search through the wine selection and talk over my shoulder. "Turn on the speakers outdoors so we can hear the music."

"What about suits? Because I really don't want to put my junk in anything where your dad's junk has been."

I snort a laugh and in my sexiest voice say, "Who said anything about suits?"

His dark brows shoot up and his eyes widen. "Yeah?" But he doesn't wait for me to respond, he's already heading toward the house's sound system on the wall by the back door.

With the wine bottle in one hand and the full glasses in the other, I step outside. Richie is already in the hot tub, the water up to his shoulders. "Until I Fall Away" by the Gin Blossoms, plays through the outdoor speakers.

I hand him a glass of wine and set the remaining glass along with the bottle on the table next to the hot tub. I remove two towels from the cabinet hanging on the wall. The air outside is cool, and as I step out of my dress, I shiver.

With Richie's hooded gaze fixed on my body, goosebumps travel down my arms. The air may be cold, but my body is hot as I take my time, reaching behind my back to unclasp my bra before dropping it to the ground. I step out of my underwear and kick them into the pile of clothes on the concrete patio.

"Get in here," Richie says, a growl in his tone.

I step into the hot tub, and the scorching water singes my chilled feet. Richie reaches for my hand and pulls me into him, pressing his slick chest against mine. The intensity of it all, the excitement of being alone, and the slight buzz from the wine cause my craving for him to deepen.

My earlier idea of dropping the bomb that I went off the pill gets pushed to the back of my mind; the topic no longer a priority. We almost lost the chance of being intimate already this evening. I can't risk it again.

Richie kisses me long and hard before pulling back and murmuring, "God, I love you." His words create a humming in my depths, the desire for him even stronger. He moves his hand to caress the back of my neck. "And I've missed you. I've missed this. So much."

"Me too." I feel like an apology is needed so I say, "I'm sorry. You know, about my dad."

He sets his finger to my lips. "Don't apologize. I know you're trying. And I'm trying to be patient." He brushes a few light kisses to my lips before pulling me into his lap.

I'm acutely aware of how much he wants me and, at the same time, realize how difficult it has been for him to be patient. I lean my head back, pressing it against his damp chest. "You've been amazing."

"Well, you're pretty amazing yourself."

He takes a long swill of his wine, so I pick up my glass and do the same. I'm ready to chuck the glass into the yard and take advantage of him, but I sense he's not quite ready, he clearly has things on his mind.

"I can't believe you would question my loyalty and the plans we made together. None of that has changed." With his arm wrapped around my body, he pulls my back closer against his chest, and relief fills me. We do still want the same thing. "I cannot wait to start a family with you."

"Yeah?" I bite my lower lip.

"Absolutely." He places his glass on the table before reaching for mine and setting it there as well. Richie flips me around and I straddle him. He pulls me so close to him, water can't even fit in between us. "Soon," he whispers.

But my heartbeat is pounding in my ears, I can barely hear him. He may as well have said, *now*. I push everything that's cluttering my mind toward the back of my brain and thrust my hips into him.

Chapter 17

Jules

As we begin the drive back to LA, it's silent and awkward. Not only is the memory of the kiss Pete and I shared fresh on my lips, but my entire relationship with Dave works its way through my mind as well. It's been over two years since I've seen him. I've long since forgiven him for treating me so poorly, but I had no idea what kind of reaction it would have on my emotional state.

Dave was not simply a random guy I dated. He was The Guy. He was supposed to be *The One*. But instead, he became the one who broke me. The one who couldn't get over the fact that I wouldn't kick Dad to the curb.

After Dave and I split, I promised myself I wouldn't date another client or former client. I quit practicing as a therapist and began the interventionist business. I swore to strictly platonically help people.

This last thought causes the kiss to circle back to my mind. Despite the intensity creating a craving in my depths and a desire in my soul, it should not have happened. I never should have allowed it. In fact, I should've called Tess after my very first meeting with Pete and told her I was unable to help her dad. From the moment I met him, I'd been attracted to him. And I'm not referring to the first day in my office when Angie's mishap with the cabinet drawer caused me to grope him.

I remember our very first encounter. At the cemetery several months before. He had this adorkable quality to him. It was obvious he was hurting, but he had this dark sense of humor shining through.

Damn men who are both attractive and funny.

After the baseball game, once again, I should've told Tess I was unable to help her dad. That was the day I knew for sure it was more than a simple attraction. I care for him deeply, more than I should care about a client.

After what we shared tonight, I'm fairly certain he's wrestling with similar feelings. I wasn't supposed to fall for him. And he definitely wasn't supposed to fall for me. But I've seen this before, the codependent client who depends on me.

In a way, that's what happened with Dave. Although, by the time we started dating, he wasn't my client anymore. When we ended our relationship, Dave said it was because I wouldn't choose him over Dad. But later, he discovered he'd only felt drawn to me because I'd helped him overcome his trauma. And ultimately, it's what caused me to become an interventionist and what inspired the idea of the Challenge Program.

"Hey," Pete says, finally breaking our unspoken vow of silence. "I think we need to talk."

It feels as if vines travel up my body, wrapping around and squeezing me. "I think you're right," I say tightly.

"Should we go somewhere we can talk alone?"

"Sure," I say, probably too enthusiastically. While my brain screams, *No!* at the chance to be alone with Pete, my body says, *It's about damn time.*

"What about your house?" he suggests.

And I realize a moment too late he means alone, alone. As in, not alone in public. "Angie will be there."

"Then that's definitely out."

I hold in my giggle. "What about your place?"

"Nah, Tess and Richie are there." Disappointment takes over his expression.

"No, I mean, *your* house."

He glances at me before focusing on the road again. "Oh, right. I don't know why I hadn't thought of that."

"Has it been a while since you've been there?" I can't help it, my skills and need to help kick in.

"About a month."

"If you don't feel comfortable going there, we can go somewhere else."

"No, it's fine." He glances at me and gives me a closed mouthed smile. "I need to start going there more often. You know, so I can eventually move back home."

I don't argue, but simply purse my lips and fidget with my globe pendant.

For the rest of the drive, we make small talk, mostly about Dave's house. It's good I don't have to focus much on the conversation because the blood is hot in my ears. I tell my mind, along with my lady parts, to calm down; nothing is going to happen between Pete and me. Because nothing *can* happen.

Besides feeling unethical, I get the impression Pete's not ready to move on. I think he wants to be, but he's not. Requesting we go somewhere to talk is probably so we can sort out the kiss and set boundaries from here on out. I prepare myself for this specific conversation.

We walk up the squared concrete pathway as bright lights shine inside the ranch-style home, welcoming us. Pete unlocks the front door and pulls me inside. He takes me by surprise when he pushes me up against the closed door, a hand grasping the back of my neck, and kisses me. My lady parts ignite, winning out over my brain, and I reciprocate the kiss, deepening it, and tangle my tongue with his.

He pulls back, breathing hard. "I'm sorry. I should've asked before doing that." He shoves a hand through his hair. "It's just...I wanted to finish that kiss right."

"You mean the kiss we shared earlier wasn't finished?" I chew on my bottom lip.

He gives a sexy shake of his head. "Not even close."

"And so now it's finished?" I tease, my body on fire.

"If I'm wrong, say the word." He doesn't release the pressure of his hips from forcing my back against the hardwood door. "But I think we're just getting started."

My face flushes because he's no idiot, he's reading my body language like a pro. And my body might as well be sending off flares, signaling its need for him. My hands go to the nape of his neck, and I lower his head to me, pressing my lips to his jaw. His mouth doesn't hesitate, he ravishes my own with a craving I've never felt so intensely before. I'd be stupid to question his motives, his readiness, but I do anyway. I have to. I'm unable to turn off the therapist part of my brain. I release his neck, and nudge him back.

"Pete," I whisper. "Are you sure you're ready? Are you sure this is what you want?"

Pete steps away from me, and my body heaves at the release from the pressure. He runs his hand over his lips, my own feeling swollen.

"Jules," he pants, "are you asking as a friend? Or as a professional? Or as a potential partner?"

I'm not sure how to answer. Part of me wishes I hadn't ended the kiss and opened my big mouth. But knowing him and his brokenness from losing Natalie, I'm unable to switch that off. No matter how much my entire body is on fire and craving him in this moment.

"Because the way I see it, you're here. At my house, with me, after hours. This isn't a Friday session or a challenge. You should only be here right now because you want to be. We don't have to discuss the details past that. So, do you want to be here?"

I don't hesitate, I answer with a nod of my head.

"Good. Because, man, would I feel like such a prick." He runs a palm down his face. "Here I invite you over to talk, and the second you're in my house, I put my hands all over you."

And mouth, I want to add, but don't. Instead, I try to ease his worries. "Pete, I'm here because I want to be."

Relief is evident on his face and the grin that notoriously weakens my knees forms on his lips. He rests a palm to his chest, exhaling. "Okay, let's get back to the original task. Let's talk." He takes me by the hand and leads me down a hall, passing arched doorways and into a large open kitchen. He kicks off his shoes on the way, so I follow his lead and take mine off. One shoe sort of sticks so I add in extra force, and it kicks further than I anticipated, landing in a different room than its match entirely.

Pete doesn't notice. "How about more wine?"

He's not a big wine drinker, that had been his wife's thing, so to help distract him from thinking of her, I ask, "How about a beer?"

"Now that's what I'm talking about." He opens the fridge, scanning the contents as if he's a stranger to it. "We're in luck." He pulls out a six-pack of some foreign brand I recognize. "I brought it with me a few months ago when I came to check on the house. Thought it would help me process the emotions easier. But Cora was in town, and instead of wallowing in my sorrows, the girls took me out to a club where one of my favorite bands—Ween—was playing."

"That was sweet of them." I shrug out of Pete's jacket and hang it over a stool pushed up to the large kitchen island.

"Yeah, they're all right." He winks, popping open two bottles of beer.

"If you don't mind me asking, how'd the internship conversation with Cora go?"

He pauses for a moment, studying one of the bottles in his hand before glancing back at me. "Good. She's promised to come home some weekends." He smiles and offers me a beer. I accept and decide to drop the subject. He clinks his bottle into mine. "Cheers."

"Cheers."

He stares at me, watching intently while he chugs his beer. I try to be sexy and enticing and bring the bottle to my lips slowly. It clinks against my top front teeth, and he cringes at the same time I do. I tear my gaze away from him and take a drink. But he's stopped watching me entirely. Instead, a jacket crumpled on the floor catches his attention. He walks over to it and picks it up off the floor, and now I'm focused on it as well.

"Hmm," Pete says. "Daniel must've forgotten this when he was here checking on the house." Pete lays the sport jacket on another stool and suddenly, his attention is on me once again.

Leaning against the counter, I feel vulnerable with his hungry gaze on me dressed in my spaghetti-strapped summer dress and bare feet. He clears his throat and moves next to me, pressing his back against the counter. I stare down at our feet—my green painted toenails and his black socks. I listen while he chugs his beer, and then I take another drink of mine, wondering again for the hundredth time what I'm doing here.

Chapter 18

Pete

When I invited Jules back to my place to talk, that had been my only intention. I knew it was important for us to hash out what happened in Monterey. I worry she's broken some kind of rule. At the same time, I'm wrestling with the guilt of having feelings for another woman. Natalie hasn't been gone that long. And what will Tess and Cora think about all of this?

But now that Jules is here and we've kissed again, all I want to do is continue making out with her for the rest of the night. Since I seem to have lost my courage to make another move or bring up the conversation regarding our feelings and ethics, I chug my beer and finish it off.

"Want another one?"

Jules holds her bottle up to the light and studies it. "I'm still working on this one."

"Right." I pop open another one for myself and take a long pull of the cold, hoppy liquid before I decide I'd better slow it down.

"So, you play the bass?" Jules gestures with her bottle in the direction of the instrument sitting in a stand in the living room.

"I do. Or I used to." I'm impressed she called it a bass and not a guitar. Most people get them confused. It took Natalie forever to decipher the two. "You know how to play?"

"Nah. But my dad plays. Played."

By the way she corrects herself, it causes me to pause. I decide talking about something other than our feelings, or acting on those feelings, may be a safer option right now. I put my lust for her on the back burner.

"He doesn't play anymore?"

"I don't think he remembers."

"Once you learn, you never forget. Maybe he's simply a little rusty."

"No, I don't think he remembers that he even knows how to play. It's been forever since I've heard him." She takes a long pull from her bottle, and when she sets it on the counter, I can tell it's empty. I open her a new one without asking if she wants another.

"What do you mean?"

"Remember I mentioned my dad has dementia?" She pauses, not long enough for me to interject, but long enough for me to remember our short conversation at the Dodger game. "He was diagnosed about five years ago. He was so young." She shakes her head, her hand going to the globe pendant hanging around her neck. "My mom and I didn't really know what to expect at first. We hoped it would be slow progressing, but it wasn't. One day, it was almost as if someone flipped a switch. And he forgot. Everything. Well, not everything, but it sure felt that way. Some days he couldn't remember who I was or that he even had a daughter. My mom couldn't take the episodes anymore and left. She left him, but she may as well have left me too. I know I'm an adult, but I think a child never stops needing—or at least wanting—their parents to be involved in their life. Now, I hardly hear from her and see her even less. She has a wanderlust soul."

I'm not sure what to say, so I say, "I'm sorry."

She shrugs.

"Is that why you wear that necklace? The globe pendant reminds you of her?"

Her head jerks up and her fingers fumble with the pendant. "Close. She gave this to me when she went on a trip out of the country when I was a teenager. It's really the only thing I have that makes me feel close to her. And it sort of comforts me. Silly, I know."

"Nah, I don't think it's silly. It's sweet."

She smiles at me. "Thanks for listening. I'm not used to being the one spilling my guts."

I grin at her.

Pink tints her cheeks and she smiles, covering her face with her palm. "Stop doing that," she says, her voice muffled.

I pull her hand away. "Stop doing what?" I give her a wide, knowing grin.

She looks at me. "That. That smile. Ugh. As if this alcohol isn't weakening my inhibition enough, that smile of yours is gonna turn my legs to Jell-O."

I chuckle. The thought of my smile making her weak in the knees is exhilarating. Not to mention extremely hot. It does a satisfactory job of distracting my mind from all the reasons the two of us shouldn't be here together. I position myself in front of her but pick up my beer and attempt to drink it in one succession.

Jules sets her bottle down and props her hands on either side of her, pulling herself up onto the counter. But as she slides her butt on it, her head bangs into the pendant light hovering above the island. It hits loud enough there's a *ding* that sounds out in vibration.

I choke on my beer. "Are you okay?"

Despite she's laughing, I check the back of her head for a bump.

"I'm fine." She shrugs and puts up both hands. "This is me, clumsy Jules."

I can't help but chuckle.

"And here I was, trying to be sexy and seductive." She buries her face in my neck.

Simply hearing her say the words, *sexy and seductive* gets me worked up again.

"I hate to break it to you, but you're sexy without even trying."

"Yeah, right." She groans, revealing her vulnerability before finally lifting her head to gaze at me.

"I'm serious, Jules. Stop trying, because you're killing me."

I tuck a strand of her strawberry blonde hair behind her ear. Her eyes go glossy as her stare fixes on my lips. A humming vibrates between us like an active electric current.

"I like you, Jules." I cup her cheek.

Her chin dips slightly and her lips tug to one side. With obvious desire glowing on her cheeks, she's absolutely breathtaking.

"Well, if it's not obvious by now, I like you too, Pete." She slips her warm hands inside the back of my shirt and lightly drags her fingertips against my skin.

A shudder racks my body.

"And, well, I'd really like to do ya."

She snorts a laugh.

I smile wide. "What? Is that not what the kids are saying these days?"

She shakes her head like I'm absurd. But also like I'm charming, too. "You're adorable, do you know that?"

I shrug it off and try to pull this train back on track. "In all seriousness, there's nothing I want more than to share this with you. But if we're not on the same page, it's cool. We can pretend I never propositioned you, and go back to a professional relationship."

"Pete. Just shut up and kiss me," she demands.

She doesn't have to tell me twice. Who am I to refrain from giving the woman what she wants? Palming the nape of her neck, I draw her in and press my lips against hers. This time, the kiss feels more intimate, and our connection even stronger. A lustful urge drives my movements. I shove open her legs and grip her backside, tugging her closer.

She's not close enough.

Jules wraps her legs around my waist and thrusts against my hard-on. I groan into her mouth as her tongue teases mine. She fists the hem of my shirt and tugs it over my head.

As Jules loosens my belt and unzips my jeans, my fingers tremble as I undo the top buttons of her dress. She's an angelic beauty before me with a black lacy bra holding up ample breasts. I kiss her neck and then her collarbone while she writhes against me. Gliding my mouth against her hot skin and pressing my lips to the top of her breast, I cup it in my hand. She moans and tethers her fingers in my hair.

My hormones are overloaded and I have zero patience. I hike up her dress and my head goes dizzy.

"Condom," she says, breathlessly. "Front pocket of my purse."

I straighten. "Right."

It's been forever since I've done this and I momentarily feel silly and careless. But then she says, "Hurry."

After success with the condom, I return to her more confident. I hook my thumbs into the sides of her underwear and yank them down her legs, and she gasps.

As she scoots to the edge of the island and slides against my length, I nearly come undone. The ache to be near her, inside of her, throbs unforgivingly. I ease into her slowly at first, wanting to take my time. But the precision I hoped to have goes out the window when she digs her fingernails into my butt cheeks, and releases these little murmurs into my mouth.

"You feel amazing. You're amazing," I pant, as I squeeze her backside and grind her against me.

"And you. You're so good at this."

I smile against her lips.

We find a rhythm we both enjoy and ride it out. Her moans make me insane, but in the absolute best way.

My mind buzzes with thoughts of us. I push away the old and the familiar. I don't think about Natalie. At least, not much. Because at this moment, it's only me and Jules.

It's sweet and intense.

It's animalistic and chaotic.

It's perfectly imperfect.

Her hushed begs for me not to stop are like a prayer. I grant her wish, and dive into her until I feel her topple over the edge of pleasure. I finish right after her, a whispered, *thank you* from my lips repeatedly like a chant.

With our breathing still heavy, she melts against me, and I am content. It's been so long, I nearly forgot what this feeling of delirious satisfaction feels like. We gaze at one another, her eyes reflecting a shyness I find adorable.

But a light catches in the corner of my eye at the same time I hear something—music maybe? My mind ruptures as realization sets in. I stop kissing her, and my eyes fly open.

We're not alone. Someone's outside.

My entire body freezes, and I jerk away from Jules.

"What's wrong? Are you okay? Was this too much? Too soon?"

"Shh," I say, pulling Jules's dress down and hiking up my jeans, zipping them as I shuffle toward the back door that leads to the patio. I'm acutely aware of Jules clambering off the counter and following close behind me.

"What is it?" she whispers. "Is someone out there? Should I call the police?"

I wave her off and swing open the door, taking a few steps onto the concrete patio. I'm momentarily blinded by what I see. "Ahh... gross!" I shield my eyes with my arm and whip around, bumping into Jules in the process.

"Dad!" Tess shrieks.

"Oh my word, I'm so sorry. We're so sorry." Jules tugs on my arm, pulling me back toward the house.

But instead of allowing her to and doing the logical thing, bolting, I stay put. My brain is scrambling to catch up with what exactly my eyes have witnessed. I press a hand over each eye. "What the hell, Tess? Are you two naked? In my hot tub? Are you two...?" But I'm unable to finish the question.

"Ew, Dad. Stop, don't say it."

"Me, *ew*? You're the one naked in my hot tub." There's a commotion of water splashing before Tess says, "You can uncover your eyes now. I'm covered up."

Hesitantly, I slide my hands down. Tess has a white, fluffy towel wrapped around her, my fluffy towel, and she's perched on the ledge of the hot tub.

"Jules?" Tess says, question in her tone. "What are you doing here?"

Jules's presence here feels as if we've announced our relationship. But her being here should be the last odd thing in this scenario. I feel her fidget next to me but don't look in her direction. And I don't give her the chance to respond.

"I think the bigger question is, what are *you* two doing here? Is this where you come to dodge me or something? Is this where you were last week when I asked if you wanted to watch a movie but you said you had a"—I use air quotes for a more desired effect—"prior obligation?"

"No, of course not," Tess says, incredulous.

"Pete, honest, we've never been here before tonight. We've never done something like this. Here."

"So, what then? Tonight felt like the perfect night to come over here and violate my hot tub?"

"It's not like that," Tess says, gripping the towel and tugging it higher. "Besides, what is *this* little tryst?"

I pass Jules a glance. I'm instantly aware of how guilty we look with her disheveled hair and my belt hanging undone. This is the first time Tess has to imagine her dad with someone other than her mom. And there's less imagination needed, I realize. Instead of allowing the embarrassment to consume me, I return the focus on them once again.

"So, what is it like? Tell me."

I'm not mad. This would be a funny situation, a story I'd tell my buddies later if the people in the hot tub weren't my kids. If I had caught Daniel, who has been taking care of our yard and pool for the last nine months, I would die of laughter. He's been known to use my pool and hot tub for entertaining. He has a perfectly fine set up at his own home—but there's something about him not wanting to give out his address to women on a first date. Ironically, he has no problem giving them mine.

"Dad." Tess drops her face in her hand while the other fists the towel wrapped around her body.

It's not the fact that she's using my hot tub. Not even that she's using it for *that*. It's that they clearly came here to be alone because they assumed I'd be at their place. And I gotta admit, it hurts.

"So you came here to get a break from me?"

"No," Richie says.

I put my hand up, cutting him off. I need to hear this from my daughter.

"You're here too." Tess throws it back in my face.

"This is my house." This seems to quiet her.

Jules tugs on my sleeve. "Maybe we should give them some privacy?" she whispers.

"Tell me, Tess."

Tess looks at me intently. "You really want to know what we were doing here?"

Richie clears his throat and mumbles, "I think he knows what we were doing."

"We're trying to get pregnant," Tess blurts. "There, happy now?"

I blink back my surprise. "For real?"

"Yes, for real."

"Wait," Richie drags out the word on a breath. "Really?"

Tess's face constricts. "I wanted everything to be perfect when I told you. I didn't want you to be mad."

"Why would he be mad?" I interject before Richie even has a chance to respond.

"Because," Tess grumbles at me, annoyance in her tone and her eyes glossy, "Richie thought we should wait a little longer. But I've seen what happens when people wait for things they want. They run out of time and they don't get the chance. I'm not willing to take that risk. I don't want to wait anymore," her voice rumbles.

"I'm not mad," Richie finally admits. "It's just—" He pauses, pushing his splayed fingers through his wet hair. "I haven't wanted to bring this up with everything else going on, but remember we talked about you having the blood tests before we seriously started trying?"

Tess nods slowly, her eyes watering. "I'm scared," she whispers.

Richie outstretches his hand and Tess accepts. "Me too. But you're not alone."

She sniffs. "And you're sure you're not mad?"

"Nah. I'm excited."

They exchange smiles and I can't contain my own excitement any longer.

"Aww, Tess." My stomach stirs with emotion, sadness mixed with slight giddiness. I'm a proud, elated father. A smile stretches wide across my face, and I bring my clasped hands to my mouth.

"Do you know how hard it is to do it under the same roof as your own dad?"

"And your father-in-law," Richie mutters.

"Why didn't you say that?"

"Because it's embarrassing."

"Don't be embarrassed, I'm your dad."

"Exactly. Dad's aren't supposed to know about their daughters being," she lowers her voice—"deflowered."

"De-what now?" Jules mumbles next to me.

Embarrassment creeps up my neck in a wave of heat. "That's what I referred to it as. It was hard for me when my girls grew up, okay?" I whisper. To Tess I say, "But this is different. I obviously know you two are doing it, you're married. And you're trying to have a baby." I'm practically squealing. "I couldn't be more excited."

"Really?" Tess asks, chewing on her lower lip.

"Are you kidding? I'm so proud of you, kid." I move toward her without hesitation and wrap her up in my arms.

"Thanks, Dad," Tess whispers into my neck.

After we break apart, I raise my arms wide. "Richie. Bring it in, son."

Richie clears his throat. "Yeah, I'll take a rain check." He stays seated in the tub, the water nearly up to his shoulders.

I shake my head, making a *tsk-tsk* sound. "No way. Come here, you sneaky devil, you."

Richie still doesn't budge. He glances nervously back and forth between me and Jules. "I'm a bit indisposed here."

"He's not gonna give up. Give him a hug already, and get it over with," Tess says.

Without giving it too much thought, I realize he's not gonna come to me, so I go to him and step into the hot tub. Jules gasps aloud behind me, and Richie is speechless as I pull him up and wrap my arms around his wet, naked body.

"Congratulations, I'm such a proud grandfather."

"Whoa, you're getting ahead of yourself there."

"It's only a matter of time." I rest my head on Richie's shoulder and squeeze him tight while he resists.

"Well, this isn't awkward or anything," he groans.

"Maybe at his next Friday session, you can discuss boundaries with him." Tess says, and Jules giggles.

Chapter 19

Jules

"I'm telling you, Ang, it was the sweetest and most awkward sight I've ever witnessed." I tuck my feet underneath me on the sofa at home. Kobe jumps up and curls into a ball in the space behind my bent legs.

Angie can't suppress her laughter. She nearly choked on her coffee a few minutes earlier when I began replaying my night with Pete. "Okay, okay, so you just stood there, staring at Pete's son-in-law? While the two hugged?" She busts up laughing again, clapping her hands together.

"What was I supposed to do? Look away? I mean, who's not gonna look when there's an attractive guy standing there naked?"

"And Pete walked into the hot tub fully clothed? Dude didn't even care?"

"Nope." I shake my head once, before curling my hands around my coffee mug.

"Whew." She wipes at her watery eyes. "Only you, Jules, I swear. You keep up with the job any longer, and you'll have enough content to write another book."

"Oh, I couldn't write about Pete."

She composes herself and studies my face.

"I'm serious. I said I wouldn't do that again. And I meant it."

My phone pings, and I pick it up off the arm of the sofa.

Pete: *I feel like I haven't seen you in forever.*

A second ping reveals another text from Pete. This time, it's a GIF of a puppy with the words *I miss you.*

My face flushes, and my ears burn.

Angie circles her pointer finger in the air in my direction. "What's going on here?"

The warmth from the mug radiates to my palms. I can't make eye contact with her. "I don't know what you're talking about."

"You like this guy. As in, *like* like him?" She says it like a question, but we both know the truth.

Angie and I met in college, and the two of us have been best friends ever since. She knows me better than anyone else. Especially now, since Mom is off following a newfound wanderlust craving and Dad hardly remembers who I am anymore. A few years ago, he knew me best. My hopes, my dreams, my secrets. Deciding to put Dad in the memory care facility was one of the most difficult decisions I'd ever had to make. But after four years of having him live with me, I wasn't equipped to handle the outbursts and the episodes on my own.

"Jules?"

I drop my head back. "Okay, fine. I really like him. Are you happy now?"

"Not really."

Her words surprise me, and I finally look at her, her black hair falling over her shoulders.

"Jules, do I need to remind you that Pete is a special kind of client? He's not like the others who are fully aware of how your program works. Instead, you should be treating him like you would've treated one of your patients when you were a licensed therapist. Remember, he's paying you to help him, not date him."

Her words are like ice creeping underneath my skin, unwelcomed. "Technically, he doesn't pay me. His daughter does."

"Oh"—she throws up a hand, and the coffee swishes around in her mug on her lap—"we're going off technicalities now, is that it?"

I drop my head to the side, resting it on the back of the sofa. "Ang," I whine.

"No, don't *Ang*, me." She waves a finger in my face. "This is serious, Jules. Pete only has three weeks left in the program. A program you created. One that's intended to help people. One that has a 98 percent success rate might I add. Do you really want to risk interfering with the program? With his success?"

She's right. And yet, memories from the night before play in my mind like a comforting black-and-white film. The way his smile weakened my knees, the way his lips felt pressed up against mine, among other things being pressed up against me.

"Jules?"

I snap out of my Pete-filled daze. "No, I definitely don't want to screw up the program. And I don't plan to. But..." My voice goes up, and I shrug my shoulder to my ear.

"But what? Hello? He's a widower. It's bad enough you're playing with his emotions, but you're gonna play with his heart as well?"

"I'm not trying to."

"But you are."

"I plan on telling him. You know, about the book. About Dave and starting the agency, about everything. Soon."

She gives me a skeptical look with her deep brown eyes over the rim of her mug. "And then what? You think he's gonna take it well? You think you two are gonna live happily ever after? Because that's not how your job works."

Another jab, this time in my gut. Now she's offending my job? The way I make a living? And in the process, her own. I'm not the only one who pays bills with the money made at the agency. I push back the tears burning my eyes that are threatening to spill.

"I know this isn't what you want to hear. But someone has to say it. You're playing with fire here, Jules." She pats me on the leg. "And

I'm afraid Pete's not the only one who's gonna wind up getting burned."

WHEN MY PHONE PINGS WITH A TEXT, I'M NOT SURPRISED WHEN I see Tess's name.

Tess: *We need to talk*

Me: *Is something threatening the six-week program?*

Duh, stupid question. It's me who could potentially screw up the entire thing.

Tess: *Yes.*

I puff air into my cheeks and hold it for a beat before exhaling.

Me: *In person or by phone?*

Tess: *In person.*

Of course she wants to meet in person, again. Part of me is tempted to tell her it will be an additional charge since this is beyond the normal sessions with the client. But since this little meeting is most likely my fault, I don't.

Me: *Where? When?*

Tess: *Saturday 10 a.m. We'll pick you up.*

Me: *Sounds good. See you then.*

Tess: *And bring a bathing suit and towel.*

I frown, scanning the text again to be sure I read it correctly. I need to play nice and keep my paying client happy, so I don't argue.

Me: *Fine.*

Tess: *By the way, this is going to be my dad's next challenge.*

I blink at the screen. Am I reading this correctly? Tess is hijacking my program?

Me: *I asked you to trust me.*

Tess: *I think you broke that trust when you became intimate with my dad.*

Me: *What exactly do you hope to accomplish?*

Tess: *One challenge. That's all I'm asking for here.*

Me: *So you're actually asking?*

Tess: *No.*

Me: *What kind of challenge is this so I can at least present it to your dad?*

Tess: *A beach day. With his daughters. It's something he used to enjoy.*

What Tess doesn't know is I already had a challenge planned involving surfing. It didn't involve Tess and Cora joining us, but that's fine. If Tess wants to tag along, why not? What's the worst that could happen?

Chapter 20

Tess

I planned Dad's next challenge purposely for today because Richie has a scheduled tee time with Carter and Dexter at the golf club. Not only would he disapprove of my plan, but he'd also try to talk me out of it. Where I tend to feel needed by friends and family to fix their problems, Richie is levelheaded and knows when to meddle and when to stay out of it. Nine times out of ten, he chooses to stay out of it.

I'm not exactly sure what I'm hoping to accomplish today. So far, my plan consists of Cora driving over for the day, filling her in on the latest Dad-interventionist drama, and hoping she'll help me with the rest. It's not that I want to sabotage the program because it does seem to be working. Dad's been wearing the robe less and less, and I haven't seen him lounging on the couch with an open bag of potato chips balancing on his chest for at least a week. But Jules assured me she would have a strictly platonic relationship with Dad, and after the incident last week, I assume that's not the case.

I physically shudder at the thought of Dad being intimate with a woman while I pack my beach bag with sunscreen, a magazine, a wide-brimmed hat, a frisbee, and a towel. When Mom got sick the second time, I occasionally allowed my mind to wonder how life would look after she was gone. Not only regarding Natalie's—we'd figured out most of that early on—but I found myself wondering about our family dynamic. Would Cora stay in school and graduate? Would Richie and I still live in this house and fill it with children? Would Dad begin dating and eventually get remarried?

Picturing Dad with someone other than Mom is disturbing. All I've ever known is them together. Imagining him alone somehow feels better than imagining him with another woman. And yet, I'm well aware of how arbitrary that sounds, how selfish that must make me. I suppose if he thinks he's ready to move on, he should have the chance to do so. I guess I never thought it would be so quickly. And with someone I'm literally paying.

When I spot Cora's Mini Cooper pulling into the driveway through the front window, I rush out the door to greet her. I find Dad crouched on the grass, waxing his surfboard. He puts the wax down and stands, propping his hands on his waist and waiting for Cora to turn off the engine and step out of the car.

A large-brimmed sun hat sits on her head, and she adjusts it after climbing out. My heart jumps in my chest at the sight of her. It feels good to have the three of us together. Though I remind myself, it will be four of us once we pick up Jules.

Cora and I haven't spoken again about the mix-up with the blouses. Nor about her choice to brush off the business. I'm still holding onto hope she'll change her mind. Even if it's only a small part—I want her to be involved in some way.

Cora takes a beach bag out of the back seat and hikes it over her shoulder.

"What, no suitcase?" Dad calls.

"I gotta head back tonight. Early meeting tomorrow."

Cora meets Dad on the edge of the grass, and they embrace.

"So, only here for a beach day? I guess I'll take what I can get." He gives her arm a little shake before crouching next to his board again.

"What's with this mystery beach day, anyway? One that was so important I couldn't miss?" Cora asks as she makes her way down the stone walkway, and I give her a hug before taking her bag off her shoulder.

"We're leaving soon. I'll throw this in Dad's Jeep."

"Well?" She shoves her fists on her hips, the black swimsuit cover-up sprinkled with red and pink flowers rides up higher on her thighs. It's something Mom nor I designed. Cora can have whatever she wants from the clothing line for next to nothing, but instead, she often chooses something from Target.

A prick of pain hits me under the rib cage.

"We're picking Jules up on the way." I turn and head toward the Jeep, sidestepping her question and tossing her bag into the back.

"Wait, the therapist lady?" Cora follows after me.

"The interventionist," I correct.

"Oh, is this one of Dad's challenges? Because I guess that would make sense, to get us involved in one, right?"

"Yes, exactly," I blurt. "Jules thought inviting us along would be good for Dad's recovery."

"Recovery," he mutters. "You talk like I'm a drug addict or something."

I ignore him. "Going to the beach was something we used to enjoy, before..." I let my words die, allowing Cora and Dad to fill in the blank. "Surfing is something you always enjoyed," I say instead.

"I did. I do." Dad looks at his board before glancing up at me and forcing a smile. "This was a great idea. We haven't been to the beach in a long time."

"Let's see if the old man still knows how to surf," Cora teases, sliding her sunglasses to rest on the end of her nose and waggling her dark brown brows mischievously.

"Hey, who are you calling old?" Dad takes off in a sprint, chasing Cora around the small yard before catching her and lifting her up and over his shoulder, something he always did when we were young.

My lips spread into an easy smile. The tumbling in my stomach slows down to a calm. I may have planned today for the wrong reason, but what I said wasn't a lie. A day at the beach, just the three of us, will be good for everyone.

Four of us, I have to remind myself again when Dad pulls up in front of Jules's modest bungalow and hops out of the Jeep. There's a bounce to his step as he bounds up to her front door and knocks.

Cora, who had been riding shotgun, climbs into the back seat with me, giving up the front for Jules. She adjusts her hat, and I have to scoot several inches toward the door so I don't get whacked with the brim of it.

"So what's really going on?" Cora pulls her sunglasses to the tip of her nose, narrowing her eyes at me.

"What do you mean?"

"If you wanted us to have a day at the beach, like old times, you wouldn't have invited the doctor."

For some reason, the word *doctor* doesn't sit properly with me. "She's not a doctor."

She waves a dismissive hand at me, pushing up her sunglasses once again. "Whatever. Spill it."

I hoped to make it through some of the day, or at least more than five minutes of the day, before having to tell Cora my plan. Yet here we are. I take a deep breath and check around Cora's shoulder and see Dad has gone inside. "I think Dad and Jules are...are..." I search for the correct word, unsure what the correct word even is. Especially for old people. And especially for your dad. "Messing around?" My voice goes up on the last word.

Cora tears off her sunglasses and her brown eyes widen. "As in, they're getting it on? Dad? And Jules?" Her face is amused, and I'm not so sure I appreciate her reaction. In a way, I suppose I hoped for her to be upset or hurt even, for Dad moving on so quickly. For Dad moving on in general. "Are you sure?"

"I wouldn't say so if I wasn't."

"Did you actually see something or are you jumping to conclusions? Like that time you thought you saw Mom's pastor making out with his secretary in the back row of the theater?"

I narrow my eyes and sigh with exaggeration. That incident is completely irrelevant here. It turned out it wasn't Mom's pastor. It was in fact his secretary, but she was with her husband. I'm positive about what I saw between Dad and Jules. And Cora should be able to sense it without the evidence. It's obvious in his demeanor and the extra bounce in his step. It's something I haven't seen in months.

"I'm positive, Cora. Dad's belt was undone. I think his zipper too. And Jules's hair was all messy."

She smirks and gives a knowing nod with her chin. "Sex hair," she growls.

My stomach does a somersault at the thought.

"Did you catch them at your house?"

I shift in the tightness of the backseat. "Not exactly."

"Then where?"

"At Dad's house."

Above Cora's shoulder, I see the front door of the house open and watch as Dad and Jules step out. "Let's just say, we both had the same idea of attempting to find privacy, and we both caught one another."

"Nooooooo," she says in a scandalous tone. "Now this is a story I must hear in full detail."

"Later," I assure her. But telling my younger sister about sharing an intimate moment with my spouse in a hot tub is not something I want to go into detail about. But it can't be much worse than Dad interrupting us in the middle of said intimate moment.

"Cora," Dad says, "this is Jules Sweeney. Jules, my youngest daughter Cora."

Jules climbs into the passenger side of the Jeep and shifts to the left to shake Cora's hand. "It's so nice to finally meet you. Your Dad has told me so much about you."

"Nice to meet you." Cora nods and gives Jules a friendly smile. It's too friendly. The irritation burrows its way deeper in my gut.

"Hi, Tess," Jules says. "Looks like it's the perfect day for the beach."

"Looks like it," I mumble. "Though I wouldn't mind one freakin' cloud."

Cora shoots me a look, lifting her brows behind her sunglasses. But Dad doesn't hear my comment because he's busy loading Jules's bag in the back of the Jeep, then he climbs in and slides behind the wheel. Before he puts the key into the ignition, he glances in the rearview mirror and gives Cora and me a grin and a wink.

For a moment, I'm frozen; stuck in a memory. Dad bought his first Jeep when I was nine and Cora was only four. The two of us would sit in the back seat, Cora in her booster, and we'd laugh as the wind whipped through our hair. We didn't even care that it would take Mom nearly an hour to comb out all the tangles. But before Dad would put the key into the ignition, he'd always glance in the rearview to grin and wink at us. Almost as if he was double checking we were there, safely buckled in and ready to go.

The drive is mostly quiet. It's difficult to carry on a conversation in a Jeep with the noisy wind. But you can bet I'm keeping a close eye on Dad and Jules. I feel like the parent, once again. It's like I'm chaperoning, sitting back here making sure Dad doesn't make a move on Jules. Or worse, the other way around. There will be no PDA allowed on my watch.

It's not that I have anything against Jules. I barely know her. But I know enough. After reading that entire section in her book, it was enough for me to know the kind of person she is. While her program seems successful based on all the testimonials, her methods are unorthodox. And if she thinks she's gonna mess around with my dad and shatter his already broken heart, she's got another thing coming.

Chapter 21

Pete

It's awkward having my daughters and Jules together. Especially since Jules and I haven't spoken about that night. We've texted back and forth a few times, and we sidestepped the entire fiasco at my weekly session yesterday. But over the past few days, I've come to realize that allowing ourselves to get caught up in the moment may have been a mistake. I don't even know her that well.

Besides, she's supposed to be helping me heal from my trauma. I won't lie and say that what we shared the other night wasn't helpful to my healing. But I think most people would agree we crossed a line, most importantly, my two daughters.

We arrive at Venice Beach, and I park the Jeep. The four of us pile out, unload our gear, and scope out a good location on the sand to set up for the day. Cora chooses the spot. It's close to the water but not too close to the several small children building a sandcastle. And of course, it's near the volleyball net where there are currently two all-male teams playing—shirtless, of course.

Tess doesn't argue. She simply plops her stuff down and lays out her towel in the sand. Honestly, I don't even think she notices the shirtless volleyball game happening a few feet away from her. Cora sets up a few of our folding beach chairs, hers with a clear shot of the volleyball pit.

I give her a nudge in the shoulder. "Smooth, real smooth."

"It's gonna be a perfect day." She settles in her chair and pulls her sunglasses down the bridge of her nose, staring at the buff, sweaty guys in the sand pit.

Since I haven't been to the beach in months, I'm anxious to get out in the water. "Okay." I clap my hands together. "Who's surfing?"

"I'm perfectly fine staying right here all afternoon," Cora says.

Of course she is. "Tess? How about you?"

Tess glances at the two boards, then at Jules, and then at me. "Nah, I'll sit this one out. You two should go."

"No, no, you can go with your dad. I don't even know how to surf."

"You're kidding? You've lived this close to the beach all your life and you don't know how to surf?" I ask.

She shrugs. "Guess I never really had the desire to learn."

"Or maybe, you never had the right teacher." I grin, knowing the effect it has on her and loving it.

She smiles, but it's obvious she's holding back.

"Well you're not gonna find a better teacher than Dad," Cora says from behind her dark sunglasses.

"It's true," Tess agrees. "You two go, I'm gonna rest here for a while. Maybe I'll come out later."

"Are you sure?"

"Positive." Tess is already getting situated on her tummy on the towel.

"Okay. What do you say, Jules? You wanna learn how to surf?"

"What the hell? I haven't reached my quota of clumsiness yet today, why not?"

The reminder of the clumsiness does concern me slightly. There isn't much room for error when it comes to surfing. You're either good at it, or you're not. Something tells me Jules is gonna be the latter. But that won't stop me from trying to teach her.

I give her a board, adjusting the position of her hand so she's holding it correctly. "Let's head down closer to the water." She walks next to me, not even struggling with the weight of the board under her arm. I'm impressed.

"We aren't gonna instantly head into the water, are we?"

"No way. I'll give you the basics on the sand first. Once you have that down, we'll get out and crush some waves."

I set the board down and motion for her to do the same. I go through all the basic safety lessons first. I move on to teaching her the positioning on the board, the science behind surfing, where to set her feet once she's popped up on the board, and most importantly, trusting her intuition.

"And that's all there is to it," I say after I've gone through nearly an hour of how-tos.

"You make it sound so simple."

"It can be difficult, but it doesn't have to be. Look, follow my lead. I'll tell you which wave to ride and which to pass. Soon you'll feel them and you won't even need me."

"Doubtful," she mutters.

"C'mon." I motion with a tilt of my head and step into the water, dipping my toes in first with each step. The foreign chill of the water sends a quiver through me, but it passes quickly. "First thing is feeling comfortable on the board. We'll paddle out there, past the break, and you can get a feel for it. Sound good?"

"Sure, I think I can do that."

When I'm waist deep, I turn back around and find she's barely moved a few feet. "All right," I holler over the sound of the crashing waves. "Put the board in the water and climb on."

She does, stretching out across it on her stomach. I have to look away so my gaze doesn't wander down the length of her. It's my turn to be her teacher, and I want to be professional.

"Now paddle," I say.

We both propel forward, slicing our arms into the water. The waves are calmer than usual, though I haven't been on a board in so long, they might as well be thrashing today. We both get over the first wave with no problem. But as the second wave builds, we need to make it over before it breaks. "Hurry!" I shout.

Jules navigates through the water fast and hard. Her face is set—determined. But she needs to paddle even faster if she wants to get beyond the wave. I'm over it first, and I turn back to check on her. "Hurry!" I yell again. The wave is building in turquoise and electric blue behind me. When it's at its peak, right before it breaks, she barely makes it over. I exhale a sigh of relief. But Jules starts coughing on saltwater. "Are you all right?"

"I'm fine," she spits out in between a fit of coughing.

We have to get beyond at least one more wave before we reach the sweet spot, the calm where you sit and wait for the perfect wave to arrive. My stomach twists in knots. "We have to get over one more. Can you do it?"

She nods, and this time, I make sure she gets over the wave first before I make it over myself. I won't have anyone to teach if she dies out here.

The water stills around us, and we sit up, straddling our boards. There are a few surfers on either side of us, but the most experienced ones are sitting this calm water out for the day.

"You sure you're okay?"

"You know what? Saltwater tastes disgusting."

We laugh. It eases the tension I've felt since we said goodbye on her front porch last Sunday night. It feels good to laugh with her again.

I shake out my wet hair, spraying her with tiny saltwater droplets in the process. She squeals in response. And we laugh again.

Once it's quiet between us, I rub at the back of my neck, feeling every pulse as it beats underneath my skin. Jules leans forward, her palms pressing flat on the board while her legs tread beneath the water. The olive-green bathing suit she's wearing makes her eyes pop and leaves little to the imagination. Her damp strawberry blonde hair sticks to her back and arms while sand granules dust the skin on her lightly freckled chest.

"So," I begin, tearing my eyes away from her so she doesn't catch me staring. "About last week."

"Yeah," she says. "I know."

I turn to face her. "That was..." I search for the right word.

"Intense," she uses for me.

I nod in agreement. It was definitely intense. "And..." I hesitate. "Hot."

A lump of shock rises in my throat and my face heats. Besides Daniel discussing his escapades with a long string of partners, I haven't shared about my sex life with anyone other than Natalie in years. "Yeah," the word chokes out.

"And completely ludicrous."

With those words, a stab of pain hits my gut. I'm instantly aware of what she's going to say next, so I say it for her. "It was a mistake," I blurt.

She presses her lips together, and instead, says nothing at all.

"That's what you were going to say, wasn't it?"

She looks at me, her gaze wandering over my body. I think about it too late to suck in my gut. Those few beers here and there and the lack of working out much the past few months have surely caught up with me.

But she simply pinches her light brows together and looks away.

So I do what any man does when put in an awkward situation, one they can't easily walk away from, I make it worse. "Because you know, you're the professional. And I'm your client. We probably shouldn't be mixing business with pleasure and all that. I get it. Besides, it hasn't been that long since Natalie passed. It's not like I'm anywhere near being ready to move on, right? And how would that look, the two of us dating? After I was your client and you put me through your six-week program? And then there're my daughters. I don't think they're ready for me to move on either." I hear the train wreck that is myself speaking, but I can't seem to make it stop. Luckily, Jules does it for me.

She puts up a hand. "Okay, I get it."

"So you agree?"

She exhales and opens her mouth to speak but out of the corner of my eye, I spot it—the perfect wave building. "Jules! This is it—your wave! Can you feel it?"

"What do I do? I can't remember. I've forgotten everything." There's panic in her voice.

"No you haven't. You got this. C'mon, paddle toward it. I'll take it with you."

"I don't think I can do this."

"Yes you can. I know you can. Now, paddle. And when I say pop up, do it." We navigate alongside each other toward the wave. I feel it inside my body, traveling through my bones as if this wave and I are one. I sense Jules next to me and together, the three of us are one.

I push my hands through the water, deep and hard, the spray hits my face, and I squeeze my eyes shut through it until I can feel the exact moment—it's time. "Now, Jules! Pop up!" One glance behind me, and I can see she's doing it. She's up. I do the same, and pop up onto my feet, bend my knees, and hold my arms out for balance.

The wave comes with a heady vengeance and pulls us both. I lose sight of Jules, but I'm gliding, riding on top of the wave and then through it and under the white, bubbly curl. Memories flood my mind. For months I've pushed my love for surfing—along with everything else I've ever loved—to the back of my mind. Trying to cut out all that was once good in my life. Besides Tess and Cora, I've felt like I didn't deserve anything good. If Natalie couldn't experience joy anymore, why should I? But as I finish out the wave, riding it until it dies out when it reaches the beach, I hop off and feel more alive than ever before.

"Woo-hoo!" Jules shouts from behind me.

I turn to see her unlatching the board from her ankle. When she's free, she pumps a fist in the air and runs through the shallow water toward me. And I gotta admit, I'm pretty surprised she did it. Like, actually surfed for the first time and didn't fall off. Quirky, clumsy, hot-mess Jules.

Standing next to my board, I cup my hands around my mouth and yell, "You did it!" I'm grinning like a madman. My chest expands and fills with pride. I taught her, and she did it.

She reaches me and flings herself into my arms. I catch her, and things happen so fast there's no time for thinking. She wraps her legs around my waist, and then we're kissing. The taste of the saltwater on her lips is enticing. Our skin-on-skin contact is arousing, and I want to lay her down in the sand and get it on right here.

But Jules pulls back, and I'm reminded we're not alone. Not only is the beach packed full of people and children, but *my* children. Jules slides down the length of my hard-on, and it half kills me to let her go. The restraint is painful.

"Sorry," she says, sucking in her bottom lip and tucking her wet hair behind her ear.

"You don't see me complaining, do you?" I shake out my hair again, and she shields herself with her hands and giggles.

We carry our boards back to our spot and lay them in the sand. Cora has found herself a position on the all-male volleyball team—no shocker there. Tess is sitting in a chair flipping through the pages of a women's fashion magazine. It's nice to see her at least trying to relax, but it's clearly driving her crazy to do so. She's been so busy with the store, she hardly has time to rest.

Since I'm not sure she's even noticed us, I nudge her in the leg with my foot. "How's it going?"

"Fine," she responds without looking up from the page.

I sense irritation in her tone. We towel off, and Jules puts on a white cover-up over her suit.

"Aren't you gonna ask how Jules did out there? It was her first time."

Tess finally peers over the top of the magazine. "How'd it go?"

Jules's face lights up. "Really, really good."

"She rode a wave. Stayed up the entire time."

"That's surprising," Tess says, though her expression is unimpressed. "First time surfing, you say?"

Jules ignores the question and takes my hand. "Hey, wanna take a walk?"

"Absolutely." I'd say yes to anything she suggested if it meant spending more time with her. "We'll find that shave ice stand you and Cora love and bring you back some," I say to Tess.

"But I brought the Frisbee." Tess rummages around in her bag, presenting it with vigor like it's evidence from a crime scene. "I thought we'd play—you know, like we always do. And we haven't had lunch yet."

"We're pretty exhausted from surfing." I push my toe into hers. "We're old, remember?"

She barely gives me a roll of the eyes, a typical response from her lately.

"Shave ice first. Frisbee second."

"Fine," Tess grunts.

"And, hey? Keep an eye on your sister, will you?"

"Dad, she's not a little girl anymore. She's free to make her own bad decisions. Even if it's a dumb, bleached blond volleyball player."

Jules stifles a laugh, but it's nearly impossible for me to turn off my dad mode. I pull on my John Mellencamp T-shirt, the one Tess hates, and I grab my wallet from my bag.

Jules and I walk down the beach, the taupe terrain a refreshing change from the usual office setting. The wind blows through her hair dampened from the salt water, and she looks more relaxed than I've ever seen her. I feel like this is the real her, and I want to get to know this Jules even more. The carefree, vibrant Jules who takes risks and celebrates wins by launching herself into my arms and smothering me with kisses.

We'd already discussed that what happened between us last week was a mistake. But admittedly, deep down, it doesn't feel like it was. It feels like this thing between us could be something...something real.

"Should we revisit our conversation? About last weekend?" I hedge. She glances over at me, the sun reflecting off her hazel eyes, and her expression is unreadable. I shrug. "Or not. I mean, we don't have to. You already said it was a mistake, so."

"I thought *you* thought it was a mistake."

"I didn't, I don't," I correct.

She looks like she's holding back.

"What is it? Whatever it is, just say it. Otherwise, I'm gonna start rambling again."

"Things are," she pauses, "complicated."

"Okay, yes. I can agree to that." I nod.

"No, I mean, more than you realize." She studies her toes as they dig into the sand with each step. "If we want to make a go at this, me and you *we need to talk.*"

"Uh-oh. It's never good when someone says we need to talk." I make air quotes.

"I want to be honest with you."

"Me too."

She looks over at me again, but this time, I hold her intense gaze, and neither of us looks away as we trudge along on the sand. I'm all nerves, and the silence between us lasts too long. I should say something to break it, but before I can mutter what are most likely ridiculous words, Jules trips and smacks nearly face-first into the sand.

WITH MELTING SHAVE ICE CUPS IN OUR HANDS, JULES AND I return to our spot, and I'm relieved to see Cora has returned from her game of half-naked volleyball.

"Shave ice for all," I sing.

"Finally, I'm starving." Cora accepts hers and digs in right away.

"Thanks," Tess mumbles when Jules hands her the kiwi-strawberry combo.

Jules and I join them, sitting on the low beach chairs.

"Did you win?"

"My team didn't, if that's what you're asking. But aren't we all winners after seeing that display of bare, sweaty, muscly chests today?"

Jules snorts a laugh.

Stilted quiet settles between us as we race to eat the shave ice before it melts. So we don't fall into a hole of miserable nostalgia, I'm desperate to keep us talking.

"Cora, did Tess tell you that Jules actually surfed? Stayed on the board the entire time."

"Wow, and it was your first time?"

Jules nods enthusiastically, talking around a mouthful of flavored ice, "I had a good teacher."

"Told you Dad is the best." Cora smiles at me.

It's the kind of smile that makes me feel like I really am the best. It gives me back a sliver of dad authority I've lost the past few months.

"Dad is a good teacher," Tess chimes in. "But I mean, he's not *that* good."

I blink at her, plastic spoon midair to my mouth.

"I mean, for a first-time surfer, it has to be somewhere around what, less than ten percent odds that they stay on their board the entire time? Those aren't very good odds. And that percentage is probably for an average, athletic person."

I narrow my eyes at Tess, wishing she and I had some kind of father-daughter telepathy or something, and she'd shut up already.

Tess wipes the air clean. "Not to say you're not athletic, Jules. But, for someone as clumsy as you, that percentage has to plummet significantly."

"Tess," I snap.

What is she doing?

"I'm just saying, it's almost as if you've surfed before." Her brows shoot up into her hairline. "You sure you've never surfed before?"

Jules stares, doe-eyed, before glancing back and forth between me and Tess. She clears her throat, looks pointedly at Tess, and answers, "I'm sure."

"Tess." I kick her foot, harder than playful this time. "What the hell's gotten into you?" But I don't wait for a reply because I'm not sure I want one. "Jules, you were awesome. I can't wait to get back out there with you again."

"I bet," Cora says.

I whip my head in her direction, dread sliding through me. Not Cora too.

"I saw that kiss out there."

Cool, cool. I run a hand through my hair.

"You two put on quite the show for the entire beach. I swear I saw a mother cover her child's eyes. Who knew old dad still had it in him?" Cora giggles and it turns into a cackle.

Jules dips her chin, and her cheeks stain pink.

A bit of relief inches itself into my gut, releasing some of the knots twisted there. I wasn't sure how the girls would react to seeing Jules and me together—kissing. But Cora's reaction tells me she's okay with it. At least a little, and for now, that's enough for me.

"It's nice to see him happy again." Cora takes in her last few scoops of shave ice.

Tess doesn't say anything else about the intimate moment Jules and I shared on the beach, or her opinion on seeing me happy again. She finishes her shave ice with the perma-scowl still intact which leaves me perplexed over her actions.

Chapter 22

Jules

Pete invites me back to Tess's house for dinner, but I'm not so sure Tess wants me to join them. I'm also not sure what her underlying intention was by hijacking my program and choosing the challenge for her dad. But I have a feeling it backfired. If she thought she'd push me into a corner and I'd spill my guts that I have, in fact, been surfing before, she was highly mistaken. And if she thought I'd go as far as admitting I'd been surfing on another challenge with a past client, she must've been delusional.

Tess's home is small and lovely. It's an old Craftsman-style bungalow, but it's been completely remodeled. It has enough space for a young married couple and Pete. But if one or two small children were added to the mix, it would get crowded fast. The realization of how Tess must feel having Pete living here within close proximity and the desire to start a family burrows in my chest. I know that suffocating feeling all too well. It almost makes me forgive her for earlier.

Almost.

"Make yourself at home," Tess says after we all enter, dragging our beach gear in with us. "Richie?" she calls through the house.

Not long after, Richie jogs down the stairs dressed in fancy golf clothes and greets us in the kitchen. "Hey, babe." He kisses Tess on the cheek.

The gesture feels off-putting. Like they're an old married couple rather than young.

"How was the beach today? I was disappointed to miss out." Richie rests his hands on his hips. It's a stance of power. But I'm not sure who he needs to have power over. Me? Pete? Or Tess?

Cora brushes past him. "Beach was the same as it always is." She shoots an annoyed look in Tess's direction. "Not so epic after all."

Richie frowns and glances between Cora and Tess. But Tess simply rolls her eyes. "Cora played volleyball with some guys on the beach. Gave out her number and socials a bazillion times."

"Not true. It was like four guys." She shrugs as she rounds the stairs. "Whatever, I'm going to take a shower."

"Four too many, if you ask me," Pete chimes in with a dad comment, pointing a finger after her. But no one really laughs, the air in the house is thick with discomfort.

"Oh, hey, Tess?" Cora peeks her head down below the wall so she's visible to us gathered in the kitchen. "Did you invite Jules to your party?"

An uneasy feeling snakes up my spine, and I stiffen. It's awkward, and I'm positive that's exactly Cora's intention. Not so much for me, but for Tess.

Tess's face blanches. "Uh, no. Not yet. But thanks for reminding me."

"So, Jules. Two weeks. Tess's birthday party is here at eight o'clock." Cora straightens and is out of sight as she makes her way upstairs. "That's your official invitation," she calls.

"Oh good," Pete releases an audible sigh. "I was afraid I'd be the only old person at the party."

"Hey, who are you calling old?" I smack him in the gut with the back of my hand playfully.

He exhales a puff of air, chuckling. "Okay, you're right. I'm five years older than you so I guess that makes me the only old one."

"Stop, you're not old," Tess says.

My gaze travels down the length of Pete, stopping at his midsection where his tattered John Mellencamp-Farm Aid '97 T-shirt—obviously an old favorite—has ridden up slightly, revealing mostly firm abs. I bite on my lower lip; my appetite for him rather than dinner.

"So, you're free then? Two weeks from today, eight o'clock?" Tess asks.

"I'll check my schedule, but it sounds fun." I can check my schedule now, on my phone. But it sounds better if I say that. It's noncommittal and makes it seem as if I'm busier than I actually am. Most likely, that night would have consisted of a visit to see Dad at the facility, followed by a night in watching a rerun of *The Bachelor* with Angie, rock-paper-scissoring whose turn it is to refill the wine glasses.

"Good, our friends should all be here, and you'll get to meet them."

Is that detail supposed to intrigue me, because if anything, it does the opposite. Apprehension snakes through me at the thought of meeting new people. My clumsiness heightens whenever I'm nervous. But I find myself saying, "I can't wait."

It's uncomfortable, the four of us standing in the kitchen, staring at one another.

"Who wants a beer?" Pete finally says, interrupting the awkwardness.

"Sure, why not," I say, and he passes me a smile that I catch relief in.

Meeting Tess and Richie is like meeting the parents, I realize. And it's so strange how the dynamics have shifted. The way Pete has lived his life for the past several months rolls into my mind. It's not entirely Pete's fault, it's obvious Tess has been enabling him. Taking care of her dad is giving her something to do during the grieving stage of her own healing process. I find myself questioning if she's truly ready for Pete to move out. And maybe, her inviting me today was a way to subconsciously sabotage the plan.

"Why don't you two head out back while Richie and I fix some dinner?" Tess is already pulling ingredients out of the refrigerator.

"You need some help?" I offer. I'm not the best cook, but I get by. When you have one parent who was on the road touring with his band and another who pretty much checked out, you learn how to do lots of things.

"No, no, you two go." She waves me off.

Pete hands me a beer and ushers me out the back door with a confident hand pressed to my spine. The patio is beautiful and takes up the majority of the backyard. It's constructed from large square concrete pavers, and there's a wood pergola covering it with patio lights strung around the top, cascading light onto the wood table below.

We sit next to one another with our backs to the house, and I take in the rest of the yard. There's a concrete wall stretching around the perimeter as tall as a fence. A modest patch of grass in the middle of the yard is kept manicured and privacy shrubs run down both sides of the fence. Tess and Richie seem to lead busy lives and their easy-to-manage backyard reflects that.

As I take in the view of the yard, I feel Pete's intense gaze on me. I turn and find him staring at me, a soft smile on his face. It makes me self-conscious since we haven't showered after being at the beach all day, and I'm still sitting in my suit with shorts and a tank top. I nervously run my hand over my hair. It's coarse from the salt water and feels like straw.

"Hey, thanks for this challenge today." He traces a finger over the bare skin on my arm, sending a chill shooting through me.

"It was fun."

He makes a face, like he's considering this. "It was...semi fun." He grins and I melt into a pile of goo at his feet. "You were a good sport. Those two girls are not always the easiest to get along with. I mean, don't get me wrong, I'm the luckiest guy in the world to be their dad, but"— he shakes his head—"they can be difficult."

I think about the day. The snippy comments from Tess, her change in behavior toward me, her nonverbal accusations that I've been surfing before, the obvious tension between her and Cora. And I can't help but wonder if I'm the cause.

"Nah, they were fine," I lie.

He leans in close to me, my entire side inflaming. "You're a terrible liar," he teases.

I want to kiss him. Every fiber of my being wants to devour him. But his choice of words stick in my gut and twist. Because I'm not that terrible of a liar. I've been lying to him the entire time I've known him.

Pete leans in even closer, the warmth from his breath on my face, and my brain yells at my lady parts to chill out already. The back door opens, interrupting our almost-kiss, and Cora tumbles out, making a grand entrance like she's the star of a show. And I think she might be. At least, the star of this show. She's definitely the center of attention in the family.

"Tess wanted me to let you know dinner should be ready soon. Also, Dad, she mentioned she needed your help with something." Cora sits in the white wicker chair at the head of the table, which happens to be next to me.

I shift in my seat, wondering why she chose this spot when there are plenty of other empty chairs that make more sense.

Pete stands and rubs the top of my shoulder. "What, Richie Rich isn't a suitable chef's assistant?"

Cora guffaws. "He doesn't make a suitable assistant for anything. I swear, it's a good thing he didn't have a hired hand for every single thing in his life or that guy wouldn't even know how to zip his own pants without help."

But Pete is already at the door and slipping back inside. So this last part feels like it was intended for my ears. The little I know about

Richie's background makes more sense with this new information. As well as Pete's nickname for him.

"So, Jules?" Cora rests her elbows on the table. "I have this wild dream of interning at a publishing house in New York. Do you have any connections?"

The favor—because let's just call it what it is—jolts me from this world into my other world. The publishing world. And the one Pete doesn't know about.

"Um...possibly." I glance over my shoulder and rub at the back of my neck where there're frizzy curls at my hairline.

"I know those jobs can be a long shot. Especially with me being so young and all. But I finished high school with over a 4.0, and I got a 1310 on my SATs. I've also worked on the college paper, and I'm sure my dad mentioned I'm interning at the Santa Barbara Independent. They all love me there."

Something tells me they do. Cora feels easy to be around. At first, her beauty is intimidating with her long dark shiny hair, but she warms quickly. More quickly than, say, Tess.

"I bet they do. And I'd love to help any way I can. Let's exchange contact info. I'll talk to my editor and see if she can give me any insight into their summer intern program."

"Really?" Her entire face brightens, her thick eyebrows lift. "Because if you could, that would be totally amazing."

"I can't make any promises. But I'll do my best."

She clasps her hands together in front of her, and her facial expression turns dreamy. "Thank you, thank you."

My chest squeezes, and it feels good to do something nice for someone. I have no idea what my editor will say, or if I even have enough rank to ask about something like their summer internship situation. But I suppose it doesn't hurt to try.

"You have no idea what this could mean for me and my future." She leans back in the wicker chair and crosses her legs. "I know I need to finish school first, but a job in publishing can't come soon enough."

"You don't like school?" I take a sip of my beer.

"It's fine. But I've always been ready to start my life, ya know? I'm ready to grow up already."

"And you don't think you're living now?"

She sighs dramatically. "Don't start talking like my parents." Then as she realizes her choice of words, her expression shifts. "I mean, my dad."

I help her over the speed bump. "I take it he wants you to finish school?"

"Yep." She leans forward in her seat again, placing her cheeks in her hands. "Which is so hypocritical of him. He never even finished college. He went for one year, met my mom, and bam, dropped out. Both of them did. But yet, it's so important to them that I finish."

"You ever think that's why? That they want you to finish because they had to do things the hard way, and they want it to be easier for you?"

She furrows her brows and frowns. I'm not sure when exactly I became the parenting expert, but I suppose I have no control over when my therapist training decides to show itself.

"Usually, parents want not only the best for their children but better than they had. It sounds like both your mom and dad worked very hard. Things didn't come easy or fall into their laps. It's difficult these days to make a decent living without a college education."

"Yeah, yeah, I've heard it all. And you're right. They did work really hard. And I'm trying to not take that for granted. I want them to be proud of me."

"Something tells me they already are."

She makes eye contact with me, and we share a smile.

"What about you? Did you have to work hard to get where you're at? Or were publishers knocking down your door to offer you a publishing deal?"

I let out a sarcastic laugh. "I most definitely have had to work hard. And no. Publishers were not begging to publish my book." I nervously glance over my shoulder again, peering at the back door, and tap my jittery fingers across the top of the table. "The idea came after a few years of work as a licensed therapist, a bad breakup, and several drafts along with my best friend's persistence. Then it took a special literary agent who actually wanted to take a chance on me and my book. And then an editor. I don't think any of us knew it would be a bestseller." I twirl the curls at the nape of my neck with my finger.

"That's fascinating." She rests her chin on her fist. "What is the best thing about having a best-selling novel? The money?" She waggles her brows.

I laugh but then go serious. Everyone asks about the money. Most novelists don't actually make that much. Most can't make a living from writing alone. And I never intended my book to be that big. But even still, it's not like I'm rich.

"Helping others."

She deadpans. "Seriously?"

"I'd like to think that's the best thing for every author of a nonfiction book. Especially a self-help book."

"I mean, yeah, it sounds good. But I doubt anyone actually means it."

"Well, it's true for me."

"Are you trying to tell me that you 'dated,'"—she uses finger quotes—"those men solely to help them? And it wasn't the slightest bit of fun?" Her lips quirk.

I should deny it. *No, it was torturous.* But I'm having a difficult time trying to lie to this girl. "Okay, fine. Most of the time it was fun."

"I knew it!"

"But it wasn't what you think. When I was hanging out with those guys, I didn't have to try to impress them. I got to go on dates and have fun. After I ended a serious relationship about two years ago, I pretty much gave up on men and dating."

"Why'd you end it? You know, the relationship?"

I look at her, almost afraid to answer truthfully, and swallow. "The guy couldn't get over the fact that my dad lived with me and that I wouldn't kick him out. My dad has dementia...I couldn't do that."

Cora's jaw drops and sort of hangs there open while she processes. "You're kidding?"

I shake my head. "Nope."

"Is that how you got started with the whole interventionist thing?"

"Pretty much."

"Does Tess know this?"

I hesitate. "I don't think so."

"Wow." She sits back in her chair. "It all makes sense now."

"What does?"

"Why you do what you do. Why you and Tess understand each other but at the same time, butt heads. You're too much alike."

"You think so?" I wince without intention.

She nods. "Okay, tell me the best date you went on. You know, with one of the guys who went through your program."

I think long and hard about it, and then one comes to mind. I tell her about Dave. The two of us dated for real after he finished my program, but his challenges are some of my favorite ones. One of his challenges was speed dating. It was something he and his wife did on an occasional date night. Strange? Yes, I thought so too. But Dave assured me it was all in clean fun. I had to remind Dave that in the end, his wife cheated on him and left him for another man. Regardless, since it was something Dave once enjoyed, and something I thought he could try after finishing my program to meet someone new, we went.

"You're kidding?" Cora gasps.

"Let me tell you, it was the most ludicrous, most fun date I've ever been on. In one hour, I met twenty men, all of which spent their three minutes talking themselves up in whatever way they could and pointing out their most valuable qualities. For some, this meant how well they load a dishwasher or change the oil in a car. For others, it was sexual, how much time they spent on foreplay. One guy told me how he was guaranteed to never go bald and even showed me pictures of his great-great-grandfather when he was over one hundred years old, still sporting a head of thick, luscious white hair." The harder Cora laughs, the harder I laugh. "And all through the night, Dave is giving me I-want-you eyes and gestures and sending me texts about how aroused he is. I couldn't figure out how meeting these strange people was turning him on."

The two of us are laughing so hard my stomach hurts and tears are gushing from Cora's eyes. It's at that time Pete, Tess, and Richie come out of the house carrying serving platters.

"What are we missing?" Pete smiles, setting a tray down before rubbing the tops of my shoulders and sending goose bumps shooting down my arms.

"Yeah?" Tess narrows her eyes. "What's so funny?"

"It's nothing," Cora says, waving them off and trying to compose herself.

I wipe my eyes and try to do the same.

"Really, it's nothing." Cora looks pointedly at Tess, as if to say, *Don't ask.*

"Fine," Tess says, defiance in her tone and a glare in her eyes.

If I didn't know better, I'd say Tess is jealous. She and I may have more in common, but Cora is much easier to get along with. And that seems to rub Tess the wrong way.

Chapter 23

Tess

Cora's failed to notice the daggers I've been shooting her way all evening. While her and Jules have been busy getting all buddy-buddy, I'm the one who's been cooking and cleaning. Despite this being my home, Cora is usually quick to offer to help. But it's like she doesn't even notice I've been back and forth from outside to the kitchen all evening.

Cora hadn't totally been on board with having Dad go through Jules's program, but now she's acting like they're best friends. Does Cora not see how unethical their relationship is? I'm well aware of the double standard. But as I slice the knife through the apple pie with exaggeration, I don't care.

"Hey." Cora breezes inside the house from the back door. "What's taking so long with the dessert?"

She's teasing, but the words crawl under my skin like an infectious disease and fester there. "Maybe if someone offered to help me, instead of laughing it up with your new BFF, you'd have your dessert," I bite out.

She freezes halfway between the back door and the kitchen

island where I'm at. "Whoa." She blinks, wide-eyed at me. "Excuse me for being nice."

I exhale and roll my eyes dramatically. "Oh, c'mon." I point toward the door with the knife. "That was more than simply being nice. You two might as well have exchanged numbers and socials. You can send each other funny GIFs or memes or whatever."

"Actually, we did exchange numbers," Cora says, stepping lightly toward the island.

"Are you kidding me?" I breathe out.

"No, I'm not kidding. Jules is smart and she has a career that actually helps people. She's also got connections in the publishing world."

"Oh, so what? The lady is a hot mess. And if you came home more often, you'd know that." I raise my voice and stab the apple pie, slicing another piece.

"Maybe I would come home if I had a home to come home to," she yells. Her voice echoes in the space around us and vibrates in my chest.

It's only a matter of seconds before Dad comes in here to find out what all the noise is about.

"Instead, when I come 'home'"—she uses air quotes—"I have to come here. Because if I go to my real home, no one is there."

A painful feeling works its way into my chest, coiling around my heart. She's right. When she comes home on the weekends, she stays here. Not only did she lose Mom, but in a way, she lost her home as well.

"Look, I'm sorry," I say, my tone softer. "Sometimes I forget how things are from your perspective."

"It's easier to not come home at all."

Dad opens the back door and peeks his head inside. "Everything okay in here?"

"Yeah, we're fine," I say, brightly. "Cora's helping me with the pie."

"Awesome." He grins before closing the door.

"So, Jules has connections in the publishing world, huh? What does that mean for you?" I change the subject.

She sighs. "Well, I'm thinking of another summer internship. Preferably in New York."

"Wow." The thought of having Cora so far away is unsettling, but I try not to allow my emotions to show. "New York, huh?"

"It's not for sure. Obviously. Internships at publishing houses are way different than a newspaper. But if I had a connection, maybe it would be easier." Cora opens the silverware drawer and pulls out some forks.

I bite my lower lip while I scoop vanilla ice cream from the tub.

"What?" she bumps the drawer closed with her hip.

I dollop the ice cream on top of each piece of apple pie. "Nothing."

"I know you want to say something, so spit it out already."

Without looking at her, I say, "New York is far."

"And?"

Her glare presses into me. "And what if that sets Dad's progress back?"

She slams a fork onto one of the plates. I jump.

"Are you kidding me right now? I'm supposed to put my life on hold because Dad might still be 'healing'?" She uses air quotes again. When did she start doing that? Or has she always done it, and it's only now annoying me? "Besides, by the looks of things, he seems to be doing much better. He's sure come a long way from the surprise college visit a few weeks ago."

"I'm not saying you should put your life on hold. All I was trying to say is maybe consider applying for an internship that's closer to home. There are plenty of opportunities right here in LA."

"Maybe I don't want to stick around LA. Did you ever think about that? Maybe there're too many memories here. Maybe I'm more like Mom. She hated it here."

My heart feels like it wants to wiggle out of my chest. "She didn't hate it here."

"No? Well, she sure didn't love it. I think she was happier in Seattle."

"You don't know that. You can't know that. You were young when we lived there." But she's not wrong, Mom was happy in Seattle. But she was happy in LA too. Truthfully, I think she would've been happy anywhere Dad was.

"It doesn't matter anyway. And regardless of how you feel about Dad's new girlfriend, I'm gonna apply for internships in New York with or without her help," she snaps, picking up two of the plates.

"Fine, do what you want, Cora. You always do." I pick up the other two plates. "And she's not his girlfriend."

We head to the back door, pie plates in our hands, and we look like the perfect sisters. We smile and laugh as we catch the tail end of some crack Dad is telling Jules about not letting us fool her because we used to go at it like professional cage fighters when we were younger.

Behind my smile, I grit my teeth, and Cora mumbles so only I can hear her, "She looks a lot like his girlfriend to me."

Dad has his hand on the nape of Jules's neck, his fingers trailing down the skin there and twirling in the loose hair that's fallen from her ponytail. It's natural and not the least bit awkward at all, and my stomach does a flip-flop at the realization. He really likes her.

The feeling is unsettling.

AFTER WE FINISH THE PIE AND ICE CREAM, DAD DRIVES JULES home. I busy myself in the kitchen, cleaning up the dinner and dessert mess, and try not to think about how long it should take Dad to drive to Jules's house and return. I play a little game in my head; if I rinse four dishes and stick them into the dishwasher, then I can check the time flashing on the stove. But I'm losing at my own game because I'm glancing at the time on the stove basically ten times before another minute has passed.

Richie carries in wine glasses and beer bottles from outside and sets them on the kitchen island. "That's everything." He tosses the bottles into the trash. "You wanna hand me a towel, and I'll wipe down the table out there?"

"Sure." I get him a wet towel and hand it to him, smiling. "Thanks."

He returns the smile and before he goes back outside, he says, "You can thank me properly later." He winks.

"Ew, gross," Cora says, sauntering into the kitchen.

"Why is it gross? I'm your sister, we should be able to talk about this stuff."

"Yeah, well, our age gap sometimes makes it feel like you're a lot older. And when I'm around you two, it sometimes feels like you're my parents."

"Gross," I mutter.

"So," Cora takes a seat on a stool shoved under the island counter. "You wanna finish discussing Dad and his not-girlfriend?"

I glance up at her while cleaning a pot in the sink, surprised she wants to continue our earlier conversation. But also not wanting to. I'm tired— tired from the day, tired from the topic. "I'm not sure that's a good idea."

"I get it, okay? I get your reservations about seeing Dad with someone new."

"It's not that," I interrupt.

"No? Then what is it?"

I hesitate, chewing my lower lip and scrubbing the pot with more force.

"It's Jules? You don't like her?"

"It's not that I don't like her. But you don't know her as well as I do. I told you, she's a mess." I glance at her.

Cora shrugs this off. "She's really smart. And did you know her dad was living with her up until about a year ago?"

I glance over my shoulder to look at Cora and shake my head.

"I guess he has dementia, and her mom left him because of it a few years back. Jules felt bad and had him move in with her. But no matter how difficult it got, she didn't have the heart to put him in a facility. It wasn't until there was some kind of an incident that she realized she wasn't equipped to handle him on her own."

"Wow," is all I can say.

Questions swirl around in my mind. Is that why she'd been willing to take on Dad as her client when she'd been hesitant at first? Because she's aware of how hard my situation is? Suddenly, things begin to fall into place, clicking in my mind, words spoken and actions made by Jules. My heart squeezes as the guilt pinches around it. I haven't given her much of a chance. Especially as being a potential partner for Dad.

"That has to be hard," Cora says, but I hardly hear her over the swishing of the regrets in my mind. "Our dad may have reverted to a child again, but at least he knows who we are."

"Right," I mumble.

"And even though her dad doesn't always know who she is, she still goes every week to visit him. She brings him books. I guess he loves reading."

My jaw hangs open before I find words. "How do you know all of this?"

Cora smirks at me. "It's called asking questions and listening. That's what people do when they want to get to know someone. Duh." Cora stands. "Do you honestly believe I care about her dog Kobe? And how her roommate can't stand the thing and how she has to try to keep the two separated constantly? Not one bit. But you know why I ask?"

I don't even shake my head, Cora continues.

"Because I know Dad likes her. I can't let him fall in love with her without knowing what kind of woman she is."

Her attention to detail and her strategy astounds me, and a stab of guilt hits me in the chest for not giving Cora more credit—she deserves more.

"You think I'm some flighty, silly girl, but I'm not. While you've been busy designing clothing and working on opening the store and planning to start a family with Richie, I've grown up. And whether you like it or not, Dad is eventually gonna move on. He's fun and goofy and smart. And even if we crack jokes about his age, he's not that old. Do we really want him to be alone for the rest of his life?"

I stare at her for a minute. She threads her arms across her chest with a little defiance, as if she's waiting for me to debate this further. But I'm not willing. I'm exhausted. And she's right—about all of it.

I exhale and say it out loud so she can hear it too. "You're right. I may not like the idea of Dad moving on without Mom. But he really is a catch." I smile and Cora does too. "And obviously"—I throw my hand up in the air—"I don't want him to live with me anymore. Which is the reason we're even discussing Jules to begin with." Leaning against the counter, the hard granite edge digs into my back.

"It's not like I love the idea. But Jules seems pretty great. And I trust Dad's judgment."

Her words stick in me like a broken record, playing on repeat, and they'll haunt me for days. Because is it really Dad's judgment? Or is it mine? I'm the one, after all, who stuck the two of them together.

Chapter 24

Jules

I purposely cut my workday short on Friday. It's Pete's second-to-last session. I only scheduled him and one other client who is just beginning his six-week program. I planned Pete's challenge for this afternoon. It's a rarity to schedule a challenge for the same day as a client's session, but this was the only time slot that worked.

Pete stares at me with desire burning in his green eyes while I feel the slightest trickle of sweat work its way in between my breasts. Since our relationship beyond interventionist-client has progressed, my focus on the task at hand has become erratic. It's proving to be near impossible to get through my checklist for today's session.

When I glance up at Pete, leaning back into the sofa, his vision drags up the length of my bare legs beneath my short green dress.

"Pete," I warn. "Focus."

"I could say the same thing to you." He grins. "You've been staring at your black iPad screen for at least sixty seconds while fiddling with your necklace."

He's right. The iPad screen has timed out and I've been staring at it while my mind wanders back to last weekend when Pete drove me home after our dinner at Tess and Richie's. I'd planned on giving him a lingering kiss goodbye on my front porch. But one thing led to another, and upon finding Angie out, I invited him in.

Pete knew Tess would be back at her home, climbing the walls waiting for him to return, so we got right down to business. We were like ravenous teenagers, acting as if our parents might come home any minute and catch us. Our clothes were stripped in record timing, and he thrust me onto the sofa, his foreplay skills quick and efficient. His kisses had been like fire against my skin, his tongue making quick work between my thighs. The love making session was so intense it could've reached an astounding eleven on the Richter scale.

Pete clears his throat, and I blink up at him, feeling flushed, and adjust in my chair. I unlock the iPad screen, my eyes quickly scanning over the checklist to find my place. "Yes, here we are. So, what did you think of your last challenge?"

"What did I think?" he repeats the question, incredulous, and rubs at his chin.

"Yes. Was it challenging?"

"I mean..." He sits forward. "Yeah, at first."

"How so?"

"Spending a lazy day at the beach was something we used to do as a family. When we needed to unwind or reconnect. Surfing, shave ice, Frisbee, were only a few things we enjoyed. The four of us."

It's as if my lap gets weighed down by bricks, one after another being laid on top of me as the realization comes into full form. In some kind of a twisted joke, Tess had hijacked Pete's challenge in order to recreate their family trip to the beach. Then purposely attempted to sabotage it by having me admit to knowing how to surf. Which would possibly cause me to admit to the usual structure of my program.

But I'm not sure why she'd want to hurt her father. Or ruin the program.

"But having you there helped tenfold. You can't imagine how much of a relief that was. If Tess had planned a beach day, it would've been just me, her, and Cora. And maybe Richie. Which would've been worse."

Little does Pete know, Tess did plan the challenge.

Something about Pete's last sentence digs in my brain. "Why would it have been worse if Richie had been there?"

"Look, don't get me wrong, Richie is great. When he's with Tess, she makes him better. She grounds him. But without her, he comes off looking like a big douche. Somehow, together, they work."

I consider this. My first impression of Richie was close to that. I pegged him for a pretentious douche. But I like how Pete explained Richie and Tess's relationship in this way—together, they work. Isn't that how a relationship should be—each person complementing the other and making them better because of it?

"So again, thank you for my last challenge. It was enlightening, to say the least."

"How so?" I'm not positive if I'm asking as an interventionist or as his girlfriend.

Am I his girlfriend?

"I've been so scared to enjoy things again like I used to. I felt guilty for laughing, for having a good time. But when I was out there on that surfboard riding the waves, I felt carefree. I felt like myself for the first time in a long time." His face is open, and he nearly smiles, almost like I can read the relief on his expression.

"That's really great, Pete. Letting go of the guilt you feel for moving on when your loved one can't is a monumental step." I feel as if I've said too much. I fold my lips in between my teeth. Because maybe him moving on and not feeling guilty about it can mean he has a right to move on with me. That we have a chance at a real relationship.

He nods, his attention fixated on his shoes where the laces are about to unravel. It's as if the air in the room is being sucked up with a vacuum. I need to bring him back. "Do you want to know your next challenge?"

He glances up with wonderment shining in his green eyes and

maybe a little excitement. He seems to be enjoying these challenges. "Give it to me, doc." He winks, causing goosebumps to flutter down the bare skin on my legs.

"As I told you on the phone, this one has to be done this afternoon. I typically like to have at least a day in between a session and a challenge, but this afternoon was the only opportunity."

"I'm intrigued." He waggles his dark brows.

It sends a throbbing between my thighs, and I'm tempted to hurl myself onto his lap, and beg him to deflower my office.

I swing by Tess's house to pick up Pete around one o'clock. Because of my last encounter with Tess, I text Pete from the car and let him know I'm here. A few moments later, he climbs into the passenger side, pressing a kiss to my cheek, and I stiffen. This feels very date-ish when it should feel more challenge-ish.

"Hey, Pete. Ready?"

He clicks his seat belt into place, and I pull away from the curb.

"You're being awfully secretive about this challenge."

"That's because this is your surprise challenge." I glance over at him, and his dark brows furrow.

"What's that mean?"

"Exactly that. It's a surprise."

"But what is it supposed to accomplish?"

I flip the signal and turn right, taking us out of Tess's neighborhood and back into the city. It's strange taking this route to a place I could probably drive to with my eyes closed from my own house.

"Jules?"

"Right. Um...the surprise challenge is supposed to accomplish trust. You need to learn to trust someone again. Trust they know you well enough to plan things—such as outings."

"As in, a date?"

"Not exactly."

"Sounds like a date to me." His voice sounds husky, and it makes the skin on my neck tingle.

We reach the memory care facility, and Pete is quiet next to me. I assume he's still trying to put the pieces together. I pull up in front of the main doors and climb out of the car. A moment later, Charlene pushes Dad outside in a wheelchair. The sight causes the air to expel from my lungs. But she rests an assuring hand on my arm.

"It's only to get him out here quicker and to make it look as if I'm taking him out for a stroll," she whispers, conspiratorially.

I bend. "Hey, Dad. It's good to see you." I search his eyes for recognition, my stomach tight with apprehension.

"Good to see you, honey."

I exhale audibly and give him a quick kiss on the forehead. Okay, this is going to be fine.

Pete gets out of the car, and I realize that I forgot to give him instructions.

"Hey, you wanna help me get him into the car?"

He checks over his shoulders nervously. "Uh, sure."

I pull Dad up underneath his elbow and when Pete goes to his other side to do the same, Dad shakes us both off. "I'm not an invalid. I can get into a car by myself."

Worry bubbles in my chest, and I whip my head toward Char.

"Mr. Sweeney, I presume?" Pete asks.

"Let's save our introductions until we're in the car, shall we?"

Dad folds himself into the passenger seat, and I close the door behind him. Pete gets into the back without another word. I look to

Char for a warning that this is a very bad idea. But she takes my hands in her clammy ones, squeezing them.

"Don't worry. He'll be fine. It's a good day."

Her eyes are sincere and persistent, I trust her. And she obviously trusts me to put her job on the line.

"Thank you."

"But you call me if there's any problem. I have one of the nurses on the ready, and we'll be there in a jiff." She backs away, moving closer to the main doors.

I make brief introductions between Dad and Pete. Thankfully, Dad is cordial, and Pete doesn't ask too many questions, though I hear him repeat Dad's name under his breath several times, like he's trying to figure why it sounds familiar. The two remain mostly quiet until I pull up in front of a large historical apartment building in Beverly Hills, and we climb out of the car.

"Where are we?" Pete whispers when he comes alongside me.

I hold up a finger to him.

"And please tell me we didn't just break your dad outta that place without permission?"

"Then I won't tell you," I say flatly.

"Dad." I hook my arm in the crook of his elbow. "Do you know where we're at?"

Dad stops abruptly, his gaze travels up the building until it reaches the top. "I have my suspicions."

The three of us enter the lobby, and it's all marble floors and tall cathedral ceilings with chandeliers. A massive gas fireplace adorns the wall, and a man dressed in a black suit stands behind a large desk before directing us to the elevator and buzzing us up to the thirteenth floor. This building is so fancy it's rendered Pete speechless. But Dad is taking it all in, the memories flooding his mind.

"Jules," Dad whispers, "this is a wonderful surprise."

My heart swells, and I have to remind myself, not only am I doing this for Dad but for Pete as well. Two birds, one stone.

We knock on the door for apartment 312 and are greeted by a

smiling, well put together woman with etched wrinkles and a large pearl necklace wrapped around her neck.

"Hello, my name is Jules Sweeney. We spoke on the phone."

Her smile turns brighter, and she welcomes us inside. "Yes, please come in. It's so nice to finally meet you. Harry has been going on and on about your father."

We step inside and enter a foyer that's nearly as impressive as the building's foyer, though the ceilings are slightly lower. There's a small round table in the middle, and I never understood why people place a table directly in the middle of a foyer. We enter a living room, and on a well-manicured chair sits an older man with a balding head and a navy cardigan. He stands when he recognizes Dad.

"Jimmy? You really have aged. Look at you. Gray hair and all."

I stifle a laugh.

But Dad isn't laughing. Instead, he's emotional, fighting back tears. "Harry, it's good to see you, my friend."

They embrace, and regardless of what happens when I take Dad back to the memory care facility, this moment will make it worth it.

"You too."

He pulls back. Dad says, "And who are you calling old? At least I have hair."

Harry points a finger at him as if to say, *Aah, you got me there, old-timer.*

Pete nudges my arm, leaning toward my ear. "Is that—Is he... Harry Brooks? Bass player for The Hughes?"

"It is." I smile, fighting back my own tears at the sight of this reunion. It's only been about five years since the two have seen one another, but a lot has changed in that time. Dad's health declined, Mom took off, and Dad moved into the facility.

I glance at Pete and see his jaw is hanging open.

"Hi, sweet angel." Harry wraps his arms around me. His height towers over me, and he plants a kiss on the top of my head. I breathe in his musky scent. It brings along waves of memories with it. For years I watched the two of these men play together. He pulls back and eyes Pete. "What's with this guy?"

"This is Pete Redd. He's a fellow bass player."

"Is that so?" Harry gives him the once-over, as if sizing him up. "Okay, let's see what you can do."

Pete blinks at him. "Pardon me?"

"That's the reason you're here, isn't it?"

"I, uh…I'm not sure." He glances back and forth between me and Harry.

"My dad is Jim Sweeney, guitar player for The Hughes from 1978—1989," I say by way of explanation.

Pete rubs a hand over his mouth and crosses one arm over his chest. "I thought you said he played bass?"

"He does. He also plays guitar. And drums and keyboard."

"Jack of all trades?" Pete raises one dark brow, impressed.

"I brought you here to not only meet my dad but also Harry. And to play with them."

Harry shuffles past us, giving a flick of a wave over his shoulder. "C'mon."

We follow like obedient schoolchildren, walking down a long hallway with tall closed doors on either side until we reach the room at the end. Harry opens the door and enters, the rest of us close on his heels. The room is a small but fancy high-tech recording studio. A variety of instruments line the walls with a control board covered in a multitude of buttons and switches.

Harry gives Dad a guitar, and without hesitation, he pulls it over his head and sets his hands on the strings as if the instrument were a missing limb. Harry removes a bass from a stand and hands it to Pete. He accepts it like the gift it is, taking it carefully like he's holding a newborn baby.

Harry sits on the leather chair in front of the control board and begins pushing buttons. "Let's start with something simple. 'When You're in Town, Look Me Up.' You know it?" He glances over his shoulder at Pete.

Pete nods enthusiastically. "Yes, of course. Do I know it? There was a time I lived and breathed 'When You're in Town, Look Me Up.' I learned how to play bass by studying how you played," he says to Harry.

Harry chuckles under his breath. He waves me over. "Jules, you sit here and move this switch up or down depending on the instrument sound. And turn this dial if the background voices grow too loud or too soft."

"I think I can do that," I say.

I take a seat, and my eyes move across the many buttons while my fingers twitch. There are so many switches. When I turn my head to look at the three men, Pete makes a face at me with his mouth hanging open as if to say, *Can you believe this?* A warming sensation fills my chest, and I smile at him.

Harry takes another bass from off the wall and adjusts it in his hands. He directs me to press the big round black button before counting the men off. They begin playing "When You're in Town, Look Me Up" with the band's vocals singing along in the background. They have a bit of a rough start. I can't remember the last time Dad played. But it doesn't take him long to pick it up again.

I realize I've never actually seen Pete play before, and I wish I had sooner. He looks at one with the bass. He plays with ease and confidence. This is not only something that brings him joy, but it makes him shine.

I have to remind myself to pay attention to the sound and remember to move the dials and levers as Harry instructed. But I'm distracted by this vision of these men playing together. All three are clearly talented, and it doesn't matter how long it's been since they've picked up an instrument or how old they are. Once the music gets ahold of them, there's no loosening its grip.

Dad looks more alive than I've seen him in years while he strums the strings of the guitar. It's as if the instrument has rolled back the clock somehow. It's also as if the dementia has no effect on him while he's playing. His thumb works the chords, and he sings along with the words, not missing a beat. Unwanted tears work their way up my throat and sting my eyes. I swipe at them quickly with my fingertips and don't think the men notice. They're completely transfixed by their music.

After their jam session, Harry's wife, Rita, brings us homemade cookies and tea in fancy cups on saucers. It feels very different from the In-N-Out burgers, fries, and milkshakes I used to consume with the band after jam sessions when I was a child. It brings me back to reality, reminding me that these men aren't the young guys they once were. Their balding and gray heads, wrinkled hands and faces, and slow-moving bodies are suddenly front and center in my mind.

"You're not too bad," Dad says to Pete over the brim of his teacup.

"Thank you. You're not too bad yourself." He grins.

"I never would've thought my daughter would end up with a musician." Dad shoves a cookie into his mouth in two bites.

My face blanches. On our drive over to Harry's, I explained to Dad that Pete is my client. I never mentioned we were dating. But I'm having a difficult time finding the words to correct him.

"Why is that, Mr. Sweeney?" Pete asks.

"I always thought she hated how I was on the road all the time. You know, touring with the band. I missed out on a great deal of her childhood."

My heart rate accelerates, and I worry he's going to bring up Mom. If she comes into the conversation, Dad may get upset, and I could lose him. Not to mention have a hard time getting him into my car and back to the facility.

"But when you were home, you always made the best of our time together. Like all the basketball games." I remind him, trying to keep the conversation positive. "And it was only for a few years."

"That's true," Harry chimes in. "But what a whirlwind those years were."

Dad and Harry both smile. I imagine all the memories they share in that one smile.

"When Jimmy decided he needed to quit the band and be a more present father, I went solo."

"It was the best decision I ever made for you." It's obvious it's intended as a joke, but I can't help but pick up on the slight edge to Dad's voice.

I've always wondered if he regretted quitting the band. I felt responsible for his decision. But I also remember the fights he and Mom would have over him being away on tour and how she never planned on being a single mother. It was that reason they never had more children. I think I was a surprise.

"It's true. My solo career was a good one. I have no complaints. But the best thing was when I retired and I met this wonderful lady." He smiles up at Rita, a look of endearment shining in his eyes.

"I can't complain either."

"So, Jules," Harry begins, "you ever pick up learning an instrument? You think about following in your father's footsteps?"

"Oh, no." Embarrassment creeps up my neck with a tingle. And maybe a bit of worry. The talk of my lack of musical talents somehow brings with it the conversation of my clumsiness followed by a possible episode for Dad. I can't risk that. Not today. "I think my talents are more suited toward helping others. And pointing out their talents."

"Is that what you're doing here? With Pete?"

"Um...sort of. Yes." I finger the globe pendant around my neck.

Pete looks at me and gives me a closed mouth smile.

"My wife died a few months back. It hit me harder than I thought it would since we knew for a while it was coming. Jules is helping me discover how to do life again. How to enjoy life again."

"I take it you once enjoyed playing bass?" Harry asks.

"I did. I do."

"You're quite good." Harry doesn't throw compliments out like Oprah on her gift-giving episodes. He keeps them guarded and close to his heart, only handing them out when he feels they're most deserved.

Pete seems to understand this because he nods reverently. "Thank you."

"You know, it's never too late to pick it up again. Playing an instrument is like riding a bike; once you've got it down, it sticks with you. It can be a refuge in times of trouble, grief, doubt. It can fill that emotional hole and take the place of a lover too." Harry glances at Rita, taking his free hand in hers. "At least until you're ready to fill that hole with a physical being."

Pete's eyes flick toward me as if on instinct alone, and I think it surprises not only me but him as well. It sets my skin on fire, and I want to tell him so many things at this moment. I want to tell him that there are things he needs to know before I can fill that hole. Things that could make him change his mind about me entirely.

Chapter 25

Pete

Today is my last session with Jules. I enter the elevator of her office building feeling light on my feet and push the button with a sense of ease. Even the uncertainty of the rumbling floor underneath me doesn't alter my mood.

And when it spits me out into the main office, I'm prepared for it, and I glide out easily. Angie is seated at her desk, feet out of her shoes and propped on the desktop. She gives me the usual once-over, and I'm tempted to ask if she'll ever not check me out when she sees me— my guess is no.

"Morning," Angie singsongs, fluttering her long fingers in my direction.

"Good morning, Angie. Always a pleasure." I tip my imaginary hat at her. This grants me a grimace along with a giggle nonetheless. "Is she in her office?"

"Yep. Eagerly awaiting your arrival, I'm sure."

Her comment sends an eagerness of my own deep within me, and I turn the knob slowly before pushing the door open. But when I peek inside, Jules isn't sitting on her chair near the sofa, where we usually have our sessions. And she's not seated at her desk either.

"Jules?" I search around for her.

"Pete?" a muffled voice calls out.

"Where are you?"

"Don't come in here," she warns.

"Too late, I'm already in."

"Fine, just don't come any closer." Her voice sounds frantic now.

"What's going on?" I finally find her wedged underneath her desk in a position that looks uncomfortable. "What the hell?"

"Go away! And go get Ang, will you?"

"What are you doing down there? Are you okay?" I crouch beside her.

"I'm fine," she pouts.

"You don't sound fine. Were you trying out some kind of sexy move or something?"

"What?" she shrieks. "No! I was trying a new office exercise I saw on Pinterest."

I drop to my knees and attempt to help untangle her. From this angle, the unnatural position looks even worse. "Did the exercise work?" I tease, reaching underneath her arms and pulling her out.

"Shut up," she mutters in between a string of *ouches* and curses.

Once I have her seated in her office chair, pink crawls up her neck and tinges her cheeks. She adjusts the green dress at the neckline and over her legs. I worry I should've listened to her first request and fetched Angie. But I'm fairly certain she would make a bigger deal out of this than I will.

I crouch next to her again and push the strawberry blonde hair out of her face. "You okay?"

"I'm fine. Thank you." She straightens, then winces.

"Why don't you come by tonight. We'll see if we can work through some of that tension." It isn't my meaning, but my words come across as if I'm propositioning her. I only wish I was that smooth of a talker.

This lightens her mood a little, and she gives me a soft smile without revealing her straight white teeth. "I don't want to intrude on Tess. She made it pretty clear she'd rather the two of us not date."

"Not to Tess and Richie's place. To mine."

She eyes me skeptically.

I scratch at the scruff on my chin. "I moved some of my stuff back home earlier this week."

Jules's hazel eyes widen. "Really? Why didn't you tell me?"

Her expression reveals she's hurt by this. During our texting exchanges this past week, I hadn't mentioned anything about it. I think I wanted to shock her with the sticker price.

"Guess I didn't think it was that big of a deal." But of course it's a big deal—I've decided to move back home—it's a *huge* deal.

She seems to consider my response, but she's not buying it. "What did Tess say?"

"I haven't told her yet. So far I've only taken a few things over. And I haven't slept there—yet." I waggle my brows at her.

She blushes, tucking her hair behind her ear. "C'mon, session time." She slides to the edge of her seat before pulling herself to standing.

"You sure I need it?" I grin at her, hoping my boyish charm will get me off the hook and the two of us can head to my place now.

"It's your last session. I never let a client leave unsatisfied." She smirks, and fervor rises in me. Her innuendo is impeccable, and I'm impressed.

"Yes, ma'am." I take my seat on the sofa. When she joins me, sitting in the chair adjacent to me, I say, "Can we skip to my last challenge already?"

"Always the eager student," she teases again and pulls up my file on her iPad.

I glance at the lit screen in her lap but she holds it away so I can't read what she's written about me. I'm curious now, why so secretive? "Hey, let me see. Whatcha got written there about me?" I reach out my hand to push the iPad down.

She snatches it further out of my reach. "No way. Hands off. This is for my eyes only."

"Can you at least tell me, am I passing?"

"There's no pass or fail here. You should know that by now."

"But c'mon, there's some way of you knowing if I successfully made it through your program, right?"

"Well, yeah. Of course."

"Then at least tell me that."

"This is your last session, is it not? And you only have one more challenge left. You complete those, you complete the program. Simple as that."

But it doesn't feel like enough—it doesn't feel simple. Getting through Jules's last five sessions and last five challenges have been exactly that—challenging. Not all of them, of course. Because Jules has been there for most of my challenges, each one has felt easier and easier to complete.

Once I finish the program, what will happen to me? And to us? Will I be able to do life without her insisting I complete these challenges? Or will her presence be enough for me to keep going? To keep inching forward in this game called life.

I push the worries away. As long as I have Jules at my side and Tess and Cora in my corner, I can keep going. I have to. Because I don't have a choice. My daughters need me. And I promised Natalie I wouldn't fall apart without her. Before meeting Jules, I'd broken my promise.

When my last session draws to an end, the finality of it all sits low in my gut, and I feel uneasy rather than light like when I'd first walked into Jules's office. I began this program defiantly, practically kicking and screaming, and now I find myself not wanting it to end. These sessions have been sacred, on my calendar for six weeks, every Friday. Giving me somewhere to be—something to look forward to.

"So," Jules says, stretching out the word as she leans forward in her seat. "You ready for your last challenge?"

The sunlight catches the globe pendant dangling from her neck.

The neckline of her dress is cut low, and I imagine telling Angie to hold Jules's next client and locking the door, and forgetting about all the finality of this session.

But instead, I say, "Go for it."

"This last one is a biggie." She crosses her leg and my vision dances up her creamy skin starting at her ankle and working up to her thigh where she subconsciously tugs at the hemline of her dress. "You, my friend, are going hiking."

"Hiking? As in a day hike? Or an overnight?" I'm momentarily stunned. This is not what I had expected. Hiking is easy. Jules said this last challenge was a biggie. Hiking has never been a challenge for me.

"Just a day hike. And you can choose to go at it alone or invite someone else." A smile spreads across her sweet face, taking it over. "But seriously, I won't be offended if you don't take me."

"I wouldn't dream of doing it alone," I say hastily.

"Pete, I'm serious. I don't think you understand the implications here."

"Hiking is easy. Hiking is something I used to enjoy." I wave her off and relax into the sofa. "Natalie and I—" I stop, the words lodging in my throat. They'd begun so easily. But now, everything rushes toward me—weighing me down—the past flooding my mind and taking over my present.

My present may be easier to handle and live in lately, but my past will always be there, sometimes haunting me and hindering my hope for my future. Will it always be like this? Will it always hurt this severely when the memories come at me, pinging from all directions?

Jules gives me a sympathetic smile. "It's okay," she reassures me.

But it's not okay. The sense of defeat from these emotions I've pushed away for the past few weeks drench me, weighing me down. I clear my throat past the lump there. "Why do I feel like I've suddenly failed the program?"

Jules slides off the chair and joins me on the sofa. She rests a gentle hand on my back and another on my arm, caressing me there.

"You haven't failed. This is a successful program, yes. But it's not foolproof. The design is to help you overcome your trauma. It's not a miracle program." Her hand slides into my hair and sends a shiver all the way to my toes. The touch is exhilarating and comforting all at once. "It doesn't take away your memories, or your past hurts," she continues. "Nor should it. Those memories are important. And special. I'd never want to take those away."

She's right. I hadn't agreed to this program in hopes of forgetting about Natalie and the life I shared with her. I agreed to satisfy my daughters. I'd agreed because deep down, I knew I couldn't go on with the despair I was feeling. Looking into Jules's hazel eyes, I see hope shining back at me. I outstretch an open palm on her lap, and she slides her hand into it.

"When?" The word comes out as a rumble in my chest.

"Tomorrow."

"Will you come with me?"

She answers with a soft and meaningful kiss to my cheek. I turn toward her and press my forehead into hers, pinching my eyes closed and inhaling her intoxicating scent of cherry blossoms.

If anyone can get me through this last challenge, it's Jules.

Chapter 26

Tess

The weeks of the countdown until the store's opening is in the single digits. But this weekend, I attempt to push every last detail surrounding the store, the designs, and the grand opening, out of my mind. I attempt to focus on my birthday party. The one I insisted I didn't want help with but am now scrambling to get things done.

Cora worked it out with her peers at the paper and was able to come to LA and help, and I'm immensely grateful. My birthday party was supposed to be low-key. An intimate setting at home with a few friends. But Richie and Cora insisted I invite more than a few friends, and somehow, nearly fifty people have RSVP'd. I'm not sure how my small home and modest yard will accommodate that many guests, but I'll have to make it work.

"Stop stressing," Cora says, reading over the to-do list I've handed to her. "This is gonna be easy. A few snacks, some drinks, extra napkins, and plates. Chill, we got this."

"It's not just a few snacks," I huff, peeking over Cora's shoulder to get a look at the list. "We have to make all of those." I point.

"I don't see why you didn't arrange to have this thing catered."

"Because, that's not the intimate party I wanted."

"Well, is fifty-two guests the intimate party you wanted? Because that's a whole lotta people to be throwing around the word *intimate*." Cora tosses the to-do list onto the kitchen counter.

I sigh and wipe the imaginary sweat off my forehead with the back of my hand. The stress ball in my stomach is manifesting. "Not really. But it's too late now." I bite the inside of my cheek, holding back from reminding her it was her idea to invite so many people.

"True. Guess we should get to work then."

"Thanks for your help."

My phone rings and the sound causes anxiety to course through me. The only time my phone has rang in the last six months has been related to the store. And it's not usually positive news. But when I pick up my phone, my doctor's office number flashes across the screen.

I answer but shuffle out of the kitchen. "Hello?"

"Is this Mrs. Cavanaugh?"

"Yes it is." I glance at Cora, who's reading over the to-do list again, and I make my way out the back door.

"Hi, Mrs. Cavanaugh. This is Victoria, calling from Dr. Miller's office. I'm calling to schedule your appointment for your blood test and genetic counseling."

"Right." In all the chaos, I'd forgotten I sent a message on the online portal requesting an appointment.

"Dr. Miller has an opening in two weeks from today at 9:00 a.m. Does that work for you?"

I don't check my schedule. I decide if I have anything on my calendar, this test is more important. Discovering if you carry the same cancer gene that is responsible for taking your mother's life is important. "Yes, that works fine."

"Great. I've got you down. Be sure to check the patient portal on our website for instructions before your appointment."

"I will, thank you." I turn back toward the house. Cora stands there, arms crossed and face questioning. I suck in a breath. "You scared me."

"What was that about?"

"Nothing. Issue with the store," I lie.

"Everything okay?"

I rush into the house, pushing past her. "It's fine."

"Because if you need help taking care of something"—she pauses, following me back inside—"I can go with you."

"No, it's fine. It's not a big deal. It can wait."

Cora is being more persistent than usual, and maybe she knows I'm lying. But I don't want to tell her I'm going in for the test. When the two of us spoke about it a year ago after Mom's cancer returned, Cora said how stupid the test was. She said a positive result could steal joy from years of being healthy, and a negative result could give you false hope because it doesn't mean you won't ever get diagnosed with cancer, it simply means you don't carry the gene. But I need to know, either way, joy-stealer or not.

"C'mon, we have lots of work to do," I say, changing the subject and hoping it's enough to distract her from my phone call.

Dad returns home when it's nearly dark. "Hey, I'm home."

I peer down the hall at him, hands pressed to my hips, and wonder if he plans on mentioning where he's been all day. I bite my lip, hoping I won't have to pry. "Hey."

He takes a seat on the bench in the entryway and slips off his shoes. "How'd everything go today? Get everything ready for the party?"

"Almost. Cora was a big help. We'll finish everything in the morning."

He nods. "Awesome." He sets his shoes inside the entryway closet and squeezes my shoulder as he passes. "Cora still here?"

"Yep. Eating all my favorite ice cream."

"Hey," Cora interjects, pushing herself up and peeking over the back of the sofa. "You said I could. If you didn't want to share, you shouldn't have offered."

Dad walks over to Cora and pats the top of her head, messing up her hair. "Hey, kid." He plops down next to her on the sofa, sliding his phone from his front pocket when it pings.

Richie is stretched out across the sofa on the opposite wall, snoring. I squeeze in at the end, hugging the armrest in an attempt not to wake him. Work has been extra stressful the past few weeks, and he's exhausted.

"So." Cora waggles her brows, combing her fingers through her hair. "How was your session today?"

A smile stretches across his lips, one that's genuine and creates a warm stirring in my chest. He's happy. He taps away on his phone before placing it facedown on his thigh and resting both arms on the back of the sofa. "The session was good. Jules had on this olive-green dress that really made her hazel eyes pop."

"Dad." Cora pushes her fist into his leg. "We don't want to hear about Jules."

He chuckles to himself. "Fine. Let me guess. You're only interested in what she's given me as my last challenge, right?" He raises his brows.

"Duh, of course."

"Hiking," he says flatly.

"Hiking?" I question before the memories roll in, and I realize what this last challenge could do to Dad. I fidget with the threads from the holes in my denim jeans. "Do you think you'll be okay?"

He shrugs a shoulder. "I'm sure the memories of Mom will be present in my mind while I make my way through the terrain, but I've survived the last five challenges without her, so this one should be no different."

"I'm not so sure your first challenge went as well as you think." Cora snickers.

"Hey, I didn't say it went well, I said I survived."

"And is Jules planning on joining you?" I hedge, unsure how I want him to answer.

"I asked if she would, and she agreed, yes."

"You sure you wouldn't rather do this challenge on your own?" The worry bubbles in my stomach.

"I think it's safe to say, as Cora pointed out, I don't handle these challenges so well on my own." He smiles to himself, and Cora and I share a look from across the room. Happiness radiates from him. "Besides, I enjoy her company. She's pretty cool."

"Well, she's much cooler than you, that's for sure," Cora teases.

Dad puts her in a gentle headlock and gives her a noogie on the top of the head, and they laugh. But my stomach is still tied like a pretzel. Now that the challenges and sessions are over, had Dad passed the program? And will Jules be done with him? Or will this "relationship" continue? Was it real for her too?

"Where were you all day?" I ask, my tone unintentionally sounding accusatory.

"If you must know, *Mother*"—he exaggerates the word mother—"I went to Pismo Beach."

"Really?" I scoot to the edge of the sofa cushion. "Did someone put in an offer on Dave's house?"

"Yep." He grins. "And Dave accepted. The house is sold."

"Way to go, Dad." Cora high-fives him

I reach across for a high five as well. "We need to celebrate."

"Nah." He gives a dismissive wave.

"C'mon, it's been a while since you've sold a house," Cora reminds him.

"It's no big deal. Besides, I've got plans."

"Plans?" I run my palms over my thighs.

"With Jules?" Cora presses.

He shoves a soft fist into her leg. "No, nosy." His phone pings and he smiles so big it stretches across his face as he glances at the screen. "Actually, Dave had a couple extra boxes so I brought them back."

My eyes go wide, and my jaw drops.

"Don't look so thrilled, jeez. You could at least play it off that you're sad I'm gonna be out of your space soon."

"I am. I'm...surprised is all." My words come out jumbled and broken.

Cora scoots close to Dad and rests her head on his chest, her toffee-brown hair splaying out and around his shoulder. "You sure you're ready?"

He wraps his arm around her and shakes his head. "No. But it's time."

It has been nearly ten months since Dad moved in and rumpled my home and life. There was nothing I wanted more than to get him back on his own two feet, back in his own house, and have my privacy back again. But now that it's about to happen, it feels as if there's a gigantic hole in the cavity of my chest.

Jules really did it.

Just as she said she would. She promised he would complete her six-week program successfully. And he did. So how come it doesn't feel like a success? How come it feels like a failure instead?

"You know you don't have to go," I insist, my words vibrating in my chest as tears threaten.

He huffs. "Yeah, right. It's nice of you to say, Tess, really. But you and Richie are trying to have a baby, and I'm getting in the way. Not to mention, I've nearly finished Jules's program. It feels fitting to complete it by moving back home."

"I'm not gonna lie," Cora mumbles, "I'll be happy to have our home back too."

Dad smiles and brings her in closer, pressing a kiss to her forehead. "I know, kid."

Tears spring to my eyes, and I blink rapidly to prevent them from fully forming.

"Well, you said you didn't want to celebrate, but you wanna join us for ice cream and a movie?" Cora says.

"Rain check? I'm actually gonna start packing some things, and Daniel is gonna help me take the boxes over to the house. Then I'd better get to bed. I'm picking up Jules early." He stands and pats Cora's leg and then squeezes my shoulder. "Night, kids. Don't stay up too late." He winks.

"Night, Dad," we both call up the stairs in unison.

"Wow," Cora says once Dad is gone, falling back against the sofa. "I can't believe it worked."

I move to join her on the sofa. "Me neither," I say on an exhaled breath.

"You and Richie are getting your house back."

But it doesn't feel like I'm gaining anything. In a way, it feels like I'm losing him all over again. Just like I had after Mom died.

The soothing sound of the bass begins to drift from upstairs. Dad is playing "Jack and Diane." For the last week, he's been playing the bass again. The sound is both soothing and unsettling.

Chapter 27

Jules

It's Saturday morning and today is Pete's last challenge. I'm all nerves and agitation as I fret in front of the full-length mirror. Part of me assumed Pete would attempt this challenge on his own. But the other part of me was thrilled he'd asked me to join him.

Despite his progress—cutting ties with the robe, selling a house, and slowly moving back home—he still has issues he needs to work through. I'm sure that will always be true. No one is instantly healed after completing my program. Life, in general, doesn't work that way. If it did, entire professions and pharmaceutical companies would go out of business.

Angie enters my room dressed in workout clothes, her black hair pulled into a high ponytail. I'm busy shifting this way and that, posing in front of the mirror. She's awake early for a Saturday. She met a new guy at the gym last week and is meeting him for a workout date. I make a mental note to add that as a challenge idea for a future client.

Kobe jumps off his bed and trots over to her, grunting and jumping on her legs.

Angie steps back and hollers at him. "Down, Cujo! Don't you dare even think about pissing on my new Nikes."

"Kobe, bed," I command. He hesitates but ultimately gives up on receiving any attention from her, and returns to his bed unsatisfied.

Angie tilts her head to the side, inspecting my outfit choice: A pair of olive-green linen shorts, a cotton black tank top and hiking boots.

Nerves creep up my spine and into my neck, creating unnecessary tension. "What? What's wrong with it? Should I change?" I talk to her through the mirror.

"Nah, I mean...I guess not."

I turn to face her, throwing my hands up. "What's that supposed to mean?"

"I guess I thought you'd go with something more fitted, sexier. Since you clearly aren't taking my advice and you're still dating Pete." She leans her back on my dresser, crossing her arms.

I exhale a dramatic sigh through my nose. "We aren't dating. We aren't labeling it. He asked me to go with him, and I thought he shouldn't do this challenge alone. Hiking was a big part of his life before..." I let my words fall, not bothering to finish the sentence. The look in Angie's creamy-brown eyes says I don't need to. I tie a flannel around my waist and throw snacks, a few favorite hardback books, and a couple Hydro Flasks full of water into my backpack.

"Yeah, maybe. But he could've asked one of his daughters. Or a friend."

"Well, he asked me."

"And I'm sure you were quick to oblige," she sarcastically teases.

I pause from packing my backpack and look at her. "I know you don't approve. But Ang, I'm actually happy. Being around Pete makes me happy, okay? I spend all my time and energy visiting with my dad, transporting books back and forth. I strive to help people succeed in my program, assuring they'll end up happy. Don't I deserve a happily ever after?" Pushing aside the backpack, I slump onto the bed.

"Of course. God knows you've been screwed over enough times in your life by men. Scratch that, by people. Your mom included. All I've ever wanted is for you to be happy. But—" She pauses, and for a moment, I think she's going to sit by me, wrap her arms around me, and tell me everything will be okay. But this is Angie, and she's not the nurturing type. "But at what cost? At whose cost?"

"Ugh." I bury my face in my hands. Why does she always have to be right? "Why does it have to be at anyone's cost? Why can't things just work without anyone getting hurt?"

"Sadly that's not how things work. Especially if you're not completely honest with someone from the start."

"Stop making so much sense," I mumble from behind my hands.

Angie pats my shoulder, her *attaboy* gesture and I slide my palms down my face, glancing up at her.

"Hey, I'm not saying it can't work out. I'm saying, maybe not now."

A tiny smidge of hope stirs inside my core, and I pull my hair up into a ponytail. "I hope you're right."

"Get him through the program. Then be honest with him and see where it goes." She gives my shoulder a shake. "I know your old lady parts went through a dry spell but have some self-control, woman."

She gets an exhaled laugh out of me. "I'll try my best."

"Good. That's my girl." She turns around and walks out of my room.

"But I'm not making any promises," I holler after her.

PETE PULLS UP IN FRONT OF MY HOUSE AT 7:00 A.M. WITH THE top off the Jeep. To bypass the awkward interaction between him and Angie, I've been waiting on the porch. He climbs out and comes around the front of the Jeep, dressed in tan shorts and a green T-shirt stretched over his tight abs. Fervor radiates through my chest, and I inhale a deep breath before averting my eyes.

This is not a date, I remind myself as I lug my heavy backpack down the cement walkway.

"Hey," Pete says, sporting his signature adorable grin and I resist from melting. "Hope you brought lots of water. It's supposed to be really hot today."

Oh I think we've already reached a record-breaking heat level for the day. Sizzling in fact.

He meets me in the middle of the walkway while I fan myself with my shirt and suck my lower lip in between my teeth. "Let me get that for you." He reaches for my backpack.

"I brought a lot. Like, more than a human possibly needs to drink in a day."

"You aren't kidding. Did you pack some bricks too?" He struggles as he throws the pack into the back of the Jeep.

I ignore the question and climb into the passenger side, buckling my seatbelt.

Pete mumbles under his breath as he slides behind the wheel and starts the Jeep. Then I hear him more clearly. He's not mumbling, he's singing. It's so quiet I almost can't hear him. He sings the lyrics to Nelly's "Hot in Here," and I try to refrain from giggling but fail. He blushes but then proceeds to sing the next line louder, adding a bit more confidence as well. The two of us laugh, and I join in with the chorus and even dance a little in my seat.

It feels like it takes an eternity to get out of the city, and I've already drank a full water bottle to find some relief from the sun beating down on me. The road to the hiking trail turns from asphalt to gravel, then to dirt. California live oak trees line the road, gifting a bit of welcomed shade. Pete parks the Jeep in the designated area and sits for a beat, staring out the windshield and holding a blank expression. I decide to give him a moment to collect himself, and I climb out, stretching my legs and arms.

Pete gets out and grabs our backpacks, one in each hand, but he struggles with mine as he sets them both on the ground.

"Seriously, what did you pack in this thing?"

I dip my chin. "A couple water bottles and..." I hesitate telling him the rest.

"And?"

"Books."

"Books? Again with the books?" He shakes his head and rubs at his brow, but he's grinning. "And plural? You actually thought not only would you have time to read one, but more than one book?" His brows lift.

"Fine, I'll take out a couple." I crouch down and unzip the backpack, reluctantly removing two hardbacks.

He laughs. Full-blown, out loud belly laughs as he claps his hands together once and bends at the waist. "Hardbacks even."

I try to find the humor in this and not get offended. "Well, paperbacks could get all bent up shoved in the pack." He's standing upright now but still hasn't quit laughing, so I smack him in the gut with one of the books. He doubles over as the air expels from his chest. "Here, why don't you carry this one for me?"

"Okay, okay, I'm sorry." He chuckles once more before taking all the hardbacks except for one. He stuffs them into the glove compartment of the Jeep and locks it. "We should probably hit the restrooms before we head up the trail. There aren't any once we're up there."

"Good thinking." The bottle of water I chugged on the drive over is already sitting uncomfortably in my bladder.

Because the top is off the Jeep, we can't leave the packs unattended, so we take turns standing by them while the other person to uses the restroom. I insist Pete go first, though I have no idea why as I'm practically hobbling around in pain.

After it's my turn, I make my way back from the restroom and find Pete scrolling through his phone. I almost panic, thinking I may have missed something already, and maybe I should be checking my phone also. But when I pull it out of my back pocket, there's zero notifications.

"Everything okay?" I hedge.

He glances up and smiles at me. It calms me in an instant.

"Work."

"Really?"

"Well, not really work. But Daniel is still sending me listings."

"And?"

"And...I gotta admit, this one looks pretty great."

"Yeah? So you think you'll take it? You look excited."

His expression changes and his mouth goes slack. He quickly shoves his phone back into his pocket. "Nah. It's not that good. Besides, I don't have time." Pete takes ahold of the flannel tied around my waist and pulls me toward him. He wraps an arm around my lower back, pressing me tight. "My time is valuable right now because I want to spend it all with you."

My face flushes and heat tingles up the back of my neck. As much as I want to pull him the rest of the way into me, Angie's words are heavy on my mind. Pete has nearly completed the program. Once he's done, being honest with him about how my program usually works and about the book will need to take precedence. I'm holding onto hope he will give me grace and understand why I agreed to Tess's plan. And that somehow—someway—we'll end up together. But Angie is right, I've been dishonest. When he discovers the truth, he has every right to walk away from me forever.

I press my palm to his chest and give him a gentle push, but it fractures my heart to do so. I force a smile. "C'mon, we better get going if you want to finish this challenge."

One last challenge—then I can tell him everything.

Confusion swims in his expression but he doesn't question it. He picks up my backpack. "Here, turn around, and I'll help you with your pack."

I turn my back to him, tethering my arms inside the straps. I'm about to clasp the brace around my waist when Pete lets go of my pack to put on his own, and it's then I'm aware of how heavy it really is. The weight comes down on my shoulders, and my attempts at fighting against the force fail. I sort of half-jog three or four steps before the weight is too much and flings me backward. My pack lands with a thud, but it breaks my fall, so at least I'm not hurt.

Pete whirls around barely in time to see me impersonating a turtle lying on its back with its limbs flailing. "Are you okay?" He hurries to my aid, taking both of my hands in his and hoisting me back up to my feet. This time, he holds onto my shoulders to steady me and doesn't let go.

I stumble until I get a good footing. "Well, that was embarrassing." I blow air out the side of my mouth at the loose hair flopping in front of my eyes. Luckily, he's not laughing. If he were, I might suggest we skip the hike and ask him to take me home.

"How about you give me a couple of those water bottles to carry for you?"

"Are you sure? Because then your backpack will be heavy."

"It's fine. I can take the weight." He waves me off and helps me out of my pack. "Besides, I can't have you falling backward on the trail every twenty feet." He laughs to himself as I hand him three water bottles. "Things are always exciting when you're around."

I dip my chin, hiding my reaction to his words.

Once we both finally have our packs on our backs, mine still heavy but manageable at least, we set off for the trail. Pete leads but stops at the bottom near the sign. "Hold up. Let's take our picture. Then we'll take one at the view point. We'll have a sort of before and after shot."

"Um...okay, yeah." It's the first time we've taken a picture together. It feels like a pivotal moment in our relationship.

He holds his phone up with the camera lens facing forward, and we stand close with our heads tilted together. He inspects it before showing it to me. "It's good, right?"

I nod. "Yeah. And nice choice with the trailhead sign next to us."

"Do you realize we've never taken a picture together yet?"

"Really? I guess I hadn't noticed." I lie, biting my lower lip.

He's still staring at the photo. "We should do it more often. We look good together."

My legs go weak, and my desire for him burns through my core. When he says things like that, it only makes me fall harder for him. Because he's not wrong. We do look good together. And like a genuine couple. A bit of anguish slithers through me.

One last challenge.

Chapter 28

Pete

The trail is the same as I remember—flanked by yellowish-white Ageratina adenophora carrying a carrot-like scent—and yet, it's different. I'm not sure if it's because Jules is with me or because it's been a while since I've hiked it. When Natalie and I would come here, she had a quicker pace than I did. Probably because she always kept in better shape than me. Now, with Jules, the two of us seem to go at the same pace.

I pull my Hydro Flask from my pack and twist the top off, chugging for several minutes and allowing the cold water to wet my dry throat. Jules drinks hers but with less enthusiasm than me. She peers at me with intensity over the brim of her bottle while she drinks—sending an attraction buzzing south.

So far, I've been able to push most memories aside and focus on today. I'm not sure I'm capable of thinking of the future yet like Jules had asked me to do. In a way, it feels as if I've been planning for my future the past few weeks without even realizing it. Thanks to Jules's program. She's some kind of magician, skilled in her profession to perform a trick right in front of my eyes without me noticing. Or it's simply her captivating smile, adorable freckles, and mesmerizing hazel eyes.

Jules swipes the back of her hand against her mouth and twists the lid closed on her bottle. "How ya doing?"

"Good." I nod once. "What about you?"

"A little out of shape," she answers honestly.

But I don't see the out-of-shape body she does. I see someone confident in her own skin. That's more attractive on a woman than a perfectly toned body. Jules is sexy just how she is, with slightly knobby knees, a flatter backside than most guys would appreciate, and freckled skin that's more noticeable when she's not wearing makeup like today. All of those aspects make her more appealing to me, not less.

"I'm right there with you." I take another drink of my water before capping it and shoving it back into my pack.

"What are you talking about? For someone who sat around for several months eating chips, you sure bounced back into shape quickly."

"Nah." I wave a hand, dismissively.

"Have you forgotten? I've seen you with your shirt off."

"Right. Would you like to see again? Because that can be arranged." I make like I'm going to take off my shirt, but she puts her hand on mine to stop me, her face turning several shades of red.

"No, no...that won't be necessary." She stifles a laugh.

"Okay. But the offer will be a standing one." I grin.

She gives me a playful push in the chest. "Why don't we get moving again?"

"Fine," I reluctantly agree, though I can't help but feel like she's distancing herself from me.

There's not much shade on the trail, and there's a steady incline. Since we got a later start than most, it's fairly empty of other hikers. The ones we do pass are coming back down rather than going up.

When we reach the top, there's a stunning view of the valley on one side and the city of LA on the other. Because of the Pacific Ocean, it remains cooler up here than down at the bottom of the trail. Jules comes alongside me, glances down, and gasps. Bigberry manzanita trees speckle the landscape, and quite a few mariposa lilies remain from their early summer bloom. I've seen this view more than a dozen times, but today I'm trying to see it through Jules's eyes—as if it's for the first time. She's not wrong to have the sight take her breath away.

"Wow," she says, hands on her hips and her chest rising and falling in rapid succession. "It's stunning."

"It really is, isn't it?" I take the view in again for a beat, and we stand in silence as we both stare at it. Then I take my pack off my back and unhook the bag that holds my hammock.

"You brought a hammock?" She takes one end of it and we stretch it out.

I help Jules take her pack off. "This is the best part of a hike. A little R&R before we make the trek back down the trail. I brought some snacks, you brought a book"—he winks—"it should be fun."

"It sounds like a perfect day."

It takes a bit of searching, but we manage to find two sturdy trees with the right amount of space between them, and Jules helps me attach each end of the hammock. I climb in first, leaving adequate room for Jules to fit in snug next to me. Plus, I figure if I get in before her, she can't flip over in it.

She chooses a book from her pack and squeezes in. I rest my arm under her head. The hammock forces our sweaty bodies to crash together, colliding like unstoppable freight trains. This hammock has a mind of its own, and I gotta say, I'm not complaining.

"I want to stay squished next to your sticky body forever," I mumble before pressing a kiss to the top of her head. "What book you got there?" I give a nod with my chin to the book pressed to her chest.

"*Where Rainbows End* by Cecelia Ahern."

"Is it any good?"

"I'm enjoying it."

"You want to read some of it?"

"Out loud?"

"Sure." I shrug underneath her head. "Why not?"

She begins reading and at first, I pay attention to every word. But soon I'm entranced by her voice, it soothes my soul, and I want to drink it in. Scanning Jules's body, I attempt to memorize every inch of it. I move my hand to her hair and wrap a strawberry blonde strand around my finger. She stiffens next to me, resistance in her demeanor. Fear slides through me, worried I'm pushing this relationship too far, too fast.

But after a few minutes, Jules reassures me when she stops reading, shuts the book, and tosses it to the ground. She tiptoes her fingertips up my chest before resting her palm there. My nerve endings tingle and I crave her touch. She nuzzles into my neck, and I turn further into her, running my finger down her jaw and pressing my lips to her forehead and then the tip of her nose. She giggles, and I kiss her soft lips while my heartbeat increases.

"So," I mumble against her smiling mouth, "did I pass?"

She looks at me curiously.

"Did I pass the program?" I explain further.

"Let's see...six sessions, six challenges, you've ditched the pink robe, and you're moving back home." She smiles sweetly and whispers, "I'd say you passed."

My own smile starts in my chest, and reveals itself on my lips as the pride I feel over something that's probably completely ridiculous settles on me. This woman pressed against me is responsible for my transformation. What I feel for her is too much to bear. I'm grateful, I'm inspired, I'm enamored.

I'm aroused.

I nuzzle my lips into her neck and ask, "You ever made love in a hammock before?"

RICHIE AND I HAVE DONE LITTLE TO HELP WITH THE PLANNING of Tess's birthday party. This is one of those times I'm extra thankful for Cora and Tess's good friends Alissa and Cheyenne, who pretty much handled every detail. All I had to do was RSVP.

I'm the oldest one at the party since Tess decided she didn't want to invite her grandparents or aunts and uncles. Usually, that doesn't bother me, but when Jules arrives dressed in a low-cut red dress that hugs her hips in a second-skin sort of fabric, she looks about ten years younger than she is. My jaw nearly plummets to the floor, and I can't help the bit of jealousy that snakes up my spine.

Jules only has those mesmerizing hazel eyes set on me as she saunters past other party guests and makes her way toward me. My heartbeat picks up speed, racing like the roadrunner from the cartoon. The heat in the small house rises, and I tug at the tie around my neck, the air suddenly feeling constricting.

"Good evening," Jules says, her voice low and seductive.

"You..." I'm at a loss for words. "You look amazing. You're radiant."

The smile she gives me is thanks enough, and I pull her in at my side. I press a soft kiss against her lips, worried about messing up her lipstick. But when she slips her finger in the knot of my tie and gives it a tug, I can't help but deepen it. In a matter of seconds, we're nearly making out in the middle of Tess's living room with an audience of party guests.

"Ahem," someone clears their throat.

We break the kiss. I reluctantly tear my lips and eyes off Jules. When I do, I find Alissa standing in the entryway of the living room, a pointed look on her face.

"Alissa." I raise my voice an octave. "Always nice to see you. How are you?" I take Jules's hand and don't let go when I bend and give Alissa a side hug.

She gives my arm a pat. "I'm good. In fact, I'm better than good now that I can see this for myself." Her eyes dart between Jules and me.

I use this as my prompt to introduce Jules to her. But apparently, she knows all about her already. Though I shouldn't be surprised Tess told her.

"I'm so happy for you, Pete." But Alissa's face doesn't match her words. Instead, her expression is challenging. "Who would've guessed you two would actually hit it off?"

"Not me," I say, squeezing Jules tighter to my side. "But I'm so grateful we did." I plant a kiss on her temple.

"I'm sure," Alissa says.

Cora enters the kitchen and it feels like an eternity since I've seen her. "Will you please excuse us? Cora's here."

Jules and I shuffle past a few people I don't recognize. "Hello, daughter. What do you think you're doing?" I catch Cora at the exact moment she's chugging a glass of champagne. She practically chokes on it and swipes the back of her hand over her lips.

"Dad! Holy crap, you scared me." Setting the now empty glass onto the counter, she wraps her arms around me in a tight embrace. The alcohol is fresh on her breath.

"That's enough, okay?" I say into her ear. "This is Tess's big night. We don't want to ruin it."

She pulls away. "I'm a responsible adult, Dad. You raised me, remember?"

"Good to see you again, Cora." Jules gives her a friendly smile, her lipstick smeared below her bottom lip, and I suck my own in between my teeth subconsciously.

Cora hugs Jules like they're old friends, and it shouldn't affect me like it does, but I can't help it. Their embrace causes my heart to swell until it's nearly bursting at the seams.

We make small talk with other party guests until we spot Daniel. My insides give a silent heave, a release, because not only is it great to see my best friend, the knowledge that he's a year older than me gives me a sort of pleasure. I take Jules by the hand to introduce her.

Besides my friendship with Natalie, Daniel is my longest. The realization of this is saddening. Not that having Daniel as a best friend is a bad thing, but that he has had to fill that void in my life. That's a monumental responsibility, and I put him in that role unintentionally.

"Daniel," I say, holding out my arms to him, ready for an embrace. We don't do the manly handshake-pull-into-a-hug thing. We do full-on hugs, front-to-front contact, and there's no shame in it. Not for us anyway. We don't care how uncomfortable we make the people around us.

"Pete." He hugs me, his hands firmly pressing into my back.

In the last ten months, I've been more grateful for this friendship than I've ever been before. He stepped up as a friend, taking care of my yard and maintaining the pool. He checks in on the girls often too. He's not a silent godfather, rather more like their uncle. He gets overprotective and worries about them like an uncle would. And sometimes, as a father would.

"Thanks for coming." The words come out thick and full of emotion.

"I wouldn't miss it. You know Tess is like the daughter I never had."

"It's not too late." I pull back and squeeze his shoulders, waggling my brows at him.

He waves me off, swiping a beer off the table. "Nah, I'll live vicariously through you. That life isn't really for me, ya know?"

"Yeah, I know." I want to tell him it can be if he really wants it. But I don't because he truly doesn't. I rest my hand on Jules's lower back and push her forward a step. "This is Jules Sweeney. Jules, this is Daniel Russo."

Jules smiles brightly, reaching out to shake his awaiting hand. "Ah, the best friend."

He winks at her, that Daniel charm unstoppable.

"In the flesh. And, the therapist?" He raises a quizzical brow.

"Interventionist," she corrects.

The two share a smile.

Richie gives me a pointed look and a nod from across the living room—signaling it's time to give Tess part of her birthday gift. I tap Cora on the shoulder and whisper in her ear, "It's time."

I snatch my bass I'd left hidden behind a curtain near the back door, and Jules and I follow Cora outside. I glance around at the space—the acoustics should sound amazing out here with the small proximity of the backyard and the concrete brick wall surrounding it.

Tess requested I play, "I Could Use a Love Song" by Maren Morris. Part of me thinks she was giving me a challenge of her own, forcing me back into playing the bass again. Forcing wasn't necessary. I picked up my favorite bass a few weeks ago after my visit with Jules's dad and Harry. But I have a surprise of my own for Tess.

When Richie escorts her outside to the back patio and she finds Cora standing at my side, she's confused. "What is this?" Her brown eyes dance between the two of us.

"We're singing a duet," I say proudly, my head held high.

"Dad and I have been practicing for the last few weeks," Cora admits.

"When? How?" Tess is touched and already crying.

I find I have to fight back my own tears.

"You know that thing called FaceTime? You know, technology?" Cora teases. "Now stop your blubbering so we can get on with it."

"What she said," I say.

I glance at Jules, who's sitting in a patio chair, legs crossed and a glass of champagne dangling between her fingers. My nerves jumble in my stomach as I realize she's never heard me sing. But I attempt to push them aside and make room for the excitement I'm feeling as well.

I cup my hands together and yell, "Hey everyone, if you could make your way outside, Tess has requested a special birthday present." I wait for a few more people to file out of the back door and onto the patio. Others sit in empty seats outside. "Tess's sister, Cora, and I are going to sing."

We are going acoustic, no plug-ins, amps, or mics. Only me, my bass, and our voices. I strum a few chords on the bass, Cora hums, finding the correct note, and we begin.

Cora sings alone on the verse, and we come together on the chorus, mixing her young but solid alto voice with my tenor. I'm not gonna lie, we sound good together—better than good, fantastic. When I glance at Tess, tears stream down her cheeks, but she's smiling through them.

We finish, and the crowd breaks into a standing ovation. Cora gives me a quick side hug, and I whisper my congratulations into her ear. Tess wraps the two of us into a hug, crying and telling us how good we were, how proud of us she is, and how lucky she is. But with my two best girls in my arms, I'm the lucky one.

Jules waits to congratulate us. I think I adore her even more for the patience she gives us before intruding. Though, it doesn't feel like an intrusion. Even Tess hugs Jules, and as a bystander, it looks genuine.

"I'm so glad you came tonight, Jules. Thank you." Tess squeezes her hand, and the gesture tightens around my heart.

"I appreciative the invite."

"You're always welcome." Tess drops Jules's hand and saunters away to visit with her friends.

Jules and I share a look, both of us clearly touched by Tess's words.

"That was epic, Dad," Cora says. "Now I'm off to visit with Tess's boring friends."

"Okay, kid. Great job, again."

"That was seriously amazing." Jules stands in front of me, the glow from the moon catching in her eyes, darkening them.

I wrap my hands around her middle, pressing them to her lower back and pulling her in close to me. She winds her hands around my neck and twists her fingers in my hair. "You're amazing," I whisper before lowering my lips to hers.

Each time I kiss her, it feels like the first time. Exciting and new.

When we break apart, Jules sucks her bottom lip in between her teeth. It's irresistibly adorable and sends a craving deep inside me to relish her again. But she pulls back.

"Do you think we could go somewhere quiet and talk?"

I glance around at the nearly empty backyard. "It's quiet here." I grin.

She hesitates and looks over her shoulder toward the house. "Yeah, okay. Why don't we sit."

She takes my hand in hers, so natural already, the two of our hands fitting together like they're the other's missing match.

"Is everything okay?"

"It's fine. It's just...there's something I've been meaning to talk to you about."

"Okay." I try not to worry. She says it's fine, but it feels as if my stomach plummeted all the way to my feet.

"Hey, you two," an accented voice calls from the back door. It's Tess's friend, Cheyenne. "Tess is getting ready to open gifts."

"Okay, be right there," I call to her. I turn back to Jules, intertwining my other hand into hers. "What did you want to talk about?"

Jules fidgets with my fingers, studying our caressing hands. "Nothing. Never mind. It can wait." She smiles at me.

"Are you sure?"

"Yeah...we can talk tonight after the party."

I hook her arm into the crook of my elbow and escort her inside the house through the back door. Inside, everyone is gathered around the small living room while Tess sits in the armchair. She has always hated being the center of attention, especially while opening gifts.

I take a seat on the edge of the sofa, squeezing in next to Cheyenne. Jules sits on the arm of it and drapes her arm around my shoulder. Her fingers dance across my collarbone and chest. It's distracting as all get-out. But it's not like I'm dumb enough to ask her to stop.

Chapter 29

Tess

In an effort to get out of the spotlight, I open my gifts quickly. First, I unwrap a bottle of my favorite perfume from Cheyenne. Dad's gift is Dodgers season tickets with infield box seats. I tear the wrapping paper off a large painting Daniel had commissioned of one of Mom's earliest designs; a long bohemian chic dress with multiple colors. I try to hold in my emotions, not wanting to risk crying again. I already had to fix my makeup after Dad and Cora's song. Daniel must be having a difficult time as well because he chooses now to say goodbye and gives me a tight hug before leaving.

I open several more random gifts along with gift cards and a Coach purse from Cora. There's a small gift on top of the remaining stack sitting in front of me. I search for a gift tag or card but come up empty-handed.

It's a book. And not *any* book. I recognize it right away. This is Jules's book. I lift my eyes to her, confused. Why would she gift me her own book?

"Um...thanks, Jules." I shove it underneath my thigh, face down into the sofa, hoping Dad doesn't notice.

"That's not from me," Jules mutters, her usual rosy color draining from her cheeks.

"I'm sorry, I just assumed." I lift the few sheets of ripped wrapping paper, searching for the tag I must have missed.

"You already opened our gift," Dad says. "The season tickets were from the both of us."

"Right."

"The book is from me, silly," Alissa squeals. "I thought you should have your own copy. You know, because you're so close with the author now, I figured you can get it signed." She smiles wide in Jules's direction.

I shift uncomfortably on the sofa, watching as Dad tries to play catch-up. He searches around the room, looking genuinely confused.

Alissa snatches the book from underneath my thigh. "Alissa!" I whisper-shout.

She gives me an eye roll and mouths *What's your problem?* She crosses the room. "So what do you say, Jules? Will you sign Tess's book?"

I can see Alissa's hopeful eyebrows all the way from my side of the room. This is not going to end well. How could she not have known this was a bad idea? What was she thinking? Dread fills my body, weighing me down.

"You could write something clever, like *Happy birthday to my future stepdaughter.*"

I gasp.

Jules stands, ready to accept the book and whatever else is to come now that we're basically caught.

Cora zooms toward Alissa, snatching the book from her before she can give it to Jules. "What a fun idea, Alissa," she says, her voice dramatic and loud. "To ask everyone to sign this for Tess's birthday. What a nice keepsake it will make."

Alissa gives her a dumbfounded look. "What are you—?" Realization dawns on her face and she winces.

But it's too late.

"Why do I feel like I'm missing something here?" Dad stands and glances at everyone in the room.

My other friends appear as confused as he is. They all look around as well.

Cora hugs the book to her chest. "Don't be so nosy, Dad. You'll get your chance to sign the book." She fake laughs, "Ha, ha, ha."

I drop my face in my palm. The lies, the scheming, the past few weeks all tumble to the ground. I push my gifts off my lap and prepare myself for the inevitable.

"Give me the book, Cora." Dad holds out his hand.

Cora winces and hands the book over reluctantly.

Dad stares at the cover for a moment. It's a nice photo of Jules sitting on top of her desk in her office. But there's a person with only his back visible. It's likely a man. He's kneeling before Jules with his hands clasped together like he's begging.

"You wrote a book?" Dad looks to Jules. She fidgets with the pendant hanging from her neck. "That's amazing. Why didn't you tell me?"

Jules remains silent. Waiting.

He reads the book jacket before thumbing through the pages, starting back at the beginning again. It feels like the entire room is holding our breath together as one—wondering when he'll realize. It takes him what feels like an eternity to put the pieces together. And when he does, my regret is instant and unfathomable.

"What is this?" He looks at Jules, dark brows furrowed, confusion taking over his expression. "You used to be a licensed therapist?"

Jules doesn't answer, simply bites her lower lip. It's as if she's waiting for the blow just like I am.

"What is this section? Referring to a fake dating program? Where you're a fill-in girlfriend, and there are challenges?" But he doesn't show Jules what section he's referring to.

He doesn't need to. She knows. We all do. He looks at her again, hurt shining in his eyes.

"Jules, what the hell is this?" Now he holds the book in the air.

"If you would let me explain," Jules says, her voice small and cracking.

"Explain?" he says in a strangled tone. "Yeah, I think that'd be a good idea. Because what it looks like to me is that you put me through your Challenge Program, which is actually a fake dating program. Please tell me that isn't true," he pleads.

"Can we go somewhere we can be alone? I'll explain everything." She reaches for his hand, but he pulls it away. Jules flinches, and I think I do too.

"No, no," he breathes out, pacing the floor. "I think you should explain here. Now." He whips around to face me. My heart stops beating. "Because suddenly, things are beginning to make sense. And I have a feeling...you're not the only one who has some explaining to do."

"Dad." The word slides out of my throat with a croak, tears spill from my eyes. How do I explain something like this? How could I have been a part of something like this?

"Okay," Richie says, suddenly at my side. "Party's over, friends. Thank you for coming, but if you wouldn't mind showing yourselves out."

"Oh, no you don't," Dad says, moving to block the doorway of the living room, rubbing at his temples. "I need to know. Who else was in on this little game of yours, Jules?" The way he says *game* sends an ice pick into my heart. "My lovely daughters?" He lifts his brows, fire burning in his eyes, and I swipe at the tears on my cheeks.

"Pete, please," Richie pleads. "How about we let everyone go and we'll talk about this. Only the family."

"That sounds like a grand idea, Richie Rich."

The nickname sounds foreign, it's been weeks since he's used it.

"But I have a feeling it wasn't simply you and my daughters who were in on this." He glances around at my confused party guests. "Let me guess. Alissa? How about Cheyenne? Not sweet Cheyenne? But alas, yes, you knew as well. That means your hubbies were in on it too."

"Hey," Dexter says, holding up a hand in surrender, "if it's any consolation, I told Tess that pimping out her father was a bad idea."

The tears come easier now.

"There." Dad slams his fist onto the cover of the hardback before pointing at Dexter. "At least he had the decency to call it what it is."

"It wasn't like that, Dad," Cora says.

Dad whips around to face her, his previously hurt face now overtaken with stony anger. "No? Then what was it like, huh? You all got together and thought I needed a pity screw and hired the best person for the job?"

His words slice through the room and my heart in the process.

Jules is trembling while she cries. "Pete, it wasn't like that."

He looks at the book again. "A New York Times best seller. *Pft*. What kind of dates did you take these other men on? Did you take them to meet your dad and Harry too? Hiking and sex in a hammock?" Dad sets his cold, hard eyes on Jules. "Surfing?"

She hesitates before nodding and swiping at her wet cheeks. "Please, just let me explain," she pleads.

"Don't bother." He throws a hand in her face. "But you two, you three—" he points between me, Richie, and Cora. "You three are my kids. You're all I had left when I lost everything, when my life went to crap."

"You still have us, Dad," I say, finally finding my voice. "We only wanted to help. You were so depressed. We were worried about you."

He puffs out a breath of air, as if he doesn't believe a single word I say.

"We only had your best interest in mind," Richie says.

"That's bull, and you know it. You wanted your precious house back. And me out of it." Dad sets a card into my hand. "Here, I made you a playlist of all your favorite songs, sung and played by me. Happy. Birthday. Tess." He brushes past me, and I can feel the iciness straight to my bones. Before he leaves, he turns back around. "Kudos to all of you for succeeding in your plan. I moved back home. And I'm all alone. Congratulations."

He slams the door, and I jump.

"I'm so sorry," Alissa whispers. "I wasn't thinking. I thought he completed the program. I thought he knew."

She tries to comfort me, but I don't want it. I don't deserve it. I stiffen. "Just go, please," I whisper.

"All right, now the party is over," Richie says. "Thank you all for coming."

"Yes, thank you," I mumble nearly incoherently before rushing out the back door. I slump onto the step of the deck and bury my face into my palms, sobbing inconsolably.

Chapter 30

Jules

My heart is screaming at me to go after Pete, but my head is instructing me to stay and make sure Tess and Cora are okay. But Tess has already disappeared out back, and Cora rushes after her.

"Is there anything I can do?"

"I think you've already done enough," Cora bites out before stepping out the back door.

If my heart wasn't already shattered into a million shards her words would have done it. I back away. Cora's reaction is a reminder of where I stand, and it's not with Pete's family. And I can't lie—it hurts.

Richie hands me my sweater and purse. "Give them some time. They'll come around." He offers me a hopeful smile.

But it does nothing to lift my spirits. "Thank you." I pull an envelope from my purse with Tess's name scrawled on it, and I leave it on the kitchen counter before I show myself out. I run down the front steps, hoping to catch Pete.

I worry about him driving in his condition, but my apprehension eases some when I find him pacing on the sidewalk, his cell phone in his hand.

"Pete!" I call.

He doesn't bother turning around, he continues stalking down the sidewalk.

"I am so sorry." My words rattle from my vibrating chest, directed at his back. "Please, the least you could do is let me explain."

Pete whips around. "The least *I* could do? Jules, you fake dated me. And you got paid to do it."

"It wasn't like that."

"No? Let me lay it out for you: I was under the impression we were dating, and my daughter was paying you. What am I missing?" He throws up his hands.

It feels as if I've been struck by them. I hold back the sobs that threaten to burst out of me. I am a professional, a grown woman. *Hold yourself together.* "I wanted to tell you. I tried to tell you. That's what I wanted to talk to you about."

Pete glances at the screen of his phone, appearing uninterested, so he surprises me when he says, "Fine, you have a few minutes before my ride gets here. Try."

"Tess did not pay me to date you. That was never part of the plan."

"Yeah, right," he mutters.

"I'm telling you the truth. All I was supposed to do was take you through the sessions and the challenges. That's it." I refrain from telling him the details of the program and that I don't *fake date* anyone. That's not how it works. My clients come to me willingly and know full well what they're signing up for.

Except for Pete.

"Then what happened?" He shoves his phone along with his hands into his front pockets.

"Then I met you. And you had this kind face and this infectious grin. You were funny and adorable, and I couldn't help it, I was attracted to you." The tears slip from my eyes, and I try to wipe them away before he notices. "Pete, I fell—"

"Don't say it," he interrupts, holding up a palm.

"In love with you." I say it anyway because he needs to know. Even if it is too late.

"Ugh," he groans, pushing his hands through his hair. "Yeah, well, there's no one else around to see your performance now. It's only me. You can stop pretending."

"Pete." My voice breaks. "The time we spent together was the best time I've ever had. In the process of trying to help you through the steps, through the challenges, it helped me too."

"Well, isn't that nice. I'm glad I could be of service. So, you got paid and you got some inner healing as well. Three cheers for you." He turns his back to me and faces the road, tugging his phone free from his pocket to check it once again.

"Regardless of what you think, I didn't date the other men who I took through the program. I simply gave them what they needed— attention, a listening ear, a pep talk—to gain enough confidence to get through their trauma."

"Do you want a medal or something? Because I would think the title of best-selling author would be enough."

"I never meant to hurt you, Pete. That's the last thing I ever wanted."

"Who was it?"

I shake my head, confused.

"Who broke your heart? Who turned you into...into this? Someone who dates men for money?"

I don't correct him. I deserve all the hurtful accusations he's willing to throw at me. "It was Dave. But something tells me you already knew that." He presses his lips together and bobs his head once. "For what it's worth, I am sorry. And I gave back the money to Tess. It wasn't right to keep it when the two of us were..." My words fall off. I'm unable to finish, unable to define our relationship; what it was or what it is now.

A fancy sports car pulls up to the sidewalk, Pete opens the passenger door, and I catch a glimpse of Daniel waving at me from the driver's seat. I give him a limp smile. Before Pete steps inside, he gives me one last glance.

I've already explained, I've already apologized, so I say the only thing there is left to say. "I love you, Pete."

"Good luck with everything," he responds before climbing into the car and slamming the door shut with more force than necessary.

My body jumps at the sound. The car speeds off down the road, and I'm left on the darkened sidewalk, all alone.

I AWAKE GROGGILY THE NEXT MORNING TO THE UNFORGIVING sun peeking through my curtains. My only relief is when I realize it's Sunday, and I don't have any clients today. But I do have somewhere to be in the afternoon. I'd promised Dad a new stack of library books and a restock of Yoo-hoo. I groan at the thought—I'm definitely not in the proper headspace to deal with Dad or his moods today.

Pushing myself up on my elbow, my head pounds, and I rub circles at my temples. Kobe is positioned in a tight ball next to me, his snores rumbling through his nose. My tongue feels like sandpaper. What the hell happened last night? The scene with Pete replays in my mind, bringing fresh emotions minus the tears. I don't think I have any more left in me.

My bedroom door pushes open and Angie appears in the doorway holding two mugs of coffee. She's my savior. "Wakey, wakey."

Kobe stirs in the bed next to me, grunting and snorting until he's settled once again. He doesn't seem ready to welcome the new day yet either, and I'm grateful. Angie hands me a mug and climbs onto the other side of the bed, being careful not to bother Kobe.

We prop ourselves against the headboard, sipping our coffee in silence. The inside of my mouth feels like it's been wrapped in a fuzzy blanket, and my breath must smell like death. The bitter taste of the brew offsets it slightly, and I close my eyes, sucking down the caffeine.

"What happened last night?" I finally ask.

"You don't remember?"

I curl my fingers around the mug and rub Kobe under the ears with my other hand. "I remember coming home, telling you what happened with Pete, and then—" I pause, my brain playing catch-up. "You brought out the tequila." My head pounds as if in response to the memory. "I'm nearly forty. Why have I not learned by now that alcohol doesn't solve anything?"

"It may not solve anything, but it sure does a fine job at making you forget." She smiles at me. "Clearly."

"Right. Until the next day when you wake, remember everything, and feel even worse." I take another drink of my coffee. Kobe gets up, stretches, and climbs onto my lap.

"I never said it was a good idea." She shrugs.

"Actually, I think your exact words were, 'Alcohol is always a good idea.'"

She chuckles under her breath.

"And then you proceeded to tell me, 'I told you so' and that you knew things with Pete would end badly."

She cringes. "So you do remember."

"But things didn't just end badly. They blew up. In all the ways I'd imagined Pete might discover what Tess and I had planned, I'd never expected him finding out that way. Discovering my book in front of all those people. He was humiliated in front of his family and friends." I squeeze my eyes shut so hard white spots speckle behind my eyelids. All I want is to go back to last night before Pete learned about my book and tell him everything.

"Guys get over humiliation. Pete might get over it too."

"That's very unlikely."

"If he truly had strong enough feelings for you, he'll get over it. And he'll forgive you."

"I don't see how he can. How would you feel if you discovered someone you loved was paying someone to date you?"

"I'd ask for a cut." She grins.

I sigh and lean my head against the headboard.

"Even though I did warn you not to get involved with Pete, I'm sorry it went down the way it did."

I turn my head to face her. "Ang? I don't know if I can do this anymore."

She gives me a puzzled look. "Dating?"

"The business."

BY THE TIME I GET TO THE MEMORY CARE FACILITY, MY BAG filled with Yoo-hoo and new books for Dad, it's later than I usually visit. But at least my hangover has mostly worn off. Getting drunk is seriously no joke at my age. When I was in my twenties, I could get up after a night of drinking, take a few Tylenol, drink a cup of coffee, eat some Taco Bell and be good within an hour. At thirty-nine, it's taken me three cups of coffee, a cold shower, and a nap and I still don't feel one hundred percent. And I'm definitely not ready for Taco Bell.

Charlene is at the front desk, greeting me before I even make it all the way inside the building. "Good afternoon, hon."

"Hey, Char."

"Whoa. You look terrible, dear. Are you feeling all right?"

I subconsciously run a hand through my un-styled hair. "I'm fine. Not enough sleep last night, that's all."

"I hear that. At your age, you gotta be sure to get your beauty sleep. It doesn't come natural anymore."

"I'll keep that in mind," I mutter, making my way to the double doors.

"Oh, your boyfriend was here earlier."

My feet turn to bricks, and I feel as if I've smacked into a wall. Ice-cold dread trickles through my veins, and I turn back around slowly. "Who?" The word slides out of my throat like a whisper.

"That nice man you brought with you last week when you picked up your father. I'm sorry, I just assumed he was your boyfriend."

"Pete? He was here? Today?"

She nods. "Yes, that's right. Pete. Such a friendly man."

Thick trepidation fills my limbs, and my head swims while the tequila from the night before threatens to make a fresh appearance. "What was he doing here?"

"He brought your father a book."

My stomach clenches, sending another wave of nausea through me. I whip back around, and by some miracle, my feet move, one after the other. Pushing through the doors, I speed walk to Dad's room. The door is closed, and I don't even bother knocking. I push it open and step inside.

Dad is dressed in a pastel-colored Hawaiian shirt and his graying hair is neatly combed. He's sitting in his leather recliner, his face hidden behind a book—my book. Of all the times I imagined entering this room and finding Dad reading my book, I never imagined feeling so much angst.

"Hey, Dad." I step cautiously around his legs propped up on the raised footrest and go to his side to press a kiss on the top of his head.

He doesn't respond, simply keeps his focus on the page he's reading with interest. His forehead is furrowed. I silently stock the mini fridge with the Yoo-hoo before taking a seat in the chair across from him. I fidget with my phone in my hands and wait through the painful silence.

I shoot a text to Angie.

Me: *Pete brought Dad my book.*

Angie: *Whoa. That one has balls.*

Me: *He hasn't even noticed I'm here.*

Angie: *Then he must be intrigued.*

Me: *He's not gonna handle this well. I know it.*

Angie: *You don't know that.*

After what feels like an eternity, Dad shuts the book and rests it on his lap. He stares at the cover as if he's trying to recognize the woman on it staring back at him, trying to place her. It takes everything in me to not jump up and shout, *That's your daughter on the cover of that book. Your daughter wrote a book.* But I don't. Because that would most likely confuse him even more.

Dad glances up, recognition dawning on his face. "Hey, Jules." He smiles.

Okay, so maybe he's not gonna yell at me. Maybe he hasn't gotten far enough along in the book. Because surely if he had, he'd be disappointed.

He taps the cover. "How come you never told me about this?" His hurtful expression searches mine. "Unless you already did, and I forgot? But something tells me, this is the first time I've read this."

"You're right. This is the first time you've read it." I won't use his illness to my advantage and lie to him. Not even if it will get me off the hook of a handful of wrongs I've caused. "I never told you about the book. I'm not sure why." And that part is mostly the truth.

He looks pointedly at me. "Are you ashamed of yourself, or me?"

The meaning of his words slice through me and cause me physical pain. I want to shout, *Neither!* But I'm afraid the answer is both.

"I could never be ashamed of you, Dad."

"Daughters are supposed to look up to their fathers. They typically want to know their fathers are proud of them. And fathers will do nearly anything to assure their daughters are happy and feel loved."

I'm not sure what he's getting at, so I remain quiet while he continues.

"When your friend Pete brought me this book, he said his

daughter set the two of you up and that she didn't go about it in the traditional way."

Embarrassment travels up my neck, spreading into my cheeks as the mortification sinks in. Pete really came here, gave my father my book and then told him everything?

"Do you want to know your dad's opinion?"

I nod, but I have a sinking feeling in my stomach.

"I like Pete. I think you two should give your relationship another chance. I don't remember you being as happy as you've been the last few weeks."

It surprises me when he says this. Sometimes Dad can't remember yesterday. But he's noticed I've been happy? I'm not sure what to say to him. My throat thickens. "Maybe, Dad."

"What are you so afraid of?" Dad's eyes feel as if they're peering into my soul.

"I'm not afraid of anything," I lie.

"I'm your father, I know this isn't you." He holds my book in the air. "Helping people, yes. But not like this. You're better than this." He slides the book on the table with a huff.

I want to argue, but my words sit caught somewhere between my brain and my throat.

"Are you doing this because of your mom and me? Because we didn't work out?"

"Dad," I finally find my words, and they come out too loud, too forced, and vibrate in my chest. "It wasn't that you just didn't work out. She left you. When things got tough, she left."

"And that's on her." He stands and grabs a Yoo-hoo from the fridge. "Are you afraid to commit or something?"

Tears burn at the corners of my eyes. "I did commit, Dad. And he left. When things got hard, he left. You remember what happened with Dave?"

"Dave was a putz, and he knew he didn't deserve you." He twists the cap off the Yoo-hoo and takes a drink. "And I hate to say it, but that's the risk you take. It's all a part of life. A part of loving someone."

"It's too hard. Falling in love is too hard."

He sits across from me. "Listen to me"—he takes my hands in his — "even if I had known how the journey between Susana and I was gonna end, I still would've gone on it with her."

I'm crying now. I don't believe him. But I want to.

He takes my chin in his hand, lifting my gaze to him. "And I'm not only saying that because it gave me you." He smiles and his eyes crinkle. "Love is a gift. It's precious. If you're lucky enough to find it, take a leap and grab ahold of it with two hands. I can promise you it's worth it."

I sniff and wipe my nose with my shirt sleeve and whisper, "What if he doesn't want me?"

"What is there to not want?" He teases. "But if so, you send him here. You may have to remind me who he is, what exactly he did to hurt my girl, and probably remind me who you are. But then, I'll really let him have it."

I laugh-cry, swiping at my tear-stained cheeks. I wind my arms around his neck, breathing in his musky scent, and hug him before he forgets who I am.

IT'S BEEN FIVE DAYS SINCE TESS'S PARTY—MEANING IT'S BEEN five days since I've heard from Pete. I had Angie cancel all of my clients for the week, but who am I kidding? I have no plans to continue my interventionist business.

My last conversation with Dad has been circling through my mind on repeat. Giving Pete and me another chance isn't that simple. I hurt him. He has every right to never speak to me again. And maybe that's the worst part of the entire conversation with Dad. I'd give my heart right over to Pete without hesitation.

I'm sprawled across the sofa, Kobe stretched out at my side while I scroll through Netflix for the hundredth time. Finally, I settle on a romantic comedy I've seen a dozen times. I pop a peanut butter M&M into my mouth and scratch Kobe under his ear while contemplating shutting my eyes for a nap.

Angie struts into the living room, dressed in a nice pair of dark jeans and a red silky tank top, her iPad tucked underneath her arm. She slowly shakes her head at me while pressing a hand to her jutted hip.

"What?" I ask accusatory, my eyes wide.

"What?" she repeats. "How long is this gonna go on?" She wipes her hand in the space over me.

I roll over, nearly crushing Kobe, and reach my hand into the bag for a couple more M&M's. I sarcastically chuckle under my breath as I read the bag. *Share Size*. Fat chance of that. "I don't know what you're talking about."

Angie exhales dramatically before planting her butt on the coffee table, blocking the TV and the bag of M&M's. She bends, leaning in closer. "I know you're devastated over what happened with Pete. I get that. I do. But you can't mope around and be depressed forever."

"It's not forever. It's only been a few days." I push off my elbow and sit up, my head pounding from the lack of movement I've done lately. "And I'm not depressed," I protest.

"Five." She holds out an open palm at me. "It's been five days. And all you've eaten is M&M's and wine. I'd call that being depressed."

I bite the inside of my cheek. I have zero energy to argue with her. Pushing my hand through my hair, I'm surprised to feel the greasiness on my fingers. When was the last time I washed it?

"Look, while you've been lying around this week, I've been busy. I wanted to wait to talk to you about this until you were feeling up to it, but I'm starting to wonder if that's ever gonna happen." She holds her iPad out to me. "I have an idea."

I glance at her, then down at the iPad, and back up at her before I take it. I scan the words on the screen, my brain muddied and trying to catch up. The fog I've been in for the last five days is worse than I thought because it takes a few long moments before I realize what Angie is proposing.

"So, what do you think?"

"You want to start...a dating service?"

"Not just a dating service. It's like a dating app but in person. I want to match people based on their profiles—interests, values, beliefs—and then send them on dates, challenges if you will."

I quirk an eyebrow at her. My brain is slowly waking up, but my body flutters with a mixture of apprehension and excitement. "I had no idea you were interested in doing something like this, modifying the Challenge Program, I mean."

"When things between you and Pete blew up, I knew you couldn't go back to running the program. But you've always inspired me with the way you help your clients. I didn't want to see it end completely."

My throat thickens. She wouldn't want me to point out her compliment and what it means to me, so I push my emotions down. "This could really be something great." I glance over the iPad and the relief Angie must feel is visible. Her shoulders relax and her smile beams. "I mean, I definitely need a cup of coffee before my brain can fully comprehend what you're proposing, but it sounds fresh and new."

"Right." She stands. "I'm meeting with a loan officer at the bank this afternoon. But my hope is that you'll allow me to use half of the office space and we can do this together."

I hand her the iPad and scrub a hand down my face. "Ang, I can't. You just said it yourself, I can't help with dating or challenge stuff anymore. I'm sorry."

"Oh, I know I did. But that's not what I'm talking about." She slides an envelope from the back pocket of her jeans and hands it to me. "This arrived for you."

I stare at the printed words on the envelope, and unintentionally my eyes fill up with tears.

"I'm guessing this is the form to renew your therapist license?"

I nod, slowly.

"It's a sign. Renew it. You made a damn fine therapist." She shrugs. "It's your thing. Helping people is your thing."

My chest expands while the tears threaten to spill because I can feel it. She's right. And Dad was right. I can't allow a broken heart or my parents' severed marriage to dictate my life any longer.

"Now, take a shower and get dressed. We've got a lot of work to do."

Chapter 31

Pete

Waking up in the house all alone is as bad as I imagined it would be. Waking up in the bed Natalie and I shared for all those years is even worse. I push back the covers, set my feet on the hardwood floor, and allow the memories to wash over me like a waterfall. I assumed it would get easier with time.

It hasn't.

It's been six days since I've spoken to both Tess and Cora. I'm certain we'll work this out—eventually. Natalie would be upset with me for giving our girls the silent treatment for this long. But I need more time. In a way, it feels as if I'm right back where I was ten months ago, like I'm losing Natalie all over again. Like I'm all alone.

I throw on an old Rush T-shirt and pad out to the kitchen to fix a cup of coffee. Natalie used to prepare the coffee the night before and set the timer so it would be ready when we awoke the next morning. Then we'd have our coffee together outside on the back deck. It was our routine—our reset button from the day before.

Since I haven't learned how to set the timer, I prepare the coffee and wait for it to brew. The sound of the percolator is satisfying, but it feels as if it's taking a hundred years to finish brewing. I grow impatient and pull up my email on my phone, stepping through the back door and onto the deck. The air is thick today. It seems to fit my mood—this sort of unsettling mixture of uncomfortableness and heartache.

There's a new email from Daniel. It's a listing for a home he thinks I'll be interested in. This isn't anything new. He's sent me a listing or two that might catch my eye or cause me to bite nearly daily for the last ten months. But this particular listing does catch my eye. And not only because he's sent three separate emails specifically for it. This one is for a home in the outskirts of town, on the hillside, near an area Natalie and I used to go hiking.

The coffee machine lets out a string of three loud beeps, signaling it's finished brewing, and it snags my attention away from the email. I snatch my laptop from the kitchen table and pull up the listing so I can see the pictures on a larger screen. Tapping through them, something thrilling stirs within my gut. It's a familiar feeling, but one I haven't felt in a long time. Besides selling Dave's house, this feels different. It feels raw and exciting.

I fix my cup of coffee, scooping several teaspoons of sugar into the mug until I've lost track of how many. I tap Daniel's number on my phone, press it to my ear, and carry my laptop and coffee out to the back deck.

"Hey," Daniel greets. "I've been expecting your call."

"Give me the details." The words tumble out of my mouth. It feels like an eternity since I've spoken them, and yet at the same time, it feels like yesterday.

"I thought you'd never ask," Daniel says.

My first instinct when I get off the phone with Daniel is to call Jules and ask her if she'll come with me to check out the home. But I don't. Jules practically handed my last listing to me wrapped up in a box and tied with a bow.

This one, I need to do alone.

But before I make the drive to check out the listing, I need a good omen. I need to work things out with my girls. I send a group text.

Me: *I'm not mad anymore. I get why you did what you did. But maybe I needed more time. And still do. I love you both.*

I don't wait for replies—I turn my phone on silent mode and shove it into the center console in my Jeep. I set the satellite radio to a Tom Petty station and sing along as I back out of the garage. The top is off the Jeep, and the sun is still hidden by a decent cloud coverage that I find both soothing and welcoming today.

The home is Mediterranean style, situated on a hill and three acres. Those three aspects alone are enough points to sell this thing almost immediately. But I need to get a closer look to be sure of its condition.

Once I get the key out of the lockbox, I unlock the front door and step inside. And it's perfect. I knew it would be. The cobalt-blue tiled floor and the brick accent wall in the living room send a zing of excitement shooting through my bones. The black iron banister leading to the matching upstairs balcony causes my heart to beat rapidly. My mouth goes dry and begins to water all at the same time.

After I take one lap around the perimeter of the home, I scroll to Daniel's contact info and press my phone to my ear.

He answers with, "What'd I tell ya? Perfect, right?"

I sigh. "You were right." As much as it pains me to admit it, he's a genius when it comes to real estate. "I want it."

"I knew you would." He chuckles. "It's yours."

"No, I mean, *I* want it."

There's a short pause. "What do you mean, *you* want it?"

"I want to buy it. For myself."

"Dude, seriously?"

I'm not even sure how the words formed and left my mouth because I hadn't exactly planned them in my head. But now that they're out, they're the truth. I do want this home. "Seriously."

"Well, okay then. Let's meet up and go over the deets."

"Text me the time and place you're available." I'm about to disconnect the call but quickly add, "And, Daniel, send me another listing."

"You got it, man."

DANIEL ISN'T FREE UNTIL EVENING. I HAVE A SNEAKING suspicion he purposely planned it this way so we can meet over dinner and drinks. His meetings can never be simple. They have to include a meal or alcohol, and I wonder if him still being single has something to do with it. Then I wonder if this will be me someday soon.

It's eight o'clock when I pull up to the curb of Paradise Bar and Grill and hop out of the Jeep. I toss my keys to a kid working valet who looks like a preteen sporting a Tom Selleck mustache. He looks relieved after handing him the keys to a Jeep rather than a sports car worth over one-hundred grand. In this part of LA, those are the norm. Daniel drives a Porsche 911 Carrera. He's the one who says something douchey to the valet like, "Watch the paint job," or "Don't wreck it or I'll wreck you."

Daniel is standing next to a table near the back when I step inside the dimly lit bar. The men-to-women ratio is less than twenty percent, and I'm instantly aware of why Daniel chose this place to meet. When I approach him, he's busy flirting with two women.

"Pete," his voice calls with an exaggerated enthusiasm. "You made it."

We do our whole full-on-front-to-front hug thing before I step back and nod at the women. They don't give me much thought, but Daniel's intimate hug with me causes them to look dreamily at him.

"Pete is one of LA's top realtors. Alongside me, of course."

The women look at me with fresh eyes, taking me in as if now considering I may be worth their time. Daniel might use his profession and high salary as a way to pick up women, but that's not something I've ever needed to do. And I don't plan on starting now.

"Wow, that's so impressive," one of the women says to me, pressing her hand to my chest and running her fingers down the inseam of my sports jacket.

"Yeah, thanks," I mumble, backing up to put distance between us. I knew the jacket was a mistake but had no choice. Paradise doesn't let you through the doors without it. "Ladies, would you please excuse us? We're here to discuss business tonight."

Daniel whips his head in my direction. "Right, we are. But—"

"Time is money, am I right?" I smile.

Daniel sets a hand on the back of one of the women and says, "He's right. Gotta work to make the big bucks. Maybe I'll catch up with you later?" His dark-brown eyes are hopeful.

She presses her chest into his and whispers loudly, "I hope so," before her and her friend saunter off.

I slide into a seat while Daniel watches the women leave. When they've disappeared into the crowd, he joins me, slumping into the chair across from me.

"Dude, what was that about?"

"You know I'm not here for that." I peruse the drink menu so as to not look at him. It gets old constantly seeing disappointment on someone's face.

"Yeah, but you could've done it for me."

I toss the laminated drink menu onto the table. "Do it for you? That's all I ever do."

He holds out his palms. "Okay, okay. That may be how it was with us before, but for the past several months, I've been the one catering to you. Now"—he leans forward—"I'm not complaining, that's what friends are for. But a little thanks would be nice."

"You're right." And he is. I've done very little to keep this friendship afloat in probably closer to a year. He put up with me during both times Natalie was sick. Then during the gloomy months following her death, and then again, in the last few days while in my slump after things blew up with Jules. "You've been great. I appreciate you being there for me."

"And?" His brows shoot up.

"And...I'll try to be better about showing up for you too."

He eases back into the chair. "There. Now was that so hard?"

I rub my brow. All day, I've been antsy about meeting with Daniel to get down to business. I want to discuss details of the house and go over more listings. "Okay, you ready to go over details of the house or what?"

"Hell yes I'm ready." Daniel takes a drink of whatever he ordered before I arrived, a beer of some kind. I try not to be annoyed he didn't order me one as well. "Do you know how exciting this is? I'm so proud of you, man. It's like I'm the mama bird and my baby bird is finally leaving the nest."

"And I'm the baby bird in this scenario?" I resist the urge to remind him I got married when I was twenty. I've owned my current home for almost fifteen years, and I've raised two children. But I'm fairly certain that's not what kind of "leaving the nest" he's referring to.

Daniel holds up a finger to signal our server. "Let's get baby bird a drink and discuss the deets."

Chapter 32

Tess

With both of Richie's hands enveloping mine, it keeps me from bolting from Dr. Miller's office. As much as I want to know the results of the BRCA test, having her call me and request I come into the office to hear them in person is not a good sign. After receiving the call from her assistant yesterday afternoon, I decided to bring reinforcements and have Richie accompany me.

My nerves have spiked to an all-time high, and I have no chill. So by the time Dr. Miller enters her office, greeting us with an apology for her tardiness, I exhale an audible, "Finally."

Richie squeezes my hand. I'm not sure if it's a warning to not be rude or if it's a reminder he's here to support me. Either way, it snaps me out of my impatience, and I smile up at Dr. Miller in anticipation.

She takes a seat in her modern high-back office chair and removes a folder from a stack on her desk. "Now, I know it's unusual to be called in for lab results, and the last thing I wanted to do was worry you."

Well, you did, is what I want to say. Because I *am* worried. Mom was diagnosed with breast cancer twice. And she only beat it once.

That sick feeling permeates my stomach again, familiar and like it's making a permanent home there.

"Please, give it to me straight."

Dr. Miller smiles warmly at me, taking off her glasses. "The results for your BRCA test are negative."

My previously straight and stiff body melts like an ice cube on hot asphalt, and I collapse into Richie's chest. He wraps his arms around me, holding me close, and kisses my hair. The tears form without warning and spill over my cheeks and onto Richie's shirt.

Dr. Miller moves around to the other side of her desk and hands me a tissue. I pull away from Richie and wipe at my tear-stained face. "Thank you, thank you," I mumble in between the quiet sobs.

Leaning against her desk, Dr. Miller crosses her ankles and says, "There's one more thing."

At first, I think I misheard her, but Richie stiffens next to me. A lump forms and lodges in my throat. What else could they have found? A different kind of cancer? Lymphoma? Uterine cancer? My mind scrambles as I try to think of all the blood tests performed.

"I wanted you to come in today so I could tell you the news in person. Your mom was a special patient of mine, and I still think of her often."

"Um, thank you," my words croak out.

"Tess, you're pregnant."

My jaw goes slack. "Excuse me?"

Richie grabs ahold of my shoulders, a huge smile on his face, and he shakes me. He pulls me in for a hug, and his arms cocoon me. I sink into the weight of his comfort and love.

"Are you sure?" I ask, my words muffled by Richie's neck. I finally pull away and turn to look at Dr. Miller. "You're sure? I mean...how? When?"

"We did a blood test, just to be sure," she confirms.

"But I've only been off the pill for a few months."

"Then consider yourself one of the lucky ones." She smiles.

"We do," Richie answers for me, planting a kiss on my temple and still squeezing me to his side.

"Very lucky," I agree.

"After your last appointment a few months back, I knew this would be good news for you."

"It's fantastic news." I wipe the tears off my cheeks that won't seem to stop falling.

"Good." Dr. Miller nods once. "We'll set you up with an appointment in the next week or so and check everything out. We should be able to determine the due date and maybe even hear your baby's heartbeat."

My baby's heartbeat? The words sound foreign. I never expected to hear them so soon. If I'm being honest, maybe not ever. Richie and I stand. I can't help myself, and I fling my arms around Dr. Miller and thank her profusely. After Richie pulls me off her, he shakes her hand.

"Make an appointment at the front desk on your way out and we'll see you soon," Dr. Miller says.

We leave the doctor's office hand in hand and step outside into the hottest temperature of the day. But I hardly notice, I'm still in shock. I pull back on Richie's hand to stop him. "We're having a baby." I laugh with giddiness.

Richie chuckles too. "Sounds like it."

"This is a happy surprise, right?"

"Of course." He lifts my chin with his finger and kisses me. "Guess it's perfect timing." He presses one more kiss to the tip of my nose before taking my hand again and leading me to our car.

I can't help but feel a stab of remorse at his choice of words. *Guess it's perfect timing.* Why now? Because Dad has finally moved out? Truthfully, it feels like questionable timing. Natalie's grand opening is only weeks away. How am I going to run the store and keep up with the designs after I have the baby? At least if Dad still lived with us and hadn't gone back to work, I'd have his help.

My first doctor's appointment confirms I'm about ten weeks along. Richie holds my hand, and when Dr. Miller quickly finds a strong heartbeat, I cry right there in the office. At least this time, I can use the excuse of pregnancy hormones.

I haven't told Dad and Cora the news. I wanted to wait until after my first appointment to be sure things looked okay and that this is real. I'm actually pregnant. I'm going to have a baby.

Since Dad and I haven't been speaking regularly, both of us entering a silent agreement that some much-needed space was due, I hesitate before calling him. And instead, decide to make up an excuse to ask Cora to come home for the weekend so I can tell her and Dad together.

She surprisingly answers after only the second ring.

"What's up? What's wrong? Is Dad okay?"

"Hey, Cora...we're all fine."

"But you're calling. Instead of texting."

"Yeah," I exhale a light laugh. "I thought it would be easier."

"Okaaaaaay," she draws out. "What's up?"

"I was hoping you could come home this weekend. You see, there's this—"

"I'm already planning to come."

"Oh, really?"

"Yeah, I thought you knew. Dad's moving into his new house this weekend. I said I'd come help."

"Wait. What?" Surely I heard her wrong. Dad's moving? Into a new house?

Cora exhales dramatically into the phone. "Don't even think about getting out of helping. If I'm making the drive and coming for the entire weekend, you and Richie better be helping. You know how much crap Dad owns, right?"

My cheeks go hot and it feels as if flames are licking up my neck as the realization sets in. Dad bought a new house. Dad is moving. And he didn't even tell me. "Well, maybe I'd be willing to help if I had known," my words bite out.

"Whoa, hold up. You didn't know which part?"

"All of it."

"Dad never told you he sold the house?"

I shoot to my feet. "Dad sold the house?" My head goes light and dizzy. I clutch the back of the chair for stability.

"Well, yeah. He sold it after he bought the new one. You haven't seen it yet?"

"Cora," I half-scream into the phone. "How could I have seen it when I had no idea he bought a new house?"

"Hey, I'm sorry things with you two have been weird, but don't take it out on me. I'm over here trying to do my thing, trying to have a life while he's over there making drastic changes to his. Ones I'd assumed you've been supporting."

I have no words. I'm both hurt and saddened by the news of the house and that Dad didn't tell me. Was he even going to let me say goodbye to the old house? To the memories?

"I'm sorry. I honestly had no idea things had gotten so bad between you two."

"I didn't either," I agree, slumping back into the chair.

"So, will you come over to the house this weekend? I really don't think I can handle seeing it empty. It was bad enough going without Mom there, ya know?"

"Yeah." I do know. I returned nearly once a week to check on the place during that first six months because Dad could hardly bring himself to go. "Of course, I'll go with you."

"Thanks, sis. Okay, I gotta go. A few of us interns are going out. There's a band playing at an underage club where the guitarist may or may not be a guy I'm sort of seeing."

"You're seeing someone?"

"Sort of," she reiterates. "It's not serious. We're not labeling it."

I have never understood the whole thing of not labeling relationships. When you put a label on a relationship it helps you to know where you stand, where your boundaries are. It also lets other people know where you stand. How does Cora not see the importance of it? But I suppose Cora and I have never agreed on most things.

"Well, maybe I'll get to meet him someday."

"Not likely. I mean, don't count on it or anything."

"Fine. I won't bug you. But if for some reason the two of you are more serious or official by the time of the grand opening, you should bring him along."

"That's not for a couple more weeks. It's doubtful we'll still be seeing each other by then. But yeah, okay."

I disconnect the call and stare at the unlit screen of my phone. Things are such a mess. How did we get here? My family used to be my rock, the one thing I knew I could count on. And the house was my refuge. After moving from Seattle when I was only six, that house is all I really remember from my childhood. I went there to sleep all those nights after Mom's chemo. And that last week before she died, I couldn't bring myself to leave her side.

Rather than having another drawn out and emotional phone call, I decide to text Dad instead.

Me: *Cora told me about the house.*

Dad's text comes almost instantly.

Dad: *I meant to tell you but didn't want to bother you since you're busy with the store.*

Me: *Cora wants me there this weekend. At the old house.*

Dad: *Me too, kid.*

Me: *When were you planning on telling me?*

Dad: *Undecided.*

His last text jabs me in the gut, and I have to take a few deep breaths in and exhale before replying.

Me: *I have news. I'll share this weekend when Cora is here.*

Dad: *Sounds great. Can't wait to see you. It's been too long.*

Me: *Yeah.*

Me: *Congrats on the new house I guess.*
Dad: *I'm anxious for you to see it.*
Me: *Saturday.*
Dad: *Awesome. Love you, kid.*
I hesitate, my fingers hovering over the keypad.
Me: *Love you.*

SATURDAY COMES FITFULLY SLOW. MY STOMACH IS A BALL OF nerves, and it does nothing to help the morning sickness. But lucky for me, morning sickness doesn't come until evening—combined with relentless heartburn.

Richie left for a business trip to Texas, leaving me alone to deal with Dad and the whole house thing. Both the old and the new. We meet at the old house first. Cora says it will be easier to accept the new house if we say goodbye to the old one. She's probably right. But I don't want to say goodbye at all.

When I reach the house, I have to park on the street. Dad's Jeep and a moving truck fill the driveway. I stare at the house with fresh eyes, paying attention to every detail and hoping they'll make a permanent mark on my brain so I don't forget them. Dad taught me how to ride a bike out on the long sidewalk. In the large patch of grass in the front, he taught me how to wax my surfboard. In the pool in the backyard, he taught me how to swim. Mom used to decorate the inside of the garage for our birthday parties. She would spend weeks leading up to the party making sure every square inch was covered in the theme so it didn't resemble a garage at all.

The inside of the house is bare. The walls have been stripped of family photos and paintings. I run my hand along the nail holes where the Sheetrock has bubbled up, remembering exactly which photos hung where. My heart squeezes at the memories, and I force myself to move further inside.

The fancy dishes have been removed from the built-in shelves in the kitchen, the curtains Mom picked out while on vacation in France have been taken down, and the furniture they special ordered from a family friend's business in Seattle is gone. I wonder if Dad moved them to the new house or if he got rid of them entirely. An eerie feeling snakes through me, and I shiver as a result, wrapping my arms around myself despite not being cold.

"Hey, kid," Dad's voice calls from behind me.

I spin around slowly. "Hey."

He moves toward me, and I can't help but meet him halfway, and we embrace. It doesn't feel awkward, and I want to cry because of it. Instead, I breathe in his scent, all saltwater and sunscreen. I grasp his T-shirt in my fists, clinging to his sturdiness.

After I pull away, I swallow back the tears. "So, you're really doing this, huh?" I take in the space around me again, and the weight of the emptiness of it all consumes me.

"I am." He nods, hands on his hips. "It was time."

I'm not sure I agree with him. It's only been less than a year since Mom died. But, maybe for him, living here without her was too unsettling. So I suppose for him it was time.

"And you think you'll be happy in the new place?"

He looks pointedly at me and tilts his head. "Tess," he sighs. "I don't think it's about happiness, necessarily. But I couldn't keep waking up here every day without her."

My heart hurts, and I rub my hand against my chest. All those months he drove me crazy, moping around like a slug in my home, and all I wanted was for him to pick himself up and get over it. Selfishly, I wanted him to be a dad because I needed a parent. Most of the time, I forgot he lost his partner, the love of his life. I get it now. The shame coursing through me is too much to bear.

"I wish you would've told me."

"I know, me too." He smiles and puts an arm around my shoulder, bringing me into his side. "But I'm glad you're here. And I know Cora will be glad you're here too."

"I think she'll be glad to have help unpacking all your junk." I laugh.

"Hey." He pulls back, looking at me. "I packed everything myself. With the three of us and Daniel, we should be able to handle it easy peasy."

Cora bounds down the stairs. "I told him he should've hired movers."

"Where's the fun in that?" Dad asks.

Cora and I hug.

"It's not like he can't afford it," I say, agreeing with Cora.

"I needed the project. The distraction."

"C'mon." Cora holds a hand out to me, and I slip mine into hers. "Let's go say goodbye to our old rooms."

My steps are heavy as I take the stairs, one at a time, my fingers finding the grooves in the banister where Dad attempted to fill in the gouges Cora and I put there from riding the laundry hamper lid like a sled down the stairs. In the hall is our growth chart. One line even reflects Dad's name and date. He wanted to mark the day we grew taller than him.

Inside Cora's room, the walls are thick with multiple layers of paint. Each time she changed her mind on her favorite color, Mom was happy to oblige and repaint Cora's walls. Mom was amazing like that. She never complained about Cora's mood swings or her change in taste.

Cora stands in the middle of the empty room, spins in a complete circle, then places her hands on her hips and sighs. "I've had some good times in this room. Mom used to sit on the foot of my bed while I cried about a bad grade or a stupid boy way too many times to count."

I fight back the urge to cry now. The tears sit in my chest, heaving, thrashing to come out. I'm the big sister, so I try to keep my emotions under control, but the pregnancy hormones are threatening to consume me.

"But probably the best memories are all the nights Scott Stevens snuck in through my window and...who I ultimately lost my virginity to."

I gasp. "You lost your virginity to Scott Stevens? In your bedroom?"

"Oh, c'mon, did you really think I was still a virgin?"

To be honest, yes. But also, I guess I haven't given it much thought. With the age gap, I've been having sex probably long before Cora even knew what it was. "I mean, I guess not. But that's your best memory?"

She laughs. "We're talking about Scott Stevens. You do remember how hot he was, don't you? So, hell yes, that's my best memory."

I laugh too. But then, Cora takes me by the hand again and pulls me out of her room and into mine. I'm not ready. My stomach twists with knots, and all kinds of emotions course through my veins. It's silly. It's only my childhood bedroom. And I have my own house, my own children to have, and new memories to make. But with Mom gone, it feels harder somehow.

Cora sits cross-legged on the floor in the middle of my room. I join her, running my fingers over the pink nail polish stain on the carpet. Dad was so angry he'd refused to replace it, so Mom bought a rug to hide it. She promised me we'd fix it one day, but with the rug covering it, I'd forgotten all about it.

Dad appears in the doorway, leaning against the jamb. "Got room for one more?"

I smile and scoot closer to Cora, patting the carpet. "Of course."

He sits, completing our circle. The reality of our new family unit sinks in. This is it now, this is us. Regardless of how things have been going the past few months without Mom, we're still here. We've only got each other. And in a few more months, I'll need their support more than ever.

Cora sits back, resting on her palms. "So, what's this big news?"

"Right." I exhale and fidget my hands in my lap, staring at the nail polish stain until it becomes a pink blur before my eyes.

"You okay?" Dad presses. "You and Richie doing okay?"

I clear my throat. "Actually...we're better than okay." I smile and force the words around the tears working their way up my throat. "I'm pregnant." A single tear slips out, and I'm not sure why I'm crying. From happiness, maybe? Pregnancy is already doing weird things to my emotions.

Cora shoots up to her knees and then flings herself at me. I catch her in a hug, and we fall to the floor in a heap of laughter and tears. Okay, I'm crying and Cora is laughing. Dad sort of dogpiles on top of us, wrapping us up in his arms.

"This is awesome," he says. "Best news ever."

My emotions are taken over by the little being forming in my stomach and I allow it. I continue to laugh and cry at the same time, and then I hear it, Dad is crying muffled tears too. It sends a pang in my heart, and I can only hold onto the hope that he's crying happy tears.

Chapter 33

Jules

Angie and I sit on the throw rug in my office, our backs against the sofa as we eat Chinese takeout from Fortune Cuisine. The savory broccoli beef tastes extra garlicky and it's a good thing Kobe is at home today. He'd be trying to sneak a piece every second I'm distracted. "Hey Girl" by Lady Gaga plays from my Spotify playlist while I tap the keys on my laptop. We're taking a break and allowing the soft blue paint to dry in the new waiting area.

"What about...reunite?" Angie glances up from her iPad.

I scrunch my nose and shake my head. "Nu-uh. It sounds like they've already met. Like they're having a reunion."

"Yeah, okay, you're right." She fixes her attention on her screen again while I open a carton of chow mein, the delectable tangy scent wafting to my nose. "I got it!" she says. "Huddle."

"Hmm...no."

She blinks at me, her jaw muscles clenching.

I shrug my shoulders. "It isn't you."

"Okay fine. What about...unite, gang up, gather, meet up, congregate?"

I hold up a finger and make check marks in the air. "No, no, no, no, and no."

She tosses her iPad onto the table and pinches her lips together.

"Look, I'm sorry." I reluctantly set the carton of chow mein down. "But choosing a name for your business is a big decision. It should be perfect."

She huffs out a breath. "Exactly. *My* business."

"And you asked for my opinion."

"I did, but that was before I knew you were gonna get all high-and-mighty and pull the boss card on me."

I sigh. "I'm not pulling the boss card."

"You've had your turn to be in charge, and now it's my turn. So you can veto as many names as you want to, but in the end, it's my decision." She narrows her eyes and crosses her arms defiantly.

Inhaling a deep breath, I scoop up her iPad off the table. "You're right. It's one hundred percent your decision."

Her eyes go wide.

"Don't look at me like that. You know I'm always on your side." I wave her off and scroll through some ideas she's listed on her note app.

"True, I know that. But I don't think you've ever said I'm right." She snickers.

I ignore her, and my mind starts spinning, taking words from her list and piecing them together—combining them to make a full name. "Hey, look at this. What if you use a few words that have similar meaning? Or a few words that have conflicting meanings?"

She peers at the list, watching as I take two or three words and combine them into small phrases. I hand her the iPad. "These are simply some ideas. What do you think?"

"This could work."

While Angie contemplates the business name, I take the chow mein into the new waiting room. The soft-blue paint gives it a warm, welcoming feel. I cross the area and enter Angie's office. It's empty now, but soon it will be full of beautiful furniture, decorations, and people. Allowing my mind to wander over the possibilities of all the amazing things she's going to accomplish here—that *we* are going to accomplish here, together—my chest expands. I get a bizarre sense of confidence and slide my phone from the back pocket of my shorts. I send Mom a text informing her of what Angie and I are doing here and about my renewed license.

My mind shuffles to Pete, as it often does these days. I want to text or call him. I want to tell him about the new business and my new career. But he's better off without me. What I did to him is unforgivable. And the last thing I want to do is interfere with his growth and moving on.

Angie bursts into her office where I'm gazing out the window at the busy street traffic below. I spin around and return my phone to my pocket.

"I've got it." Her smile shimmers. "And no vetoing it this time. I've made up my mind so don't bother trying to change it. I've even got an idea for a logo." She holds up her palms theatrically, completely unlike her, which makes me realize how excited she is. "Flock Together."

I smile, lifting my hands at my sides. "It's perfect."

She pumps a fist in the air. "I told you." Then she jumps up and down before tackling me in a hug.

BEFORE I HEAD TO THE FACILITY TO SEE DAD, A TOTE BAG FULL of new books slung over my shoulder, I check the mailbox. Pulling out the stack, I take it with me as I climb into my car and flip through the mail, mumbling to myself, "Bill, bill, Ang, bill, Ang." I pause when I come across a large manila envelope with my full name printed in the window. The return sender info in the left corner informs me it's my therapist license renewal. "Impeccable timing," I say aloud but find myself smiling as I continue sorting the mail.

I freeze again when I come across a light-blue envelope with my name scrawled across the front in black calligraphy. I glance at the return sender information. I set the stack of mail onto the passenger seat and slide my finger inside the blue envelope, tearing it open, my heart beating fast.

I scan the card inside as I read it aloud. "You and a guest are invited to the grand opening of Natalie's Clothing Boutique." I check the return sender name again—Tess Cavanaugh. I press the invitation to my chest and gaze out over my steering wheel. Tess invited me to her grand opening? I would've preferred if Pete had invited me. But that's wishful thinking considering I haven't heard from him in weeks.

I enter the memory care facility, but Charlene isn't behind the desk to meet me with her usual greeting. Instead, Dorothy, the fill-in person is behind the desk. It throws me off, but I suppose Charlene could be out sick or on vacation. I don't bother asking Dorothy, only give her a wave after she buzzes me through the doors.

Dad's door is closed. I stand in front of it, collecting myself and preparing for a rough visit. Bowing my head, I exhale the deepest sigh known to man and push the door open. "Hey, there," I announce my arrival—though to my surprise—not soon enough. Dad is sitting in his usual spot, in his recliner, but there's a woman on his lap, straddling him. "Oh, gosh!" I jump back and think too late to shield my eyes. I've seen everything. "What the heck?"

I spread my fingers, watching dumbfounded as the woman shoots off Dad's lap like his crotch is on fire and adjusts her skirt. My eyes widen, and I do a double take, pulling my hands away from my face. "Charlene?"

Charlene wipes her mouth with the back of her hand and winces. "Jules! Get out!" Dad yells.

I cover my eyes again and whirl around, cursing under my breath.

"What were you thinking, walking into my room without knocking? You're always walking in here like you own the place."

Still facing away from them, completely grossed out and mortified, it dawns on me—Dad called me Jules. Dad remembers me. And remembers that I've been coming to visit him. I whip back around. "Dad, you know who I am?"

"Of course I do," he says, annoyed and flustered and shifting in his chair. "And you gotta stop barging in here completely unannounced."

"I'm so sorry, Jules," Charlene says.

But as much as I want to sprint out of here, tears spring to my eyes. For whatever reason, on this day, God has decided to shine down on me and throw me a bone. Dad not only remembers me but remembers that I've been coming to see him. This is huge. I need to take advantage of the moment. I rush toward him and throw my arms around his neck, ignoring the awkwardness in the room.

"Jules, this really isn't the time for this," Dad mutters.

"I know, I'm sorry." I pull back and wipe away my tears.

"We're the ones who are sorry," Charlene says. "We didn't want you to find out this way."

I look at her, really look at her. Sure, she's sort of annoying with that raspy voice and knack for gossip. But something tells me this is not the first time she and Dad have fooled around.

"You two are...an item?"

Charlene glances at Dad, and they share a look. If I'm not mistaken, there's a whole lotta love in that one shared look. Dad smiles and nods at the same time Charlene says, "We are."

"How? When?"

Charlene's cheeks blush full-on red. "I'm not really sure how. It just sort of happened."

I try not to think about the logistics of their relationship and how this has to be against the facility's code of ethics, but I can't stop myself from asking, "This has to be illegal or at least against the rules.

I mean, you're not one of his caretakers, but you're an employee here."

She presses her lips together before sucking in a breath and saying on an exhale, "Not anymore." I blink at her, unable to speak. "When I realized Jimmy and I had something special here, I put in my notice. We have a lot of the same interests. And I know the disease well. I understand it."

"And you're okay with it? With him not knowing who you are?"

She smiles at Dad. "Oh, he knows who I am. Even when he doesn't. Deep down, they never forget their loved ones. And despite the rough days, he always comes back to me." She turns to look at me, taking my hand in hers. "Exactly like you. You come back each time because you love him, and you know that one of the times, he's gonna remember you."

Her words comfort me in a way no one else's has. No one has quite spelled out the disease that way before. It warms my heart and gives me hope. And maybe she has something to do with his recent progress.

"Thank you," I whisper.

"And you were just leaving, right?" Dad's thick brows raise, insistent.

"Right," I blurt and turn to leave. But I whirl back around when I remember the other reason why I came today—besides refilling Dad's stockpile of library books. "I almost forgot, here."

"I thought that was my thing," Dad chuckles.

I hand him a handwritten card informing him of my new title: Jules Sweeney, LMFT, along with the official date I begin taking patients. I also included the name of Angie's business, Flock Together. I figured writing it down for him was a good idea in case he forgets.

"You're really doing it."

I smile and shrug a shoulder. "I guess I am."

"Now that's my girl."

Chapter 34

Pete

After two weeks in the new house, it's starting to feel more like my own. I haven't added too many personal touches. I think keeping it plain will make it feel more like mine—bare walls and no silly, pointless dust collectors taking up space. Cora has decorated her room, choosing to keep it simple as well. She picked out a new black metal bed frame, a white comforter, white linen curtains, and a cobalt-blue area rug along with throw pillows in alternating shades of blue. She says it matches the vibe of the home. And I kinda love that.

It's Saturday and the grand opening of Natalie's. Seeing the place Tess has worked so hard on, as well as seeing Natalie's designs on display, is going to be another hurdle to overcome in my recovery. Selling the home Natalie and I shared for all those years was painful enough.

But I feel ready for the next step.

I shuffle into the kitchen and pour a mug of hot coffee waiting for me in the programmable pot. Taking the filled mug into my room, I exit the French doors that open to the back patio. The sun streams through the wood slates of the pergola Daniel helped me build last weekend. Choosing to use the smaller room on the main floor for my bedroom rather than the largest one upstairs was a solid plan. I love walking through the French doors and coming out onto the patio. But it isn't my favorite room in the house.

My favorite room in the new house is my studio. In the past two weeks, that room has gotten more use than my bedroom. It's also where I've spent most of my money. The room has been sound-proofed for better acoustics. I've placed Natalie's piano in one corner and hung my bass guitars and Cora's guitars on the walls. On the piano is a framed family photo. It's the only picture of Natalie I have on display in the entire house.

After I finish my coffee and scroll through home listings for a new client, I jump into the pool and swim several laps to work out the nerves I'm feeling regarding tonight. When my arms feel like Jell-O and no longer want to cooperate, I finally climb out of the pool on shaky legs. As I towel off, my phone dings. I pick it up and see Daniel's name on the screen with an incoming text.

Daniel: *Running a little late.*

Me: *Dude. You better not be standing me up. You're my plus-one.*

Daniel: *Would I ever?*

Me: *Yes.*

Daniel: *Don't worry.*

Me: *And you better not let down your goddaughter.*

Daniel: *I'll be there.*

I toss my phone onto the lounge chair and finish drying off, hoping and praying that Daniel doesn't end up as a no-show. A bit of regret slides into my mind, causing my stomach to flip-flop. Choosing Daniel as my plus-one was risky. But like I'd invite anyone else. Jules and I haven't spoken for several weeks, and it's not as if I've been out looking for anyone new. Besides, Daniel is Tess's godfather, he'd be there even if I hadn't invited him.

Tess and Richie have spared no expense in the store's grand opening. When I pull up in front of Natalie's, there's a valet booth set up on the sidewalk. A man dressed in a red vest rushes to the driver's side of my Jeep. I've barely put the vehicle in park when the guy yanks open the door.

"Good evening, sir."

"Yeah, hey, buddy." I'm familiar with the drill and hand him my keys. "Watch the clutch, will you?"

"Yes, sir."

I catch the eye roll and am fairly certain I've earned myself a scratch in the paint at the very least. Two women hold the double glass doors open, greeting each guest as they enter. I glance over my shoulder, hoping by some miracle I see Daniel's car in the valet line. I don't, so I say hello to the women and step inside.

My breath catches, and my walking ceases. My hand goes to my chest while I take in the space around me and tears burn at the corners of my eyes. In a way, it feels as if I'm being reunited with Natalie the more my eyes scan the shop. Clothing in alternating shades of burgundy, gold, and green are everywhere. Dresses, shirts, and pants are draped on hangers and folded on white, glossy shelves. The walls are painted white, causing the display bursting with white blouses to become nearly camouflaged. There's a sign above them that reads *White blouses are magnets for spills. Always keep spares on standby. Buy two, get one free.* An ache sits heavy in my stomach. Tess took my advice on her predicament with the multitude of white blouses. And it only forces me to think of Jules more.

Right away, I catch sight of Tess. She is busy working the room. She's stunning in a burgundy fitted dress, a tiny baby bump showing, and of course, burgundy high-heeled shoes to match. Her dark hair is pulled back on one side while it cascades over the opposite shoulder. Richie is next to her with his hand pressed to her back. It makes me proud that my daughter chose a partner who is so supportive of her.

Tess spots me, and her face brightens. She waves high in the air to me. I make my way toward her as she excuses herself from her other guests and meets me halfway.

"Hey, Dad. I'm so glad you're here." Her eyes water.

"Hey, kid." I pull her in for a hug. "There's literally nowhere else

I'd rather be." I grin at her, refraining from revealing my own emotions. Because one of us should be strong, and I'm assuming it should be me.

She pulls back and swipes a finger under her eyelids. "You're lying. But thank you."

"Hey now, no I'm not." I tug on the sleeves of my sport jacket. "Okay," I sigh. "Maybe I'd rather be dressed in something more comfortable. But other than that, I'm thrilled to be here. You gotta know how proud I am of you?"

"I do." She nods, still wiping under her eyes.

"And how proud Mom would be." The words release easier than I thought they would. More tears spill down Tess's cheeks and I wince. "I'm so sorry. I didn't mean to make you cry more."

"It's fine. At least I can blame it on the hormones." She laughs.

Richie appears at her side again and hands her a tissue. "Hey, Pete." He puts out his hand, and I take a hold of it, pulling him in for a hug. We clap one another on the back.

I've told him congratulations about the baby in a text but not yet in person. "Richie"—I resist the urge to say his nickname—"again, congrats on the baby, man. I'm so happy for you two."

"Thank you." He smiles at Tess and rubs her back. "We're really excited. Oh"—he turns to look at me— "and congrats to you as well, Grandpa."

"Whoa." That title is still too new and I'm not sure how I feel about it. "Easy on that for now."

There's a poke in my back and I whirl around.

"It's only a matter of time, Gramps," Cora says, teasing.

"Not you too."

Tess and Cora laugh at my expense. When they finish, I wrap my arms around Cora and then palm her face like a football, an action she hates but I find hilarious. I drag my hand down her face, and she shrieks.

"Dad!" She steps back, nearly tripping into the guy kitty-corner to her. "Stop doing that." Her face blushes.

The guy looks familiar. I squint and let my mind sift through memories. Cora must notice me sizing him up because she clears her throat, and I pull my attention away from him.

"Dad, you remember, Gavin?" Cora smiles wide. "Gavin, this is my Dad, Pete Redd."

I tilt my head, still trying to place him as I shake his hand.

"Nice to see you again, sir."

Sir is what does it. I'm instantly transported back to when I first saw this guy and where. This is the hipster douchebag who had his hands all over Cora at the college party. The one who took off after I'd caught him.

I look at Cora, who's not letting go of the guy's hand. What is she thinking? Is she actually dating this moron? But when she gives me a pleading look with those big brown eyes, all I can do is push aside my dad worries and try to play nice. The only way I can is by telling myself this can't possibly be anything serious.

"And nice to see you again as well." I force the words out and even plant a fake smile on my face.

"Gavin is also interning at the paper this summer as an arts intern." Cora beams while holding tightly to Gavin's hand.

"That's...interesting."

"I told Cora she should bring him tonight," Tess says.

My attention slides to her. So she knew Cora has been hanging out with this guy all summer and hadn't told me? That's not how I hoped things would go after Natalie died. The girls were supposed to start telling me everything, like they used to with their mom. But instead of being jealous, I'm grateful they're confiding in one another.

Gavin is dressed in black slacks and a gray sweater and doesn't look as douchey as when I first met him. But you can only hide douchiness for so long before it reveals itself. I don't realize I've been glaring at him while my mind zoned out until Cora elbows me in the gut.

"Dad, did you hear him?"

"What?" I shake my head and rub at the back of my neck. "I'm sorry, you were saying something?"

"I was just apologizing. For the first time we met. At the party?" he hedges.

"Right," I say, stretching out the word as if I'm only now remembering. "You mean when you acted like a complete ass?"

"Dad!" Cora shrieks.

"Exactly, yes," Gavin agrees. "I'm really sorry about that. I have no excuse. I've gotten to know Cora the last few months, and she deserved more respect than I gave her that night. And so did you."

When I don't respond right away, Cora stares at me with widened eyes and brows raised so high they nearly disappear altogether.

"Fine," I mumble. "Thank you. I suppose I can give you another shot. Ya know, at proving your worth to date my daughter."

"Dad," Cora shrieks again. "We're not *dating* dating," she mutters.

Tess leans in. "You brought him here, where you knew your family would be. I hate to break it to you, the two of you are dating."

"She's right," Gavin admits. "I assumed we were official. I mean, I'm not seeing anyone else. Are you?"

She puffs air out her cheeks. "Wait, so not only are we official, but we're exclusive too?"

"I mean, yeah. If you wanna be?"

Cora hesitates, chewing on her bottom lip. I'm not sure how I want her to answer the question. She smiles and nods. It's obvious Gavin wants to smush his douchey lips against hers but is very aware of my presence, so he settles for a kiss on her cheek.

"Uh, Dad, your date has arrived," Tess teases. "Let's go say hello before someone gets Uncle Daniel going off on a tirade about real estate."

I hold out my arm to Tess, and she loops hers around it as I escort her toward Daniel. He's just taken a glass of champagne off the table by the door when he sees us.

"Tess, sweetie." He holds his arms out and wraps her in a hug. "Congratulations. I'm so, so proud of you."

"Thank you, Uncle Daniel."

He wraps me up in a quick hug next.

"Nice of you to finally show," I mumble into his shoulder.

"Sorry, I was in Malibu showing a house to this hot young couple. Completely filthy rich, of course."

"No real estate talk tonight," Tess warns, waving a finger in front of his face.

"I'm perfectly okay with that rule," I say. "But I don't think Daniel knows how to talk about anything else."

"He can talk about women." Tess gives him a sly grin.

He winks and holds up his champagne glass to her. "Touché," he says before taking a sip.

I shake my head and then I see her—Jules. There's a split second when I get to take her in before she sees me too. My mouth goes dry, and my lips part while my knees literally go weak. I feel like I need to reach out and cling to something to be sure I stay upright. She's radiant in a dark-green dress, not too fitted, with a low-cut neckline and her favorite pendant necklace dangling into her cleavage.

Jules turns her head midway through a laugh, so when she sees me, her face is already bright, and she's smiling. The sight causes my heartbeat to quicken, and a smile pulls at the corners of my lips. She tilts her head before glancing back up to give me a more purposeful, yet not as wide of a smile.

When Jules doesn't make her way toward me right away, my chest caves. My legs feel heavy, and my head spins. Is this how far we've come? Is this where we are now? In the short time I've known her, Jules somehow morphed into one of the most important people in my life, and now we don't even say hello at a party?

"Why didn't you tell me you invited Jules?" I still don't tear my eyes off her as I ask Tess.

"I wasn't sure how you'd react. Are you mad?"

I turn to face her and she's wincing. "No, of course not. I'm glad you did. She's been really excited for you."

"Go talk to her," Tess says.

Staring into the amber-colored liquid in my glass, watching as the bubbles zoom to the top and then pop, I weigh the words of what I might say to her in my mind, rolling them over and under one another.

Daniel nudges me in the back. "Go, man. You know you wanna. Besides, I haven't seen you this hung up on a woman since...since..." His words taper off.

We all know what he was going to say—since Natalie.

But comparing the two isn't merited. Because the two of them aren't comparable. Not only are they different in so many ways, my feelings for each of them are also different. With Natalie, there was that first lustful feeling, then first love, the wanting-to-spend-every-second-with-them feeling. Then it turned into, *I'll do anything for her*, and the desire to take care of her. Especially after she'd been sick that first time. When I realized I could actually lose her.

And then the second time, when I did.

With Jules, I also have the feeling of wanting to spend all my days with her, and do things for her, but it's different. I want to be her partner, her equal. I want us to take care of one another and support one another. To be there on the good days and the bad. But how do I tell her those things when I'm the one who not only pulled away but pushed her away?

I'm not sure how, but I need to try. My heartbeat grows faster, pounding in my chest like a racehorse as I reach for a second glass of champagne from the table and head toward her. She sees me coming and at least doesn't make a run for it. She dips her chin and tucks her strawberry blonde hair behind her ear, revealing the lightly freckled skin on her neck. My desire to be near her kicks up a couple hundred notches.

"Jules," I say, her name sounding perfect on my lips. "Champagne?" I hold it out to her.

She glances at Angie, who's standing across from her, and I realize too late I should've brought a glass for her as well.

Angie puts up her hands. "Hey, don't mind me. I'm only here for moral support." She gestures at Jules. "But some champagne would be nice, I'm not gonna lie."

"Did someone say, champagne?" Daniel swoops in from out of nowhere it seems, and is at my side, handing a full glass of the bubbly liquid to Angie.

Her expression melts as she accepts it, as every woman's does when they first meet Daniel, with his tall, dark, and handsome facade. "A gentleman? Impressive."

"Daniel Russo."

She shakes his hand. "Angie Phillips."

"You wanna take a walk with me? You see, I know the owner of this place and I can give you all the insider tips." Daniel grins.

"Really? You tempt me with a discount, and I'll go anywhere with you." She winks.

"I might be able to arrange that." Daniel hooks his elbow for Angie, and she slips her arm through his. They shuffle away looking like a power couple, and my chest tightens. Those two together definitely mean trouble.

I clear my throat. "So, Jules, how've you been?"

"I've been good, actually. Really good." She gives me a tight smile.

I'm thrilled she's been good, really good. But a part of me wanted her to say she's been as miserable as I've been. "Awesome."

"And you? How are things going? Are you still back home? And working?"

"I'm not living with Tess and Richie if that's what you're wondering. I actually sold my house and bought a new one—it's a Mediterranean style."

"Wow, really? That's great, Pete. You did it, you made your dreams come true."

I want to say, not all of my dreams because I don't have her. I want to tell her I've missed her every second of every day since we've been apart. I want to tell her I love her.

But I don't. Instead, I say, "Maybe you could come by and see it someday."

Her eyes widen. "Um...yeah, maybe."

There's an awkward pause so I say, "You look really nice."

She blushes and tucks her hair behind her ear again, exposing the soft, pale skin there. I want to put my lips on that spot, press gentle kisses down her supple neck and onto her bare shoulder.

"Thanks," she says. "You don't look too bad yourself."

Her compliment sends a fluttering in my chest and I push through. "So, listen—"

"It's okay," she interrupts, looking pointedly at me. "We're okay."

"Are we? Because it doesn't feel like we're okay." And I don't want to just be okay.

"I'm still so sorry for what happened between us. For what I did to you."

"I know. And you already apologized. I wasn't ready to listen. I don't blame you. I understand why Tess did what she did. And I understand how your feelings may have gotten mixed up in you simply trying to do your job. I only wish you would've told me. About how your program usually works. And about your book."

"I wish I would've too." She looks down at her feet. My attention goes there too, but my eyes get distracted as they move up her silky-smooth legs. She's got an old bruise still healing on her shin. It makes me laugh to myself.

"So, anyway...it's good to see you, Pete. I'm so glad to hear you're doing well. And congrats on the new house."

"Thank you."

"I know it probably doesn't mean much coming from me, but I'm so proud of you for the progress you've made. And you look happy."

"It actually means a lot coming from you." She doesn't say anything, instead gives me one of those full body nods. "You look happy too." I'm thrilled about that, but it also makes my chest tight—she's happy, she's moved on, and is doing fine without me.

"You take care of yourself, Pete," she says, backing away. "Oh, and congratulations."

I raise my brows in question.

"On the baby. Tess's baby." She smiles.

I give her one nod. "Thanks." It's obvious she wants to go. As much as my chest hurts and I want to plead with her to stay, I say, "Keep it real, Jules." Whatever that's supposed to mean.

I mentally kick myself, running my palm down my face as she backs away. But my attention snaps up when I hear a crashing sound. Jules has backed up into a server carrying a tray of champagne glasses.

Shards of broken glass and liquid scatter on the floor, and Jules is on her backside amongst it all. Attention is fully on her, and I hurry to her side, reaching out a hand to help her up. Her face is bright red, and her eyes are shining.

"Hey," I yell to the server who is hunched over the tray and piling it with broken glass. "Why don't you watch where you're going? Someone could've been really hurt here."

"It's not his fault," Jules whispers. "It's my stupid clumsy self. You know that."

I do, but that doesn't mean I'm gonna allow her to feel more humiliated than she already does.

"Everything okay here?" Tess asks, her forehead wrinkled with concern.

"Everything is fine. Don't worry. And look, they're already cleaning it up," I say, pointing to three servers who are working diligently to get the glass and liquid wiped up.

"Are you okay, Jules?"

"I'm fine. But I'm so sorry to ruin your party." She adjusts her dress.

"You didn't ruin anything." Tess waves a hand around. "Look, everyone seems to have already forgotten."

"Well, thank you again for inviting me. And congratulations. On the store and the baby." Jules hugs Tess. "I need to get going. I have a busy day tomorrow."

"So soon?" Tess asks.

The loose strand of hair falls into Jules's face but this time she doesn't bother with tucking it behind her ear. "Yeah. Thanks again. Goodnight." She only gives me a nod before turning and heading toward the door, the back of her dress damp from the spilled champagne.

"Dad," Tess growls, "go after her."

My chest pounds and I don't hesitate. I jog after her, reaching her right after she's exited the store. "Jules," I call, feeling like Prince Charming trying to catch Cinderella at midnight.

She stops but doesn't turn around.

"Hey?" I move around to face her. Already, tears are sliding down her cheeks, and I want to wipe them away for her. I want to kiss them away. I want to bury my face in hers—but I lost that privilege. She's not mine to touch or comfort. "Are you gonna be okay?"

She swipes at her cheeks violently. "I'll be fine. Maybe a little sore tomorrow." She forces a laugh.

"That's not what I'm talking about."

Her shining hazel eyes focus on mine, looking into them deeply. I wait for her to tell me she's missed me. That she loves me and doesn't want to spend another day without me.

"I am so sorry, Pete. Truly, sorry," her words vibrate. "But I'm gonna be okay. And you're gonna be okay too."

Her words crush me to dust.

She heads to the valet booth.

This time I need to let her go, despite the unforgiving ache in my chest, pleading with me to make her stay. I gaze at her for a second longer before I turn and walk back into the store, nearly bumping into Angie on my way.

She gives me a pained smile and rubs my arm as we pass.

"Take care of her, will you?" I whisper.

She nods and rushes out the door.

Chapter 35

Jules

Angie and I are up early on Sunday. We grab coffee on our way into the office, shocking Derrick, my favorite barista at Starbucks, by ordering the larger size. I hold Kobe's leash in one hand and my coffee cup in the other, releasing a sigh of relief when my olive-green blouse survives the Temple of Doom.

The office has been given a drastic makeover in the last few weeks. Rather than Angie's desk and a row of chairs taking up the space of the large waiting room, we've converted over half of it into a small office for Angie. On my office door is a shiny new nameplate. *Jules Sweeney – LMFT*. There's a light flutter in the center of my rib cage, and I hold my head high.

I open the door of the kennel we've set up in the corner of the waiting room, and Kobe trots inside. Assuring I'd keep Kobe contained was the only way I got Angie to compromise in allowing him to come into the office with me. I glance over my shoulder at Angie, and I swear her creamy-brown eyes are glossy. "Well, you ready for this?"

"Hell yeah. I'm more than ready." She smirks. "I've learned from the best. I mean, I was your assistant for two years."

Warmth expands in my chest. "You're gonna do great."

Angie's new office door features the same nameplate as mine in shiny gold, only hers reads *Angie Sanders, Flock Together CEO*. She pushes open the door, and I follow her inside. It's filled with bold-colored furniture and navy-blue curtains draped to the floor, and a large metal-topped desk shoved to one side. She spins in the center of the room, stops, and looks at me, wiping at her eyes.

"Thank you," she whispers.

Her vulnerability hits me in the center of my heart, and I want to scoop her in my arms. Because it's not me she has to thank. Flock Together was her idea. I have nothing to do with it.

My fingers go to my pendant. "You're welcome."

She pulls me into a hug, and I can barely reciprocate because my body is shocked by her rare physical contact.

"Hey, this is all you."

We pull apart and she clears her throat. "We're in this together." She gives me a fist bump before setting her purse on her desk.

My phone pings, and when I glance at the screen, I'm surprised to find a response from my mother. It's been a few weeks since I texted her.

Mom: *Sorry for the late response. I just got back into the country. Congratulations on your new job! I'm making a trip to LA at the end of the month. Can I come by and see your office?*

I fiddle with the globe, my mind turning her words over and over and reading further into them than I should. Voicing her desire to see my office rather than see me is obnoxious, but I suppose it's progress all the same.

Me: *Thank you! I'd love for you to come by.*

Mom: *Great! I'll text you when it gets closer. Looking forward to it.*

Me: *Me too!*

Angie snaps a finger in front of my face. I pull my attention to her and away from my phone.

"C'mon. It's almost time." Her face is full of elation.

I check my Apple Watch—she's right. Her first group of Flock Together participants will be here in a matter of minutes. Today, they'll meet one another, complete a more detailed profile page than what they filled out online, and then be dispersed into pairs. From there, they'll be given their first challenge.

Since today is a Sunday, I don't have any patients scheduled until tomorrow. But I came into the office to help Angie with whatever she needs, as well as to train our new assistant—who should be here by now.

"Here," Angie says, handing me a stack of printed pages. "Do you mind stapling these packets together?"

"Sure."

"Looks like your new assistant is late. I don't think your previous one was ever late." She gives me a smirk.

"Ha, ha," I say sarcastically and swipe the stapler off the assistant's barren desk.

The elevator dings and I lift my chin, expecting to see a few young people stumble out, dazed and confused. Or preferably my assistant. But instead, who I see exit the Temple of Doom causes me to feel lightheaded. I inhale a sharp breath.

Straightening, I attempt to talk past the lump in my throat. "Pete? What are you doing here?"

Chapter 36

Pete

Taking in the sight of a confident and put-together Jules is like looking at a beach sunset. She's breathtaking, the color of her shirt causing her hazel eyes to pop. It brings a memory of her front and center in my mind—her amid the waves, straddling the surfboard, wet hair clinging to her pale skin and green swimsuit, with a bright smile on her face.

I tear my gaze away from her and clear my throat. I glance around at what once was a spacious, bare waiting room consisting of mismatched office furniture and a Keurig sitting on a metal file cabinet. It looks like I've stepped into an entirely new office space. It smells new too. The recently painted light-blue walls carry a clean, fresh scent.

"Hey, Jules." I shove my hands into my pockets to keep from reaching for her and bounce on my toes. "I heard about your new business and needed to see it with my own eyes."

She lets go of the papers she's shuffling, and her fingers fly to the globe pendant around her neck. Now knowing the story behind the necklace, my chest warms at the action. It's a comforting reminder for her, and fingering it soothes her anxieties. But I wish she didn't feel anxious around me.

She swivels each way and gestures to the space around her. "Well, this is it. It's not much, but I suppose it's not the office that matters, it's what we do here."

I enter farther into the waiting room, peering at a new office where the door is open and then glancing back at Jules's office. A new nameplate mounted on her door confirms what Tess already told me. And what Jules's website confirmed. I'm not dumb enough to go into this thing blind again. This old guy's heart can't take another beating. It just can't. This time, I did my research.

"And tell me, so I don't get it wrong. What exactly is it that you do here?" I ask so I can hear the truth from her lips.

She tucks a strand of hair behind her ear and glances at her closed office door. "I've renewed my therapist license. So I'm back to strictly in-office sessions. No more Challenge Program. No more programs of any kind." She dips her chin as if she's having a difficult time making eye contact with me.

"That's good," I assure her. "Our counseling sessions helped me a ton. It wasn't only the challenges."

She smiles though she's still holding back.

"And explain Angie's business?"

"Coincidently Angie's idea for an in-real-life dating app cata-pulted off my original Challenge Program. But she's made a big change—she doesn't accompany anyone on the challenges." She finally looks at me, her cheeks blushing.

She needs me to let her off the hook for the wrongs she caused. But until seeing her now, I wasn't sure I could. In my mind, I thought I had forgiven her, but it isn't until this moment, seeing her accom-plished smile and hearing the details of the businesses they're running out of this office, that it hits me in the chest. It's like an explo-sion underneath my ribcage, centering around my heart.

Behind me, the elevator dings, followed by voices. I spin around and see about six people stumble off the elevator. They look confused, and a few of them laugh. I stiffen and hold my breath, wishing I would've come sooner. There are so many things I still need to tell Jules. So much we need to talk about.

"Welcome to Flock Together," Jules greets, handing each person a stack of paper. "Please take a seat and begin filling out your packet. You'll receive further instructions once the remaining participants have arrived." She holds out a cup of pens to them.

"Sorry about that," she apologizes to me. "Our assistant is late."

I rub at the back of my neck. "No problem." I stare at my shuffling feet.

When the elevator dings again, I push my fingers through my hair, feeling annoyed. But at the same time, my brain doesn't seem to want to cooperate and form words. A few more people step off the elevator, appearing as dazed as the first group.

"Jeremy," Jules says, relief in her tone. "Finally."

A young guy probably in his late twenties, saunters toward her, smiling sheepishly and pushing bleached blond hair out of his eyes. His skin is tanned, and he probably has washboard abs underneath his black dress shirt. He bends, hugging Jules, and my insides blaze—I don't have a right to be jealous, but I am.

"Sorry. Traffic was killer today."

"Here." She hands him the huge stack of paper from the desk. "Can you please give a packet and pen to each person who comes off the elevator?"

"Sure." He smiles wide. His bright white teeth blind the entire room, and I resist rolling my eyes at his actor-from-a-toothpaste-commercial vibe.

"I'll be with you in a minute," she says before scooting around the cluster of people. She gestures with her hand for us to move further away from the elevator. "So sorry about that."

"It's fine." My shoulders are tight with anxiety. I feel panicky—the result of Jules's busyness and the commotion surrounding us in the office. This is terrible timing, but I'm so afraid that if I don't say what I need to now, I won't get the opportunity again.

Angie parades out of her office and into the waiting room looking like a woman in charge—chin up, high-heeled shoes. "Pete?"

I nod. "Angie. Once again, always a pleasure."

She checks me out, head to toe. "Same to you."

"I hear congratulations are in order."

"Thanks." She smiles. Then calls to the group in the waiting area. "All right, come on in, Flockers."

A few in the group chuckle.

Jules snorts. "Nice, Ang. Real professional."

After most of them follow Angie into her office, it's less chaotic.

Jules touches the sleeve of my shirt. "Is everything all right? Are Cora and Tess okay? The baby?" Concern shines in her eyes, and it confirms the one-millionth thing I love about her—the kindness and care she has for others. Which is exactly what she was attempting with her Challenge Program. And she helped many people as a result —including myself.

"Everyone is fine." I scratch at the stubble on my chin. "Everyone except for me."

She glances up and her eyes dance back and forth between mine before they finally focus. "Pete," she whispers. The sound of my name on her lips causes a sensation of desire to travel south. "We already said our apologies and our goodbyes last night. Don't make this harder than it has to be."

I reach out and rub her arm, my fingers grazing down the length of it until I'm holding her hand. "Last night you acted like you wanted nothing to do with me. Like you couldn't get away from me fast enough. You pretty much told me to have a good life and you'd be fine without me. I wanted to respect your feelings, but there was so much more I needed to say. I shouldn't have let you go."

Her eyes plead with mine, but she doesn't speak.

"Why? Why are you pulling yourself away from me?"

She glances down for a brief moment before looking back up again, her eyes now wet with tears.

"Jules...why?" I persist.

"I don't know. I guess…I thought you'd be better off without me. I'm no good for you. You are an honest person and…you deserve better." She wipes at a single tear on her cheek.

"You're wrong. You're perfect for me."

She chews on her bottom lip.

"I read your book. You helped a lot of people. And look at this." I gesture in the office space. "Look what you're doing. You're gonna help a bunch more. Jules, you believed in me when no one else did." I pull her closer into me, reaching my free arm around her back and pressing my hand there.

"Of course I did. I've always believed in you. I want the best for you. And I never meant to hurt you," she rambles.

"Jules, I know that now." I hold her in my arms, and she melts into me. "Please, just let me say what I came to say." She folds her lips in between her teeth. "I love you, all quirks included. And I'm not running."

She raises her light brows in surprise. "Even when things get tough?"

"Especially then."

She smiles brightly through her tears. "You love me?" Her tone sounds teasing.

I move my hands to her neck and run my thumbs along her jaw. "Heck yeah I do. So, what do you say? Do you still love me?"

"What do I say?" She tethers her arms around my neck, her fingers pushing through my hair sending tingles shooting down my limbs. "I say…I love you, Pete."

"Thank God," I say on an exhale, releasing all my pent-up worry that we wouldn't get another chance to do this right. I pull her into me, our bodies pressing together and closing the gap between us until our lips finally touch. I devour her mouth earnestly, like this could very well be our last kiss. A moan escapes from her throat, and the sound sends a zinging sensation throughout my entire body.

Our lips part reluctantly, slow and lethargic. But our hands still cling to one another as if we're afraid to let the other go.

She presses her forehead to mine. "Were you honestly worried?"

"Nah," I answer, mustering up waning confidence. "Okay, when the tan buff dude walked into your office and hugged you, I may have had a smidge of worry."

She giggles, and it gifts me with a fluttery feeling in my gut. I grin and then kiss her smiling lips.

It feels as if I've come full circle in the past year. And even though this is far from where I imagined my life would be, I'm grateful. Before Natalie passed, I promised her I'd continue to be an excellent dad. She also wanted me to promise I'd be open to someone new if that's where my journey led. But I couldn't promise her that. Back then, I couldn't fathom falling in love again. And definitely not so soon. Besides, Natalie was the dream pursuer—the risk-taker—not me.

Yet here I am, dreaming and risking the most important thing—my heart. Jules's love and support have released me from my depression and given me wings to fly. To finally be free and soar. And it feels not only right, but heroic. Because why shouldn't I be the hero of my own love story?

Acknowledgments

First, and foremost, I want to thank God for the ability, drive, and talent to be a writer. I am especially grateful for his grace.

To my husband Jeremy—*Wow!* When I mentioned the idea of self-publishing this book, (and I was terrified) you instantly supported me. Not only that, but you also pushed me to take the leap and do it! For that, and so many things, I am eternally thankful. This is just one example of how you have shown your love for me over the years. Thank you!

To my kids, Jensen, Jaidyn, and Jace, you all got on board with my dream to put this book out in the world and I'm so thankful. You each put up with my Paul Rudd fangirling and still love me. I am truly a blessed mom!

A big shoutout to my brilliant editor, Jeanine Harrell who was patient, and not only fit me into her schedule, but allowed me to work on edits behind her so I was able to meet my deadline. You are amazing and I will sing your praises to all.

A special thank you to my proofreader, Krista Dapkey who made this book shine! Your attention to detail was impressive, and this wouldn't be as pretty as it is without you!

To the fabulously talented Enni with Yummy Book Covers, thank you for creating the most epic cover. Even better than I could've imagined. Thank you for bringing Pete Redd, (Paul Rudd) to life!

To my biggest cheerleader, and bestie, Bethany Dodson. Words are not enough. You always encourage me in all that I do, but especially when I go after my dreams. Thank you for reading all the terrible drafts, and for still telling me how amazing of an author I am. I love doing life with you!

To my ride or die beta reader, Lissa Ruck. Thank you for being willing to read every story I write. You not only rave about them but urge me to send you more! Thanks for always shouting about my books on social media. I adore you and our friendship, and I'm so glad Bethany introduced us.

Thank you to my parents, in-laws, siblings, and extended family, for the support, love, prayers, and encouragement!

Thank you to my beta readers and CP's on this book who encouraged, and gave insight, and for your treasured friendship: Bethany Dodson, Lissa Ruck, Kristine Akenson, Lauren Sprang, Diane Rubatino, Janine McCoy, Savannah Hendricks.

To my ARC team, a huge thank you for your time and willingness to give this book a chance and for the early reviews. Thank you to my online support system, the friends, connections, bookstagrammers—I am forever grateful for you. Thank you to everyone who pre-ordered, purchased, read, and reviewed this book. Thank you for not only believing in this book but believing in me as well.

A special thank you to the many, MANY people who, upon discovering I was writing a book with Paul Rudd as the inspiration for the hero, not only encouraged me to publish it, but supported, shouted about it, and loved on it. Regardless if the only reason is because you adore the charming, ageless, and adorkable Paul Rudd, I'm so grateful for you!

About the Author

Starla DeKruyf is a romance author of books that play like movies in your head about characters you wish you could hang out with. Her books always end in happily ever afters. As someone who struggles with mental health and lives with chronic illness, she often includes these topics into her books. Follow her on her socials so you can have fun and be awkward together! When Starla isn't writing,  she's probably drinking coffee and spending time with her husband, kids, and her rescue pup.